Train to Trieste

Domnica Radulescu

Doubleday

LONDON · TORONTO · SYDNEY · AUCKLAND · JOHANNESBURG

TRANSWORLD PUBLISHERS
61–63 Uxbridge Road, London W5 5SA
A Random House Group Company
www.rbooks.co.uk

First published in Great Britain
in 2008 by Doubleday
an imprint of Transworld Publishers

A CIP catalogue record for this book
is available from the British Library.

ISBN 9780385613682

Addresses for Random House Group Ltd companies outside the UK
can be found at: www.randomhouse.co.uk
The Random House Group Ltd Reg. No. 954009

The Random House Group Limited supports The Forest Stewardship Council
(FSC), the leading international forest-certification organization. All our titles
that are printed on Greenpeace-approved FSC-certified paper carry the FSC logo.
Our paper procurement policy can be found at www.rbooks.co.uk/environment

Typeset in New Baskerville

Printed and bound in Great Britain by
Clays Ltd, Bungay, Suffolk.

2 4 6 8 10 9 7 5 3 1

For Alexander and Nicholas

Train to Trieste

PART ONE

Orange Moons

I HAVE LEFT THE BLACK SEA, my skin golden and salty, and my tangled hair brighter from the sun, to take the train that crosses the land by the violet-blue waters and the yellow sun-flower fields, then cuts through mountains into resin-pungent forest.

I am seventeen. Every summer my parents and I leave the hot streets of Bucharest to spend two weeks on the beaches of the Black Sea, after which we spend two months of summer in my aunt's house in Braşov, the city at the foot of the Carpathians. I always rush to the mountains, hungry for the cool, fragrant air and sparkling sunrises.

This time I have come only with my mother. The night I arrive from the sea, I want to go out for a stroll around the neighbourhood right away. My aunt Nina tells me I should rest first and not go off like that, all heated up and sweaty. She always gives her advice in a timid, soft way, as if worried she might upset you, unlike my mother, who blurts out her judgements in shrill tones, demanding that you listen.

My younger cousins Miruna and Riri want me to stay and play with them. Miruna, who is almost ten years old now and has the bluest eyes I have ever seen, starts crying, and she says I never play with them any more and that she hates me. Riri, only five, with dark eyes like blackberries, throws a wooden toy box at my head. I tell them I'll play with them later. The only one who doesn't care what I do is my uncle Ion, who is snoring loudly on the sofa in the kitchen, too exhausted from work to even go to bed.

I need to cool off my sunburned body in the fresh mountain air, and I fly down the marble staircase, out into the fresh night, before either my mother or her sister Nina can say another word. By June, I desperately want to leave Bucharest, with its tired crowds and heated pavements, its French-style heavy grey buildings, and its slow-moving trolleybuses. The detour by the Black Sea is like a short leap into a fairy tale. The sight of the emerald-violet sea sparkling in the morning as I look at it through the perfect white columns at the edge of the beach always transports me to the times of Ovid, once exiled on these shores. I like to think of myself as a naiad walking dreamily on the burning sands and gliding slowly into the waters filled with lacy algae and pearly shells. By the end of the second week, my body aches from the sun and from the Bucharest crowds filling every square metre of the beaches with their improvised tents and coloured sheets. That's when I start longing for pine trees and cool shade.

Up here I finally feel at home, not in a fairy tale, not in a place I want to run away from, but in a place where my body feels whole and where my heart has a steady beat. There are children's voices coming from behind the thick stone walls that line the streets. Blood-red poppies and orange marigolds grow in little beds along the pavements. Right around the corner there is a large open market, and I can hear faint echoes of peasants' voices advertising tomatoes and radishes, watermelons and spring potatoes. The summer open market is the only place where you can still buy food without a huge queue. In Romania, we eat better in the summer.

I run into my childhood friend Cristina. Her two chestnut plaits are wrapped around her head, and she gives me the news breathlessly, without any word of introduction or a hello, as if she had been expecting to meet me in the street tonight.

"Did you hear about Mariana? Mihai killed her," Cristina says.

"The two of them went on a three-day trip at the end of April. They were coming down the Rock of the Prince, trying to get back to their tent before dark. He was walking behind her, and he accidentally kicked a rock loose. It hit her in the head and killed her, just like that."

Cristina breaks into sobs. She was a good friend of Mariana's and learned about kissing and lovemaking from her, which she would then tell me. I try to picture Mariana. I used to admire her. I envied her raspy voice and the way she blew rings of cigarette smoke. I loved the way she would throw herself carelessly into her boyfriend's lap, swirling her gypsy skirts. But mostly I picture her boyfriend, Mihai Simionu. He has green eyes and long lashes, and he would pluck the strings of his guitar and play melancholy songs. Cristina's news of the accident horrifies me, but somehow I don't feel sad for Mariana.

Mihai and Mariana are four years older than Cristina and me, and we used to be fascinated with them and their love. We sometimes followed them and spied on them. I used to watch Mihai from the corner of my eye as he walked holding Mariana's hand and whistling. Now I picture him walking like that, but there's no one holding his hand.

Instead of heading towards the boulevard, we turn back to our neighbourhood. Cristina doesn't want to be seen crying by the whole world. We pass a row of neatly lined-up yellow, peach and blue stone houses towards the park at the end of the street and see Mihai walking circles in the shadows around the wooden bench where he and Mariana used to kiss and sing until late at night. He is unshaven and wears check knee breeches, boots and a wrinkled short-sleeve shirt. Cristina starts crying again at the sight of him, and I tell her to go home and leave me alone with him.

I watch him smoking those unfiltered Romanian cigarettes called Carpaţi, Carpathians, almost like a cruel joke. I never understood why such stinking cigarettes are named after our most beautiful natural assets. Romanian cigarettes are the worst cigarettes in the world, bitter and sour. Suddenly my heart aches for him as he smokes and walks furiously, hurting from his loss. I go straight to him, cross his path shamelessly so he can't avoid me. He has to look at me. And he does. He gives his anger a rest and smiles a little, squinting his green eyes in the smoke. I ask if he wants to walk with me. He nods.

The moon is full, hanging low. He has his head down and walks fast. I can't keep up with him. My face is still burning from the Black Sea sun and from the summer night, from the full moon and his green eyes. I am burning like embers. I am glowing in the dark.

There is no meat in the shops and no toilet paper. Flour, oil and sugar are rationed. People say it's about as bad now in 1977 as it was during Stalinism. The worst of it is that there are men in black leather jackets with small eyes who watch at every corner, on every floor of every building, and who listen on every telephone line. They want to know if you are complaining, if you make jokes, if you speak with foreigners, if you plan to leave the country, and where you got your Kent cigarettes. Somehow, many people manage to escape the country. There is news almost daily about so-and-so who left on a tourist trip to Germany and never came back or who went to Yugoslavia and then somehow ended up in Italy. *Lucky them,* we always say. *Smart people, good for them,* we also say.

In school, between our organic chemistry classes and our comparative literature or Western philosophy classes, we study the five-year Socialist plans of the cooperative farms and the production of tools and tractors, and about the utopia of Socialist happiness in a not-too-faraway future, where people will give only according to their ability and receive according to their need. We seem to find ourselves in some kind of a transitional moment, when, except for the important Party leaders and secret police who shop at special, secret government stores, nobody is really that close to getting even the most basic needs met. The grocery shops are empty, and the steel shelves are shiny and clean to the point that you can see your face reflected in elongated shapes in the metal surface of those shelves. If you are lucky, at the most unexpected times of the day there might be a transport of cheese or chicken wings in your neighbourhood, with long queues formed instantaneously. The last people in the queue generally look demoralized: there won't be anything left on the shelf, they know, by the time their turn comes. They will leave with their empty bags and try to find other queues throughout the city, where they might have the chance of being the first in a line for butter or sardines or toilet paper. The running joke is that Romanians don't need toilet paper any longer because they have nothing to shit.

This summer I am seventeen, I am bursting into being a woman, and I don't care about empty shops and sugar and flour rations. My blue eyes are blazing. My long limbs are taut and restless. I have wild wheat-coloured hair that flies in all directions and a great hunger in my flesh. All I care about is that this man who is grieving for his dead lover turn his eyes on me, notice my sun-bleached hair, my burning face and shoulders, and play one of his melancholy guitar songs for me. For me alone. The smell of earth and death coursing through his heart makes me wild with desire. I want to be there in the centre of his heart where it smells like raw earth. I want him to be my first lover: bitter, raging, smelling of unfiltered Romanian cigarettes, and hurting for a dead girl.

This is the year of the big earthquake, and blood and pink flowers seem to bloom all at once out of the cracked earth. The greedy, unforgiving black earth! I wonder if Mariana had any time to think, to worry, to gasp at the thought of her own impending death. I wonder if Mihai was just careless when he kicked that rock downhill or whether there was anything else that Cristina hasn't told me or that she doesn't know herself. I know other men were in love with Mariana. I know they all went in big groups on their mountain trips. Maybe Mariana had flirted with Mihai's best friend, Radu, a little too much, as she sometimes had the habit of doing. Maybe Mihai flew into a jealous rage. Maybe this was a crime of passion. I remember their fiery fights late at night at the edge of the park where all the kids in the neighbourhood gathered. Mariana always broke into tears and smoked one cigarette after another and swirled her coloured skirts in a move to leave. Then Mihai would grab her violently, and in a second his mood changed from angry to tender and they would start whispering and kissing. I used to watch them with fascination and with an intimation of delicious pain.

As I walk beside Mihai, I am thinking that there never has been such a full orange moon and such a fresh, raw-smelling place in someone's heart for me to install myself like a greedy queen.

"They shaved off her hair," he is saying. "She had a big hole in the back of her head. They shaved off her beautiful brown curls to look at the hole in the back of her head. Why did they have to do that?"

He crushes his cigarette on the ground and stares in the distance. We walk some more, and the moon is swelling in front of us, orange, round, wicked. I want to take his hand and make him look at me.

I stumble in my flimsy, worn-out sandals. My feet are blistered from the sand and the salt that had gathered in my sandals at the beach. My feet burn with every step as if the earth were boiling. I steady myself by holding on to him and making him stop. His fingers on my arm burn my skin.

"Let's go and get something to drink," I say. "Today is August the fifteenth, Saint Mary of the Assumption. It's my name day."

"I thought you were a pagan," he says.

"I am. I just like to drink on my saint's day. I celebrate my name."

"Your name is Maria? Your aunt Nina always calls you Mona."

"My aunt Matilda, my father's sister, prayed to the Virgin Mary during my birth, so I had to have her name, too, for protection. Mona Maria."

"Mona Maria." He smiles and says he finds the alliteration amusing. He says it's like a movie star's name.

We pass by my aunt's house. I hear my mother call me from the balcony, saying it's late and that I have to come home. I shout up to her to leave me alone; I am old enough and I can stay out as long as I want. We keep walking.

Mihai says there's a liquor store next to the railway station. We walk for a long time without talking. We see a train smoking its way out of the station and a couple kissing at the street corner. I'm jealous of all lovers, dead or alive. I am thirsty and giddy and I fall in love with every step I take at Mihai's side, as I watch his profile. His thick black eyelashes and sad green eyes. Tonight, on my saint's name day, I don't care about sugar and flour rations, so long as the store has vodka, and it always does.

We buy cheap vodka, *ţuică*, made from fermented plums, and walk back to our neighbourhood. But just as we are about to cross the street towards my aunt's building, I take Mihai's hand and pull him onto a side street. The darkness smells of my special flower, *regina nopţii*, queen of the night. We drink from the bottle in the middle of the street to celebrate my name saint.

I laugh so hard that tears burst out of my eyes. The moons are multiplying. It's wonderful to have moons scattered like stars above your head and to smell the queen of the night and to hold the hand of this sad man who is already thinking about how he will kiss me. I am alive. I am here, laughing in front of him, ablaze and golden and seeing many moons in the sky. I lie down on the strip of grass at the edge of the pavement, under a line of poplar saplings, next to the iron fence that separates the street from the park in front of my aunt's building. The neighbour who lives below my aunt's apartment walks past me carrying a bag of potatoes. She shakes her head and mutters something about "city girls".

Mihai lies next to me, and we look at the sky and at the many moons floating in orange halos. Time stops passing. Time stops mattering, just as when Faust asks the devil to freeze a moment because it's so beautiful. I have just read *Faust* in my comparative literature class. I go to a special literature high school in Bucharest. We read all the books in the world. I have friends who go to the English school or to the French or the Italian schools. My father and his poet and artist friends think it's some kind of a fluke in the system. The Party must have overlooked the threat of comparative literature courses, being so busy destroying everything else. I don't like *Faust*, but I like that phrase about wanting the present moment to stay because it is so beautiful!

This moment – now – this Romanian summer in a small town in the Carpathian Mountains, I want it to last for ever as I lie on the earth. It is there in the middle of Mihai's heart and the over-turned earth: I see myself blooming, the queen of the night, fra-grant and plump.

I don't know what happens after that. I wake up in my aunt's house in bed, next to my two cousins. My aunt and uncle and my mother all scold me. Several days go by and I don't see Mihai. I seem to be sleepwalking.

Then it's August 23, the Romanian national holiday, the Communist holiday when people are made to march in the streets with little red Party flags and chant *Nicolae şi poporul, Nicolae şi partidul,* Nicolae and the people, Nicolae and the Party. If you don't chant loud enough, some man in a leather jacket may notice. My aunt and uncle have to go and demon-strate. All the adults are gone, my cousins are at a neighbour's house, and I am alone.

I walk to his street, two blocks away from my aunt's apart-ment at the end of the row of pastel houses. His house is larger than the other ones and is grey, not peachy, not lime. It is a stone house with a red tile roof. There are three apartments in the building, but it still looks like a house, and the front gar-den is separated from the street by a brick-coloured iron gate. I know his apartment is on the first floor, because in previous summers I used to see him and Mariana through the open win-dows close to each other, whenever I walked around the neigh-bourhood with Cristina. Sometimes we spied on them, and we saw their heads glued to each other, kissing. Other times he played his guitar for her, and the sounds of his strings flew out of the window like whimsical sparrows spreading throughout the neighbourhood. A sentimental song about the mountains in the moonlight.

I walk back and forth on his street, spying on his house. A woman passing by stops and asks if she can help me, if I am lost. I say, "No, thank you. I'm just waiting for someone." Then, as if it were true, the heavy glass door to his building opens, and Mihai comes out, wearing the same wrinkled shirt and check trousers he was wearing a week ago, but now he is shaven. He is walking with his little sway on one side, as if he were limping. I walk to meet him. We stop and stare at each other.

"Come, I'll show you a place in the mountains," he says as if he has been expecting me. "Somewhere you've never been."

"I'm not dressed for mountain climbing," I say. I am wearing a gauzy blue dress and the same flimsy, worn-out sandals.

We take a bus to the end of the line, the foot of the mountain, then a lift takes us midway up the mountain. He leads me to a trail through the forest. There are bright green ferns and blue bellflowers on the forest floor, and the afternoon light is filtered through the branches of the birch trees and the heavy oaks. Our steps reverberate in the silence of the forest, broken only by nervous woodpecker sounds or by a plaintive bird. The air is sparkling with specks of light. Then the path becomes steeper.

I stumble up the road. Pebbles collect in my sandals. The blue dress my mother had sewn from the material of an old curtain is wet with mud. It catches in the bushes that close in on the trail, hiding where it goes. I am red and sweaty as he pulls me by the hand, up and up.

We see wild raspberries, and he leans over to gather them. He feeds me the wild berries, one by one. I taste the tart fruit together with the pine resin on his hand. I know my lips are redder from the raspberries and that he wants to kiss them.

We hear thunder. The rain starts with such fury that I see water rushing down and spurting upward. He makes a sharp turn onto another path, and suddenly we're under a wooden shelter. We're soaked. My blue dress clings to my body, and I can see my nipples through it. Every part of my body is outlined clearly under the gauzy soaked dress. From the pocket of his knee breeches, he produces a piece of thick white cloth. Winking at me, he says: "You've got to be prepared for everything in the mountains."

He starts wiping my face, my hair, and my neck with the white cloth that miraculously absorbs the water. He is meticulous and precise. The cloth moves to my shoulders, my breasts, my stomach, lingering an equal amount of time on each body part. I feel a strange heat radiating from my body. I am hypnotized. I don't want him to ever stop drying me off with the white cloth.

"There you are. Much better. You can't stay wet for long in the mountains. You can get pneumonia."

I know that when I am old and decrepit and ill, and even on my deathbed, I will remember this moment in the summer rain as I am staring at the lips of this man who knows the mountains and has dried my body with a white cloth.

We stare at each other, but we don't kiss. I can feel his breath on my neck. He pulls me close to his chest and holds me, stroking my hair. I am breathing into his chest, sheltered from the rain.

"It's stopped. We can go now," he says and takes my hand again.

As we get back to the path that climbs the mountain to some mythic rock he knows, we see pink and blue and violet clouds rising from the valleys and surrounding us. The valleys below hang in dazzling, multicoloured mists; the dark green chains of the Carpathians surround us like a magic ring. Through one opening in the clouds, we can see part of the city, as if through an enchanted keyhole.

"It's a rare phenomenon," he says. "The clouds are moving on, as the sun is trying to come out. It's reflecting itself in the clouds."

We finally reach the big rock. It is a white, sharp rock with a cave at the bottom. The dogs are barking in the valley, and we hear the bells from the Black Church, the Saxon church, which was saved from a big fire centuries ago. We can almost make out the outlines of the church through the violet clouds as well, its straight, dark, burnt Gothic walls and towers shooting upward. The bells echo all the way to where we are, and as we lean against the white rock looking down at the pink clouds in the valley and at the sunset over the city, he tells me I have little stars in my eyes. The church bells sound on and on and on.

I taste the raspberries on his lips. I want to melt into the pink clouds and this kiss that tastes like the wildest fruit of the earth. The church bells toll, and my body is taking the shape of the full moon and the fragrance of the wild raspberries.

The rain has pulled down the banners for the August 23 celebration. When we return from the mountain, we find the streets filled with thousands of torn, wet red paper flags. People are moving hunched and soaked through the puddles and stepping on the red flags. I don't really care. I suddenly feel like I don't live in this country any more. His hand is squeezing mine as we approach my aunt's apartment building. He asks me to come over to his apartment tomorrow, early in the morning.

It's from this day forward that I start sneaking down the stairs early before everybody is up. I wash my hair in icy water, because we get hot water for only one hour a day, or for two hours every other day, and are not supposed to use it up frivolously. Sometimes we don't get water at all early in the morning or late at night. The Party is always trying to make us economize for something, heat or energy, frantically pushing us towards the Socialist utopia that will be here any day now. I wash my hair with laundry soap in the bathroom sink, as quickly and quietly as I can, hoping the anaemic stream of tap water won't stop and leave me with my hair all gooey and whitish with suds. The mornings are always chilly; I shiver as I shoot down the marble stairs, wet strands of hair falling down my neck and shoulders.

He plays Grieg for me. He first blows the specks of dust off the record, then he places it gently on the turntable and lets the needle drop with one swift, delicate gesture. He stands unmoved for a few seconds, listening to the music with a contented smile.

"Listen, it's like the rain. *Peer Gynt*. I love it, don't you?" he says proudly, as if it were his own music.

"Yes, it's beautiful. I've never heard this before."

"You're trembling," he says. He puts his hands on my shoulders.

Drops of sound enter every pore of my body. His bedsheets are starchy and cool. As I take off my blue dress, the same dress I wore on the mountain in the rain, I see through the open window the portraits of Marx, Engels, Lenin and Nicolae Ceauşescu, the *Father of the Nation*, hanging on the building across the street. They are ugly men and they scare me.

I seem to know it all, to understand with precision every detail of every little caress on my body. I am not shy. Waves of heat and sound rise in my body. Limbs, whispers. He bites into my shoulder, I bite into his. I am dazed, curious at what's happening. I hear children playing outside right below our window, a ball hitting the pavement stubbornly, monotonously.

The bearded faces of Marx, Engels, Lenin and the unbearded face of Nicolae Ceauşescu watch us from the building across the street. I can see them right from where I lie, through the window. I close my eyes and don't think of anything. Grieg is playing. Clear notes dripping like rain. Mihai's body is wiry and taut and it smells of pine resin, as if he's sucked all the smells of the mountains into his olive-coloured flesh. I lose myself in this tangle of limbs, in this melting of flesh into flesh. Every part of my body wants to scream and moan as he holds me. Purples and reds burst in my head behind my closed lids and shoot through the veins and muscles in my body. I hold his hand, as he lies next to me, sweaty and trembling.

The lacy curtains are moving in the breeze. Through them, above our heads, the three Marxist leaders and the fourth one, our own *Father of the Nation*, are staring at us. We laugh and make faces at them; we tell them to go way deep into hell. He draws the curtains together and comes back next to me to whisper in my ear. He says I am his little wild raspberry and he will eat me all up. He says he'll kidnap me and run away with me into the forest where nobody can find us, and we'll live there for ever like two savages, surviving on berries and roots. Then we roll among the cool sheets laughing.

I swirl through the summer, oblivious to everything and to everyone around me, rushing up and down the stairs at dawn, my hair always wet, illicitly clean. We lie in the many forests he knows, under fir trees and in secret meadows by a secret stream, the smell of fir and of earth rubbing against me. At night the moon wakes me, and a golden string seems to tie my thoughts to his, my desire to his. I leave my aunt's apartment in the middle of the night and climb like a thief through his window directly into his bed. I hold his warm, resin-smelling body. I bite the back of his neck, his shoulders, his lips. Always his lips.

When the time comes to go back to Bucharest and start the new school year, there is drizzle and fog on the heads of the mountains and at our white rock. The summer usually ends abruptly in the mountains and turns to autumn over several days during which the nights grow chillier, the morning light has a deeper golden glow, and the air seems to be quivering like a sigh in anxious anticipation of the cold weather. I am starting my third year of high school, and the university entrance exams loom ominously at the end of next year. I feel like I have to grow up overnight, mature like the summer light moving into autumn. The future seems as unclear as the mountain peaks capped in white mist.

The day before my departure, Mihai's mood becomes dark, and he talks about Mariana, about how she used to have toothaches and put vodka on her aching teeth. He remembers how she was running down the rocky path that afternoon, careless and happy. He remembers how his foot accidentally hit a big rock and sent it down the path. He says *accidentally* with a special stress, as if stumbling over the word. It's as if he were enveloped in a shadow. Suddenly he frightens me. He is sitting at the edge of the bed, his head in his hands. Maybe he killed

Mariana. Maybe that rock wasn't an accident at all? Maybe I'm in love with a murderer. I startle myself from my dark reverie. I find myself strangely enthralled by the idea. Crimes of passion fascinate me. I've never really thought anyone would actually kill someone else because they are too jealous or too in love, except in a novel. And yet I want to erase the memory of Mariana from his heart for ever. I hate how her absence sneaks in between us. I get up from the bed in a swirl of jealous anger and am ready to leave without saying good-bye. He is sorry for his own sadness. He takes my hand and licks my palm and the tip of every finger. He tells me he doesn't want to lose me.

"I'll kill you if you die," he says.

Then he embraces me fiercely and holds me like that until I am gasping for breath.

"I'm like the thistles in the field. We go on, and on, and we never die," I say laughing, as I move away from his tight grip.

I prick his arms and neck with my nails, to show how I am like a wild rambling thistle. He smiles. He has forgotten Mariana.

I have a dream about the two of us alone at night in the middle of the street, carrying the old suitcase my great-uncle Ivan was carrying when he came back twenty-five years after everyone had given him up for dead and then disappeared in the Soviet Union again. We sit on the suitcase, there are two moons in the sky, and Mariana comes out of the fog. She comes over to us, smiling. We see she is toothless, that she grins a frightful toothless smile. I feel sadness as deep as death.

Floods, Wars and Great-grandmother's Mirror

THE SUMMER WHEN I AM SEVENTEEN and I fall in love with Mihai, I am drawn to Great-grandmother's silver mirror. It has been sitting on the mahogany chest in my aunt Nina's living room for as long as I can remember. I stare at its chipped corner, its thick wooden back that once held a music box. But mostly, I stare into the glass, observing my own face as if it were someone else's: the oval-shaped blue eyes, the mane of hair, pointed chin, slender nose, and red lips swollen from Mihai's kissing and biting. The red mark on my long neck.

In this enchanted summer with the moon-studded sky and the taste of raw earth and fresh rain, I will my family stories into taking shape in the mysterious mirror. Just like the girl Lucille from a story my mother used to read to me from a miniature book of French fairy tales. Lucille got to see everything she wanted in a magic mirror that a fairy had given her: her dead relatives, the people she loved who were far away, and her future. But I am scared to see my future. I am not asking that of my great-grandmother's mirror. As I observe my own face in this mirror I want to see the past, to imagine the people in my family floating through the silvery glass and stretching their longing arms towards me.

I am afraid of Mihai's brooding silence when he mentions Mariana. I am afraid of the dream I had about the two of us sitting on an old suitcase at night in the middle of the street, and Mariana grinning a toothless smile at us. I remember my mother talking about the great loves in our family and about the women who found the men of their lives and then stuck with them. For ever. The thought of a morning when Mihai may not be in my life makes me gasp, lose my breath. I simply stop breathing at the thought. I run to Mihai to make sure he is still there, on the first floor of the grey stone building with the red tile roof. I tell him I will always love him. I kiss him until he can't breathe any more. I pray to my female relatives and beg them to protect my love with Mihai. Somehow my dead female relatives seem more reliable to me than the God or the Mother of God that my aunt Matilda always talks to me about. I want to be like the women in my family, the strong and lucky-in-love ones.

My great-grandmother saved herself from the big floods of 1918 by floating down the river Nistru on a big wooden door and holding to her chest a silver mirror with a music box that used to play Beethoven's "Für Elise". That was in the Moldovian city of Cetatea Albă, the White Citadel, in the region of Bessarabia, before it belonged to the Soviet Union.

She is floating on the relentless river that is sweeping along wardrobes and vegetable gardens and chicken coops, with her long, blond hair flying in the wind, holding to her breast the square silver mirror as she listens to the music over and over again, turning the key in the music box every time it stops. After many hours, the door she is floating on bumps against a tree. Somehow she manages to climb the tree while still holding the mirror, and waits, barely conscious, in the nook of its thick branches, for someone to find her.

At sunset, with the waters still rushing madly by her, the sky soaked in ominous violet-reds, a man in a rescue boat approaches the tree and hears a faint tune, like someone plucking a strange instrument. He finds my great-grandmother among the twisted branches, holding tight to the mirror and whispering notes like a lullaby.

Vania Golubof lowers her into his boat. He wraps her in blankets and makes a nest for her, then pulls hard for the distant bank. He tries to find out who she is, what happened to her family, what part of the town she is from. All he can get from her is her name, which she keeps repeating: Paraschiva Dumitrescu. She whispers her own name like a song, like a lullaby, just like she did the tune of the music box.

He carries her to the house where he lives with his mother and lays her in the main room, asking his mother to help him undress her and to get her some dry clothes. They live at the edge of the town where the waters don't reach, in a small white stone house.

He falls in love with the lost yellow-haired girl as she goes in and out of her delirium, talking about wild horses and soldiers floating on the river, as he makes her drink little sips of water to bring her fever down. One night, after three days of her rambling talk and fever, he thinks she is going to slip away from him. Her pulse slows down, and she burns so fiercely that the air around her is hot.

His mother helps him wrap her in cool sheets at night and gives her cool teas made from Russian herbs. He talks to the girl continuously as if his words, which by dawn become as confused and meaningless as hers, could pull her out of her illness and away from death. And they do. One morning, with the first sunlight, when Vania's mother finally goes to her own room to rest, Paraschiva suddenly stares at Vania. It is the first time in a week that she is calm. She looks at Vania as if she has known him all her life. She is neither terrified nor surprised to find herself in a man's house, in a man's bed, after having floated for days on rampant waters. She asks for her mirror – did he find her mirror with a music box on the back? He shows it to her. It's safe, see? Just a bit dirty, he says, wiping it with his sleeve. It still works, he tells her, and he begins to wind the key. She stops him, gently touching his hand.

He silences the stray notes. He places it in her hands. "Keep it," he says, "for good luck. It brought me to you."

She starts laughing. Then he laughs, too. They are shaking

with laughter when Vania's mother comes in. She watches them laugh and realizes that Paraschiva will live, and that she will be her daughter-in-law. She is happy for her son, who has finally found his bride.

It is 1918, and the war has swallowed up thousands of young men in its fields; the floods have swallowed up muddy villages and more lives. Now famine sets in. If you are lucky, you find your mate in some depth of calamity such as this; you save someone and are saved yourself. It's how people find mates, ravenously, recklessly, amid putrefying corpses, at the very edge of life and death. With her parents now dead in the flood, Paraschiva counts herself among the luckiest. She has been found by someone with a white stone house at the end of the town where the waters don't reach, a house with a small vegetable garden, a patch of corn, and a few white hens.

In the summer, they get married in the little garden with the village accordionist playing his two tunes for them over and over again, a happy one and a melancholy one. They drink *ţuică*, the brandy made from fermented plums. They eat *mămăligă*, the cornmeal mush that peasants eat instead of bread and sometimes instead of everything else, and they dance till dawn to the same two tunes. That night she wants to turn the key in the music box and listen to "Für Elise" again in the same bed where Vania pulled her away from delirium and the edge of death with cool compresses and Russian herb teas.

The summer with many orange moons when I discover the greed of my own body, I am also my great-grandmother who listens to Beethoven in the music-box mirror she saved from the floods. I want to be Paraschiva as she bites Vania's shoulder in ecstasy and sinks her nails into his back. I want to be her in the little squeaky bed in the white stone house on the side of town that was not touched by the great floods, as I smell and lick the body of this young man in this bed where I struggled for several days between life and death, soaked in fever from the infected river.

Paraschiva and Vania have two boys, Ivan and Victor. Ivan will get lost in the Second World War, and found through the Red Cross twenty-five years later, when his mother is already dead. Victor is going to be my grandfather, the one always gentle and sad from the loss of his brother. They say that as she got older, Paraschiva would put on her best clothes and her green felt hat on some cool and sunny afternoons, would say she was going into town, and instead would go inside the large brown wardrobe the family brought with them when they moved into the apartment next to the railway station. She would come out after a few hours and say everything had got so expensive in town. One day they found her dead inside the brown wardrobe, amid old coats, party dresses and mothballs, holding to her chest one of Ivan's jackets from when he was a boy. This is how the stories are kept in our family: a few big events, major catastrophes and one or two scenes, some invented from saved sepia photographs, others handed down and retold many times over the years, to the point where they have become vague and misty like fairy tales.

Mona Maria Manoliu
Growing Up in Bucharest

I WAS BORN IN THE SUMMER, in old Bucharest, when the streets were filled with linden smells so heavy and so sweet that one would keep wanting to be born again and again on a summer night such as this one.

It is three o'clock in the morning, the eerie hour of births, deaths, accidents and metamorphoses. My mother is sitting at the edge of the bed in the rented room, after her water has just broken, in her one black dress, with a little bag on her knees that she has prepared for the hospital. She is silent. She's in mourning for her mother, Vera, who died only a month ago, falling in the street from a stroke, and for her aunt Nadia, who died at the beginning of the year, falling dead in the old house on the street lined with chestnut trees, holding a postcard that her husband, Matei, had written her from political prison.

My father has just gone to the public phone in the street to call the ambulance, the hospital, or a taxi. Their apartment is right in the piazza with the statue of the famous Romanian king Michael the Brave, who withstood the Turks and united the three principalities Wallachia, Moldavia and Transylvania into one country for the first time, four hundred years ago. He is on his horse with his formidable sword pulled out for battle. My father is staring at the statue from the telephone booth, which is right next to the majestic grey stone government building with the faces of the Communist leaders hanging larger than life at its entrance. The streets are deserted, except for a drunken man who never made it home after work and ended up drinking plum brandy in the corner tavern for hours. My father is flustered and trying to light a cigarette while calling and while buttoning up the trousers that he has pulled over his pyjamas. His lighter doesn't work, so he asks the drunken passerby for a light as he is still holding the phone and his trousers are falling down. He manages to make the phone call and an ambulance comes to pick up my mother one hour later.

I was born in the morning to the smell of linden trees, to the sound of my mother's sobs. I was born in the wild disorder of pain and mourning in my family, greedy for life and for my mother's breast.

My mother is still crying in the ward immediately after my birth. The doctors don't know what's wrong, and she doesn't stop for hours. The linden smells rush through the open windows. They say I was red and scrunched up and had a lot of light hair stuck to my head. They let my father inside the ward a few hours after the birth. My father, Miron Manoliu, who had never seen a newborn baby in his life, says I am an ugly baby. Then at last, my mother, Dorina Golubof, laughs in the middle of her crying.

They name me Mona Maria. Mona from a character in a Romanian novel my mother was reading while she was pregnant. A love story that takes place in a mountain resort during summer vacation between a young actress, Mona, and an aspiring writer, Ciprian. They are both trying to get away from the dust and bustle of Bucharest. She is working on a new part, and the writer is trying to write a new play. They sit and talk until late at night on the front porch of their villa and watch the galactic journey of the morning star. My mother thinks it will be a lucky name. Nobody in our family has ever been given such a whimsical name. I also have to be called Maria, because it is important to my aunt Nina. It was on 15 August 1959, on the holiday of Saint Mary of the Assumption, that Aunt Nina and my mother, Dorina, caught a glimpse of Uncle Matei as he was brought into the courthouse in Bucharest from the political prison in Jilava. I don't know why I have to be named in memory of a family tragedy, but my aunt Nina insists. And then Aunt Matilda, on my father's side, the religious aunt, says she prayed all day to the Virgin Mary during my mother's labour, which lasted an ungodly twenty-seven hours. So I have to carry the name of the Blessed Virgin because, apparently, it was thanks to the prayers of my aunt that I was born healthy, though a little blue from having the umbilical cord wrapped around my neck.

I grow up in a minuscule apartment that faces the sunset and the little four-hundred-year-old church where my parents got married in secret, because you can't have a religious wedding in the Communist state. There is a lilac bush behind my window, whose sweet fragrance in the spring fills our tiny apartment and makes me long to go out and play all the time.

My parents are always worried about something. They speak in whispers. My father wakes up at night cursing the secret police and coughing until I am afraid he will explode. When the doctor comes to our house one night and finds my father coughing and smoking his unfiltered cigarette at the same time, the doctor gets angry and leaves without even examining him. My father says he's had too much suffering, with the war and the famine after the war, and with Stalinism after the famine. And on top of it all, now a man is following him everywhere and checking on how he teaches his classes.

After the doctor leaves, my father curses him. "It's too much. They're killing me. Isn't it enough that my poor mother had to scramble in the ground for roots to feed us during the war, and that I saw soldiers' skulls crushed by dynamite, and that I survived on ale and mouldy bread as a student, isn't it enough, hm?" Exasperated from lack of sleep and the constant drama my father makes of his life, my mother tells him, "Yes, it's enough. Calm down now, Miron, and go to sleep, for God's sake!"

When my mother leaves me in school, I always feel like crying. I have to wear a white ribbon on my head as part of my school uniform, a blue shirt and blue-and-white jumper. I hate the big white bow on my head. I feel like a big egg as I'm walking to school in the morning.

I enjoy the reading book with the picture of a girl named Lina working in the field of wheat. She is wearing a pioneer's red scarf and is cutting the stems of the wheat with a tool that resembles a new moon, and the sky is all blue with one white cloud in the corner. The writing says: *Lina is happy because she lives under the blue sky of the Party.* I want a tool like a new moon just like the one Lina holds in the picture.

There are always people in our house until late at night, poets and teachers and artists. One artist draws the Walt Disney *Snow White and the Seven Dwarfs* figures that my aunt Matilda took me to see in the big cinema next to the pastry shop, where they have the best cream puffs and éclairs in the world. I had never seen a cartoon film in the cinema before. Aunt Matilda works at the cinematographic studios in Bucharest, and she got tickets for the film before any of my school friends were able to see it. My father's friend draws each of the Seven Dwarfs and Snow White with what seems like one flick of the wrist. He teaches me how to do it, too. When all the people come to our house, they smoke a lot and drink wine, beer and then *ţuică*. They talk about Ceauşescu and the bad things he does, like censorship and following people so they can't talk, sending their friends to the secret police, who are called Securitate, punishing people who are good and just want to talk a lot.

"They know everything: they know what you say and what you eat and what you shit. It's going to get worse soon, you just wait!" my father tells everyone and drinks another shot of *ţuică*.

"They just want to intimidate us all into silence, they want us to believe they are listening to us all the time, but I don't think they actually are. Some of these Securitate are imbeciles. Let's not give them the *credit*," says the artist man with a beard who can draw Snow White so well. He's drunk quite a lot of *ţuică* by this time in the night.

His paintings are exhibited in the big gallery in the centre of the city near the cinema, but they are all coloured circles and squares that my parents call *abstract*. I don't know why he doesn't exhibit the Snow White and the Seven Dwarfs drawings. He says that the Party asked him to stop painting *abstract* and told him to take inspiration from the people working in the textile factory.

"Nonsense," says my father and lights up another cigarette, and my mother is angry and tells him to stop smoking and drinking so late at night. "This child has to go to sleep and she has school tomorrow."

I am waiting for everybody to leave so my mother can come to sleep next to me the way she always does, except when she leaves in the middle of the night because she has a headache and she has to sleep with my father.

"Pure nonsense!" my father says again. "Who says that the Securitate are intellectuals? Stalin didn't build his regime of terror with philosophers and artists, did he? It's the proletariat, remember? But they are just cunning enough to find out everything about everyone. Rest assured that they have a nice little file they are keeping for each and every single one of us. Particularly if you are an intellectual."

"You know, they are not treating their own proletariat too well either, are they? In any case, they can all fuck themselves," says the artist. My father agrees and says an even worse expression about body parts, and my mother scolds him for being vulgar and vile.

It's the August when I am eight years old. We just came back from our vacation in the mountains, after our vacation at the seaside. Everybody is worried: the Russians have just driven their tanks right into the middle of Prague. People were shot in the middle of the street, and one student set himself on fire in the main square in Prague as a form of protest. Everybody says in whispers they will come to Bucharest, too. I'm frozen with fear about the tanks that will surely *invade* us. I draw many, many Seven Dwarfs and Snow Whites and stick them all on the wall to make myself a little less afraid. I can't stop thinking about the student, a boy all ablaze like a human torch in the middle of the enormous square in Prague.

My mother takes me to the park with the lake and the swans in Bucharest, and she buys me corn on the cob from the woman sitting on the ground with her legs crossed. Then she buys me candyfloss from the man in the candyfloss booth. I stare at the white sugary fluff moving in circles, and I hope it won't all be gone by the time our turn comes. I ask my mother about the Russian tanks, and she scrunches up her face the way she does when my father makes her nervous or upset with his cigarette smoking and his swearing, and she says the tanks won't come to Bucharest, Prague is far away, and our president won't let the tanks come to our country. I am all sweaty because it's so hot in August in Bucharest, and my feet hurt from the tight patent-leather shoes I am wearing. The candyfloss tastes funny after the corn on the cob, and I feel sick. My mother says, "I told you so," but she's not really paying attention to me. Her mind is on something else. I ask her to please get me a bottle of Coca-Cola from the little restaurant on the lake, but she says that she doesn't have any more money, and that I shouldn't have got the candyfloss if I wanted Coca-Cola. I just drink water from the stone water fountain in the park, and my dress with blue circles and ruffles gets all wet from the jet of water. I want to cry because my mother is angry and everything seems so wrong today when the Russians drove their tanks into Prague. Then my mother takes me on the big Ferris wheel from where you can see the whole city of Bucharest, or almost, not all the way to where we live, but up to the statue of Michael the Brave. I hold my mother's hand on the Ferris wheel ride, and when we're at the very top of the wheel my mother kisses me and tells me we'll be all right, not to worry about the tanks, and she'll get me Coca-Cola when the ride is over. I don't want this ride to be over; I hold on tight to my mother's hand and admire her pretty profile and her taffeta grey dress with its pink daisies.

Right before Christmas, there are many students in the street holding burning candles, for a *protest*. I don't know what a protest is, but I want to go with a burning candle into the street where all the students are. My parents are very excited and happy about the protest, and I want to start a protest, too, to make my parents happy. My father says the students are so courageous. After the protest, everybody has Christmas break, because the students stood in the streets with candles and asked for Christmas break. I get a huge ball and a Snow White doll for Christmas, and I am happy about the protests, too. Happy and relieved: no student set himself on fire like the man did in Prague.

My mother has just had a grey dress made for me, out of the special thin woollen material called *tergal*, by the same seamstress who makes her own dresses. It's my autumn and winter dress, and the *tergal* makes me itch. I am too hot in it in September and too chilly in December. I will never wear *tergal* dresses when I grow up, I decide. My mother wears a white-and-grey dress also made out of *tergal*, and her hair is blond and combed up like a balloon. I'm wondering why did my mother have to ask the seamstress to put a white bow on my grey *tergal* dress. I want a dress with violet and lime circles all over it and with no white bows. I like violet and lime together. I saw these two colours together once in the special sweetshop next to the music conservatory where my mother teaches foreign languages to music students so they can sing operas in Italian or in French. These sweets were violet and lime both, and they made me feel not afraid. I want a dress that makes me feel brave.

Sometimes, when I wake up from my nap in the afternoon, my father talks to me about Romanian grammar and how there are more words that come from the Romans than from any other language, that's why it's called Romanian. But there are fourteen words from the people who lived on this land before the Romans, who were called Dacians. They were blond and had blue eyes. The Dacian words are *copil, moşneag, barză, tîrnă-cop. Child, old man, stork, hoe* . . . and I can't remember the rest. I like the Dacian words a lot, and I want to be Dacian from before the Romans came. I don't like the Romans, how they invaded and killed the Dacians and how they stole all of their words and left them with only fourteen.

I want to write a poem with my new coloured pens that are called *carioca*. I want to write a poem in purple. I sit down at the big black wooden desk with sculptures that my father got from his father, from the times when they had the house with the orchards before the Russian soldiers stole their electric sockets and cut up my father's dog to pieces. I sit down and I like to feel the cool glass that covers the wood of the desk against my elbows and my arms. I look at the picture of Nora that's on the desk.

She is my mother's old schoolmate, her best friend from ever since she was my age. Nora ran away to America three years ago; she sent us a picture of herself sitting in an orange tree in America. She is wearing blue jeans and a white shirt and is holding an orange, and she's smiling the biggest smile I have ever seen. I look at that picture and I think Nora is so beautiful, with her black hair and her green eyes. The way she's just sitting there in the tree holding the orange makes me feel cheerful.

I try to write very fast the way I see my father write when he writes his articles about Romanian poets and the language they use. I make lots of circles and wavy lines with my purple pen on the white paper. Sometimes I write a word I learned how to spell, like *copil*, which is a Dacian word, and then the word *pasăre*, which is a Roman word, and I write a poem about how I ask this bird to come to me at the Danube River so I can feed him. I want to send my poem to Nora in America where she's sitting in the orange tree and smiling the biggest smile I have ever seen. America is very, very far, my mother says, and I wonder how long it would take for my poem to reach Nora.

Uncle Ivan's Return and My Aunt Ana Koltzunov Who Has Been to the USSR

AFTER THE STUDENTS' PROTESTS everyone has Christmas break, and we get to go to the mountains twice a year now. When we go to my aunt Nina's house in the mountains for the new Christmas break, the neighbours slaughter a pig, a whole live pig. I hate hearing the pig cry out so loud when they cut him up to make sausages. The next day the ice in the backyard is red with frozen blood, and we slide on the frozen bloody patches pretending we're ice-skating. Sometimes in the afternoon the blind violinist wanders through our backyard in a worn-out tuxedo and plays the Kreutzer Sonata, with such wailing sounds that our hearts melt in an agony of sadness and joy as the winter sunset bleeds and we glide on bloody ice.

In the summer when I visit my aunt in the Carpathians again, the gypsy girl with her basket of fresh berries wanders through our backyard. My cousins and I beg our mothers to please let us get a cup of the juicy, tart fruit from the gypsy girl with the string of coins sewn onto a black velvet collar around her neck. We wait for her to fill the tin cup with the dark red raspberries or blue berries, and we watch the strands of her hair that slip out from the red scarf tied around her head. I want to be the gypsy girl who wanders through people's backyards carrying a basket of dark berries. In secret, I make myself a black velvet collar that I tie around my neck whenever I go out to play with the neighbourhood children.

One summer when we're visiting my aunt and uncle in the house in the Carpathians, I hear that Great-uncle Ivan, who got lost during the war and was believed dead for twenty-five years, has now been found and is coming to visit us. As a child, I never fully understood the disappearance of Great-uncle Ivan inside the gigantic Soviet Union, but I have always imagined it like this: The sun is aslant on a field covered with corpses sunk into the mud. One brother is looking for the other. The mother is looking for both her sons and is tearing at her hair. She finds her son Victor, but not the other. Her heart breaks in two in the dusk that smells of raw blood and flesh. Ivan is gone. He will be dead for twenty-five years.

My grandfather Victor tells me that he has found his long-lost brother. When he tells me that he found him through the Red Cross, I imagine that a nurse in the Red Cross uniform has been looking for my grandfather everywhere, and when she found him, she ran back to his brother Ivan in Russia and told him she had found Victor. My grandfather is nervous and pale before going to the train station to meet his brother. We all go with him. The train rushes in with a swirl of white smoke. I miss the moment when Great-uncle Ivan gets off the train, but suddenly I see everybody rushing towards a man with a long white beard, and crying and laughing at the same time.

Then Uncle Ivan sees me and tells me, "You are *krasivaia devochka.* You are a beautiful little girl. Come to Uncle Ivan!"

He swings me with one arm and kisses my face. I am terrified when I notice that Great-uncle Ivan is missing one arm, that his right sleeve is empty, just hanging there without an arm in it.

This special night, my uncle Ion opens a bottle of *ţuică* and a different bottle of another plum drink that is stronger than the first one and is called *pălincă*. My grandfather Victor and my great-uncle Ivan cry and laugh and hug each other the whole time. Then they look at the silver mirror, the one their mother had saved from the floods of 1918, and they both cry again. The queen of the night flowers are in bloom, and the smell is floating into the house through the open windows with the fresh night breeze. I hear the whistling of the trains coming and going. The talking, the laughing, the cigarette smoke and the smell of the queen of the night envelop me, and the empty sleeve of Great-uncle Ivan does not scare me any more.

Ivan spends two weeks at my aunt Nina's house. Nina keeps making huge pots of cabbage soup and is cheerful and talks more than ever, happy to have her whole family around her. The apartment is full of noise and so crowded that everybody sleeps in all the beds and on all the sofas, even the sofa in the kitchen. My father, who has arrived from Bucharest, drinks a lot of *pălincă* with Ivan and Grandfather Victor and Uncle Ion. They stay in my aunt's kitchen till late at night swearing at the Communists, at the Soviet Union, at the Romanian president, at the Russian president, at the Americans who split and divided zones of influence with the Russians after the war; they smoke Carpaţi cigarettes and eat pickled tomatoes from my aunt's jars in the pantry. Ivan tells everybody that life in the Soviet Union is so hard that four families would live in an apartment the size of this one here. And that all they ever eat is *cartofeli*, potatoes. But now Russia is his home, bad as it may be.

When Great-uncle Ivan leaves to go back to Moscow, my grandfather Victor cries at the train station, and he embraces his brother for a very long time. Great-uncle Ivan picks me up and kisses me on both cheeks the way he did when he first came. After that we never hear from Uncle Ivan ever again. Grandfather Victor says he is happy they got to see each other one more time, that Ivan must have just gone back to his life in Moscow, which is different from life in Romania, and he isn't at home here any longer, after twenty-five years.

The summer after Grandfather Victor and his brother Ivan are reunited I go to the seaside with my parents and with my aunt Ana Koltzunov. She is my aunt twice removed – the fat sister of Matei, Nadia's husband. I love my aunt Ana and I think she is twice removed because she lives two cities away from the city with the Black Church. She speaks a lot but very slowly with a strong Russian accent, so all the stories she tells last for a very long time. My parents took her along to make her feel better after the death of Matei from pancreatic cancer. I think Matei was so sad because of the death of his wife, Nadia.

I love the Black Sea in all kinds of weather. My aunt Ana takes me one afternoon to meet a Russian friend of hers who lives in a white stucco house with an apricot tree in her backyard. The two women talk and whisper in Russian for a long time on the front porch. All the women in my family except for Aunt Matilda on my father's side can speak Russian from the times when Great-grandmother Paraschiva and Great-grandfather Vania lived in the former Bessarabia, before it was taken away by the Russians a second time because of what everybody in my family calls the Molotov-Ribbentrop Pact. They speak Russian when they don't want me to understand something. I some-times repeat the words *Molotov-Ribbentrop* like a chant whenever my relatives speak Russian, and then they stop and look at me with a fearful look and tell me to not mention that again. It must be something bad like Stalin.

My aunt Ana is very upset and cries because her son Petea has trouble with the secret police. People are always made to disap-pear when they get in trouble with the secret police, like if they say something bad about the president or if they don't go to the demonstrations in the big squares to cheer and shout about the Party and the *Father of the Nation*. Ana's son Petea made fun of the president at a demonstration; he imitated how he talks and how he always moves his hand up and down. A man took him away, and Ana didn't see him for a week, then he came home beaten up and with a broken arm. I heard my parents talk about Petea, but Aunt Ana doesn't know that I know about how they beat up Petea and broke his arm. She cries so hard that her friend holds and rocks her and says many Russian words that sound like calming words because they have a lot of *sh* and *ch* sounds.

I eat so many of the golden juicy apricots while my aunt and her friend are wringing their hands and crying over Petea that I get sick. A wind starts, and the apricot tree is shaken by the wind. The heavy fruit drops to the ground and breaks open.

My aunt grabs me by the hand and leaves in a rush and gets lost in the town by the Black Sea. I'm scared of the wind and thunder. The storm comes suddenly, and I'm soaked in rain and my own tears. Then, in the middle of the street, my aunt holds me and tells me I am her little *krasivaia devochka*. She uses the same words that Great-uncle Ivan had said to me when he got off the train after twenty-five years of being dead. She says she wishes she could find her son Petea.

I feel that something very important is happening, and that it's an awful thing to be a mother and to love your son so much that you forget something as simple as the way home from a friend's house.

At every corner, the sea appears at the end of the street, greenish black and wild. I love the sea like a sister. I want to go and watch the storm by the sea, but my aunt pulls my hand and crosses herself. Ana keeps saying, "Don't worry, Monichka, we'll find our street." But every time she thinks she has found it, it turns out it's a different street that only looked like our street for a second, in the rain and the dark. After two hours of going in circles in the storm, all soaked and trembling, we finally find our way home.

My aunt Ana Koltzunov says to me, "Monichka, my Monichka, how could you think we were going to get lost in a little town like this? Didn't you know your aunt Ana went all the way to the Soviet Union and back, all by herself?"

She is soaked in rain and tears. I jump into her arms and tell her I know that she is brave and of course I never thought she was lost. I tell her Petea will be all right, and she holds me and cries some more.

Before we had our trip to the seaside when we got lost in the storm, my aunt Ana brought me a big doll with long blond plaits from the USSR. I named her Tania. She brought my mother an amber necklace that she had traded for a roll of Romanian horse salami and a pair of Romanian tights. I think that my aunt is intrepid and courageous to have made such a long trip to a country so big that it could hold the entire Black Sea in it, and there would still be room left for a city or two.

In the autumn after we get back from the seaside with Aunt Ana, I hear my parents say that Petea has been made to work for the secret police so they'll forgive him for making fun of the president in the middle of a demonstration. But then he disappears again. Aunt Ana always waits for him in the evening with dinner ready, and she becomes fatter and fatter until she dies of a heart attack from never seeing Petea again and from eating all the dinners that Petea didn't get to eat. I put Tania, the big Russian doll that Aunt Ana brought me from the Soviet Union, in the corner of my bed where I can see her before I go to sleep every night.

Three Deaths, an Animal Flower, and the Word *Dor*

THE WINTER AFTER PETEA DISAPPEARS, there is the sad time when everybody in my family starts dying. My grandfather Victor, who holds me on his lap and tells me stories of Roman emperors and aqueducts, dies. My grandmother Virginia, my father's mother, who tells me the story of the golden apples and the prince who cunningly picks them, also dies. And Uncle Matei, Nadia's husband, who had been a political prisoner at the jail in Jilava where they lock up and torture all the people who don't agree with the new government, died some months ago in the beautiful house on the street with chestnut and linden trees in Bucharest.

I hide in my aunt's wardrobe and tear my ugly blue tights with the scissors because I hate how they scratch my legs and because I am afraid about all the people dying. I think that if many more people die, our family will just disappear from the face of the earth and I will be alone. I hold on to my bare knees in my aunt's wardrobe where Great-grandmother Paraschiva used to pretend to go to the city, and where they found her dead. I rock myself back and forth, hoping that nobody else in our family is going to die, at least for a long time.

They will put the dead grandmother and the dead grandfather in the ground, in deep holes. Everyone dresses up, and we go to a party and there's food but no laughing allowed. I get to see my baby cousin Miruna, who is the first baby in our family since I was born. She is two years old, and her blue eyes are so big that they seem to occupy half of her face. When she walks she looks like a wound-up toy that moves quickly, with small steps. Then she falls on her face, and she gets up again. She got into her mother's bag and ate up all the lipstick. They shouldn't leave lipstick near Miruna. I hold my big Russian doll, Tania. She won't die. She has long yellow plaits.

I watch my cousin Miruna who is a baby. She is not dying, she is screaming, and she's all round and pretty like my doll. The little lost kitten mewing in front of the door is not dead. She wants to come in. But my mother and my aunt and everybody else chase her out and tell me I can't let her in. I so much want to let the lost kitten in.

For my grandfather's funeral, the neighbours make the special chocolate cake called *televizor*, television. My aunt makes the special food for the dead, *colivă*, which has little balls of wheat inside and is creamy and has powdered sugar all over it. I like the cake *televizor* so much that I hide some in a corner of my aunt's wardrobe for later. Men play a very sad song with their trumpets when they take the dead to the cemetery, and it's so sad that I think everybody is going to melt and die and disappear. I am going to eat the cake all by myself.

My body feels like it has ants in it all the time, and people don't sleep at night. I don't like it when everybody dies in our family, and I don't like it when everybody talks about Stalin. Everybody is also talking about Nicolae Ceauşescu, our new president who talked back to the Russians all the way from the Palace Square in Bucharest and told the Russian president that he won't allow any of their tanks to come over to Romania. A bad man is following my father, and other bad people are following everybody else, and we go to the cemetery a lot. My father says this man comes into the amphitheatre where he lectures at the university and takes notes during his classes. He says *the bastard and the criminal* wants to find out if he talks about any *dangerous capitalistic influences* and about *metaphysical ideas* or *forbidden authors* to his students. Then my father says the bad man can *go to bloody hell, he is not going to stop him from doing his profession the right way.* My mother scolds my father again for the bad language he uses in front of me.

I like the cemetery. There are always flowers. I sometimes get to eat the food left for the dead, the sugary *colivă* from other people's funerals. There is a special flower on my grand-mother's grave that is called the eight o'clock flower because it opens up at eight o'clock every evening and makes a little sound like *pop* when it opens up. My father and I always wait until eight to see the flower open up. I watch it very closely. Slowly the petals move, and by eight-fifteen on my father's watch the whole flower is open, so yellow with a little black soft stick in the middle.

The yellow of the eight o'clock flower makes me not itch all over my body and makes me laugh. I like to go to my grand-mother's grave in the cemetery. My father always makes me remember Grandmother Virginia, who wore round glasses and who used to scramble in the earth for roots to feed him and his sister Matilda during the war so they wouldn't starve. And we remember the game Virginia used to play with me about us hav-ing guests and serving them walnut preserve and the time I told all the imaginary guests to go away because Grandmother was tired and wanted to go to sleep and I ate all the pretend pre-serve by myself. And then I ate half a jar of the real preserve and became sick. I think she is the one who makes the flower open up every evening, because she wants to talk to me and she can't. But she can talk to me through the yellow flower, which I believe is an animal flower because it moves and pops. I want to have an animal flower of my own.

When I am ten years old, I have to write a composition about why I love my country. I stare and stare at the white page and cannot bring myself to say why I love my country. I know I love my country: the beautiful mountains, and the sea, and the old buildings, and the universities, and the wheat fields, but every-body will say that. It's what all the literature books tell us: they tell us why we love our country, and they tell us how beautiful and rich our country is, and that we all love it.

Then suddenly it comes to me. I love my country because I *miss* my country, like I miss my mother when she is not with me. But I live in my country. Why would I miss it, if I am in it all the time? But I know what I know. I miss the country I once saw in my father's eyes as he was telling my mother and me about his childhood before the war, about the cherry orchard where he used to run with his dog that was cut to pieces by the Russians and was left to rot in the front room for them to find when they came back from their hiding place during the war. This was my father's favourite dog: a female wolf dog called Nera that followed my father everywhere and slept next to his bed every night. The Russians even took the electric sockets out of the walls, and they killed the dogs, and they would cut people's hands off to get the watches from their wrists. And Grandmother Virginia had to spend two full days cleaning up after the Russians, and the house still looked devastated. "Our house never looked the same after that," my father would say, "the Soviet sons of bitches."

"I saw them cut off people's hands on the train platform once as they got off the train, I swear. They cut off people's hands," my father repeated.

Then he talked about how beautiful it all was, before the war. There was nothing like the orchards in the spring, with all the apple and cherry trees in bloom, just like paradise.

"And there was freedom," my father said, hitting the table with his fist.

His eyes filled with tears, and he started crying with little choking sobs. I felt embarrassed for him and confused and full of pity to see my father cry like that. I envied him that childhood in his cherry orchards.

All I have is the dusty Bucharest pavement in front of our apartment building where I play hopscotch for hours or hide-and-seek, hiding behind the parked cars. My mother always calls me from the balcony and tells me to stop hiding behind the parked cars because it's dangerous and a child in the neigh-bourhood had been run over like that. My favourite game is the skipping-rope competitions, when we see who can do the most tricks and who lasts the longest without stumbling or getting the rope entangled.

I cannot say all of that in my composition. But I know I can somehow say it without saying it. I know I can describe that country and describe how I love my country because I miss my country, without mentioning the Russians who cut off people's hands and who ripped up my father's dog. I hang onto a word, the one word that Romanians are so proud of because they say it can't be translated into any other language. The word *dor*.

My father explains this word to me often. "It means some-thing like a longing, like a yearning that you can't explain and you don't know why you have it. It hits you when you look at cer-tain landscapes and listen to certain music, such as music played on special Romanian instruments whose names are untranslatable, flutes with many tubes and instruments like huge horns. Then you see the mountains where your ancestors lived and fought the Turks and the Huns and the Visigoths, and where they looked at the sky and dreamed the way you look at the sky and dream now. You look at all that, and you become melancholy and you yearn for something. That's what *dor* means."

My father gives me little lectures when I ask a question and I always listen enraptured, trying to be the best student he has ever had.

I hang onto that specific word that seems like the key to why I love my country. I write about all the things that would give me that special feeling of longing, of unquenched yearning, if I ever were to lose my country, just like what I would feel if I ever lost my mother. I write about the country I saw in my father's eyes, full of cherry and apple orchards and with snow so big and so white that it was blue. I try very hard to avoid saying anything about the ripped-up dog and the electric sockets, though I want to very badly. Instead, I imagine the colour of the orchards and I describe the hills and valleys. But I do write just a little bit about the Turks and the Visigoths, and about how brave our ancestors were to fight and free our land and bring us freedom. I say that "our fearless ancestors freed our land from the invasions of the tribes and peoples who tried to steal our freedom and enslave us and take away our green pastures and our rolling hills. But our ancestors were braver and stronger because they loved their motherland more than anything." And when I write *freedom*, I know I mean the freedom I saw in my father's eyes, because I had never seen that freedom with my own eyes. I've just heard about it from my relatives and from my father, as if it were some kind of mythic creature with wild hair flying in the wind. All I write is the word *freedom*. Only the white page knows everything I'm thinking about when I write that word.

I win the first prize with my composition about why I love my country. This is the happy time in our country, when you find even dates and bananas and red caviar in the shops without queuing, and when my mother wears her grey dress with fuchsia daisies that swells and swirls like a balloon every time she turns around.

"Soon things will get bad again, mark my words," my father says. "They're just tricking us, and the West, too. They're trying to make us think we're free. They say it's a period of *liberalization*, but in fact it's all a scam to show the Western countries what a *liberal* president we have because he stands up to the Russians. But in reality," he says, leaning close, "the Russians are in on it. Ceaușescu throws us just enough scraps to keep us from howling. This liberalization is a scam, mark my words."

I don't know what *scam* and *liberalization* mean, but I'm afraid about the scam part. I think that maybe the scam is when the black van will come in front of our building and take my mother and father away, or when the Russians will start ripping up dogs and cutting off people's hands in the street and will leave us without electricity again, with big holes in the walls in place of the sockets, like during the war. I'm so afraid of that *scam* that I don't want any *liberalization* either. I tremble at night when I hear airplanes, in the summer night of Bucharest that smells like linden flowers and burnt asphalt. I'm only happy again when I hear people talk and laugh in the street. I think this is the happy time in my country as I fall asleep and I feel the yearning in the word *dor*.

Aunt Matilda and the Earthquake

I REMEMBER MOST VIVIDLY the Sunday mornings stretching like a long string of beads from my childhood to my adolescence. I measure time by the new dresses I get every couple of years when the old ones become so small that my arms stick out like thin tree limbs, and by the new textbooks I receive in school, in which there are no more pictures of Lina uttering simple sentences under the blue sky of the Party but real texts by Romanian writers and complicated literary analyses.

On Sunday mornings I go to the Romanian Atheneum in the Palace Square of Bucharest to listen to concerts of classical music. We go with the high school as part of our musical education classes. We put on our best clothes and fall into long colourful dreams on the red velvet chairs as Chopin's études trickle their melancholy notes into our souls, as Mozart's symphonies race through our hearts, as Beethoven's Seventh Symphony gallops its mad swirls through our flesh.

On such a Sunday afternoon, after the concert, I visit my aunt Matilda, who wanted me to be called Maria because she had prayed to the Holy Virgin the day I was born. She lives near the Atheneum on a little side street lined with chestnut trees. She writes plays and makes the most delicious walnut and rose-petal preserves in the world. My aunt Matilda has a white round face with velvety brown eyes and very dark hair that falls in waves down her back. She has graceful, slow gestures. When she laughs, she throws her head back like an actress. She isn't married. She says I am her *one big love*, but I know she just wasn't lucky in love. I know that there were men who lied to her and cheated on her. I know that deep down she is as sad as a weeping willow. She writes children's stories and plays, which she has a hard time getting published or produced, because the editors and the directors think she's not *contemporary* enough. "What exactly is there to be contemporary about?" she asks after every rejection. "Elena Ceauşescu?" She laughs at her own joke and throws her head back, showing her beautiful teeth.

Just then I see the crystals of her chandelier sway and tinkle. This chandelier comes from the same house from which my father inherited the black mahogany desk, where we keep the picture of Nora in an orange tree.

Aunt Matilda also has a Greek icon of the Virgin Mary with drops of blood on her face. Matilda says it is real blood. She says the icon was found floating in the water by a Greek soldier, who stuck his knife in the face of the Virgin to rescue it, and it bled real blood. Suddenly the crystals are jingling louder, and the whole house is shaking like a boat. Something like an end-of-the-world howl fills the air. A roar of metal and earth and strange wild animals hurts our ears and dizzies us. We stand holding each other in the middle of the room. I bury my head in the fragrant softness of my aunt's breasts while she prays frantically to the Virgin Mary who is bleeding in the Greek icon.

I am waiting to die, to disappear, to feel the worst pain I've ever felt. Now the house is shaking so much that we can barely stand. My aunt is holding me, and she is praying. I squeeze my eyes shut as hard as I can, and a white emptiness fills my head, the bright light of the impossible noise. I'm thinking that the Russians have finally invaded us and are bombing all of Bucharest. In a few minutes, only piles of mortar will be left of my aunt's house. We will be under the bricks, with everything we have and with everything we think, with the music and the dreams of music . . . It will all come down and crumble like the very end, the very end of the world.

When it stops, we grab our coats and rush out onto the marble staircase. There are fallen bricks and cracks in the walls and hot water spurting from broken pipes. Hundreds of people, some dressed, others half dressed, are running in all directions. The building right across the street is an enormous pile of bricks and mortar. Screams and wails are coming from everywhere. The air is filled with white dust, and everything beyond looks unreal, grey and watery. A woman is running towards us tearing at her hair and screaming. As we walk towards University Boulevard, the crowds become so thick that we can hardly move at all. We have to push through; we use our elbows to make our way. There are crumbled buildings on both sides of the boulevard, and screams are coming from everywhere.

There is the building where I used to eat the special cream puffs with my father – now a mound of white plaster. The grocery store where they sometimes have butter or cheese is half collapsed. The half that remains is gaping wide open. There is a toilet hanging from a pipe, a wardrobe ready to slide down a twisted floor. A mashed leg with a shoe on it sticks out from beneath a fallen wall of stone. Somewhere else, an arm is waving; someone is calling; someone stops moving and is silent. We are walking in the direction of my parents' apartment. I don't want to think of our building, of my father caught under a mound of bricks, of my mother lying in the street. Why would they have survived wars, the Russian and German and American bombs, just to die in an earthquake?

"An earthquake is the last thing these people need" are my father's first words as he sees us approach.

"Neither of you is hurt? Thank God!" my mother says, rushing to put her arms around me.

"Thank God and the Virgin Mary!" adds my aunt. "God help us, and the Blessed Virgin help us!" she wails and crosses herself.

Both my parents are standing at the street corner. Our building is still whole, but the one beside it has crumbled. My mother is sobbing as she hugs me, and though she squeezes me to her so hard it hurts, I don't want her to let go.

Here the streets are strangely quiet. Everyone has fled towards the big boulevards, and we stand alone at the corner of a street as silent as a cemetery. There is thick white dust swirling around us, and the smells of blood, mortar and hyacinths. It's spring, the spring equinox, and the death around us is so huge there are no words for it. But we are alive.

"We are so lucky," says my father. He turns and takes a few steps towards our home, then stops and looks up at the hole in the sky where another building had stood.

"This looks just like after the war," he says, talking to himself. "If a war ends, then there's hunger. If we get enough bread to fill our bellies a little, then there's terror. Just when we start to have a little hope, then this comes . . . comes down on us like a fist."

This is the spring before the summer when I discover my first love, sprouting from raw earth, raw flesh, misery and death. My love among the rocky, dark Carpathians grew like a stubborn plant, like a wild creature, like the colour pink in the middle of the rainbow, like the yellow hyacinth blossoming from the cracked, bleeding earth.

Secret Activities and Typewriters

THE YEAR WHEN I FALL IN LOVE with Mihai, my father is involved in secret activities he talks about only in whispers with my mother. I'm not supposed to have a boyfriend because *you never know*. I tell myself *Screw it all* and cling to my green-eyed mountain boy. I tell Marx and Engels and Lenin and Ceaușescu to *fuck off* every time we make love in Mihai's room and I catch a glimpse of their monstrous portraits spying on us from the building across the street.

We can't own typewriters any longer. They're illegal. A policeman comes to our house one evening to ask us if we have one.

"Good evening, Comrade Manoliu," the policeman says ceremoniously. "We're checking to see if you own a typewriter. It's just a routine check."

I can see my father's jaws clench with anger and his eyes flash. He waits a moment, drags on his cigarette, trying to contain his fury.

"I'm curious," my father says. "Why is it that you need to perform such routine checks?"

The officer is taken aback. Romanian policemen are notorious for how dumb and illiterate they are. This one must be no exception, I think, as I watch his self-important pose, his scrunched-up small forehead.

"Perform?" he repeats as if he were insulted.

"Yes," my father says. "Why do you need to perform such routine checks?"

He purposely stresses the word *perform*.

"We are not performing, sir, we are checking, just checking," says the policeman proudly.

My mother stares at my father, then blinks, then winks, as if wanting to say: *Just say no and get it over with, stop all this useless talk.*

"We do not own a typewriter," answers my father, as if having understood her silent admonishment. "But you are free to look," he says. "Please, go and check, look under our mattresses, look under our beds, look inside our toilets. Go and see for yourself if we own a typewriter."

The policeman looks embarrassed and moves towards the door, as if trying to escape my father's onslaught.

"No, sir, there is no need to bother yourselves. But if you know someone who does, would you be so kind to inform us?" asks the policeman as if it were an afterthought.

This time my father does not even make an effort to hide his disdain. He sends a swirl of Kent cigarette smoke right into the policeman's face.

The policeman takes some notes in a little notebook, probably the clandestine typewriter notebook. He turns on his heels and leaves muttering a "Yes, sir, good-bye, sir." After the policeman leaves, my father is overjoyed by his own cunning and courage.

I go to the oven where my mother hid our Zinger a few days ago, when the news went around that they were checking for typewriters. I take it out from among our pots and pans. I carry it to the mahogany desk with the picture of Nora smiling in that glorious orange tree in America, and I write a letter to the boyfriend I'm not supposed to have, on the typewriter we're not allowed to own.

Now that vacation is over and I'm back in Bucharest, Mihai and I pine for each other like Bedouins in the desert pining for water and an oasis. The daughter of a friend of ours has been run over *accidentally* on the pavement. I don't get why all these people keep driving on the pavement.

"It's bad," my father keeps saying. "And it's going to get worse, mark my words," he says, staring into the cigarette smoke.

It must be bad, because you can't be safe anywhere. You can't even own a sorry old Zinger typewriter, and you get killed for walking on the pavement. You're better off walking in the middle of the street. I wait for Christmas; I long for the white snow in my aunt's town. I long to be with Mihai on the same paths where we were this summer, lying on the fresh, glistening snow.

In December, Mihai is waiting for me at the train station, morose and unshaven, leaning against a wall with a cigarette and wearing a black leather jacket. I'm startled, and for a moment I want to run away when he takes me by the arm and ushers me through the crowd on the platform. There's a new confidence, even an arrogance, in the way he moves, the way he takes charge of me, and his black leather jacket annoys me. I try to push back my instincts. Not all secret police wear black leather jackets, I tell myself, and not all men who wear black leather jackets are secret police. That would be too obvious even for a stupid little dictatorship like ours.

When we escape from the crowded station and find ourselves in the street under the winter sky and the light snowflakes, he holds me in a tight embrace and kisses me in the middle of the pavement. I kiss him back, heedless of the people edging by and staring at us. I don't care about Zinger typewriters and my father's secret dissident activities any more. The streets become dark and empty as we walk. They remind me of the night of many moons, my dream of a toothless Mariana grinning at us. I push all the bad dreams and troubling thoughts far down where I can't hear them calling me. I concentrate on his profile, on the way that the snowflakes get caught in his dark eyelashes and melt on his red lips.

I start my shuttle up and down the stairs, back and forth between Mihai's and my aunt's house. His body seems warmer and more delicious than ever between the starched bedsheets. Soon I don't give a damn about his black leather jacket. He plays Grieg for me again, and sometimes we dance in his room to Western music, Ella Fitzgerald and Nat King Cole, Elvis Presley and the Beatles. He teaches me dance steps. We swirl and bump into his furniture, fall onto his bed laughing, sweaty with desire. American jazz is seeping into my Romanian veins. Thank God it's winter and the windows are closed so I don't have to see the three bearded Communist gods and the *Father of the Nation* grotesquely watching us from the building across the street.

One evening we talk politics, and I make so much fun of the *Beloved Leader*, imitating his ignorant drawl, that my eyes water with laughter.

Mihai gets mad and says, "You really shouldn't talk like that, Mona."

His tone is harsh, reprimanding. He startles me, and the moons and toothless Mariana rush into my head.

We go out for a walk in silence. I sit in the snow in the middle of the street. I lie down in the middle of the street as a form of protest. He looks at me and starts laughing.

"I don't think it's a bit funny to speak in defence of a tyrant and an illiterate criminal," I yell in the middle of the street.

I think of my father's worried face, of the spiteful look he gave the cop who asked about the typewriter. Nausea rises in my throat as I lie on my back in the snow, under the winter stars. Then suddenly Mihai lies down next to me and takes my hand.

"No, it's not funny," he says. "I was just teasing you."

Now I'm all confused and don't know whether to kiss him or slap him. He's just teasing, I think. He listens to Ella Fitzgerald and the Beatles. I can trust him. I can love him. I hear a train whistle. Something like the approach of death flutters through me as I lie on my back in the snow.

I stand up and drag him up as well. As he stands in front of me, I see him again as I saw him that afternoon at the white rock, above the phenomenon of pink and violet clouds: wild, dark, proud and with luscious red lips.

The next morning my father calls from Bucharest and says I have to return home immediately, it's urgent. But I don't listen. There's no urgency in my life beyond Mihai. I spend my days going up and down the stairs. I hold his warm body at dawn and in the afternoon. I walk through the snow on his arm, my head wrapped in a silky blue babushka shawl, like Katharine Hepburn in a film where she rides teary-eyed in what looks like a carriage or a horse-drawn sleigh next to Spencer Tracy. From five to seven in the evening we sometimes get foreign films on Romanian national television, sandwiched between news about the latest achievements of *our beloved leader and his wife.* Those same hours there are queues in the street for beef, cooking oil, bananas, menstrual cotton. It's a rich country after all. We pass by the queues and smile disdainfully. We don't need any of that. We make do without just about anything. We make love; we walk in the snow. Sometimes we drink vodka straight from the bottle and eat a lot of bread. We avoid politics. I forget my bad dreams for a while.

Until one afternoon a week later when my mother calls with a weird shake in her voice, telling me to come home right away. This time I'm scared. I buy my train ticket back to the capital.

We make love until half an hour before the train pulls out. I can't find my stockings. I have to wear my Bulgarian boots over bare legs and feet. My feet hurt and are cold as we walk to the station, the same road we'd taken when I arrived and he'd kissed me in the middle of the street, under the snowflakes, under the scornful looks of strangers. He does the same thing now, right in front of the station. He stops and kisses me in front of train conductors who have finished their shift, gypsies with heavy sacks on their backs, old people dragging huge suitcases tied with rope.

There's an overwhelming confusion in my head. Pink fogs are mixed up with blue snows, toothless grins, huge suitcases, cars running over people on pavements. Huge red moons like stars are covering the sky, and queues for food are swirling around every building on every street, in every city, like ugly serpents. I am thinking that maybe I am losing my mind. Then I know I have to run for my train. I know I have to get on that train and leave Mihai there in the middle of the platform, morose and unshaven. I watch him stand alone on the train platform while my train is slowly moving away and I try to shape his image in my mind with utmost precision as I am waving at him and as he is getting smaller and smaller: his head leaning to one side, one hand in his pocket, one hand waving at me with a steady motion.

Secret Police and Symbolist Poets

W HEN I GET BACK TO BUCHAREST filled with the sadness of having just separated from Mihai, my mother is in a strange mood, conspiratorial and unusually calm. Her head is covered in pink hair rollers. She says my father hasn't come home for three days.

"What do you mean?" I ask, not really understanding my mother's calm. The thought that my father might actually be among those *taken away* by the Securitate jolts me out of my love dreaminess.

As if to distract herself, she starts rambling about the women in her family, the Slavic side, passionate women who came through floods and famines and bombings. I feel them in my blood: Nadia and Vera, Ana and Nina, and the fierce Paraschiva. My great-grandmothers, grandmothers, aunts and great-aunts. These women who lived for love and died instantly, who saw their houses turned to dust by American or Russian bombs, women who weren't afraid of Nazis or Soviets. Are we like them, I wonder. We need that same fierce courage all over again.

Mostly I think of Nadia, the glamorous, tragic great-aunt whose story always brings tears to my mother's eyes. I am back in the terrifying fifties, with the notorious black vans of the secret police stopping in front of people's houses and taking them away from the dinner table, from their beds, from the side of a sick child or a dying mother, and locking them up for unfathomable reasons: the job they held before the war, a sentence they uttered at a party, a joke they made to a friend, an attitude, a gesture, something that someone else reported about them, or nothing at all. This is how Matei Varnitski, Nadia's dashing officer husband, is taken away one evening in the middle of one of their elegant parties in Bucharest, in the beautiful house with marble fireplaces on the street lined with chestnut trees.

Nadia is talking to one of the guests and drinking champagne. It is one or two in the morning. Suddenly she has a queasy feeling that something is happening. She sees Matei stand in the doorway and turn his head towards her right before he disappears, flanked by two unknown men. He is smiling at her. *Don't worry,* he mouths to her. The last thing she sees is a little stout man with a face like a chimpanzee grinning at her, and the bald head of the other one, pushing him out of the house. Through the glass of the front door she sees the ugly van move away slowly. She wants to scream, but the scream gets stuck in her throat; she wants to move, but her feet are stuck to the shiny floors. Through the side bay windows, she sees the van turn the corner and move out of sight. Matei is gone, and she doesn't understand why the party is still going on, as if nothing had happened. Everything becomes quiet and starts moving in slow motion: the drunken guests waltzing and stumbling, the guests bragging loudly about their war experiences, the more subdued guests talking softly about the latest trends in poetry. Then it all becomes still and completely quiet.

I imagine Nadia through the long ordeal that follows. I have always thought she could have been the one member of our family escaping disasters and having an unscathed and happy life. I watch Nadia move through the lonely years that follow Matei's arrest. I see her move slowly about the beautiful house, gliding as if in a dream, stroking the gleaming cherry and mahogany furniture, letting her dress and her slip glide off her body at night before getting into the lonely bed. Two, three, five years go by like that. Then my aunt Nina moves in with her to keep her company in the empty house with its sad ballroom. One day when she picks up the mail, Nadia sees Matei's handwriting on a crumpled, yellow postcard. I picture Nadia feverishly looking at the piece of paper. Every time I hope for a different ending. I am hoping the words on the yellow postcard say: *Coming home next week. Matei,* instead of what they really say: *Am fine. Will write more soon. M.*

The postcard does nothing to comfort or reassure her. The ambiguity of those few words is unbearable to Nadia. And the incompleteness of his signature terrifies her. He had never signed a note or a letter with anything other than his full name. She had wanted them to grow old together. She is still young, but for her it is all over. She stares at the words on the postcard until dusk has enveloped her in the empty house. The linden smells are rushing into the house through all the open windows. She hates summer and she hates the odour of linden. Matei was taken away on a night like this, she thinks. My aunt Nina finds her later that evening dead on the floor, under the crystal chandelier, still holding the postcard from Matei, her Siamese cat mewing on her shoulder.

"This group your father is involved with," my mother is saying the words slowly. "They've been trying to organize an uprising. And I suppose somebody must have turned your father in. They arrested him." I look at my mother in disbelief, Nadia's story throbbing inside my head like a crazed bird. The two women, my mother and her aunt, seem to merge into each other. Maybe my father will disappear for many years like Great-uncle Matei did and my mother will fall dead in the middle of our minuscule apartment.

"Your father is in trouble, Mona. He's been doing things . . ."

"Things? What things?"

"I told you, aren't you listening? An uprising, something like a coup, they are trying to make Ceauşescu resign."

"What uprising? What coup?" I ask. "What are you talking

about?" It all seems unreal. "Who in their right mind gets involved in a coup now," I ask her, shrieking in disbelief, "when you can get thrown in prison just for having a typewriter?"

"Exactly," says my mother. "The typewriters are crucial." Her face looks strained, and for the first time I see two deep lines stretching across her forehead. But because of the crown of pink rollers circling her head, her serious frowning face looks almost pathetic. She is wringing her hands as she often does when she is nervous and playing with the heavy golden ring on her middle finger, which used to belong to Grandfather Victor. She stares one moment at the door, as if waiting for it to open and for my father to walk through it; the next moment she stares intently at me. I feel sorry for my mother. She looks so small and both funny and sad as she sits in the middle of the sofa slowly swinging her legs back and forth. Her eyes look bigger and rounder than usual.

She tells me there are antigovernment manifestos being copied by the thousands on typewriters. The police are matching the type on the manifestos with the typewriters registered with the government.

"The old Zinger," my mother says. "Your father got it from the university. He thought no one wanted it. He didn't realize," she tells me. "It had been registered before he borrowed it."

My head is spinning. It's just a matter of days before we'll be *accidentally* run over while standing in some stupid queue for butter or toilet paper. Or before a big ugly van will stop in front of our apartment building and take me and my mother away, too. I am sure my mother knows more about my father's arrest than she lets on. Maybe they will kill him or put him in prison for a long time the way they did to Great-uncle Matei. And to think we had imagined Ceauşescu was going to be better and was going to turn things around, away from the Russians, after his big courageous speech in the Palace Square in 1968. My father had been right then, to say it was all a scam to mislead the West into believing Romania was going towards some kind of liberalization and was breaking away from the Soviet Union. I have no idea why my father thinks this is the right time to start writing antigovernment manifestos. His words from so long ago, when I had no idea what they really meant, appear clearly, ominously, to me now, as my mother's face seems strangely similar to Nadia's face in the one sepia photograph we have of her. Dusk is slowly creeping in. The room is wrapped in shadows. I sigh, and the ashes from my father's ashtray fly in all directions. I make an effort to open my mouth to speak, but I am choked. Finally, I decide to try to get her to tell me the whole truth.

"Where is he?" I ask her. "Where is Father? How do you know he's been arrested? How do you know he's not dead by now? And have you heard from him? Tell me!" I yell.

"Stop asking so many questions," my mother says icily. "His friend Darius from the university came over and told me he saw him get into a black car right in front of the university as he was leaving after his classes on Monday. There were two other men in the car. He said your father was calm and waved at him as he got in. Miron's friend from the philosophy department, Tudor, is also part of the group . . . I trust him. He's safe. He's being released soon. I think," she adds faintly. She gets up from the sofa and tidies the objects on my father's little desk: his Pelikan fountain pen, a few books lying around, and some white sheets of paper. She moves on to tidy up the rest of the room, which doesn't really need tidying.

I can't quite process all these bits of information. This moment seems distant, in black and white on a screen. I am not involved in this. It does not concern me.

"There is nothing to do right now but wait," my mother concludes in a strangely calm voice, placing her clasped hands gently in her lap. Then she changes her tone again and asks: "Did you tell anyone?"

"Tell anyone what? And who? What would I tell?"

"That friend of yours," she says, fussing with the rollers in her hair. And then she meets my eyes. "Be careful. He might be one of them."

"One of who?" I ask, furious. "Who, Mother? What are you talking about? Who's *he*? Who's *them*?"

Pronouns have lost their meaning. Nouns are too dangerous to pronounce, so we replace them with vague pronouns, until no one knows any more who is who, who is following whom. I am shouting again, and my mother looks at me with pursed lips, stubbornly.

"Your *friend*," she says. "I have a feeling . . . I think . . . Mihai is . . . might be . . . are you sure about him?" But she calms herself down, sits back on the sofa, and takes a few breaths. Then she starts talking to me again, only this time in her sweeter voice. "You know, when your father and I met in the fifties, we were both sure of each other . . . we would have stuck our hands in the fire for each other. And those times were even worse than now. I knew your father would have died before doing anything – you know – selling out or betraying me." Her eyes meet mine again and hold them. "All I'm asking you, Mona, is can you say the same about this Mihai of yours? And by the way," she adds, taking a slightly harsher tone, "I hope you are not doing anything . . . you know, stupid or dangerous . . . it would make me so sad."

It drives me crazy the way my parents always call him *this Mihai of yours* and the way my mother makes it sound so tragic that Mihai and I might be lovers. How can she be so naïve not to know already? But mostly it drives me crazy that I cannot really give a wholehearted yes to the question about whether I am sure of Mihai the way my mother was of my father. I hate my doubts, and I hate my mother for making them even worse. I conjure up Paraschiva and Nadia, who were sure of their loves until the second when they both died their sudden deaths. I beg them to help me through my gnawing uncertainties, to help me make sure Mihai is brave and honest and not a traitor. But then I realize I would still love him even if he *were* a traitor. My stomach knots up at this sickening thought.

That night, as I try to fall asleep, I strain myself to see it, and suddenly there we are, amid a sea of clouds, next to our white rock, the two of us, Mona Maria and Mihai, embracing above the city with the Black Church. We kiss as history, with all its bleak queues for food, its pavement accidents, and its typewriters, keeps rolling on and on.

Miraculously, my father returns the next day, grubby, dirty, and tired, and with a wild expression in his eyes. He has an ugly bruise on his cheek, directly under his right eye, and he is limping. My mother, who during the long nights of his absence had managed to write an entire volume of bleak poems, is revived at the sight of my father. She starts boiling potatoes and carrots, the only things in the pantry. My father recounts feverishly what happened: that one of the interrogators turned out to be a former student of his – Petrescu. "He's a big shot now, a colonel." My father smiles with disdain. So they ended up discussing the Romantic and the Symbolist poets. They roughed him up at first, made some threats, he tells us, but then let him go.

"You know, this Petrescu individual," he starts as if recounting a funny story from work, "did a thesis with me on the influences of French Symbolism on Romanian poets. It was a pretty good thesis, actually. About symbols of emptiness in the poems of George Bacovia," my father goes on, as if any of this mattered. "Emptiness." My father laughs. "Can you imagine?"

For a moment, my father looks as satisfied as if he had given a lecture to an amphitheatre full of eager students. But then his face changes again. I am staring at him in disbelief. What does he think he can achieve with his manifestos, I wonder. But how can I tell him to stop? His face is changed in a way that worries me. He keeps staring wildly in the distance as if fixed on some terrible memory. I think of Great-uncle Matei and how Aunt Nina and my mother always described his face that August 15 in 1957 when they saw him for a few minutes as he was being brought into the state courthouse in Bucharest for the trial of *political treason*: gaunt and with a wild look staring at something that only he could see. This was after Nadia had already fallen dead in the hallway of their elegant house, holding on to his postcard.

Even if my father does have some old student acquaintance among the secret police who helped him out this time, he cannot possibly trust or count on his protection for ever. It suddenly hits me: my father could be killed. In his great idealism, he thinks he can overturn the government by writing up some antigovernment manifestos and throwing them around University Square. He thinks he is going to keep being lucky because a student of his who happened to like the Symbolists showed him some pity after his men had already beaten him up. If others have disappeared or were run over on the pavement for less than this, he will certainly find a violent end before too long.

At the dinner table, my father starts sobbing over the boiled potatoes and carrots with the same little sobs as when he told us the story of his childhood orchards and the Russian soldiers who cut up his dog. My mother is undoing her rollers at the table instead of eating, and she piles them up neatly in her lap, staring at the wall. I choke on a potato and I don't miss my country any longer the way I once did in my composition. As I watch my father's tears and my mother's hair fall down on her face, I want to get out of my country. I want us all to be somewhere else, where it's safe and where we can have a better daily diet. I hate the manifestos.

Dangerous Carnations

THEY MEET IN BASEMENTS AND ATTICS: workers, students, artists. They meet in places with rats and roaches where the wind howls through broken windows and doors won't close, places that smell of urine and vomit. This is in the newly built apartment buildings near the Bucur Obor Market, which isn't a market any longer because it is always out of everything. Sometimes the attic or the basement sections are left unfinished by the construction workers and become festering locales for vermin, drunkards and delinquents. Or meeting places for would-be revolutionaries. At other times the group meets at someone's house in the old Turkish and Greek section of Bucharest, with the little consignment boutiques and the buildings in the eighteenth-century Brancovan architectural style: white stucco with lacy brown verandas and woodwork. I know about the meetings because I followed my father a couple of times to two different meeting places and waited in a corner, behind a glass door, or in the hallway of an old building with a squeaky staircase, listening to their meeting. It was late at night, and I walked a certain distance from my father, feeling like a detective from an Agatha Christie novel, my heart pounding crazily out of my chest. They get together a few times a week and change their meeting places often, sometimes from one day to the next. They all have one book of our classic writers like

Sadoveanu or Arghezi with them, in case they get caught, to show they are just meeting to discuss our immortal classics.

Mostly they write manifestos, talk about censored poetry, and prepare for something. It's not clear just what. They even talk about weapons, though no one seems to know how they work or where to get them. They talk about throwing the manifestos – they are just leaflets, really – from all the scaffolding in Bucharest. Since the earthquake, there's a lot of scaffolding. They also mention trying to get information to Radio Free Europe about the human rights violations in Romania, "so the West can hear it, too, so the whole world can know what we are going through". The big news is that Ceauşescu's right-hand man, General Pacepa, defected to America, where he was given asylum. My father says this is a huge blow to the system and it's the right time to do something. I hear my father's resounding voice during the meeting in the new building near the Bucur Obor Market. Then I hear people shushing him to talk softer, what if someone is listening. Others also mention Pacepa and say that he will probably try to help dissident movements from abroad, wherever he may be. And communicate via Radio Free Europe with the ones inside. At that point I tiptoe back out quiet as a cat.

Autumn is slowly settling in over Bucharest, and the poplars in front of our windows are shaking their pointy heads, sending droves of swirling yellow leaves into the wind. I shiver at the idea of the impending cold weather and the growing dangers every time I get into bed. My father is absent from home more often and looks more fierce and distraught than ever. At the dinner table he stares into his plate as if he were searching for something. After dinner he spends a lot of time with his head glued to his Grundig trying to get clear reception of Radio Free Europe. Usually the static is overpowering, and my mother screams at him to *turn it the hell off.* But once in a while, the voices come in clearly, with an echo as if from a different universe: deep, conspiratorial, mentioning dissenting authors and their actions of resistance or interviewing émigré writers about the abuses of the Romanian Party and leadership. My father's face brightens up as if in some kind of ecstasy. My mother's poems go on about death and imaginary places covered with snow.

One afternoon, soon after I come home from school, I hear my father tell my mother in a hushed voice that his old friend, an electrician by the name of Dumitru Iordache, was arrested according to Article 166 for throwing manifestos from scaffolding in the Lipscani neighbourhood with the Turkish bazaars, where the gypsies sell their tin pots, wooden spoons and roasted pumpkin seeds. The manifestos are calling for the people to replace Ceauşescu as Party and state leader. "They will probably kill Iordache," says my father in a resigned tone.

My mother is silent, and I hear the anger in her silence, in her quick breathing and her sighs. Then she blurts out: "You are all idiots. Don't you realize the danger for Mona?"

My mother is crying, and my father lights up another cigarette. The windows are slammed shut by a gust of wind, and I am so startled that I fall off the chair where I'm perched secretly listening to my parents' shushed conversation. My father pushes open the door to our improvised living room and sees me struggling to get up and act as if nothing has happened. He holds me to his chest for a few long seconds, tells me I shouldn't be spying on my parents, and we start laughing about how I looked falling off the chair.

I want to forget about Iordache throwing manifestos on top of the Turkish bazaars in Lipscani, and I go to the library of the American embassy to borrow books in English. I devour everything with an indiscriminate appetite: John Steinbeck, Emily Dickinson, Eugene O'Neill, Arthur Miller, Virginia Woolf, James Joyce. I am intrigued by how Stephen Dedalus leaves everything behind in one moment of folly, in one grand gesture: country, family, religion, love. He wants to be free, to find himself.

I want to turn into a bird like the girl he sees on the beach. I want to become the bird in James Joyce's metaphor. To fly to my love in the Carpathians, surprise him at dawn, flee away across the mountains and across the wide seas. I want to cross the skies side by side with my love.

The Romanian soldiers standing in front of the American embassy watch me with blank eyes. I stare at them boldly, as if I could make them ashamed of what they have to do: inform on every citizen who enters the embassy. I even go to a movie showing at the American library, *One Flew over the Cuckoo's Nest*. I strike up a conversation with the American librarian about the movie and about Jack Nicholson's acting, although we are not supposed to talk to foreigners. A man who is not a soldier but certainly must be the library's informer is staring at me with his right hand tucked inside his blazer, as if ready to pull out a gun. The librarian, a tall man with a grey moustache, compliments me on my *excellent English* and I blush and thank him. I leave the library feeling elated by the conversation in English and threatened by the man with the hand tucked inside his blazer.

They put politically dangerous people in asylums that are worse than that in the film. People disappear inside asylums all the time when they aren't run over on the pavement. They are medicated until they don't know who they are any more and they'll say anything they're asked to say. Usually they are never seen or heard of again.

My father's psychiatrist friend Mihnea resists the internment of people suspected of *political treason* and is arrested, then released after a month with threats that he will be imprisoned for much longer if he continues to resist. He is supposed to inject his patients with tranquillizers, but he sometimes uses water. He tells the patients to pretend they're numb and tranquillized and not say anything compromising. Some eventually disappear anyway. There is little he can do in the end, he tells my father.

I now have my own personal secret-police agent, someone young and tall who always wears a suit and tie and who actually lives in my neighbourhood. The secret police are truly efficient. It must be because of my frequent visits to the American library and my conversations with Ralph, the American librarian. They must think I am trying to seduce him in order to escape to America, although he wears a wide wedding ring and has talked to me about his wife, Sally. I don't want to go to America, and I certainly don't want to marry an American man in order to leave the country. I just want to practise my English and hear Ralph talk about Chicago. He lives in Chicago, or really near Chicago, in what he calls a suburb. He tells me about the Chicago skyline and Lake Michigan and the tallest building in the world, the Sears Tower. I am having a hard time imagining the city of Chicago next to a big lake. I have always imagined Chicago as a frightening city swarming with gangsters and with cars chasing each other at one hundred kilometres an hour. Ralph laughs wholeheartedly when he hears me talk about the Chicago gangsters and the car chases and says not all of Chicago is like that. The man with the hand hidden inside his blazer is always listening to our conversations in a corner of the reading room of the library. Sometimes he pretends to be reading a book.

My personal secret-police agent lives in the building across from ours, so I have the *good fortune* to be under twenty-four-hour surveillance. When I leave the house, he's waiting outside his building. Sometimes he follows me. Sometimes he nods and smiles at me.

One evening, he pays a visit to our home. He brings a big bouquet of red carnations. He rings the bell and waits on the step with his flowers. My parents and I stand at the open door and stare at him.

He clears his throat and grins. "Good evening. I'm Sergeant Dumitriu, a neighbour. I hope I'm not bothering you. May I come in for a minute?"

"What for?" asks my father.

"Just to chat a little. If this isn't a good time, I can come again later. I brought these flowers for your lovely daughter."

And he peers over their heads at me, handing me the huge bouquet of red carnations.

"This is a bad time," my father says.

My mother and I look at each other, panicked.

"Come in, please. It's no bother," says my mother.

I hold the carnations away from my body, as if they were poisonous. I take the crystal vase on the mahogany desk and place the flowers in it, without water.

Sergeant Dumitriu walks in, and my mother motions to him to sit down. He settles himself in my mother's chair. My father is standing in the middle of the living room. I sit opposite the sergeant.

"Comrade Manoliu, forgive me, but I need to . . . to bother you with a few questions, if I may," he says. He asks my father if he knows anything about the *slanderous* manifestos going around the university and in the Lipscani neighbourhood. *Naïve, reactionary ramblings,* he calls them. *Hooliganism.* He says that his colleagues were wondering, since my father is a professor, if he might know of anyone who might be involved. Students, or even –

"And who are your colleagues?" my father asks.

Sergeant Dumitriu laughs as if he has just heard a good joke.

"My colleagues. You know . . . at work."

My mother says, "Mr Dumitriu, would you like some walnut preserve? Some cold water?"

She goes to the kitchen to bring the preserve Aunt Matilda made for us.

My father's jaws are clenched. He lights a cigarette. Sergeant Dumitriu relaxes a bit in his chair, happy to change the subject. "Yes, please. Walnut preserve is my favourite. My grandmother used to make it."

I stare at my father and then at Sergeant Dumitriu, terrified he might ask some trick question I won't know how to answer. Something about Ralph the librarian, for instance.

There's a moment of awkward silence, when the only sound is my father drawing fiercely on his cigarette. Then he looks at the sergeant through a cloud of smoke and says, "Do you have any of these *manifestos* you can show me?"

"I don't, sir. No, I don't have any with me, but I've seen some. Trash, pure trash."

My mother comes back with the walnut preserve and a glass of water. Sergeant Dumitriu eats daintily and compliments my mother. Just like his grandmother's, he says. My father crushes his cigarette in the ashtray on the mahogany desk and lights up another.

"Maybe your daughter, Miss Mona," he says, turning to me with his smile. "Maybe you've heard some talk about this, among your friends at school."

He looks at me with a strange smile. I get shivers down my spine. I hope the idiot isn't in love with me or something. I stare back at him almost with fascination.

My father's eyes suddenly flicker with anger at the sound of my name in the man's mouth. His familiarity disgusts me as well.

"My daughter knows nothing of manifestos, apart from that of Comrades Marx and Engels, of course," my father says. "She studies poetry. Ah! She has just read the *Symbolist Manifesto* of 1886. Tell me, Sergeant," he continues, "are you familiar with the French Symbolists?"

"Hardly, Professor. I'm a police officer. I'm afraid we have no time for these symbolist people, as you call them."

"Ah yes, of course. And yet I have a former student who's now a police officer, a colonel, I believe, and he's a great lover of the Symbolists. I was enjoying quite a spirited discussion with him on that very subject not long ago. Perhaps you know him: Comrade Petrescu?"

The sergeant's smile fades suddenly. "Thank you, Mrs Mano-liu, for the excellent walnut preserve. Perhaps I'll have the pleasure of visiting you again soon, but for now I must be going."

Sergeant Dumitriu gets up to leave, kisses my mother's hand, and thanks her again for the preserve. He holds out his hand towards my father, but my father stands smoking, smiling with the same look of defiance. The sergeant pretends not to notice my father's refusal to shake his hand, then nods to me and bids me good night. Again his eyes linger on my face and his mouth stretches into a grin.

"They do interrogations in style these days," says my father, as soon as Dumitriu is out of the door. "Now they bring flowers!" He collapses into his worn chair, knocking his reading lamp's shade askew. His hand trembles so violently he struggles to stub out his cigarette in the overflowing ashtray beside his stack of books. He gazes at the spray of carnations glowing obscenely red before the desk lamp. He looks at it, fascinated, as if it were a fire. I sit down at the mahogany desk with the glass top and stare at the painting of the old man walking through a field covered with snow on the wall facing me. It has been there for as long as I can remember, and it has always made me feel calmer with its bluish expanse of snow and a tired old man in a black coat and a cane, crossing the field for what seems like an eternity. The glass top is refreshing against my arms, and the snow in the painting seems deliciously cool. I am flushed and sweaty after Dumitriu's visit.

"Why flowers?" my father whispers.

Suddenly, the idea that the flowers might be bugged with a listening device possesses us like a shared madness. We start tearing apart the bouquet petal by petal, stems, and leaves, until there's a pool of red petals and broken stems on the floor. We haven't found a microphone, yet my father is sure it's there somewhere, we just can't recognize it.

"They're capable of anything these days . . ." my father whispers.

We talk in sign language and whispers. We even rip the paper in which the flowers were wrapped into many little pieces. We sift the pile of torn petals and paper scraps through our fingers and let them flutter to the floor. As the fall of red snow collects at our feet, we hear a little metal sound. We stare at one another and then dive at the pile of petals, leaves and paper, scattering them with our hands.

"Aha! Here it is. I knew it!" announces my father.

He picks up a tiny metal object that looks like a needle, but finer, like a strand of silver wire. We look at it in wonder. My father tries to crush it under his foot, then he twists it with his fingers, trying to break it. My mother tells him he's gone crazy, it's probably just a staple, or something that could have fallen out of something, a piece of jewellery, his lighter, anything.

My father's face is red. "You're the crazy one," he hisses. "You don't know how far they'll go. I *do*."

My father carries the object cupped in his hand into the bathroom and flushes it down the toilet.

"Let them listen now!" he says, satisfied.

We stare at the mess on the floor. My mother goes to the window and makes certain the curtains are pulled tight. We continue to speak in whispers and signs, unable to shake the feeling that someone is listening.

My father watches as my mother kneels and sweeps the broken petals into her dustpan with a hand brush. A look of exhaustion settles over his face.

"They were such pretty flowers," she says.

Then we look at one another and start laughing. My mother is so lovely as she is shaking with laughter. It's so rare to see her like this, her dark blond hair with reddish tints down around her shoulders, her blue eyes sparkling. My father, as he shakes with laughter, hugs her shoulders, and they rock together on the floor. Each of us knows we're laughing because we hope they can hear us somewhere, those secret police with their tweezers, inserting secret microphones into flower petals. I laugh and close my eyes and imagine the violet clouds above the city with the Black Church, imagine hovering above it all in the shape of a large white plumed creature.

"Say It's Only a Paper Moon . . ."

THE MUSIC HAS STARTED, we are in our best clothes, a slow dance. I feel his hand firmly on my back. Every muscle is tight and strong. I am happy. I'm wearing a peach satiny dress; it's New Year's Eve. A new decade will start after tonight, the eighties. We are hopeful. We have coloured confetti. Maybe our president will die and the world will change. There is food that everybody's parents have prepared for our party, which they spent whole days queuing to collect. There's the famous *piftie*, frozen gelatin filled with garlic and pork. *Sarmale*, cabbage leaves and grape leaves stuffed with rice and meat. Pickled apples and pickled tomatoes. Whoever said Romanians are starving? Mostly, I care about the music. *Do we have enough dance music?* I hate that greasy trembling gelatin anyway. All I care about is dancing and *do we have enough wine?* The party has hardly begun and we're already tipsy from the Murfatlar, red wine that is exported everywhere in the world but hard to find in Romania, because the state trades our wine, our leather and our tractors for hard currency.

The windows are wide open, and Ella Fitzgerald is singing our special song. *Say it's only a paper moon, sailing over a cardboard sea. But it wouldn't be make-believe if you believed in me.* The three giant pictures of the bearded Marxists and the fourth one, the *Father of the Nation* – even they look sort of human tonight, because we're drunk from the precious Romanian wine that somehow escaped a cargo ship to America. The four gigantic faces looming high on the building across the street look a little melancholy as they stare down at us, dancing in our depravity to the sound of capitalist music.

Everybody is kissing, touching, dancing. Now we dance to Romanian music, the famous folksinger Maria Tănase. She is singing her song about all the gifts her lover gives her: earrings and a scarf and a string of pearls. Then her lover discovers her without the gifts, and he curses whoever buys them to hang himself with the scarf and the pearls. This is a weird curse, I think, because the man curses himself instead of cursing the woman who betrayed him. I'm hopping to the fast songs and swirling to the lazy songs and bumping into chairs and tables. Then comes another song about another big love curse, that a man who abandons his lover should have to crawl like a snake and bear the burden of the ant, and then crawl like a snake again. All Romanian love songs are about curses; no wonder we're so angry all the time.

Everybody is swaying and singing with the music in drunken voices. The cool winter air is sneaking into the room through the open windows and is cooling off our sweaty, throbbing bodies. It's midnight and we throw confetti. Mihai and I kiss and kiss, standing in the middle of the room. Thank God the curse song ended! A drinking song now, about how good it is to drink with a beautiful person. Red gurgling wine, and drinking with a beautiful person. We are still kissing, and we tell each other we will always, always love each other. There are even coloured fireworks! We're so young – I feel our youth, our hopes, and our bodies so sweaty and full of desire. We will always love each other, won't we? Yes, always.

We tell jokes, all kinds of jokes. We tell political jokes about how stupid Ceauşescu is. He goes hunting and catches a rabbit and holds the rabbit down and says, *Admit it! You're a boar!* We tell obscene jokes about the national folk hero, Bulă, who gets married and doesn't know how to do his wife, so his father tells him to *put the longest part of his body into the hole.* Two hours later, they find Bulă in the bathroom with his leg stuck in the toilet. Then someone tells one about Bulă's grandmother after the earthquake *still holding on so well for her age,* hanging from a beam all stiff.

I dance on the table. I dance the Charleston on the kitchen table next to the jellied pork and the pickled apples and tomatoes. We have so much hope this New Year's Eve that somehow things will get better, that everything will be beautiful and fragrant like the crystalline winter air smelling of snow and sprinkled with stars, and that Mihai and Mona will be happy despite everything. Our friends talk about people leaving the country and about people who have left, people we know, people Mihai knows. They're escaping to Turkey or to Yugoslavia, swimming across the Danube, crossing borders at night or hiding on freight trains. I wait for Mihai to become angry. He always gets angry when he hears such stories. He says, "Who the hell is going to live here if everybody's leaving?" He shakes his head in frustration. We move away from everybody and go to his room.

Like never before, we make plans for the future. He will be an engineer soon. Next year he'll get his diploma, and then he'll try to get a job in Bucharest. I'm stunned with happiness. He wants to be with me, to have a life with me. I will finish my university studies and he will be an engineer in Bucharest. I will be a writer and an actress both, and a teacher, too. I want to be everything! Ideas open up in my head like water lilies floating on the water. Round, silky, luscious ideas like water lilies.

We hear the sharp whistle of a train leaving the station. It's past midnight, and it startles us. Judging by the hour and by the long, plaintive whistle, it must be the train to Trieste. I feel sadness mixed with joy. Mihai's wide forehead is crossed by a long, deep furrow.

"You'll leave me one day, won't you?" he says suddenly.

I'm startled by his question. I shake my head vehemently. "Of course not. Are you crazy?"

Marx, Engels, and Lenin watch us sternly from the other building. Only Nicolae Ceauşescu seems to be smiling.

"No, I'll never leave you," I say firmly.

We hold each other's hands. We look into each other's eyes like old people who have lived through everything. There's that love curse song again in the other room. *He who loves and leaves will crawl like a snake.*

"Let's change the music," I say, breaking away from him. "Let's dance! Let's dance, my love."

Say it's only a paper moon, sailing over a cardboard sea . . .

We dance more lightly than ever before, this crystalline New Year's Eve. My satiny dress is clinging to my body. The sparkling snowy air drifting into the room cools our skin. We want so much to hope, to believe it will all become true.

But it wouldn't be make-believe, if you believed in me.

In the Snow, a White Mare

O N NEW YEAR'S DAY we go to the house of Mihai's best friend, Radu, whose thick, reddish beard scratches my face as he embraces me. He winks at me and slaps Mihai on the back and wishes us a happy new year. Radu lives in the neighbourhood at the foot of the mountain and near the cemetery where my great-grandmother Paraschiva is buried. The streets here are steep and narrow, and the houses have thick stone walls like fortresses and large iron gates. We dance, we argue, we swirl. We dance the tango, waltzes, rock and roll, the polka. Then we dance the Romanian hora, then rock and roll again. There are snowflakes pirouetting by the window. They make me dizzy and languorous as I look at them while I'm swirling through all the dances of the world. Maybe this decade will bring us something good, like no food rations, just *food*, and no secret police.

I am slightly drunk and I say stupid, insulting things for no good reason other than it's New Year's Day. I feel like dancing without stopping and breaking everything.

We go outside, and Mihai drags me up the hill behind the house. The fir trees are heavy with snow. The air smells like fresh, raw snow and wood-burning stoves. Veils of snow fall on me when I touch a branch and wrap me up like a gauzy shroud. He pulls me higher, then throws me to the ground. The steep snow-covered ground is hard, cold, frozen. Mihai makes love to me with the snow falling on us and sneaking up under my skirt along my thighs. I am looking at the grey winter sky above me, sliced by the bare branches of the oak trees and the dark green pointed firs. Veils, shrouds of snow, are wrapping us this first day of the year, in our rage and in our love. His eyelashes are fluttering on my cheeks. My thighs are cold and hot in the incomparable snow.

In the evening, we make love again in his apartment. We're all heated up and drunk. We roll in those white starched bed-sheets of his where my flesh howls and whispers and bursts into bubbles of light.

When I leave his apartment, gliding happily on the snow, a shadow comes after me in the dark and follows me. I don't like shadows, and I don't like steps behind me. I had always thought I was free from shadows following me here in the mountains, and that once I left Bucharest everything would be normal and clean. I run like mad to reach the street corner of the building where my aunt lives, but suddenly the steps rush behind me, and a hand grabs me before I can breathe again and whips me around.

The shadow is a woman, a scrawny dark-haired woman with thin lips and a very long mouth. I discover I'm not afraid – I'm angry. I want to beat her up and scream at her, *What the hell do you think you're doing?* I've dealt with stalkers throughout my adolescence. Male stalkers, following me after school. I always managed to scare them away, either by screaming at them in the middle of the street or hitting them over the head with my schoolbag.

But this woman doesn't seem to be a stalker. She is standing very close to me and I can feel her breath on my face. She smells of the nasty Carpaţi cigarettes. She grabs my arm with a tight grip. She looks straight into my eyes and tells me through her teeth, with rage and yet with a tone of pity, "He's secret police, you stupid girl! Stay away from him, you stupid, stupid girl. Stay away from him!"

Then she lets go of me and walks away hurriedly through the snow in the direction of the railway station.

I am biting my lip and scratching my palms to make sure I'm awake. I feel that I'm in a nightmare, struggling to be awake and screaming in the frozen New Year's night. But my lips feel the biting and my palms feel the scratching and my feet are cold. Black nausea, fear and sadness spill into my heart, my boom-boom mad, breaking heart.

As I hurry to my aunt Nina's house, I rerun the whole scene in my mind, this delirium in the glittering snow. The woman was real. I know it happened, because my arm is burning from her grasp on me, and there are her footprints in the snow. Maybe she was a madwoman who mistook me for someone else. Did she say his name, did she say "Mihai" or "he"? I don't remember now. But something in her tone demanded that I pay attention and take her warning seriously. I see her face, her look of rage – or was she also afraid, was she maybe trying to get away from someone? Why would she have grabbed me like that and then run away so suddenly? Now my memory insists she was also being followed. I convince myself I heard other unmistakable, blunt footsteps echoing in the cold air, echoing in the white snow like inside a huge white bell.

As I finally turn the corner and enter my aunt's building, I sense another shadow gliding past me and disappearing. It's a shadow with hands in its pockets, sure of itself, sure of the fear it causes, gloating in the snow. I run up the stairs to my aunt's apartment faster than I've ever run before, thinking of nothing else but locking the door, getting into bed, forgetting the shadows. I think of the stories of my family, the bloody stories of whole fields covered with the corpses of dead soldiers and two brothers looking for each other and calling out each other's names in the dusk that rushes mercifully onto the bodies lying in the mud. These terrifying scenes from my family's history are perversely comforting to me as I tremble under the bedsheets, next to my cousins, thinking of the shadows and the woman with the long, thin mouth calling me *stupid, stupid girl.*

I rush to my sleep imagining that Mihai slits my throat just after we've made love. My fantasy melts into a nightmare. He makes tender, undulating love to me, and we're surrounded by sparkling snow in the metallic dusk of winter. Then Mihai takes a beautifully crafted knife, with a long, sparkling blade, dips it in snow once, and says, *I have to do this, my love, for your own good. I have to, so you can be free.* He carefully, artfully slits my throbbing throat. I turn into a white mare, a wild white mare running with its mane in the wind like wings. But not even as a wild mare am I really free. I'm trapped in a clearing. It's a small, beautiful clearing covered in snow and surrounded by dark fir trees, black trees like prison bars. I run in circles like mad with my white mane flying in all directions and my throat burning and my heart aching and breaking into a million pieces with the sound of glass, because my heart inside the mare's body has turned into a block of ice that breaks with a loud crack.

The morning is greyer than any of my mother's grey dresses, and I prefer my dream of white mares and throat slitting on the snow to this grey morning, waking with a feeling of something twisted and wrong in my head and in the world, both. It takes me a while to remember why, then the image of the woman grabbing me in the night jumps up clear and sharp in my memory. I have a nagging feeling like a bad cough stuck in my throat that I'm not comprehending something important. Mihai is secret police? It can't be that. And yet I can't ignore that sentence scratching at me through the night like a bad conscience. Why can't I ignore it? Why can't I just go to Mihai now and make love to him again and dance again and go for a walk in the snow again and make love over and over again?

I know why I can't ignore it. If there is the smallest chance that the woman's warning was meant for me, that she wasn't just another schizophrenic wandering the streets at night, then Mihai would want information from me about my father. Mihai would try to find out where he goes, what he does, what he writes, who he sees. And *Does he have any Kent cigarettes?* I think, laughing to myself. What have I told Mihai already, in moments of the sharpest intimacy?

Mihai. Mihai. I want to cry his name, already sounding alien to me. The sound of it twists in my mind until I think of *Mata Hari.* I saw a photograph of her once in an old magazine of my father's, the legendary spy of the First World War, wearing a long, silky dress, her eyes dark with kohl, a white flower in her jet-black hair. I have fallen inescapably in love with a male Mata Hari who will send my father to prison. *Stupid, stupid girl.*

On this grey morning, I go out for a walk around the neighbourhood, thinking that the cold winter air will help me clear my thoughts. I run into Cristina, who is bundled up in shawls and seems frazzled. Her hazel eyes are shinier than usual, and she is biting her fleshy lips. At the sight of me, she smiles her warm, innocent smile that she has kept intact since she was a little girl. But her slightly unkempt appearance and her rushed manner make me think there is something wrong. She grabs my arm and begs me to go into town with her.

"Come on, girl, let's go! Since you have your lover boy, you never spend time with me any more," she says playfully, pouting.

Her cheeks are flushed from the cold, and her chestnut plaits, usually neatly wrapped around her head, are hanging down her shoulders loose from under her many shawls. I am tempted to go. Now that I'm with her I realize how much I've missed our long strolls to the centre of town, our whispers about boys and sex and menstruation, our stealing the special sour cherry brandy from her parents and getting loud, laughing drunk. My vacation days with Mihai are precious, and I'm greedy for him. I've neglected all my childhood friends rather than sacrifice a morning or an afternoon beside him in his white sheets.

But last night's strange occurrence and the troubling dreams about Mihai have soured the sound of his name in my thoughts. It will be comforting to my disoriented mind to hear Cristina's voice, her laugh ringing in the clear air, and not have to think about Mihai for a few hours.

We spend the morning walking through the centre of town to the plaza near the Black Church, talking and laughing like we used to. We go to the pastry shop where we went as children, after we had saved enough money to buy one cake and share it between us. The cake and pastry shelves are half empty, and the cashier standing at the counter looks sleepy and depressed. We buy our favourite cake, the *cataif*, a Turkish cake with little sweet sticks made of fried noodles and lots of fluffy cream. There is one man in a grey coat in the corner of the pastry shop, with his back turned towards us. A young couple with a little girl stuffing herself with the last éclair on the shelf is sitting at the table next to ours. Suddenly, Cristina starts talking about Mihai.

"So, how is it?" she asks.

"How is what?" I pretend to not understand.

"You know, *in bed*," she says quickly, blushing.

Before I had fallen for Mihai and experienced *in bed*, I used to love our discussions about romance and sex, since it was all hearsay and imagination. Now I feel a strange shyness talking about it, even to Cristina. But I don't want to disappoint her.

"It's like" – I laugh – "it's like you forget yourself and . . . it's really, really good." I feel my face burning as red and hot as a boiling lobster.

Cristina, for once, doesn't press me for more. Suddenly she becomes very serious.

"Be careful," she says, looking down at her pastry. "Just . . . be very careful, OK?"

"Oh, don't worry," I tell her. "We're not fools. I always wash with vinegar afterwards, you know. You can't get pregnant that way."

"No, I don't mean that," she says, though now she is the one who blushes. "I mean . . . you . . . you know."

"No, I don't know. In fact, I have no idea what you're talking about," I say, raising my voice.

"Be careful what you say," she says and stuffs her mouth with the sugary *cataif.*

My mouth is hanging open with bits of fried sweet noodles from the cake falling out, like a child who's had enough and can't eat any more. The woman, the shadow, the dream about Mihai slitting my throat, all rush back to me, and I feel faint. I don't understand anything any more.

I try to compose myself and wipe my mouth with a napkin. "Why are you saying this, Cristina? What have you heard?"

"I'm just worried, that's all. I'm scared all the time. Look around you, Mona. Open your eyes." She's looking at me with an intensity I've never seen in her. She's tired and very pale. She is biting her lips again. "You can't trust *anyone,*" she says, picking up some cake crumbs off the table. Her face is very close to mine, and I can see the glow in her skin that I have always admired.

"I trust you," I say hurriedly.

She blinks rapidly, holding back tears that suddenly well in her hazel eyes. "Maybe you shouldn't," she says. "And you've known me since we were two," she tells me. "Remember? You know my family. We're practically like sisters. But, Mona, how long have you known Mihai? What do you even know about *his* family?"

I know his parents both work in a factory, I tell myself. I know his mother is a good cook. She makes pickled tomatoes and cucumbers and apricot preserve. But most of the time when I visit Mihai, they're both at work, and I've barely exchanged ten words with them.

"So what?" I ask defiantly. "So what if I don't know his parents or his grandparents or his great-granduncle on his cousin's side? So what if you know of a girl who had a lover, and she got run over on the pavement? So what, so what, *so what*? Does that mean I can't trust anyone, I can't love anyone ever? Is that what you want?"

My voice is high again, and my tears are getting mixed with bits of the *cataif* cake, and I know I must look like a total idiot.

The man and woman at the table next to ours turn around and glance at us disapprovingly while the little girl is giggling in her éclair.

"Forget it," Cristina says. "You're in love. I'm happy for you. When is the wedding?"

I've never seen Cristina so bitter, and so old. Sitting there in the pastry shop with five tired cakes on the shelves, I just want to keep on loving Mihai. I want to be oblivious to the rest.

Cristina pulls me closer to her by my jacket collar and whispers in my face:

"I am seeing someone . . . a foreigner! I don't know what to do. But I'm also terribly in love!"

I understand now for the first time that Cristina is truly scared and she has serious reasons to be so. Her face is strained, and her eyes have a wild glitter. Why of all the things in the world did she have to get involved with a foreigner? That may also mean she is planning to leave the country.

"Why?" is all I can ask, and I become self-conscious of the stupid ring of my question, as the sad-looking cashier lifts her eyes from the register and stares at us for a second. Maybe she is an informer, too; Cristina is right, you can't trust anyone.

Cristina produces a little giggle and says breathlessly, in quick whispers: "Why? How can you ask that? Because this is how one falls in love, you never know where it's going to come from! He is a Tunisian student at the Polytechnic. Mona, I'm crazy about him. But I know I am being followed everywhere. It's awful, I can't stand it."

She nods quickly in the direction of the door towards the man in the grey coat, and I get it. *We* are being followed. Now that she is seeing a foreign student, and I am her closest friend, of course I am among the suspect ones as well. Between my father's Radio Free Europe and manifestos, Cristina's love affair with a Tunisian student, and the idea that Mihai might actually work for the secret police, I feel I don't stand a chance at happiness, at a normal life, that I'm trapped and running in circles in a tight clearing with no way of ever getting out. So if there is the slightest chance that Mihai is secret police, then that concerns Cristina as well. We were all once just children playing in the marigold- and poppy-filled park in front of my aunt's building and listening to Mihai play his melancholy mountain songs on his old guitar.

I look at Cristina and see two lines of tears streaking down her face. Her brown plaits are undone and she has white sugary cream on her lips, like a little girl. I want to hold and protect her. She *is* just like a sister. Except for her own older sister Simona, she has no one else in the world. Her mother died last year, only a year after her alcoholic father died of cirrhosis. She is the orphan on the block, and all the neighbours whisper words of pity about her whenever she passes by. I am overtaken by an impulse to be Cristina's sister and mother, her family. I stroke her cheek and wipe the tears off her face.

As we are standing up to leave, the man in the grey coat sitting at the table in the corner looks at us sideways. He is small and scrawny and looks like a rodent. I have a wicked impulse to do something childish, to show the rodent man I don't give a damn. So I stick out my tongue at him as Cristina and I are leaving. He gives me an ugly look, and as I go out of the door I have the gnawing feeling I've seen him before.

I pull Cristina by the hand and start running in the snow-covered street, gliding in the snow, making her chase me like we used to do when we were small, throwing snowballs at her and sliding on patches of ice in the street. I am running and laughing and refusing to believe we live in this place. I am running like the white mare in my dream, wanting to believe there is a place for me to love and play in the snow. Cristina catches up with me and tries to sneak snow down my collar, like she used to. We stand in the middle of the street, wet from the snow, red faced, with tears in our eyes, holding on to our childhood for just a little bit longer.

My Mata Hari Lover

HARD AS I TRY, I cannot pretend the evening with the woman shrieking in the street and the shadow following me did not happen. Everything becomes twisted, broken, double. Every moment with Mihai is torn between the painful confusion of not knowing who he is and the impossible love I have for him.

Our lovemaking becomes even more furious. I close my eyes and bite hard into his flesh. Thoughts of Mata Hari cross my mind, thoughts that I am like the men she used to seduce for secrets. Every time he mentions my father, I try to guess from his eyes. He asks me about the courses my father teaches and the book he is working on. *Is he still such an anti-Communist?* he asks. Maybe he was asking me questions about my father before. I don't remember. I don't know what I do remember.

I adapt my memory either to fit my suspicions or to erase them completely. *No, he never used to ask me about my father. He never cared about him.* Or *Yes, he often used to ask me about him, and always said he admired him so much, so what's the big deal now?* I don't tell Mihai anything real about my father. I say he's a dusty, crazy old man, lost in his books about dead old languages. *Child, old man, stork, hoe.* His fourteen Dacian words. *How can anyone write so much shit,* I ask Mihai as we share a cigarette, *about fourteen words?* I become cold and reticent, and almost shy. Sometimes I'm mean. He wonders what's wrong with me.

I ask him what he thinks of Mata Hari. I ask him if he would ever become a spy like Mata Hari, seducing people for their secrets. If he would ever use me and make me believe he loves me, but really spy on me and betray me like Mata Hari.

He looks at me with big surprised eyes, asks if I'm drunk or hallucinating. He says, "Who do you think you are? You think you're so important some Mata Hari would bother to seduce something out of you?" He looks at me like I'm a crazy person. "What kind of secrets would *you* have?"

"Very important information," I tell him lazily. "I happen to have the world's biggest secret about all the bombs in the world, and not even Mata Hari could get it out of me."

He pretends to be a spy. He plays with me like he is a British spy, trying to seduce me. I laugh when he tickles my neck and fakes his awful British accent in my ear, and I fight him and beat him to make him stop. I start to cry, and then we're laughing. I think I must be losing my mind in such a major way that I've finally become incapable of distinguishing between fantasy and reality.

Then something in his voice, in a small gesture, like the way he has of tucking my hair behind my ear or the sad look in his eyes when we talk about my leaving soon for home, jolts me, drives me mad with sadness. Lust and love drum through my heart and through my body. I bite and lick and kiss him to forget everything. I want to get drunk on the scent of his flesh. I want to beat and kill the suspicions and the fear, to keep our love in its glowing cocoon of mists and to spread over it veils of sparkling blue snow. I want to protect it from the mean woman shrieking in the night, to protect it from the menacing shadow of Mata Hari in her shiny, silky dress.

This is the winter in the first year of the new decade. I become more and more fascinated with Mihai. I think I'm just like the generals were with Mata Hari, spilling out their secrets for a touch, a kiss, a whisper, for the feel of her black hair with the white orchid. I find his white face whiter, and the black hair blacker, and the red, rounded lips redder and more fragrant. I find his touch sweeter and more repulsive at the same time. I sink into a deep, inescapable attraction, as if a strong liquor were flowing in my veins and numbing my conscience.

I am happy when I have to go back to the capital. I get on the train with glee, thinking I'll be free from this torment of love and fear, from the fascination and suspicion. I'll be the free mare running wild in a white field, without any fir trees blocking my way. Just the white field.

For the next few weeks, I drown all my torments, my love and my hatred, in reading for my university entrance exam. I read by the light and by the heat of the gas burners in the kitchen, because we only get two hours of heat a day and sometimes not at all. The state and the Party are economizing again in order to pay the national debt and to achieve that Socialist utopia where everybody will be equally and inescapably miserable. I'm shivering in my winter coat inside the apartment. I turn on the oven as well, hoping it will produce a little bit more heat. One evening in late February, I hear my father exclaim loudly: he has just managed to get past the rumbling static on his Grundig radio and hear the faraway voices of Radio Free Europe. We find out that the Munich headquarters of the station have just been blown up by a hit man sent by Ceauşescu to stop the broadcasting of news about General Pacepa. My father is beside himself and smokes one cigarette after another, cursing constantly.

"The bastards, the criminals, I wish they . . ." He doesn't continue, but the wild look in his eyes is telling enough. He goes on listening to Radio Free Europe and the news of the attack. Despite the increased static over the next few days, somehow he always manages to get just the right wave and capture the resonant voices that ring differently, both bolder and more real than any of our radio and television broadcasters relating news of the latest accomplishments of the Party: a new quota in the production of bulldozer parts, or a new visit of Comrade Ceauşescu at a cooperative farm in the northern Maramureş area.

And then another grey winter afternoon, as I am immersed in Thomas Hardy's *Tess of the D'Urbervilles* and my parents are having a conversation about our difficult financial situation, there's a pounding at the door. Loud men shout for us to open the door. My father tells us to go to the bedroom and to stay there.

He opens the door, and I hear men going through our apartment and pushing around furniture, opening drawers, knocking over chairs. I freeze and think again of the stories of the black van that used to take people away in the fifties. I think our time has finally come. Everything is going backwards to the fifties, it seems. My mother and I are holding hands, and I think I hear the sound of fists pounding into flesh. My mother is pursing her lips and staring at the wall. I hear my father cursing, and then the sound of something crashing through a window.

I hear one of the men shouting, "Where are they? Where are the bloody manifestos? We know everything about you and your anarchist friends!"

I am crouched on the bed and rocking myself. The man's words go through me with a thud: . . . *you and your anarchist friends.* I repeat them several times in my mind, trying to grasp them. I am afraid for all of us. I think of Cristina and her Tunisian boyfriend, of Ralph the librarian, of the leaflets asking for new Party leadership flying above the Turkish bazaars, the woman in the winter night warning me about Mihai. He might be working for people like the ones here, beating up my father.

The smell of burning paper fills the house. The men must have resorted to burning my father's manuscripts and books to force him to reveal the secret of the manifestos. But then I remember the Zinger typewriter hidden in the oven, and that tonight I had turned on the oven without taking it out, the way I usually did. There seems to be a commotion in the other room, and then one of the men says, "Fire! There is a fire. Are you burning the works of Comrade Ceauşescu? Are you? We know what you people are doing."

I remember in a spasm of fear the news that my father gave us at the dinner table a few nights ago: two brothers by the last name of Pavel had been sentenced to fifteen years in prison for setting volumes of Ceauşescu's speeches on fire in their back-yard. My father and his friends were working to get that information somehow to Radio Free Europe. Maybe my father has gone totally insane and is burning Ceauşescu's speeches in our oven. But the only volume of Ceauşescu's speeches we have in the house is the one I have from my school. I rush to my shelf of schoolbooks looking for it and feel waves of relief when I spot it: the thick book with the red Party flag on the back cover and the picture of Ceauşescu beaming his fake smile on the front.

My mother and I come out of the bedroom and see my father holding on to the door of the drawing room swaying, a thick line of blood trickling from his nose and mouth. There is smoke coming from the oven. I must have left the letter I was writing to Mihai inside the typewriter and then forgotten about it. My mother yells to call the firemen. My father says not to call them, to throw water on the oven. I realize he is worried he must have also left an unfinished letter or manifesto in the type-writer. I am holding the volume of Ceauşescu's speeches like a trophy in my right hand. The two men who were beating up my father a minute ago are flanking him and looking fierce. I hold up the book and hear myself say in a voice that doesn't sound like my own: "Here are the speeches of Comrade Ceauşescu! Here they are, I was just studying them!"

My father's eyes have a sparkle of something like pride or gratitude as he looks at me, blood trickling from his nose. I know he is proud of my presence of mind.

A neighbour must have called the fire station, because two young firemen burst into our apartment and start spraying water all over our kitchen. One of them asks, "What were you cooking, paper or something?"

"Yes," says my father, "we're eating paper. That's how desperate we are. This way we shit less and don't have to queue for toilet paper."

One of the firemen laughs at my father's joke. My mother's face turns a dark red. The two Securitate thugs are easing up on my father. They look conspicuously alike, as if they were twins: short and stout, with small foreheads, and both are wearing black suits that pull too tight over their bellies. One wears dark-rimmed glasses, the other a fedora. Where does the Party find people like these, I am wondering as I stare at them in fascination.

My father is standing in front of the stove, not allowing either of the firemen to get close to it, worried they will want to open it and will see the typewriter and then denounce him. Indeed, one of them wants to get past my father, to look inside the oven.

My father says, "Thank you, we're fine. The fire is out. Now we'll just have to starve. No more paper casserole for us tonight! Thank you. Thank you very much."

Then my father goes on, as he gets a second wind and now tries himself to intimidate the Securitate men.

"How dare you accuse me of such a thing as burning the speeches of Comrade Ceauşescu? I am a university professor and have taught these very speeches," he yells, taking the volume from my hand and waving it in their faces.

The two men look at my father, then at the two firemen with their big red extinguishers, then at me and at my mother again, evaluating the situation.

Then the one with the fedora says with a wicked grin, "We'll get you, Professor, one of these days." He pauses, smiles again. "I would watch out if I were you." He makes a sign to his colleague, and they both leave with an efficient step that conveys that they are no-nonsense guys.

The fireman tries to push my father out of the way to make sure all the flames are extinguished inside the oven. But then he sees my father's wild eyes, the blood from his nose and mouth, and backs off. They suddenly look like they don't want to have anything to do with us, as if all this was too much for them. They are moving backwards towards the door, trying to get out as quickly as possible.

"Good evening, sir, call us if you have a problem again, sir."

They both leave and slam the door behind them. The three of us are left standing in the kitchen, staring at the oven. My mother opens the oven to see if the typewriter has been destroyed. There are ashes all over the inside of the oven, but the old Zinger is still standing, a little blackened from the fire, but whole.

"These German products, they're immortal," says my mother.

The house has got warmer from the fire, but the smoke is making us choke. The living room looks the same as it did after the big earthquake: books, chairs, papers thrown everywhere across the floor in an offensive disorder. A ravenous desire to hold and kiss Mihai possesses me. I go back to reading *Tess of the D'Urbervilles*, trying to quiet the throb of my flesh and to soothe my heart in the story of a tragic heroine.

Winged Man, Ripe Tomatoes

I'VE JUST TAKEN MY ENTRANCE EXAMS for the University of Bucharest, four days of gruelling oral and written tests in the city's oppressive summer heat. For my written exam, I get two of my favourite subjects, Bernard Shaw's *The Devil's Disciple* and Thomas Hardy's *Tess*. I am menstruating and writing feverishly, page after page, about the paradoxes in Shaw's main character and the bigoted society around him, and about Tess as a sacrificial victim, about the scene at Stonehenge when she falls asleep on one of the stones of the prehistoric temple, a foreshadowing of her death. Blood and words pour out of me at the same time, in a continuous flood. I'm pale and shaky, and I've lost ten kilos in the last month. I cough all the time. I'm like a tuberculosis patient, and I feel beautiful.

I don't wait for the results of the exam, but get on the train to the mountains the very next day. I find Mihai in a strange mood, distant and malicious, as he settles himself in his worn-out chair and I throw myself onto his bed.

"What's all this studying like a maniac and getting yourself into this state?" he asks.

"What state?" I ask.

"Just look at yourself," he says. "You look like a famine survivor. What's the point?"

I'm raw, bloody and sweaty after the exams and the three-hour-long train ride from Bucharest in a hot compartment. I throw all the swear words that come into my head into his face, an endless stream of obscenities, with enormous satisfaction and relief. He smiles, and I feel like slapping him. I get up to leave, but he holds me and kisses me. He changes into his tender, loving mood just like that, in a flash.

After we make love, he comments again on my skinny body. And then he tells me it's too difficult, all this waiting for me, and the *damn distance between us*, what if he meets another girl, *there are other women in the world, you know!* I don't really get what he is trying to say. Maybe he has cheated on me, and this is his way of breaking the news. He looks dark and impenetrable like when he would think of Mariana and the accident on the mountain during our first summer together. He is wearing his check knee breeches and a clean pressed white shirt. I've never seen him in an ironed shirt before. His shirts always used to be wrinkled. He is more handsome yet more foreign than usual. Almost like a stranger. I ask him to explain himself about the distance and other women. He stares at me with an ironic look and lights up a cigarette, this time a Kent, not the odious Carpaţi. I am wondering why he's now smoking Kent cigarettes. Maybe it's one of the favours he gets for working for the secret police. Maybe he is a total stranger and turns into someone completely different the minute I leave the town of Braşov. A dangerous man that I don't know any longer. Or that I have never really known very well.

"Mona, I don't know," he says, dragging on his cigarette. "We are hundreds of kilometres away from each other, and we live in such different worlds. Maybe you should just get yourself one of those artistic Bucharest boys, now that you are a university student." He crushes the cigarette in the already full ashtray.

Why is he saying this? I turn over the ashtray, and ashes get all over the bed and the carpet and on our clothes. He stands up trying to protect himself from my fury. I stand up, too, and I kick and punch him. I kick him in the balls, and he falls to his knees, gasping. I spit in his face.

He disgusts me. I don't want him to touch me. I tell him he's a cheat, and a *fucking informer* and a traitor and a rat. He tells me to leave the house, which I do, slamming the door as hard as I can.

I go back to my aunt's house and cry in my aunt's arms, and she makes cabbage and potato soup for me. My uncle gets a huge watermelon, and my cousins play gin rummy with me. My aunt Nina has the sweetest, most comforting face in the world. Her round brown eyes and her smile always make me feel safe and cosy. I like watching her prepare her mythic cabbage soups, as her brown curls fall all over her face and as she attentively takes little sips from the soup to check it for salt. She's my second mother, I tell her. She's a forestry engineer and is out on various sites every day. She curses at the big trucks and tractors that she works with.

She knows everything about European history and, even better, she knows about the big void of many centuries in Romanian history. She says that between the third and the twelfth centuries almost nothing is known about our people. It's her opinion that during that period we were just a bunch of barbarians fighting with other barbarians, and there's nothing worth mentioning about Romanians during that period.

When she talks about the black void in our history, I feel a wild curiosity. I'd like to be a barbarian like the Romanians during our mysterious medieval period and ride a horse across the landscape, hunt and slaughter animals for food, and be too tired at night to do anything but sleep on the hard earth under the stars of fifteen hundred years ago. I want to run inside the black void of Romanian history where there is no Romania, just barbarians hunting, fucking and sleeping on the earth and writing nothing in history books.

"What good has history got us? Look at how history is tearing us apart and tormenting us," she tells me. In my black mood, I couldn't agree with her more.

"Stop filling her head with your stories," says my uncle.

"Don't you see how she gets melancholy? She's young, just leave her alone."

I cut myself another piece of watermelon. My aunt goes on about Romanian history and pretends to not pay attention to Ion.

My uncle stands up in the middle of her lecture and kisses her right on the mouth. My aunt says: "Stop it! Are you crazy?" But I know from her smile that she likes to be kissed just like that.

"Forget him," she says while I'm eating watermelon and spitting out seeds. "He's not worthy of you. Just forget him. Your uncle is right. You're so young. You'll find someone much better and more worthy of you when you start your classes at the university."

I try to do just that: forget him, and pretend that the summer smells and the orange moon do not tear my insides with pain. I pretend that I don't think of him and that I'm not waiting by the phone. I even dance with my cousins, to all the songs he and I danced to. I pretend I'm just as happy as I can be, and that the tears that soak my pillow every night are an *existential malaise*, like the metaphysical nausea of Sartre or, better yet, the Romanian *dor*. I pretend that I am finally coming into the full comprehension of that state of being by which we Romanians supposedly define ourselves.

I pretend I'm longing for something unknown, for someone unknown, like the girl in the poem by the Romanian Romantic poet Eminescu. She dreams every night about a black-haired man with wings. She dreams he descends into her room and flies away with her to his magical kingdom in the country beyond the sun, beyond the moon, where everything is golden and nobody ever dies. And this romantic winged man *does* come into her room one night and sees her sleeping. She is so rosy and beautiful asleep that two silver tears fall out of his eyes onto the girl's face and wake her up. She's immediately struck with love for him but realizes that he is too cold, too immortal, and that she doesn't want to live with him in that golden kingdom of his, because gold is cold and *life is warm.* Then he gives up his immortality for her and comes to live with her on earth, where everyone has only one short life and lovers kiss under the fragrant linden trees on summer nights. I'm telling myself that I am experiencing that kind of longing, for that kind of a mythic creature.

After ten days of this poetic agony I meet Mihai as I'm going for a walk in the neighbourhood. Then my heart is just about ready to explode into more pieces than would cover the entire street. I walk towards him, trying to look calm. He's the first one to give in, to hold me and to kiss my earlobe and push back my hair, and to tell me he will always love me, he will always feel this way, and please forgive him, please, can I forgive him for having been so mean? And that's when I don't pretend any more and when I start sobbing in his arms and shouting at him *Why didn't you call me? Would you have called me if we hadn't met today?* and *Can we go somewhere to get away from everyone and be alone?*

He takes me to a house at the outskirts of town, where an aunt of his lives. She's on holiday for a couple of weeks and has left him the keys. There's a vegetable and a flower garden and a tall fence separating us from the street. We make love among tomatoes and parsnips and basil in the shade of a cherry tree. We eat tomatoes and sour cherries warm from the sun.

"Can you forgive me? You know I would never be untruthful, never love anyone else! I was just teasing you, that's all," he says, more contrite than ever. "Sometimes I get desperate and don't know what to do. All the months that go by without you . . ." He looks melancholy and lights up a Carpați cigarette. I feel relieved to see he is not smoking Kents any more.

"So you should die of shame!" I scream as loud as I can, slicing into the silence of the sunny garden.

"Forget it, Mona. Here, take this tomato. You've never had tomatoes like these before."

I bite greedily into the ripe, juicy tomato, earthy and sunny. I fall asleep in his arms in the vegetable garden listening to the buses and the cars going by. As I am slowly emerging from my sleep, I imagine that I'm Tess of the D'Urbervilles and that I kill my lover and run away and live in the deep forest, in a place where instead of wild berries and wildflowers there are huge vines with tomatoes on them. The earth is covered in parsley, and I cry all day and all night until Mariana comes to me and tells me to forget him, to forget all about him. *You did well to kill him,* she says in my fantasy. *Now we can live together in the forest and feed on tomatoes and parsnips.*

I wake up hot, burning from the afternoon sun. He's watching me wake up. He holds me until I calm down from my dream. He brings me cold water in a tin cup.

"Here, drink this. It's from the spring behind the house. The cleanest water in the world."

My insides cool down, and my mind is clearer and – how I love him as he gives me water from this tin cup and strokes my hair. I'm quivering with love for him, for his beautiful arms, his velvety eyes. He holds me for a long, long time, until dusk falls and envelops us. We have only one little, bitty life, not an endless one like the winged man in the story. To hell with the winged man! This moment is plump and juicy like a ripe tomato in the sun.

No Afterlife

O N OUR WAY HOME from his aunt's house and her tomato garden, we run into Cristina and another woman whom I don't know. I see them from a distance, walking and talking heatedly. I'm tired and flushed from the hot afternoon, our arguing and lovemaking, and I'm not really in the mood to talk to anyone, not even Cristina.

When she sees me, she waves with great excitement and hurries in our direction. As the two women get closer to us, an unpleasant feeling creeps up inside me. When the woman accompanying Cristina lifts her head and looks straight at me, I recognize her. She's skinny with thin lips and dark, lanky hair.

The steps pursuing me in the snow, the feeling of unreality, the fear and confusion. What is Cristina doing with this woman? How does she know her? My conversation with Cristina in the pastry shop, on that cold, grey January morning, shapes itself quickly in my memory. So the two of them know each other, and they both know something I don't. Cristina gets close to me and opens her arms to embrace me. She kisses me on both cheeks, then she introduces me to the other woman.

"This is Anca," she says. "Anca Serban. She just moved here. She's going to the Polytechnic. You know, on the hill, like all of us."

Indeed, it seems that everyone in Romania is going to the Polytechnic Institute on a hill at the outskirts of the city to become engineers. I know Cristina is elated because her Tunisian love is going to the same school, but what's with this Anca character again appearing in my life out of nowhere?

"Where did she come from?" I ask Cristina, as if the woman were invisible.

"From Bucharest," Anca answers. "I'm a city girl, like you," she says with a smile.

Her voice is low and very soft, nothing like the piercing high notes on that cold January night. I'm thinking that I must be mistaken; my memory is playing tricks on me. Yet the lips are unmistakable, and the hair, and the fierce look in her eyes.

"I think we've met before," I say, smiling.

"Really! Where would you have met?" asks Mihai. "Bucharest is a big city."

"I don't think so," Anca says, firmly.

The moment she says it, I know she's lying, know that each one of these three people standing around me in the street on this oppressively hot July afternoon is hiding something from me. Each is hiding something different.

"Do you two know each other?" I ask Mihai, a knot of anger swelling in my throat.

He turns his body towards her. "I think I've seen you on the hill once or twice after the exams this summer," Mihai says. I go over the last weeks in my mind, his meanness when he first saw me, my jealousy, his excuses, our afternoon today in the tomato garden. The knot in my throat is choking me and feels ready to explode.

"Anca is going to be in my class this autumn," Cristina says happily.

I don't understand Cristina's excitement at all. But of course a whole life goes on here in my absence. Suddenly I feel like a stranger to these people and these places. Who knows what they all do here in February and March and May? Who knows what happens between all these people while I am in Bucharest studying like a maniac and worrying about my family being accused of setting Ceauşescu's speeches on fire or about prisoners of conscience locked up in mental asylums or compromising leaflets flying from scaffoldings in the centre of Bucharest? Maybe Cristina has plans to leave the country and marry her Tunisian student. Maybe Mihai and Anca are lovers. Or maybe they are both secret police, *comrades,* and Anca was just trying to get me away from Mihai last winter. Maybe Cristina is turning into secret police because she got caught with her Tunisian boy.

Mihai must be having an affair with both of them. I don't know whether this is about politics or about love, or both. Just a huge political mess with sentimental entanglements the way it can happen only in our stupid and confused country. Because not even love can be love any longer. Everything is murky and rotten. As the late afternoon sun is hitting me in the back of my head, I fantasize about Mihai sleeping one day with Cristina, one day with Anca, or maybe both of them at the same time. I hate all of them. I want to slit their throats, the way Mihai slit my throat in my dream. I want to see the three of them lying dead on the hot asphalt. So this is why Cristina was warning me away from Mihai when we were sharing our Turkish cakes, so she could have Mihai all to herself. Ah, not really all to herself, to herself and her new friend Anca.

"Isn't that nice, that you all go to the same school," I say, feeling my mouth curling into a smile and that my last bit of self-control is about to snap. "I hope you all fuck each other up on that hill at the Polytechnic."

The words don't seem to be coming from my own mouth.

There's an awkward silence. The two women look at each other, and Mihai bursts out laughing.

Anca says with a glitter in her eyes, "Now *that's* a good idea. We might want to try that sometime."

I take Anca's long, black, lanky hair and pull at it with all my might. I see myself from a distance, not believing what I'm doing, getting into a hair-pulling fight with another woman. It feels like we're moving in slow motion and my body isn't my body, until Mihai gets between us and pulls us apart. He yanks me away from the scene and sends the two women off, telling them something I'm too angry to understand.

We walk back to his apartment, where he holds me for a long time, whispering to me, stroking my hair as the hot summer light spills through the windows. He talks to me sweetly as if I were a sick child.

Mihai tells me to calm down and just trust him. Don't I trust him? I don't know what to say. I don't understand anything and don't trust anyone. My head is hurting so badly I feel it will crack, and my heart will crack. I will soon be all cracks and bruises. I want to run away. He gives me cold water. I see my great-grandmother Paraschiva drinking cold water from a tin cup in Vania's bed more than half a century ago, just after she has come out of her delirium, just after she almost died of fever from the river. I am her, in the flood and the fear, staring at a man who is a stranger and yet familiar, loving him and fearing him, giving myself to his care. Drinking cold water from a tin cup.

The summer goes by in a frenzy of heat, suspicions, arguments, interspersed with lovemaking in shaded meadows, in Mihai's cool bed, in secret, dark, humid caves dripping with calcareous water. Sometimes I just follow his instructions obediently, trust him to know what he is doing, whatever that may be, that he cannot possibly be betraying me, that it's all a bad dream, a mistake.

Some mornings I wake up in a swirl of rage and mistrust. When I see Mihai I yell at him and tell him he's a traitor. I want us to break up. I want to run away. I want to kill Mihai right after lovemaking, like a praying mantis. I want revenge. I want Mihai to scream in pain. I want to go into the depths of Romanian history and be a barbarian killing animals and other humans, maybe with one or two moments of primitive poetry at night as I'm falling asleep on the hard earth, under the impenetrable dark vault studded with millions of stars.

How did I end up lucky enough to love a man who may be secret police *and* is cheating on me? I will end up marrying a kind but boring schoolteacher and spend my days like some sorry French heroine in a forsaken Romanian provincial town, looking out the window and wishing my life had turned out differently. My father will eventually be killed by the secret police or hidden in a mental asylum, my lover will soon reveal his true colours, and my university career will be turned to trash by the secret police following me because of my father's work for Radio Free Europe. Why doesn't Radio Free Europe help me out and make me free, what's the point of all the foolish activities if we become less and less free every day?

I toss and turn in bed in my aunt's apartment and sweat profusely next to my two sleeping cousins until it is time for me to wake up and lie to everybody again that I am going to see Cristina or am taking a hike in the mountains with a group of friends. It's what I always tell them whenever I go over to Mihai's. I am myself all wrapped up in a web of lies. I invent trips I never take and tremble at the thought that Aunt Nina might be running into Cristina and ask her about our latest hike in the mountains. We all live wrapped up in our own cocoons of lies. Why should I be so hard on Mihai after all, when everybody is lying and when everybody is putting up with the demonstrations in honour of Nicolae and the Party, when even my aunt and uncle had to give in to the pressures at work and become Party members for fear they would lose their jobs, when I will probably have to give in and become a Party member myself if I want to keep my place at the university? My father was right when he once said: "We are all collaborators, one way or another; just that some are more than others."

A week later, on August 23, our national holiday, Cristina is found dead in her bed. Since she is practically an orphan, nobody in her family, not even her sister, Simona, asks to have an autopsy performed on her. If she'd been run over by a car, at least then I would have known for sure.

"How does one wake up dead from unknown causes at the age of twenty?" I ask Mihai. I want to ask Mihai if he knew anything about Cristina's Tunisian lover, but I am worried about what I might discover. I am worried that Cristina may have been keeping this information away from Mihai. What will he think when he finds out? Not even on the edge of a beloved friend's tomb can we trust each other.

"Maybe she had a bad heart and didn't know it. Or maybe she poisoned herself," he says gloomily.

Mihai smokes one cigarette after another and looks genuinely sad. We all used to play together as children, and Cristina was Mariana's best friend. They plaited each other's hair and learned how to smoke together. I see tears welling up in Mihai's eyes. Again I am struck by the feeling of being alien to this world: so many things have escaped me while I have been carrying on with *Tess of the D'Urbervilles* and *The Devil's Disciple* in Bucharest and while my father was carrying on about Radio Free Europe and being busy getting arrested by the secret police.

"Are you crazy? Why would Cristina have wanted to poison herself?" I ask. I remember how happy she was that day in the pastry shop when she told me about having fallen in love.

Mihai says he's sorry. That's all he says. He's very sorry, he says over and over, as he tries to embrace me. I push him away.

The day of Cristina's funeral I find enough courage to ask Mihai, "Do you think she might have been killed?"

"I don't know," he says thoughtfully, and this time his answer seems genuine. Maybe I have been wrong all along about Mihai. Maybe it's just the general atmosphere of suspicion and confusion that is to blame and that is getting to us all.

I look at him and try to read something in his green eyes shaded by the long curly eyelashes that I've been so crazy about all these summers and winters. He's inscrutable. The old Mata Hari feeling comes back.

I cry so hard and so loud at Cristina's funeral in the cemetery spread out on the hill at the edge of the city that Mihai makes me move farther down the pathway, away from the grave. As I'm trying to calm down and look at the people standing around the grave, I see the scrawny man who was sitting in the pastry shop last winter when Cristina and I had our *cataif* cake. Anca Serban is standing in a corner, crying silently. Then, on the other side of the grave, I notice a handsome man with dark curly hair and a moustache looking straight at the grave, his eyes shiny with tears. This must be Cristina's lover, I think, and I am not surprised that she was so crazy in love with him. I can just see the two of them next to each other, she with her brown glistening hair and he with his dark eyes, a perfect couple. Then I look and see at least three other men I don't know, whom I suspect must be Securitate. With a foreign student present, the place must be swarming with them. I feel shivers down my spine, despite the blazing sun. I look again through the crowd around the grave in the direction of Cristina's friend, and he is nowhere to be seen. I wonder if I was dreaming a few seconds ago, but the striking face with the delicate features and curly dark hair is well contoured in my memory. I wish I had met him, had talked to him about Cristina, but I seem to be living in a universe where people appear and disappear like magic. Some magic!

I remember Cristina, trying to push snow down my collar, her face flushed from the cold, framed by her chestnut plaits that were coming undone. How lonely and desperate, how cornered from all sides, she must have felt if indeed she decided to kill herself. I wish I had remained closer to Cristina. I wish I had kept alive the impulse I'd had this past winter, to be her family and protect her. It's as if Mihai has changed my perception of time, my sense of the reality around me. As if I have been living within this love like in a hot-air balloon, floating above everything and everyone. I have no idea of Cristina's life over the past two years, except for a couple of quick encounters and the conversation I had with her last winter. Then summer rushed in, and then she was dead. She was so confused, and so like a lost child without her parents, her lips smeared with sugary white cream and all excited about being in love with someone exotic, someone from Tunisia, old Carthage, where Dido had died of love for her beloved Aeneas. I wonder if she suffered much. If there is any possibility she might have poisoned herself, what would she have taken? An overdose of sleeping pills would have sufficed. Did she call for help at the very end, when it was too late? Was she scared? Mariana and Cristina, two childhood friends dead within three years, before we even had the time to fully grow up. Maybe this place is cursed and my great-grandmother's magic mirror has used up all of its charms.

I feel defeated and exhausted. I want to lie on a fresh grave covered with petunias and marigolds and go to sleep for ever. I want to run away. I do not belong in this universe. I don't understand it and I don't like it. Mihai seems like a stranger to me again. The skinny man in the leather jacket staring at us doesn't even scare me any more. Why do the Securitate wear leather jackets even in the hot summer, I wonder. I've got used to the absurdity of it all. But I don't want to get used to it. It's like freezing to death, being lulled to death, and yet having enough stubbornness in you to resist. I want to run away, I want to run away, I want to run away. That's what I keep repeating to myself as I watch the crowd leaving Cristina's grave.

The day after the funeral, I decide not to go to Mihai's and stay home to spend time with my cousins. Miruna and Riri bring out their card games. For the first time in a while I notice how both of them have grown up. Miruna's face is pale and has got longer, and her blue eyes have an even deeper hue. She is a quieter child now, whereas Riri is getting taller and looks more mischievous than ever. They both want to know about the funeral. They say how sad it is that Cristina died like that, so young. She'll meet her mother in the other life, says Miruna, her chicory-blue eyes wide and watery.

"There is no afterlife," I tell her.

"Yes, there is!" says Riri.

"No, there isn't. It's just a bunch of silly tales, about how you go to heaven and all that crap," I say.

Miruna starts crying, and Riri throws one of the porcelain gin-rummy stones at me.

"Are you a Marxist or something?" Riri yells, her face all red and her dark eyes glittering with anger.

I turn over the gin-rummy game and kick the pieces.

"I am not anything!" I say and start crying. "I'm not a Marxist. I'm not a Christian. I hate everything!"

I'm breaking down in front of my cousins who have never seen me this way. They wrap their arms around me and try to console me. They tell me they're sorry about Cristina and it's all right if I don't believe in the afterlife. Miruna gives me a piece of her chewing gum, and Riri picks up the gin-rummy pieces.

That evening, Mihai calls to ask me if I want to go out for a walk. I don't really feel like it. I'm enjoying the time with my cousins and my aunt Nina and uncle Ion. My aunt has boiled a pot of corn, and Ion has cracked open a huge watermelon. They're laughing and teasing each other.

"Yes, I want to go for a walk," I hear myself telling Mihai. "Where should I meet you?"

"Downstairs in ten minutes," he says.

It's rare that Mihai comes to pick me up at my aunt's building. We usually meet somewhere halfway, or in the park at the end of the street. He's freshly shaven, wearing a clean shirt that matches his eyes.

"I got a job in Bucharest," he announces. "At the tractor parts factory. I start in a month. See? I kept my promise, didn't I?" he says proudly.

I'm speechless, I'm in awe and I've been wrong. Mihai would never betray me. I have just been paranoid about him cheating on me and being secret police because of the overall atmosphere of mistrust. And because I've been reading too many English and French novels. After all, Mihai often talks about my father with great admiration. It's just that he comes from a different world than mine. His parents are workers, and he lives in a provincial town, but that makes him more interesting than the pretentious spoiled Bucharest boys. He loves his country and simply doesn't want all the smart Romanians to leave. It was he who only the other day told me the joke about how the last Romanian to leave the country would *turn off the lights, to save the electricity.* Then he said sadly that only the dumb ones and those too lazy to leave will remain. I build up Mihai again into the hero I've always wanted him to be as I'm standing in front of my aunt's building this August afternoon. My heart is beating so fast that I feel dizzy in the hot sun. All the fragrances of our first summer are filling the air, and I just want to look at the piercing blue sky and admire the whimsical yellow roses that the neighbour on the first floor has planted and the red poppies spreading all over the park. Mihai will move to Bucharest. I'll start my university classes, and we'll get married, and maybe if things get really bad, one day I'll even be able to convince Mihai to run away with me somewhere in the world. We'll escape to Switzerland or Canada or somewhere like that, where there will be lots of beautiful mountains and glacier lakes, where we can finally live our love freely.

Bad Cologne

I ARRIVE IN BUCHAREST the last week of August, elated.
Mihai will join me soon to start his new job, and I am about
to start my first year at the University of Bucharest, as an English
literature major. But my happiness is soon tinged with fear and
nausea again. Sergeant Dumitriu, the secret-police officer who
brought me the red carnations, is on my trail. He calls repeat-
edly, wants to meet me alone, and asks me to *help him with some
information about student colleagues at the university.*

He asks me to meet him in the University Square, right in
front of the four statues of Romania's greatest literary and historic figures. We meet in front of the statue of Michael the
Brave on his enormous horse with the fearsome sword pulled
out for battle, in the neighbourhood where my parents used to
live the night I was born. Michael the Brave must be my
guardian angel, I think, and smile as I see Dumitriu approach
me full of self-assurance. He takes my smile for a sign of glad-
ness to see him and rushes to kiss my hand. He smells strongly
of cheap cologne. I become stiff and edgy at his touch and
secretly wipe off my hand on the side of my skirt. We start walking in the direction of the InterContinental Hotel, with its con-
cave modern body of white stone looming above the city. I walk
several steps away from Dumitriu, looking around me worried
that someone I know might see me in the vicinity of this secret-

police officer. I stumble, and he rushes to hold me. I jerk my arm in repulsion and he says with a grin: "Miss Mona, I don't bite, you know, deep down I am quite a nice guy!"

I feel like laughing at the sound of the expression "deep down" but try to keep a serious, stern face. I am wondering how *deep* does one need to go to find anything *nice* in a person who is responsible for people losing jobs, being arrested, being shoved inside mental asylums, or even being killed.

He starts talking as we are about to cross the street. "It's nothing to be ashamed of, Miss Mona," he says. "You would be doing us a great service and your country and Party, too. And most important, you'd be doing yourself a great favour. Just paying attention to what some of your colleagues might say, that's all, paying attention. For instance, do you meet anyone you know at the American library, or do any of your colleagues have contacts with foreigners? Things like that, quite innocent, really."

He wipes sweat off his forehead with a handkerchief he's just produced from his trouser pocket. My heart jolts as I hear about the American library and I remember my conversations with Ralph the librarian, and the man in a black blazer always sitting at the faraway table pretending to read.

"In return," he goes on without giving me a chance to respond, "we would make sure you land a nice position after graduation, something in your field, something here in the capital – for instance, at the American or at the British library. We know how much you love to read."

We are now walking past the grandiose building of the National Theatre with its wide marble steps leading to the modern glass-and-brick façade. My heart is pounding so hard that I am almost having trouble breathing. I look back at the statue of Michael the Brave and am sorry to have left it, as if I cannot receive its protection any longer. I feel sweat dripping from my forehead along my nose, and my clothes feel heavy and bulky. My sandals scratch my feet, and my toes look all red and swollen. I stop in the middle of the pavement and tell him very calmly, very softly: "Thank you, Mr Dumitriu, for your kind offer. But I want to teach after I graduate. I don't want to work at the American library. I want to teach English. Excuse me, I am late for my classes now."

I let a young couple holding hands pass between us, and I take advantage of the distraction to start running. I run on the heated Bucharest pavement without looking back, on the side streets that I know so well, and find myself next to Aunt Matilda's apartment building. I rush inside the cool hallway and close the heavy iron door with a thump. I sit on the marble steps leading to Matilda's apartment to catch my breath. Cracks from the earthquake are still visible in the walls, and a great sense of relief overtakes me at the thought that only a floor away is Aunt Matilda with her sweet, smiling face, her rose-petal and walnut preserves in her pantry. I rush up the stairs and walk right in as I always do, for Matilda always keeps her door unlocked, except for when she leaves the house or goes to bed. "God always helps me," she says, "God and the Virgin Mary." She is sitting at the long polished wooden table under the crystal chandelier and is reading. I have never been so happy to see Aunt Matilda as I am now, running away from Dumitriu and his scabrous offers. I ask her to give me a large portion of rose-petal preserve.

I try to go about my daily business as if nothing has happened: my literature classes, meeting with a friend or two for coffee or a beer at the café next to the Architecture Institute. I sometimes notice Dumitriu in a crowded bus on my way to school, hiding behind someone and pretending to look in the opposite direction. Once I notice him at the other end of the bus I'm taking to get home, bus number 88. He is staring at me with fascination or maybe desire. The thought fills me with disgust. I would much rather he hated me and followed me for purely political reasons. I can't stand the thought of being lusted after by a bona fide secret policeman, someone who actually calls himself officer. And it's not because he is in the army.

One night, I am returning home after studying late at the library. I hear footsteps behind me, the kind that give you the creeps. You stop, they stop; you start walking, they start coming up behind you. Before I know it, I am being pushed into the entranceway of a shabby apartment building, my back against the wall, and a tall man smelling of sweat and bad cologne has me trapped. He's whispering into my ear. He is wearing the same cologne as Dumitriu did the other day. There must be a special brand of Securitate cologne, I think. I'm surprised at myself for not being scared, although it's past eleven at night and there is no one on the street. Maybe it's the cologne that turns the whole thing into a joke. People should smell of tar or cigars when they attack people in the street at night. I kick him with my knee and spit at him. He recoils for a second, enough for me to try to break away, but he recovers and traps me against the wall again with one arm, wiping my saliva from his face with the other.

"Feisty, ha?" he says, grinning.

I don't want to say anything. I don't want to scream or talk. I just want this over. I know somehow this isn't a sexual assault. I'm suddenly angry at everybody, including my own father and Mihai. Everybody has some stake in something that I'm not interested in, and I seem to be the one paying for everybody's attempts at heroism and adventure. Our lives aren't getting any better because of all the fuss with manifestos and Radio Free Europe and all the meetings about censorship taking place in grungy attics and damp basements. We are still standing in the same stupid queues for every bite we eat, and we can't even talk in public. I feel no fear but only waves of hatred and anger at the whole world. Even at my dead relatives who are letting me down.

"What exactly is your daddy trying to do, hm . . . who are his best friends?" he asks. "If your daddy continues the way he is, you'll end up like your little friend," the man whispers in my ear. "Or worse."

I find the thought of ending up worse than dead kind of funny, and I laugh. Then I shiver at the sound of *little friend* in his mouth. So maybe Cristina *was* murdered after all. In any case, even if she was made so desperate as to kill herself, it's almost as if she were murdered. Her death was just another, more perverse way of being murdered.

"You think it's funny, ha?" the man asks, squeezing both my wrists against the wall until they hurt. "But it's true. There's worse things than being dead," he says.

"So why are you whispering, tough guy?" I ask him. Cristina's death had made something snap inside me. I don't really care any more.

"YOU WANT TO HEAR IT LOUDER?" he shouts, inches from my ear. *"FINE. I CAN DO THAT."* His voice echoes down the empty street. I try to twist my head away, but he pinches my jaw with one hand and pulls my face up to his.

"You hear me now, *right?*" he shouts. It echoes down the street: *Right, right, right.*

"Yes," I say meekly. It's important to tell myself that I am only *acting* meek.

He grabs my chin and lifts my head up so I have to look at him.

"Good girl," he says and lets go of my chin.

The sound of the words *good girl* makes me tremble, and I know I am not acting any more. Now I *am* scared for my life and for my father's life. His words suddenly remind me of the girl who was mysteriously run over. Maybe she, too, was just a piece of the puzzle that they used in order to get to someone else: her parents or her lover, who knows. Or maybe it was her lover who was behind it. *Who knows, who knows,* I hear the words ringing in my head like a chant. Maybe Mihai is good secret police like my father's former student, maybe there are a few noble ones among them who actually work to undermine the bad ones. I am sure Mihai wouldn't let anyone hurt me this way and grab my chin and shove me against a wall in the middle of the night. But *who knows, who knows.* Trust your instincts, they always say. Maybe I should trust the suspicion I had for the first time when I came back to see Mihai the winter after the summer we fell in love, when suddenly he seemed a stranger, with his leather jacket and moralizing to me about my anti-Communist attitude. How can there even be good secret police?

The man with the chubby face eases off and moves a step away. Then he walks away, just like that, straightening his jacket collar. He looks up at the buildings as if he owned the street.

My legs give out, and I slip down the wall until I'm sitting on my heels. I'm shaking all over. I am exhausted from the strain of acting and also from not acting and from just being afraid. I close my eyes and I am floating on the river Nistru in 1918, rushing by floating bodies and chicken coops, and the music in my mirror music box keeps playing, a persistent string of notes carrying me through the demented waters. I climb into a tree and wait. I sing the tune of my music box, the "Für Elise" tune, over and over again. Then I am awake a week later in a strange man's bed, drinking cold water from a tin cup he is holding for me. He has soft black hair neatly combed back, a thin nose, and an elegant, smiling face. I know we will get married. I am going to plant lavender in my garden to cover the smells of rotting bodies and shit from the river. My house will always smell of lavender. And bad cologne will be outlawed from my neighbourhood for ever.

Choices

M Y MOTHER AND I ARE AFRAID every night when it gets to be past eight o'clock and my father hasn't come home yet. We sit on the living room sofa with the storage box beneath it that holds all my childhood dolls. We hold hands and stare at the door. Sometimes I want to open up the box under the sofa bed and take out my dolls and place them all around me and talk to them. Daniela the blond one, Mihaela the brunette, and Tania, the Russian doll my aunt Ana brought me from the USSR: Tania's long plaits and soulful glass eyes used to make me think people were so wrong to say bad things about the Russians.

I am waiting for something awful to happen to me any moment, to be run over, to be strangled in my sleep, to be served poisoned ice cream by the scrawny woman in a yellow dress in the corner ice-cream booth.

My mother makes leek stew every night. Now, even bread is rationed, and we run to all the shops in the neighbourhood looking for coffee. When we don't find it, she makes very strong black tea. We drink it scrunching our faces, with no sugar because we've finished our ration of sugar for the month, with no lemon because we haven't seen a lemon in two years.

One evening my father comes home looking defeated, his grey hair dishevelled and his blue-grey eyes almost teary, and announces to us he has been demoted from his position at the University of Bucharest to the Ploieşti Institute, a city that is sixty kilometres away. Another colleague of his from the comparative literature department was also demoted and made to teach high school. "I'm supposed to be lucky, actually," he says with a bitter smile. My mother says he should have expected it, with his overt craziness about Radio Free Europe and the manifestos.

"Indeed, you are lucky," my mother continues as she purses her lips with a stern expression. "They could have put you into an asylum, like they've done with others."

She sounds almost cruel. I realize that although she has stood by my father's activities, she has actually hated them and the danger for himself and all of us. She has acted as if nothing has changed, teaching her classes at the conservatory, queuing after work for a bag of potatoes or to get our oil and sugar rations, and wishing my father hadn't got involved in anything. Writing her poetry at night to forget about our daily worries.

My father now leaves home every morning at four and travels on an unheated train with broken windows to get to his new assignment at the Ploieşti Institute. He teaches foreign students from Africa who are studying in our country because Ceauşescu has travelled there trying to get more foreign currency in the country. In order to soothe the pain caused by his demotion, my father reads all the Romanian poets over and over again, in no particular order: Eminescu, Minulescu, Bacovia, Arghezi, Blaga, Barbu, the Romantics, the metaphysical, the folklorists, the Symbolists, the modernists, all our greatest. Sometimes he recites poems by heart, pacing around the apartment. Melancholy poems about being buried alive in snow, playful poems about spring and about pink and violet tree buds and a waltz of the roses, and passionate love poems about waiting desperately under the lover's window all night, under the cold, cold moon.

When he is in a better mood, and excited about his new African students who are learning Romanian, my father tells us political jokes at the dinner table over our leek stew. I particularly like the one about the two men sitting in a train compartment and it starts to rain. One of them says, *Look, it's raining again.* And the other one says, *I know. To hell with them!* My father laughs so hard he chokes on a leek, and then tears come into his eyes. We jump every time we hear steps in the hallway outside our apartment. We jump up from our chairs every time the phone rings. Sometimes my father says, "Don't answer. Let it ring."

My father surprises me one day when he tells me I have to start thinking about leaving. "It's getting dangerous for you here," he whispers. "I am afraid for you," he adds and strokes my hair sadly. I wonder if he knows anything about the chubby-faced man who threatened me that night, or if maybe he has received his own set of threats about something happening to me.

I see my mother's angry eyes. I know she's angry because he's done this to us, and now she's losing her daughter. But she says nothing, and I know they've talked this over. Now it's in the open: I have to think about leaving.

There are so many ways of escaping; all you need is the energy to go ahead and try one of them. People escape all the time. I'll have to find a way, too, by sea, by river, by train, by plane. Walking, swimming, riding, crawling across the border. Anything. At least in that respect the choices seem numerous.

As we are sitting close to one another whispering about my escape, I feel the danger emanating from all directions. I am puzzled and at the same time detached from the huge irony of Mihai moving to Bucharest just about when I am thinking of leaving the country. I can't quite process the two thoughts next to each other, so I get up from the sofa and go to the kitchen to try to find something to eat. There is nothing in the refrigerator except for a bowl of leftover lettuce and tomato salad from yesterday. I take it out and eat the soggy salad with the last slice of bread from our ration for this week.

One evening when it's cold and rainy in Bucharest, and all

the umbrellas get turned inside out, and the dead leaves are swirling in the air like in the picture of autumn I used to have in my elementary school reading books, the wife of my father's psychiatrist friend comes over wet and trembling. She says three generals in Ceauşescu's government have been executed, and everybody who is suspected of any *illegal activities* is being hunted down. My mother goes pale because my father isn't home yet; it's already eight o'clock and he was supposed to be home three hours ago after his classes at the Ploieşti Institute. She lights a cigarette from the package my father left on the table next to his bed, next to the pile of index cards for the dictionary of neologisms he's working on. She tells Liliana to take off her coat and sit down, does she want some coffee, it's soy coffee, she found it yesterday at the grocery near the Russian church downtown. No, all Liliana wants is some water. My mother asks if she knows anything about my father.

Liliana says they're all hiding. There were meetings in the attic of her house sometimes, and she admits she helped by typing, keeping records of people who had disappeared, and watching for cars or people walking by the house during the meetings.

It bothers me that she's telling us this. Why now? Why not just pretend she was never there? I don't want to hear her, and I don't want her to say another word.

"It's got huge," Liliana tells us. "They say there are men and women of all ages, lots of students. But in the end, who knows? Half of them could be informers. Then one day they round everyone up, and everyone's pointing at someone else, because this is how we are, we Romanians. And since the defection of Pacepa, things have got even more confused."

She fidgets and wrings her hands. Liliana is so small and plump that her feet barely touch the ground when she sits down. She has a whining, weepy voice that pierces like the point of a needle. Her husband, Mihnea, already spent seven years in political prison in the fifties. He happened to be at a party where someone recited a metaphysical poem of some sort, and one night he disappeared in a black van. He reappeared seven years later, barely recognizable even to his own wife and son.

Liliana is wringing her hands over and over. Her annoying voice and the rain tapping at the windowpanes sound like omens of catastrophe and misery. I am thinking that maybe I can get to Italy somehow. Maybe I can get to sunny Italy just by taking the train to Trieste, simply buying a ticket and swinging across the border.

My father appears at the door, soaking wet and looking like a fugitive. He tells my mother to pack a bag of clothes for him. My uncle Ion is coming to drive him to his relatives in the country-side. That's all the way to northern Moldavia, deep in the country where people still get their water from the village well and they light their houses with candles, because there's one electrical socket used only in emergencies. It's not like the Securitate couldn't find them even *in a snake pit,* as my father says sometimes. But they will gain time, allowing things to blow over, and maybe they can even mislead the Securitate for a while. Now my father thinks the Securitate aren't all that smart anyway and the whole system of terror is based on making people believe they are cunning and omniscient so that everybody stays intimidated and paralysed.

"If everyone resisted and did something, we wouldn't all be in the huge pile of shit we are in right now. There's the Romanians for you," he often says angrily, crushing his cigarette with an abrupt gesture.

Liliana asks feverishly if my father has heard from Mihnea, and he tells her, "Yes, he's safe." She doesn't ask for more; she knows it's all he can say, all he knows. My father gives my mother the phone number of the former student who's a colonel in the secret police and helped him out before. She needs to meet with him. Maybe he can tell her what to do to get his name off the wanted list.

I don't understand why some Securitate are helping them out. Why does my father trust people like that? He's said he knows; he has his instincts. Colonel Petrescu won't betray him.

I'm glad the world is full of my father's former students. Then I think of Mihai, and now I want to believe that Mihai really is in the secret police, but he's like Petrescu's good secret police. I want to trust him, even if he's one of them. I want to call him and hear his voice telling me there's nothing to worry about. I want to tell him everything.

While my father helps my mother collect his clothes and food, he tells us a joke. There is this man running in the street, and he meets a friend who asks him, *Why are you running?* So he says, *Didn't you hear? They're shooting camels everywhere!* And the first man says, *But you're not a camel! Why are you running?* And the man says, *I know I'm not a camel, but these guys shoot first and check later.*

I laugh at my father's joke, though no one else does. He embraces me and tells me to be good, not to stay out late at night, because *you never know.* I am so sick of that expression that I want to explode. I thought my father was always the one who knew everything. Instead, he seems more confused now than ever before, and even his running away to the mountains seems naïve and senseless. It was he who always told me that when *they* want to find you, *they* will find you anywhere, even in a bear's den, even in the darkest hole in the earth. Maybe he was exaggerating, as my father often does. Maybe he is just playing hide-and-seek with the secret police. Or maybe he is right when he says that not even the Securitate are as invulnerable and cunning as they try to seem.

Uncle Ion arrives late that night, ready to take my father to the northern Carpathians where his relatives will hide him in a basement or in a stable with the cows and the pigs and the hens laying eggs. They drink black tea without sugar or lemon and tell political jokes. They laugh out loud as if, for once, it doesn't matter. Tonight I am envious of my father and uncle, and of Liliana's husband. They seem to be playing in an adventure film, and suddenly I feel like I want to be in this film, too.

I don't know which path to choose. I feel I'm being forced to make a choice I never wanted to make. Maybe I should join the students meeting in basements and trying to change things. If my own life is in danger anyway, it might as well be in danger for something I'm doing myself, for an important cause, not because of what my father or lover does. And then what? I think of Cristina again and of how trapped and desperate she must have felt. I don't want to feel like Cristina, I want to love, live, study, be something important. I want to run away, and I also want to be with Mihai. My heart is cracking again under the weight of such impossible choices.

This rainy November night in my parents' apartment, as my father is going off to hide in the heart of the mountains, as I start to fantasize about crossing the border into Italy, I find refuge again thinking of Mihai. Soon he'll be here, living in Bucharest. But even that comforting thought seems poisoned by doubts and worry. There seems to be a worm gnawing at everything. There's terror in everything, in what we do and in what we don't do, in being with someone and being apart. At least my father and people like him, running and hiding tonight, are sharing the terror together.

I'm dreaming about the black hole in Romanian history that my aunt always talks about. That place of nonhistory, dark and mysterious like a womb, where I could curl up like a foetus and forget everything and float in the warm gelatinous waters of oblivion, waiting.

Sad Winter in Bulgarian Boots

MIHAI HAS KEPT HIS PROMISE. He's moved to Bucharest. He works as an engineer at the dreary margins of the city, in a factory that produces parts for tractors that are exported for hard currency. He lives in a rented room in another part of the city, close to where my great-aunt Nadia, who fell dead on the floor with the yellowish postcard in her hand, used to live. The streets here are wide with rows of oak and chestnut trees and turn-of-the-century buildings and houses. The room where Mihai lives is tiny, with a creaky door and a creaky bed where we make love in the evening as people go up and down the creaky staircase outside our door. There is so much creaking everywhere that sometimes we sit and listen and laugh, because we both miss the starched bedsheets and the cool mountain air coming through the windows in Mihai's room in his parents' apartment. The creaking makes us think of old age and of time passing as we stare at the ugly cracks in the walls left by the big earthquake.

Everything seems to get calmer for a while. I pack the events of the past year in a kind of mental wardrobe for memories I mustn't remember. After returning from his hiding place deep in northern Moldavia, my father becomes quieter than usual and is often brooding. He seldom leaves the house, which makes me think that his group must have dissipated and everybody must have been scared off for a while. Maybe some have disappeared or are locked up in Mihnea's hospital.

Those thoughts I had of Mata Hari now seem silly to me as I spend my days moving between my university classes and making love with Mihai in the little room with creaky furniture. I am happy as we stroll down the long streets lined with oak trees and as we shuffle through the carpet of russet leaves like an old couple.

I go to my university courses every day while Mihai works in the tractor factory. I read dozens of English and American plays, medieval plays, and Shakespeare and Restoration plays and Tennessee Williams and Arthur Miller, and I think about all the characters loving and disguising themselves and dying and killing and committing suicide and the glass figurines the woman in *The Glass Menagerie* collects and the Forest of Arden where love plays the wildest tricks.

The grey trolleybuses dragging their giant snail bodies down the boulevards of Bucharest seem more bearable and even acquire a touch of colour. The sad, dusty-looking people with drawn faces, returning from work with bags of potatoes and their sugar and oil rations, take on a certain edge of nobility. I don't particularly like the pathetic character in *Death of a Salesman*. It seems banal and uninteresting to kill yourself for life insurance. At least under Communism we have good pension plans. There are better reasons to kill yourself, like not being admitted to the university or being caught by the secret police or working every day in a tractor factory.

Some evenings, I tell Mihai I have to study for my exams, and I go to the theatre in the centre of town. I feel happy walking along the marble corridors with crystal chandeliers, looking at the elegant theatregoing crowd, women in black velvet dresses and men with bow ties.

I see *Iphigenia*, a sad play about a virgin being sacrificed by her own father to ensure the glory of his army in the Trojan War. She seems noble and melancholy, in a shimmering long white dress. She has a soliloquy about going alone to be sacrificed. I rage inwardly against the men around her, so greedy for glory at her expense. I am furious at how men use women to obtain glory for themselves. And then how they write it up so it's as if it were *their* sacrifice of their most precious possessions – their women, their daughters, sisters, mothers. How Clytemnestra tears at her gown and her long hair in despair, trying uselessly to save her daughter from being sacrificed. I will not be Iphigenia walking towards the sacrificial altar in a white gown, I tell myself almost out loud in the dark theatre. I will run for my life.

Most of all I like *The Master and Margarita*. Valeria Seciu, the best Romanian actress, is playing the role of Margarita. She appears half naked at a window, chanting her passion and her revolt. The devils plotting to take the artist's soul away are both funny and frightful. They make me think of the secret police buying people's souls, only these devils are colourful and have funny red tails.

There's nothing I would want to do more in my life than make plays like this one, with crushing passions and poetry flowing in sensuous chants onstage, with men and women moving as in a dream, faces with grotesque makeup, under red and mauve and yellow lights.

When I leave the theatre, the streets are glistening in the November drizzle. I feel sad for Mihai, sitting alone in his rented room where everything creaks and smells like it's a hundred years old.

Mihai seems smaller without his dark mountains and the hidden paths among the pine trees. He seems out of place here; he takes on the greyness of the Bucharest autumn like a hand-me-down coat with sleeves that are too short.

It's on a Sunday afternoon, this November, that we take a funny photograph we call *Just Escaped from Refugee Camp*, in the rain near the railway station. Me in my detestable Bulgarian boots and a ridiculous wide-brimmed hat, Mihai with a green coat and a big Russian hat. We're looking straight at the camera. Mihai has the beginning of a crooked smile; I have no smile whatsoever. I am stern and angry, holding his arm. You see silhouettes behind us, people with umbrellas, and the street has a slight glimmer in the rain.

My feet freeze in my Bulgarian boots. It's snowing ruthlessly, and Bucharest seems almost festive under a dusting of snow. I wear a white mohair shawl over my head.

One evening I take two streetcars and two buses to find the tractor factory where Mihai works. I wait for him at the tall metal gate of the entrance as his shift pours out. I see him in the distance, walking slowly, almost with a limp, crouched under the falling snow. I am seized with fear that the Mihai I know, the man who took me along the hidden paths of the Carpathians, knowing every secret turn, naming every flower and tree, will slowly disappear under his ridiculous Russian hat among the workers at the edge of Bucharest where heavy machinery is being built.

I know it's hopeless. He won't make it. We won't make it. This is a sad, sad winter. He hates everything, and I hate him for hating everything.

He finally sees me through the shimmering lace of snow-flakes. He's angry to see me there. He grins at the security guard at the gate who greets him, *Good evening, Comrade Simionu,* and then he's sullen again. But when he grudgingly kisses me in the swirl of snow outside the metal gate, I suddenly have the feeling I'm growing, becoming immense in my white shawl. I feel like the queen of the North Pole. It doesn't matter that it isn't going to work out. I feel white and huge like a polar bear, and I can't help swelling and flying upward just like the old man in *Mary Poppins* who can't help floating to the ceiling as he fills up with laughter. I think of the theatres at night and the yellow and mauve lights with actors reciting poetic words in melancholy rhythms. I walk next to him without touching the ground, ballooning into white fluff.

We go back to his room and sit on the squeaky chairs at his work desk staring at each other for a while. He is unshaven and I ask him if he plans to grow a beard.

"Maybe. Don't you want me to blend in with the Bucharest hippies, with your college friends, don't they all have beards and long hair?"

"I don't have any hippie friends. I like you with or without a beard," I say.

He scratches his face, holds his head in his hands, lifts his head, and stares at me. He tells me he really can't take this city. He can't take the factory, the ugly industrial district where he has to work.

"I am really trying, you know, I'm trying very hard . . . for your sake. But I don't know how you can live in this city."

He lights a cigarette and wraps himself in the blue smoke, staring at the ceiling. I find him handsome in a new way, with his beginnings of a beard, the sad, anguished expression. I hear people going up the staircase outside the room, and I know how much he hates hearing people go up and down those stairs all the time. I take his hand and hold it to my face as he looks deeply into my eyes. I grab the cigarette from his hand and take a couple of drags from it. It tastes bitter and sour, and the unpleasant taste goes well with the morose atmosphere in this room. Then he grabs my head almost with violence and kisses me on the lips the way he has done so many times in our most inebriating moments: slowly, deliberately, pressing his lips hard against mine.

"I wanted so much for us to be together always, Mona," he says sadly, and the sound of my name in his mouth sends shivers of pleasure down my spine. I want to hear him say *Mona* for ever. I see tears in his eyes and am shocked at the sight. Mihai truly does love me like crazy.

"But I am suffocating. And then there are things, things I am worried about, things I have to do. And it's better if I am away from this city," he concludes vaguely.

It's the first time I hear him talk this way, actually mentioning something that he is doing outside of his work and his mountain climbing. My heart starts pounding with anxiety. I don't want to ask him what those *things* are that he has to do. I don't want to know about them. Right now, I prefer to think Mihai is a friend of my father's student, Colonel Petrescu, working with an inside movement of people in the Securitate who wish to undermine the very organization they are part of. He kisses me again, and I let myself get carried away.

We make love in a new way, slowly, deliberately, whispering words of love and promises of eternal faithfulness, oblivious to the squeaking of the bed and of the people going up and down the staircase outside our room. It is now dark; we can barely see each other's face, and we cry in each other's arms. By mid-February, Mihai has resigned from his job at the tractor factory and is back in his beloved mountains. We'll see each other during vacations as before, and I'll be back on trains to see him. But summer is so far away and this winter seems endless. Sometimes I take the bus to where he used to live. I walk around the sooty building with the tiny room and the creaking staircase. My feet are cold in my Bulgarian boots.

Spring and Brown Soup

ONE EVENING, after I've circled the block where Mihai used to live in an agony of nostalgia as grey and opaque as this February dusk, I see a shadow across the street, hands in his pockets, sure of himself. I have the feeling this shadow is watching me. I want to run, but I don't want him to run after me. I want to be in sunny Italy, Bermuda, Valparaíso, even Bulgaria – on another continent, on another planet.

Instead of getting on bus 99 that just stopped at the corner, I run inside the building with its creaky staircase. For a moment, I forget Mihai doesn't live there any more. I rush to the room on the left that used to be his room. I try the doorknob: it's unlocked. I open the door and walk in, as if I know he'll be there waiting for me.

The room is dimly lit. Instead of Mihai sitting at the wooden table against the wall, working on some diagram of a tractor part, there's an old man who stares at me with red-rimmed eyes. He holds a spoon. Juice from a brown liquid is dripping into his beard.

I let out a scream. It's the scream I've wanted to produce for a long time, since the night of New Year's Day, the crazy woman, the shadow. I scream and scream, and the old man knocks over his soup jumping up from the table. He looks terrified, holding his hands out, trembling, panicky. He begs me to not report him because he doesn't have the key, somebody else does, please, please don't have him arrested. He starts crying.

I have no idea what anybody wants from me any more. In this moment, as I sit on the chair in Mihai's old room, with the ancient man with brown soup in his beard, I only know that I want to run away for ever. I want to be on the train to Trieste, to find myself in the exact moment where the train crosses the border into Italy where olive trees grow, where velvety, dark green pines cast their profiles against blue hills and Roman ruins, where people speak joyously in sentences that sound like opera arias and say things like *mamma mia* and *mascalzone*.

I get up from the chair and say, "I'm terribly sorry, sir. Please excuse me for interrupting your dinner." The old man looks at me with relief. I rush out of the building in a flash. I run without stopping. I don't take the bus back home, but just run like the wild white mare of my dream, across the streets of Bucharest in the icy February drizzle that mixes with my warm tears.

Once in a while I see Sergeant Dumitriu in a crowd, on a bus, like before. Sometimes he actually says hello, as if he were an old acquaintance. He has been my most loyal *follower*. I run into him when I go to my university courses. I recognize him in the street at night when I get back from a play or from the library. He is always wearing a suit and a tie. You might as well look respectable when you are following and informing on people. I don't feel like sharing any of this with my father. Why burden him with more worries or incite him to do something wild and violent to protect me, such as beat up Dumitriu in the middle of the street, the way he did once when a shady man was stalking me in Bucharest when I was fourteen.

Sometimes at night, in the menacing silence of the street, I hear footsteps very close behind me. I think I see shadows going around the corners of buildings. But since the night when the man pinned me against a wall and shouted at me, I glide through my life as if nothing can touch me.

One afternoon as I am walking home from my classes, a day in early March when gypsy women are selling the first timid sprigs of violets and hyacinths, when I've switched my ugly Bulgarian boots for my one pair of slightly less ugly Hungarian loafers, I see Anca Serban. I see her meet with Mihnea, my father's psychiatrist friend, in front of the ruins of the building where they used to sell cream puffs, which collapsed during the earthquake of 1977. There is now scaffolding all around it for the reconstruction, and the pavement is always more crowded in front of it because it is narrower and filled with construction workers. It is probably why they are meeting there, to be less conspicuous. And who in God's creation is this phantom woman who haunts my existence and who now is suddenly in Bucharest, giving a square package in brown paper to Mihnea, who works in the hospital where the secret police throw all those who are suspect for "political crimes", to rot in madness and in straitjackets, numb and tranquillized?

I try to make myself unnoticed on the pavement across the street by turning towards the flower seller in the corner and buying a bouquet of hyacinths. I am watching Mihnea get the package and talk for a few short minutes with the woman who had attacked me in the night. Mihnea looks like a spectre, has bulging pale eyes, and is thin like he has been on a hunger strike. I buy the flowers, I smell them, and their spring fragrance penetrates my exhausted body as a gust lifts the pleats of my skirt.

I smile at the woman and thank her for the flowers as I place the money directly in her cold, wet palm. I run home knowing that not even there can I feel safe and unwatched. If my father is still involved in illegal activities and with his group of dissenting friends, then my life is seriously in danger. If Mihai has the slightest connection with the secret police, then my father's life and my own life are even more in danger. This maths is very simple and I totally get it. My life is in danger one way or another, for things I've done or haven't done. I never wanted my life to be in danger in this confusing, maddening way. Wasn't it better with the bombs during the war and the famine? You just fought for survival. You survived the bomb or not. You floated on flooding rivers, scraped for a root in the ground to not starve, lived, or died, all clean and harsh.

I wish I could say that my grandparents and great-aunts who survived every possible human and natural catastrophe had it worse. I wish I could feel lucky to live in peace and have bread and potatoes and soy coffee to eat and drink every day. I wish I could say it's great I can buy hyacinths in the street on my way home from classes. But I find myself envying them. I think of my maternal grandparents in the sepia photograph taken before they went to a ball, a wartime grand ball, my grandmother Vera in a black shiny dress, a string of pearls around her statuesque neck, and a flower in her hair, and my grandfather Victor dashing, a flower in his buttonhole, ready to dance, hoping that after the war there will be peace and things will get better.

In the month of April, bursting with the yellows of forsythia bushes and the pale pinks of chestnut blooms, Rodica Ursu, the daughter of a friend of my father, gets run over by a car that didn't stop at the stoplight. My father says she was working both sides. She had been careless.

I don't understand any of this any more. Pick one side or another, but why live *two* secret lives? What's the point, really? I feel sorry for the girl, for her crushed body and her devastated parents. Maybe this is what Mihai is doing as well, having two secret lives. Is it what he meant when he had said there were *things* he had to do? And his letters have been colder than usual, just brief reports of his new job at the big tractor factory in Braşov and a few brief lines about him missing me and waiting for the summer vacation. He doesn't even say he is waiting for *me*, but for the vacation.

I'm terrified now. I walk close to the building walls and take long detours to avoid crossing the street. I take buses and move away from anyone who gets too close or who jostles and pushes their elbows in my side trying to move past me in the crowded bus. Once in a while on a bus, I find solace in watching some poor woman nursing a round baby with lips like coral, sucking at a perfectly round breast.

One evening, with smells of spring flowers and trees in bloom rushing through the open windows in our Bucharest apartment, the three of us sit talking about my leaving the country. My father is more explicit and more adamant about it than the other time he mentioned leaving.

"You see what happened to poor Rodica. Anything can happen, no matter where you stand," my father says. My mother nods. They are whispering and looking over their shoulders into the fragrant night.

"Plus, you have no future here, Mona. Things will only get worse," my father says.

I know this is the decision that will jerk everything off its hinges, the decision that, once taken, will change everything in more dramatic ways than anything else that my family has ever gone through. More than the wars, than Stalin, than Ceauşescu.

I know that hundreds, thousands, have already done it. I know that every day someone crosses the border and runs for her life. Every hour of every day, someone makes a plan. Many succeed. Trains, ships, airplanes, all hold some desperate Romanian trying to get to the other side, risking everything and rushing into that overpowering wave of total erasure, towards some freer shore. I know it, and I don't care because this is not how I thought my life was going to turn out when I was writing my composition about why I love my country. I thought things were going to get better when I met a mysterious mountain man and discovered the love to end all loves in the fragrant depths of the Carpathians, on carpets of wild berries and magical snows.

I can't stand how things have turned out. Now there's no other way. Life has become a constant race. I'm running from shadows and jumping at every whisper, every footstep. I want to crash through it all and shoot all the secret police and then, finally, shoot the tyrant who invented such a network of fear. I want to shoot everyone who's crushing everything beautiful and fine out of existence. I want to walk towards them slowly, wearing a purple silk dress that clings to my body and a pair of dark sunglasses, and I want to shoot them right in the centre of their dark hearts. Then, *puff* – a big coloured explosion will wipe out everything, and a new life will start.

My parents and I hold hands and wait in silence for a few minutes. We listen to the noises of the street. We let the seconds go. Maybe an angel has passed us in this moment of silence. Maybe an invisible presence, a messenger from our ancestors, is fluttering around the room, gently laying a blanket of golden light over our souls.

My father breaks the silence. We start making plans for my escape. I'll be leaving on the train to Trieste soon, very soon. This summer.

One Last Time, Our Rock

IT WASN'T REALLY the train to Trieste. We just called it that, because it went to the last little Romanian town at the border with Yugoslavia called Jimbolia, from which you could get to Trieste – if you took the train to Belgrade and convinced the Serbian authorities you needed to get to Trieste because you would be killed if you were sent back to Romania. They would keep you in custody for a few days, and then they would let you go on, if you were lucky. You would be on your own, taking another train if you could smuggle out enough money to bribe the conductor and then bribe the police to let you into Italy. That's what some people did. Or that's what we *heard* that some people did, from their relatives or friends or someone who knew someone.

Some swam across the Danube into Yugoslavia or Bulgaria, Romania's more moderate Communist neighbours. Others swam the Black Sea to Turkish waters. Others crawled under barbed wire across the Yugoslavian border at night, if they could bribe the border guards to look the other way. Or they just risked it and tried to trick the border guards, waiting for them to turn and crawling between two rounds. The border guards were known for their ruthlessness; they shot and killed whatever moved. Still, some people crawled out successfully.

The Trieste route was my plan. I was going to try to get to

Belgrade posing as a tourist. This wouldn't be conspicuous; many Romanians went to Belgrade on tourist visas, since it was easier to travel to other Communist countries. Romanians were so desperate to get out, to see anything beyond their border, that they took one-day trips to Bulgaria or one-week trips to Russia, just to be able to say, *Russians are much worse off than we are. You can find tights without a problem, and lots of amber necklaces. But people there are practically starving.* If you couldn't go to Paris or to Rome, you might as well go to Belgrade.

One of my father's former students was married to a Yugoslav woman called Biljana who always wore dark red lipstick and silk pants. She crossed the border to visit her husband once a month while he worked towards his comparative literature degree at the University of Bucharest.

My mother informs me that she had already tried to contact Nora, her friend who had escaped to America long ago and whose picture, smiling in an orange tree, is still standing on our mahogany desk. But Nora is nowhere to be found; she hasn't answered any of my mother's letters; she probably moved somewhere else, to Canada or Australia. Or maybe my mother's letters have just been censored and kept at the border; it's what happens all the time. So Biljana is my only ticket to freedom, it seems.

She was going to wait for me in the little Romanian town at the border, and then we would both get on the train to Belgrade. And then . . . from there on, it all seemed blurry: somehow we would just talk the Serbian authorities into letting me across the border, and then somehow I would miraculously get across another border to the West and settle somehow in Italy.

There were also those cases where the Yugoslav authorities would simply turn you over to the Romanian authorities, who would probably send you to prison. So the presence of the Serbian woman made the plan more credible to the Romanian and Serbian authorities: I would just be visiting Belgrade and staying with Biljana.

"That's all, that's all you have to tell them when they ask for your papers," says my mother, trying to hide her anxiety and anguish at the thought of possibly never seeing me again.

I spend most of this last summer in the Carpathians. My passport hasn't arrived, and August is here already. There's a good chance it will never come, and part of me doesn't want it to come. I am in Mihai's arms, on a bed of leaves he has made for me in the shade of dark fir trees, and he is feeding me wild blueberries and telling me the names of wildflowers. What more could I ask from life? But I *do* want more, and the other part of me waits in agony for that passport. I could be run over in the street, or Mihai could turn out to be on the other side of the political spectrum. He is more stern than usual this summer and often distracted. Once when I say, "Fuck Ceauşescu, I hope he dies a painful death," just to see how he reacts, he looks straight at me and surprises me by saying, "I agree, he is a fucking idiot." Something in his tone sounds strange and phony. It's what the Securitate would often do, I think, go along with a joke or a curse, or a criticism of the president and the Party that someone has uttered, just to try to get more from them, to push them and see how deep their antigovernment attitudes go.

I feel now even more suspicious than when Mihai was protecting the name of the president from my curses. I have a sense of imminent danger. I have to get out of here, I tell myself as I watch Mihai tune the strings of his old guitar in his room. I must get out of here, the sooner the better. Then he plays an old tune for me, and I am not so sure any more.

My heart still bleeds every time he looks into my eyes with his old adoring expression. It doesn't matter any more whether he likes our illiterate criminal of a president or despises him. Every second is taking us closer to that last second when I will hold and kiss him and look at him for the last time. One evening when I hear the train to Trieste whistle as it leaves the station near my aunt's house, I break into sobs. He holds me, as if I were ill or dying.

The very last day in August, when I'm packing for the trip back to the capital, my mother calls to tell me she got the red shoes. That's our code, to let me know my passport has arrived. I feel frozen, as if I'd been put in a refrigerator and turned to ice. I have to get back the next day. I cannot tell Mihai the reason that I am leaving Braşov two weeks earlier than usual. My parents made me promise that I would not say a word to anyone. "But really, not a soul," my father said, and I knew he meant not even to Mihai.

We walk hand in hand. The moon is full and the queen of the night is spreading its reckless fragrance throughout the neighbourhood. Then I thaw again, and waves of heat take over my body, and sorrow comes over me in floods, in flames, in earthquakes, in every possible form and element. I shake the way I saw the epileptic woman who lived downstairs from us when I was little shake and writhe on the floor. No human force could calm her once the seizures took her, until she fell into a deep sleep that lasted for days. I feel myself shake like that inside, and Mihai watches as I crouch down in the middle of the sidewalk and hold myself. He just stands there waiting, lighting another cigarette. I love the way he lights his cigarette, hurriedly, his hand cupping the flame, and then drags furiously two or three times in a row. How I will miss every one of these little gestures of his that I know by heart.

In the middle of my own personal cataclysm I feel something like a fine, shiny string of reason and strength. It's silky and smooth and strong, and I hold on to it and manage to calm myself.

I tell him I have to leave earlier than we planned, because the Ministry of Education wants us to do the *potato and onion practice* before we start the academic year, and we have to do it in Bucharest, in the city where our university is. I am supposed to start my second year at the University of Bucharest. We have to sort out the good potatoes from the bad, the big onions from the small. It's part of our *civic education.* We sing Beatles songs and tell obscene jokes while we sort the potatoes and onions. We sometimes speak in French or in English so the comrade who supervises us cannot understand. We comment in English on the stupidity and the ugliness and the small brain size of the comrade walking up and down the onion and potato aisles. Once my friend Ioana said, "It's too bad the government doesn't train these people in a foreign language or two," after which we all laughed hysterically. Sometimes we have potato fights, and then we get written up in the special notebook of the comrade for delinquent potato-sorting behaviour. Sometimes he also writes us up for speaking in a foreign language. I stand in front of Mihai and tell him I have to get back earlier than planned, to do the potato sorting. I tell myself I am not really lying because if I were to start my regular year at the university, I would actually have to do just that. This is our night, our last night.

I tell him, "Let's go to our rock now. Please? Let's see our rock in the moonlight."

He's not surprised, almost as if he expected this. "But you're not dressed for it," he says.

"Since when did that stop us?" I laugh.

"I'll carry you if I have to," he says.

Just like the first time, I think.

We take the last bus to the end of the line below the mountain where the forest starts. We climb in the dark. His hand is firm and strong and doesn't let go.

Our rock is glistening, majestic in the moonlight. I recognize it, though everything else is different from the afternoon when we first kissed above the clouds. I shiver a little as he gently places my back against the white stone, he takes off his jacket and wraps it around me, then holds and kisses me under the moon above the city with the Black Church. He carries me to the little cave under the rock where we make love in slow motion, undulating like in a dream, in the resin-scented night air broken by owl calls and the yelps of foxes. My body is growing into a big, plump queen of the night flower, pulsating in the wild night of the Carpathians, where I have learned to love, where I will always want to return, for which I will always yearn.

The next morning I go one last time to his house to say goodbye. Mihai isn't home. I go behind the building, where I can see into his room through the window. I take a cement block lying next to the building and climb on it to see over the windowsill. His bed is made. His room looks suspiciously tidy, as if he had gone on a trip. His check knee breeches and his hiking boots that were always lying in the corner are nowhere to be seen. I gently push the window and discover it's unlatched. I push it open all the way. I pull myself over the edge of the window and climb into his room, as I had during our first summer. I look for his trousers and boots everywhere, in his closet and under the bed, but cannot find them. Under the bed I find an old slip that I had lost long ago. It's a red slip with lace that Mihai had given me for Christmas the year of our big New Year's Eve party. It's the only gift he has ever given me, other than flowers or pinecones or fruit from the forest. Our smells, our presence, echoes of our moans of love, seem to hover in the air.

I sit on the bed and look around the room where I have spent hundreds of hours of delight and torment. The room where we had built our own universe. I have a queasy feeling like a big hole in my stomach. The thought of never seeing Mihai again is unbearable, and it translates into a splitting ache through my stomach, my groin, and my diaphragm.

I don't understand why he's not here. He had told me to stop by in the morning before leaving for Bucharest, to say good-bye. But I feel something happened and he won't be back for a while. I have to catch my train to Bucharest in an hour. Then, if things go according to plan, I am supposed to board the train to Trieste in a few days and start my journey.

I could sit here and wait to find out what has happened to Mihai. I could miss this train and all the other trains and forget about escaping the country. How can I leave without saying good-bye to Mihai, without seeing him one last time? I will tell him everything about my plan to escape. He will reveal all his secrets to me: why there are people following me everywhere, why Anca warned me he was secret police, why he himself sometimes acts so weird, as if he were hiding things from me . . . I will ask him for the truth, and this time he will have to tell me the whole truth. I am clutching the red slip in my hand. I remember how I tried it on as soon as he gave it to me, so he could take it off immediately.

I put the red slip on the bed. I spread it out very carefully and stare at it as if it were my body lying on the bed. I climb back out of the room, leaving the windows open. The room needs to breathe.

I board the train and watch the dark forests roll past. This is my last train ride towards Bucharest; the next train will take me away from it, for ever. The train to Trieste that doesn't really go to Trieste.

On the train, I write Mihai a letter, my parting letter. I want him to know all that he has meant to me, and all that he will always mean to me. I remind him of our secret paths through the mountains and of the nest he once made for me in the shade of an old oak tree at the edge of the tiniest path covered with berries and mountain flowers. I tell him I will always remember his low raspy voice in my ear, his dark hair in disarray. I tell him how I had loved and desired him with an impossible love like a hungry she-wolf, like a peasant woman lying on the earth, on the hard earth covered with berries and wildflowers. I write to him that we could just as well have been somewhere at the end of the earth, in Patagonia or Valparaíso, does he remember how he used to joke that one day we'd go to Patagonia and to Valparaíso to see the jaguars, does he? I sign with my full redundant name, Mona Maria.

As soon as I get off the train in Bucharest, I rush to the first postbox in the station to drop off the letter. I stand for a few seconds in front of the box, staring at people parting and reuniting on the many platforms. At the last second I change my mind and don't drop it in the box. Nobody should know of my leaving. Not even Mihai, or especially not Mihai. I tear the letter into many little pieces that fall on to the station floor, and I run out into the street.

The Train to Trieste

THE FINAL TWO DAYS, I move into a state of unreality. I am trying both to tear myself from everything and to absorb everything. My mother and I pack my suitcase at night in the dark, with the curtains tightly pulled, so Dumitriu the secret-police officer from across the street cannot see what we are doing and what we are putting in that suitcase. We speak in whispers in case we are being bugged. Packing my suitcase makes me sick with sadness.

I want everything to be imprinted for ever in my blood, on my retina, in my flesh.

When I board the train to Trieste from Bucharest one afternoon in September – my last train, my last passage through the Carpathians – the only memory I can conjure of Mihai is of his unshaven, morose face at the station before I would return to Bucharest at the end of vacation.

I watch the mountains, and memories rush at me in disconnected bursts: the Carpathians, with their steep valleys and peaks, their plateaux covered with velvety green pastures where sheep graze, where waterfalls and rivers rustle and rush wildly through forests of pines, oaks and beeches, producing haunting echoes. We are adolescents. We play with echoes on every one of our hiking trips. *Miruna, runa, na, aaa . . . Cristina, tina, ina, aaa . . . Radu, adu, du, uuu . . . Mihai, hai, ai, ai, iii . . .*

Mona ona, ona aaaa . . . ! Our names shoot out into the wide valleys and come back to us multiplied into many clear sounds, round and distinct like the drops of water from the foaming waterfalls. We throw echoes at one another, and the sounds of our names entangle and chase one another.

Sometimes the echoes get stuck in a valley and ramble and bounce on their own until dawn. That's what the old women in black head scarves tell us. They tell us we mustn't leave the mountain until all the echoes have come to rest, otherwise they *get stuck* and haunt the valley. *Babies will cry at night and lovers are cursed,* they tell us as they sit knitting on their front porches. The echoes of our names embrace one another breathlessly above the grazing sheep and rocky slopes. *Mona, ona, onaaa . . . Mihai, ihai, ha, ina, ai, a, mi, mo, ha, na, aaa . . .*

I find myself alone on this train crossing the mountains toward distant borders and into the world. The echoes of a crying baby on a train ride in the night. The mother is sleeping. Her head is bouncing in the red scarf wrapped around it. When the baby doesn't suckle, she cries, and the mother wakes up, giving her the nipple again. The cries of the baby are soothing. I absorb them through every pore.

I would have liked to be with a baby of my own on this train ride, fruit of my first love. I am greedy, wishing the crying baby were mine, in the train smelling of sweat and garlic and weariness, with heads leaning against the fogged-up windows. But *It wasn't meant to be,* the old women knitting endlessly on their porches in the mountain villages of Romania would say. Or who knows, I think suddenly, maybe on our last night I was careless, maybe I am carrying Mihai's child right now on this ride, and I will take it with me into the wide world. I will have part of Mihai with me always. But in the same instant I become terrified of the possibility. How would I be able to do anything wherever I may find myself, among strangers, pregnant, and then with a newborn baby. The crying of the baby on the train loses its charm and becomes annoying. I count the days to my next cycle in my mind: only five days away, I shouldn't get pregnant. I don't want to have a baby, not now, maybe sometime in the future. The thought of a baby in the future makes me even more nervous, because I start thinking about whom will I ever have a baby with, since Mihai is now for ever out of my life. For ever out of my life, the thought persists, and I pick up my luggage and move to the next compartment, where there is no baby crying.

I never got to say good-bye and see his face one last time. I also have the memory of great confusion, as if my head had been screwed on wrong, as if my head were a Dalí painting: disorderly limbs, earth and sky squished together, and a red ant climbing a huge clock. Everything in the wrong order, everything in a yellow haze. You want to scream and you can't. The person chasing you is getting closer and closer, and you open your mouth as wide as you can, but nothing comes out, and you disappear in the blackness of fear into your own nightmare. And before you know it, you're queuing on a street corner, hoping there will still be one more box of menstrual cotton left for you.

I am wearing a pink-and-white-striped dress and I'm sitting by the window, absorbing every bit of landscape that rushes past me. I am listening to people's conversations, paying attention to the sound of their words, the round vowels and the sweet or harsh consonants. My language, my first words, bouncy, playful, angry – not for much longer. Soon I will hear foreign languages, and I will look at foreign places and foreign faces. They say of all refugees, Romanians pine the most for their native land and their native language. That's what people who have talked to people who have visited people who have left the country say. They say that when a Romanian abroad meets another Romanian by accident and they hear the sound of their native language, they break down and cry right there in public, in a square in Paris or Rome.

Some people are eating bread and sausages. They talk about how they were able to find cheese and butter and tights in the

capital. They bring all that back to their little towns like tro-
phies. I see there are still six hours of travel through the night
until I get to the border town where I am supposed to meet Biljana, who will take me to Belgrade and then help me get to Trieste. I have butter and cucumber sandwiches that my mother
made for me, holding back her tears, thinking that by the time
I eat these sandwiches I'll be far away, and who knows when we
will see each other again, if ever.

I also have a little envelope of photographs in my bag, which
I hold in my lap for the entire train ride. I have the book of
grades from my university so I can transfer my credits and finish
my studies wherever I end up. I have a little wood and silver icon
of the Virgin Mary that my father gave me the evening before
my departure. It had belonged to his father, and it always
brought him luck, he said, as he passed his fingers through his
white hair, just above the scar he still has from the last time he
was interrogated by the secret police. I don't like the Virgin
Mary, although I carry her name. She is so impossibly pure. I
hold the little wooden icon nevertheless. I stick my hand inside
my bag and touch it and then pass my fingers through the photographs and take a peek at them.

I try not to think of Mihai. I think of everything ugly and
painful so that my being among people eating garlic sausages
and talking about queues for chicken gizzards, on this train
rushing towards the Yugoslavian border, will make some sense.

The train stops at a rural station. I see the moon above the
Carpathians, and I smell the evening air. The mountain air,
thick with the smell of pine resin, cools my face. I can't think of
anything ugly any more. The entire inventory of ugly things –
the food queues, the dingy buildings, the posters of the *Father of
the Nation*, the dead people beneath rubble or run over by cars
on the pavement – is still not enough to make leaving less
painful. I am leaving behind everything except . . . myself. I
remember the book from the American library, *A Portrait of the
Artist as a Young Man*. I think of how Stephen wants to leave

everything so he can write in freedom, so he can find himself. To calm my thoughts, to make the chaos in my head go away, I pretend I'm Stephen Dedalus fleeing his country.

In a few minutes the train will arrive at its final destination. There is a commotion of luggage collection and conductors giving orders. A few more minutes, and the train slows down. I take down my suitcase with the clothes my mother has packed for me in the dark, clothes for cold weather, for hot weather, and for in-between weather. I clutch my bag tight. My heart is beating faster. I feel the mountain air coming through the window and touch my own face as if wanting to make sure that all this is real, that I am real.

I get off the train and look for Biljana. It's past midnight and I find myself in Jimbolia, the border city with Yugoslavia. I've never been to this part of the country. People waiting on the platform have a different accent; their words sound more elastic and round. There are peasants and gypsies in colourful long skirts. I don't see Biljana, and a rush of fear crosses my heart. *My whole adventure is over*, I tell myself. *I'll just have to turn back.*

I realize then that I don't want to turn back. I want to keep going and going. I want to ride on the crest of this storm all night and wake up tomorrow on the sand, like a Shakespearean character, rising from a slumber to find myself on a glowing, completely unknown shore, just when the dawn starts sparkling on the sea that has sucked the past back into its roaring, green belly. Forget the calm and clarity, forget Stephen Dedalus and his bird woman. I want my big adventure.

The fragrance of French perfume envelops me, and she touches me gently on the shoulder. Her lipstick is so red it almost glows in the dark. Biljana is wearing silk trousers as usual and a red silk blouse with tiny white dots, which flows elegantly over her small breasts and thin waist. I feel a rush of gratitude and joy at the sight of her. She looks like a fairy godmother. I embrace her and wait for her to tell me what I have to do. I'm ready to follow her every step. I am thinking of nothing but crossing the border, getting to the other side.

She hands me my ticket to Belgrade.

"Do you have your passport?" she asks.

"Yes, yes, of course," I whisper breathlessly, eagerly.

We whisper on the train platform. She takes my hand in hers as if I were a little girl and leads me through the crowd of travellers and the families meeting them, towards another platform, for the train to Belgrade. We board the train half an hour later, and I start hearing another language: a Slavic language with so many consonants that I don't know how these people can fit them all inside their mouths. I keep close to Biljana as we walk the corridor to our compartment. The clusters of foreign consonants make me feel lonely and cold. My language is full of long, curved, melodious vowels, diphthongs and even triphthongs. We even have one word that has no consonants, just a cluster of four vowels, that means sheep, *oaie*. I repeat the word *oaie* in my head to protect myself from the avalanche of hard consonants around me.

The compartments in the Yugoslav train are more elegant than those in the Romanian train. We sit down by the window, facing each other, and Biljana tells me not to worry, that everything will come out all right. I feel breathless, as I did the time I rode the roller coaster in the amusement park by the Black Sea and a big rush of fear and pleasure stormed through my insides.

Soon after the train leaves, I hear the Romanian customs police start their search. I have a US one-hundred-dollar bill that my father was able to buy for me from one of his Senegalese students at the Ploieşti Institute. My mother has sewn it inside the jacket I am wearing over the pink-and-white-striped dress. Romanians are not allowed to carry foreign money across the border. If the authorities find it, I will be put in prison. If I come out of prison alive, I will never be able to leave the country again, not even to Belgrade or Bulgaria, not even to the Soviet Union to exchange a kilo of horse salami for ten pairs of tights.

They come into the compartment. Two Romanian customs officers and the Serbian conductor are checking tickets and passports. I note with surprise that the Romanian customs officers speak Serbian and the Serbian conductor speaks Romanian. The hard, unintelligible words of the Slavic language mixed with my own language make me feel lonely and worried again. The Romanian customs officers ask us to take down our suitcases and open them. Everyone in the compartment takes down suitcases, a confusion of luggage and packages. Biljana carries only a shoulder bag she has placed next to her on the seat. It is a large, elegant brown leather bag, and I am wondering what Biljana is carrying in it as I try to distract myself from the worries about my own luggage. I bring down my suitcase from the rack, and I feel sweat streaming down my neck.

One of the Romanian customs officers tells me to hand him my coat and my bag. My father had told me to put everything in my bag. *They search the least in the most obvious places,* he said. But it seems to me now this was a mistake. When they find my university transcripts, my family pictures, and my little wooden Virgin Mary icon, they'll certainly know I'm not planning to return. They'll take me off the train, and it will be all over.

I place the suitcase on the seat but hesitate handing them my jacket and my bag. Maybe they will forget about the jacket by looking at the suitcase first. I have to think which one to hand to them first: my coat, which contains the hundred-dollar bill I'll need for bribes, or my bag with my photos, my grade book, and the icon. As one of them starts probing through my suitcase, his blunt fingers going through the things my mother had packed so carefully, my underwear and clothes, the other one asks again for the coat and the bag. I give him the bag but keep the coat in my hands, not withholding it, but not quite offering it to him.

He opens my bag and starts rummaging through it. He takes out the envelope with the photographs. The grade book is just next to it, but he doesn't seem to notice it. He focuses on the photographs, opens the envelope, and shuffles through them. He stops at one, looking puzzled. Mihai and me in Bucharest, near the train station, a black-and-white picture on a rainy November day. It's our *Just Escaped from Refugee Camp* picture. Mihai with his Russian hat, me in my large brimmed hat, both of us angry and morose in the November rain. The customs man holds it out and laughs. He shows it to his fellow customs worker. They both laugh.

"Your sweetheart, ha?" he asks, and they both laugh.

"Yes, sort of, my . . . my friend . . ." I stutter, blushing.

He hands me my bag. I experience a moment of relief.

But no, now he turns serious and holds out his hand for my coat. He snaps his fingers. I hold it out as if I'd forgotten it was in my hands.

He passes it to the other Romanian officer and shifts his attention to someone else's luggage. This one is younger looking with a thin face and long nose. He runs his hand along the coat, squeezing it here and there. He is touching it just where my mother had sewn in the hundred-dollar bill. He is feeling it, and he asks his colleague for his pocketknife. I see myself in a cold basement, in a prison for political detainees and *traitors of the country*. A blackness sets inside my head, and I can't see very well around me. I hear the steady roll of the wheels on the track, and I hear hard sounds spoken in a language I don't understand, they seem to be hitting me in the head like hard pebbles, hard consonants that make no sense. Even the sounds of Romanian in the mouth of this customs worker sound like an unknown language full of clusters of mean consonants. I repeat *oaie* in my head, the word that's all vowels like a clear mountain stream.

He doesn't find his knife with which to rip open the inside of my coat; the customs worker is irritated, and the departure whistle has just sounded. The other one is holding and feeling my coat. He looks at me straight in the eyes and asks:

"What's in here, what have you got in here?"

He looks as if he's ready to tear it open with his hands. No words come out of my mouth. Nothing comes out. And suddenly, there it is, my bit of luck: the scream, the sharp, piercing scream. It's not mine, though it feels as if it were mine. A woman's scream crosses the train and the platform, enters through the open windows, and goes back out like a flash. Another Serbian conductor comes in and says something to the two customs workers, and just as they are about to rush out of the compartment, Biljana asks the Yugoslav conductor something in Serbian. In her mouth, rolling off her shiny red lips, even those hard clusters of consonants sound melodious. I'm exasperated that she has to get the men's attention and keep them there any longer. The man answers something back in a hurry and they all go away, dropping my coat on the bench next to me.

The train leaves slowly. I wish it would take off like a flash, like the blood-curdling scream crossing the night. The scream that saves my life! Like a miracle, almost unreal. I can't resist my own curiosity, so I stand up and pull down the window. I see a woman in a light-coloured summer dress running across the tracks. Then another train flashes by, and when it's gone, so is the woman in the summery dress. The night is silent and moonless. I have an acute feeling that the woman crossing the tracks was the one who has just screamed; the scream was intentional, it was meant for me. I have an even stranger feeling that I know that woman, something in her figure and in the way she has run across the tracks, with large quick steps. But I can't be sure of anything any longer. Only this train I am riding in the night is real. I and my heartbeat are real.

As the train speeds up, large tears are falling down my face in unstoppable rivers. They don't stop for hours. I think of the composition about why I love my country that I wrote when I was ten years old; in order to write it I imagined so hard how it would be to lose my country and my mother, both at the same time, that it felt like I had lost them. That's how I was able to write the composition that won me the first prize in a national competition: I got myself into a state where I felt the bleeding, the burning, cut right through the middle of my heart, the pain of losing both your mother and your country all in one second.

Now on this train taking me away from everything familiar, it feels just like it felt when I imagined it then. Only it's worse because it happens in the sound of someone else's scream, in the night, on the train to Trieste that doesn't even really go to Trieste, and I have no words for it inside me.

Belgrade

BELGRADE SEEMS LIKE AN UGLY CITY, with its factories and grey buildings resembling the Socialist constructions at the faraway margins of Bucharest. I think of the beautiful parts of Bucharest, the "Little Paris of the Balkans", with its large boulevards and parks, with its rows of chestnuts and linden trees on the wide avenues. And although I often had been weary of my native town because I yearned to be with Mihai in the Carpathians, now, as I cross Belgrade in the taxi next to the woman who is helping me escape it for ever, I realize that Bucharest is a magnificent city. In a flash, I even remember the woman selling chrysanthemums and roses at the corner of my street the afternoon I left for the railway station. I remember her radiant face, her sparkling brown eyes looking straight into mine.

I'm exhausted. My pink-and-white cotton dress stinks of perspiration. It seems I've been on trains for days and days. My body is shaky with weariness. I imagine going to Biljana's house and sleeping, and then when I wake up I'll find myself back in my own bed in our Bucharest apartment. I'll hear the sound of my mother's typing on the forbidden typewriter, typing her poems about swans and snows and death that flutter like rose petals and birds' wings. And when I wake up, I'll find in my hand a stick of Biljana's lipstick. I will think it has all been a dream, but how do I have the lipstick in my hand? Then my father will come in and tell me about the article he's working on, about the use of relative pronouns in the poetry of the great Romanian Romantic poet Eminescu, and he will tell me that even the secret police were just a bad dream, that there are no secret organizations meeting in attics and basements, they're all just bad dreams.

He will stroke my head like he always does when he is proud of me. There will be red carnations everywhere in our apartment, with no hidden microphones, and we will look at them and laugh, remembering how foolish we were to have torn those poor flowers apart petal by petal. It's not that bad, things are not that bad, after all. We will laugh and laugh, and a ray of light will come in through the gauzy curtain and catch little specks of dust in the air.

I wake up, realizing I've fallen asleep in the taxi, in front of a creamy white building with pots of red flowers on the windowsills in an elegant residential area of Belgrade. I see my face in the rearview mirror as I step out of the taxi. I look like a fish; my eyes are swollen, my lips are swollen, everything about me is swollen, but it doesn't bother me. I don't want to look the way I did yesterday. I will never look the same. I climb the marble staircase of Biljana's apartment building wearing my new face. I might as well look like a fish.

That night in Biljana's apartment, I pass in and out of sleep. There is a large party of people in my bedroom, talking politics and laughing. Some are even sitting on my bed. They are saying Ceauşescu will fall; his days are numbered. I can't move, I can't talk, and they all act as if I'm not there in the room, lying in bed with a big round fish face. Then all the people talking and laughing turn into jelly, and the room becomes watery. But before they disappear, they all stare at me and laugh and tell me, *You didn't have to leave, you know. If only you had been more patient!*

Then I see Mihai. He is holding me and whispering in my ear. He gently tucks my hair behind my ear and kisses it. He tells me he will always love me, always. Even when my hair is grey and I turn into an old woman, he will still love me. Suddenly he looks scared and tells me he has to go. Before he runs away, he asks me to meet him at our place, in an hour. But I can't remember where *our place* is. I run in the streets for hours. I know I will never see him, but I keep running through the streets, and then it seems to me I see him at a street corner. He turns the corner. I run after him, but the street disappears. I get sucked into a vortex of black. I must have screamed, because Biljana is sitting at the edge of my bed trying to make me drink cold water.

The realization of what I have done and of what I am about to do hits me with the light of dawn. So far, I'm still on a tourist trip to Belgrade. I could still just visit Belgrade, stay with Biljana until my visa expires, and go back. Nothing is irreversible. But it is. I know there is no going back. Today we have to go to the Serbian authorities, Biljana tells me. She has connections. We'll have to bargain with them to give me a visa to Italy, and then we must buy the ticket. She hands me a pair of scissors and tells me to cut the money out of the coat, for the authorities for the visa. It sounds so simple. I almost wish it were more complicated, so I will have a more dramatic story to boast of.

We go to a building with many offices that looks like the police building in Bucharest where I went to apply for my tourist visa. Biljana asks to speak with Mr Marish, and we are asked to wait in the waiting room. After more than half an hour, a man looking like a movie actor with silver hair at his temples, bony features, and piercing blue eyes strides over to us and gives Biljana a kiss on both cheeks. She talks with him in Serbian for a long time. Sometimes their voices get very low. As I watch them, I have the distinct feeling they are not talking about me and my visa to Italy, but about something much more personal. I think of my father's student who is married to Biljana and feel sorry for him. He thinks he will move to Belgrade in a couple of years to live happily ever after with Biljana. But maybe I'm wrong, maybe it's just a marriage of convenience between Biljana and my father's student, so he can get out of Romania. The secretary in the office has slowed down her typing, trying to catch what they are saying. Then suddenly I hear Biljana pronounce my name. It's so strange to hear my name, my full name, including the middle name, Maria, being spoken in a police office in Belgrade. The two names together, Mona Maria, seem like a joke. I laugh when I hear my own name. Biljana's handsome friend signals to me to follow him. Biljana comes along.

Marish speaks English beautifully, with a British accent. He asks me if I like Belgrade, and I say, *Yes, very much.* There's a scrawny little man in the room who smells like garlic and doesn't seem to speak English. He looks stern and angry. Biljana makes a sign to me to give the man the envelope with the one-hundred-dollar bill. He slips it into the inner pocket of his coat without a word.

The three of them speak Serbian for what seems like a very long time. I keep waiting to be asked something, for someone to address me in some way, but they just keep talking in Serbian, and then they laugh. The scrawny man takes a seal out of his pocket and motions to Marish to ask me for my passport. He stamps my passport in several places and hands it back to me.

Marish kisses Biljana on the cheek again as we leave. Outside, Biljana holds me and tells me I am fine, now, as far as the Serbian authorities are concerned. I have my exit visa from Yugoslavia, allowing me to cross the border to Italy.

But I still don't understand how I get into Italy – don't I need an Italian visa? I picture the border as a crack in the earth, like the cracks in the street after the earthquake. My brain feels like there are hundreds of threads tangled up inside it. Whatever happened to my search for clarity? I try to hang on to one simple thought at a time. I can leave Yugoslavia; I can leave this city and never have to return.

As we walk, I ask Biljana if we're going next to the Italian embassy.

"With a Romanian passport?" She laughs. "No. There's no use. The Italians will take one look and know what you're up to. They don't want any more immigrants in their country. Everyone's sick of immigrants.

"It's different once you get there," she says. "Once you find a way to get into Italy, then they help you. What are they going to do, send you back to the Communists in chains? They have no choice but to give you asylum; they are a democratic country, after all."

We go back in a taxi to Biljana's. Belgrade looks more beautiful this morning than when I first came. The Danube is shining in the morning sun, and the grand Gothic cathedrals and medieval buildings are reflected in it. There is an air of prosperity on the streets, which is new to me: foreign cars, elegant women. Some of the boulevards remind me of Bucharest, but the buildings are creamier, the streets less dusty, and there are flowerpots on most of the windowsills. When we pass the busy port, I realize with a start that I'm looking at the same Danube that flows into Romania and ends in the pelican- and cormorant-filled delta at the Black Sea. I'm tempted to beg Biljana to let me stay one more day with her, just to see more of the city, to look at the Danube, to walk free in the streets.

But as soon as we find ourselves in her apartment, she tells me to get ready, that there's a train to Trieste that same night. "I am ready," I say. We still have to buy my ticket for the train to Trieste. For the *real* train to Trieste.

"But I have no visa," I say stubbornly, glaring at Biljana. "What do I do when they ask for my papers?"

She laughs. "How do you think all the others do it?"

"I don't know. How?"

She sighs, exasperated. "They get on the train and wait. When they get to Trieste, when the Italian customs come to check the passports, they catch them in the corridor, ask them to let them in without a visa, say that they're trying to escape. Or they don't say anything, and they just wait and hope the customs workers are busy and don't check every last paper. I know lots of people who escaped this way."

I feel too tired and afraid to beg customs workers to let me in without a visa. What if I can't convince them? What if they send me rolling right back to Belgrade on the same train, and then back to Romania, flanked by police?

"There are two passport checkpoints, one on the Yugoslav side for the exit, the other for entering Italy. You're already through the first. Maybe the Italians will assume you're OK." Biljana shrugs.

"You just have to find a way," she insists. "Lots of people do it. You can try hiding in the toilet, or you can jump off the train when it stops, or . . ."

I'm not listening to Biljana any more. Fatigue spreads through me like a slow poison. I feel like sleeping. I don't understand why I decided to leave. I know that now that I've started, I have to somehow see it through, to keep going until I reach my destination. But what is my destination? There are still so many kilometres, so many checkpoints and chasms ahead of me, until I can start over, until I can begin my new journey.

The Yellow Fiat

THE BELGRADE TRAIN STATION WAITS for us like a monument with its ornate sculpted walls, its forged iron gate, and the impatient clock. It had rained overnight, and parts of the façade are reflected in the puddles and shimmering in the afternoon sun, like mysterious pieces of a puzzle. There are massive crowds going in and out of the station in a steady rhythm. Just as we are about to cross the street, a Serbian police car pulls up in front of the station. We watch as two officers in uniforms lead a man and a woman down the steps and into the car. They keep their heads down. I wish I could know if they are Romanian, but I know it doesn't make a difference. I turn to Biljana. Her face is pale, her red lips tight.

I see several cars with Italian licence plates passing us by. I smile at my sudden thought, and I feel fully awake. I have my bag in one hand and my suitcase with clothes for all kinds of weather in the other. I know I have to choose. I know my bag is more precious, but what will I do without any clothes other than what I am wearing?

I kick my suitcase farther down onto the pavement. I step off the pavement into the road. I take off my jacket and swing it carelessly on my shoulder as if I were going for a walk. In one quick move I take off the white taffeta ribbon holding my hair in a ponytail. I shake my hair loose. I feel the sensuous comfort of my hair coming down around my face, my neck, and onto my shoulders. I feel a jolt of wild energy in my body, as if I am the wild mare in my dream. I am rushing across borders, my wheat-coloured mane flying in the wind. The muscles in my back, my calves, my shoulders, tighten up and I feel all tingly like before sex. Cars are passing by me, and some are honking at me to get out of the road.

I see Biljana's puzzled face. I love Biljana so much. She truly is my fairy godmother. I see a small yellow Fiat, with Italian licence plates, so yellow that it shines in the night. I am trying hard to distinguish who is at the wheel. It's a middle-aged man, grey haired, glasses, suit and tie. I am not scared.

"Do it!" says Biljana, understanding my wicked thought right away.

I stand in the middle of the road and wave my white jacket like a flag. It all happens in a few seconds. Like a miracle, he stops. I have never hitchhiked before. I am bursting with excitement. I ask: "Trieste?" The car makes a full stop, and all he yells from the window is "*Senza la valigia.*" I know what he means; it sounds almost Romanian. I'm so happy I can understand Italian, *senza la valigia*, without the suitcase. His car is very small and already filled with luggage.

I embrace Biljana and see tears in her eyes. I look at the suitcase and ask her to take it, the suitcase that my mother had packed for me with so much care, even putting a volume of Romanian poetry in between the clothes for all weather. "Be careful," Biljana says and squeezes my hand one last time.

I get in the car next to him, and I'm not afraid. I'm not tired. He accelerates through Belgrade towards the highway that will take us to Trieste. The thought that he may be taking me elsewhere crosses my mind once or twice in the first silent minutes of the ride. I don't want to think about it, and when I see a wedding band on his hand I feel relieved. He is the first to start the conversation.

This is how I begin to learn Italian: I add *o*'s to Romanian words, then repeat his words when he corrects me. I put together words I remember from Italian men I heard at the seaside, on the beach. Italian feels delicious in my mouth, a crisp fruit, both tart and sweet. My heart is beating so fast. I am focused on this moment in the yellow Fiat next to the Italian middle-aged man who is going to take me across the border somehow. I don't even worry about it, watching him shift gears and gun the engine to pull onto the highway. His name is Mario, he tells me. *E Lei, come si chiama?* Mona. Mona Maria. *Ah, che bello!*

I've heard about Italian men, that they are all gigolos and Don Juans, that they think of nothing else but seducing women. But Mario talks to me about his wife, *mia moglie,* and offers me a sandwich, which he says his wife made for him. She was supposed to come with him, he explains, but changed her mind at the last minute. *Le donne,* he shrugs. Women. He smiles at me. Little by little I understand he is a salesman, but I can't figure out what he sells. He travels a lot, and he's even been to Romania. He says my country is *molto bello, molto molto bello,* but Ceauşescu is *pazzo,* crazy, and also evil, *cattivo.*

I think of Biljana with sadness. I wouldn't be on this road to Trieste if it hadn't been for her. I think of her smooth, comforting voice, her silkiness, her smile. I settle into the worn seat of the Fiat and begin to doze to the buzz of its little engine. I picture the train to Trieste. It is a train I'll never have to ride.

We ride into the night in the yellow Fiat, past forests and factories and more forests and more factories, and little villages and fields, and towns with names swollen up with consonants like Sremska and Bijeljina.

We reach the Italian border at dawn. I've fallen asleep in the car and open my eyes to see the first rays of the sun pierce the clouds. I hear Italian voices, and turn to watch Mario take out two passports and hand them to the border officer. In my semiconscious state I remember Mario telling me that his wife had changed her mind at the last minute; he must still have both passports; I have to pass as his wife. The border guard looks at the first passport while he and Mario exchange a tangle of Italian words, and then he hands back both. I am holding my bag, everything I own, pressed against my chest. My university records, the icon, the packet of photographs.

Then suddenly I hear and feel something new, something I don't remember ever having heard or felt before. An ease, a breeze of freshness, in the way the border guard says *grazie*, in the carefree voices of people laughing and talking, in Mario's confident smile as he slips the two passports into his front pocket. I keep my head turned away from the border officer, but he shows no sign of doubting that I am Mario's wife.

Siamo in Italia, Mario says. We are in Italy.

This must be what freedom feels like, this is its smell, its sound. It is raw and unexpected. It chuckles, and it flutters. I have no comparisons, no metaphors that describe this freedom. I've never experienced this before, only heard about it. I had imagined it: a wild creature with dishevelled hair. But it's not like that. It's the sound of laughter, an inflection in the voice. The way Mario said *grazie*.

Tutto Sarà Bene

I SPEND THE NEXT TWO WEEKS in Mario's house. He puts me in the care of his wife, Luciana, and his sister-in-law, Letizia, as if I were a convalescent, a cancer patient in remission. The first day both women greet me with open arms, as if they had been expecting exactly this, some refugee from Romania with all her belongings in one bag and smelling of sweat, suddenly appearing at their doorstep. They feed me minestrone soup. I am so tired and disoriented that I start crying. My tears fall into the minestrone together with my hair, when my head droops over the bowl as I sob. I haven't eaten soup in more than a year, since my aunt made me her delicious cabbage and potato soup. I cry even more ardently because it's so ridiculous to cry over a bowl of soup. It's not as if I've been starving. But in a way, I have been. It's too hard to admit that I've been craving soup.

I remember foods, fruit, so delicious that the memory brings on a new wave of tears. Berries of every colour, the berries that Mihai had fed me in the forests. Tomatoes ripened in the sun of the mountains, and the television cake I used to hide in the wardrobe when I was little. The special sheep's milk cheese made by shepherds in the mountains where the alpine pastures stretch endlessly and the grass is a light, velvety green among white rocks and blue bellflowers. But I haven't tasted these in so long . . . I cry because I am hungry and I don't want to admit it to myself or to the Italian women, who talk in their operatic trills, worrying about me.

For two weeks in Trieste, in the house of Luciana, Letizia, and Mario, I eat and sleep in a regular rhythm, trying to convince myself I'm on a vacation and trying not to think about whatever I have to do next. Strangely, I don't want to see the city, except for the Berlitz building where James Joyce used to teach when he lived here. Mario and Luciana set about locating that building for me, wondering why I don't want to see the rest of their beautiful Trieste.

I saw Trieste at dawn, the morning I first entered it in the yellow Fiat, my mind somewhere on the cusp between unspeakable fatigue and dizzying excitement. I wasn't expecting a beautiful city with canals, with pink and orange Renaissance buildings and piazzas where people stand around and talk joyously. Reflections of the old, ornate buildings swayed lazily on the mirrorlike surface of the canals sparkling in the morning sun. I had thought Trieste was going to be an improvised city, small buildings built in a rush at the frontier with Yugoslavia to welcome refugees who had crossed the border. Somehow I saw the city in my mind as a transitional place where the train to Trieste stopped, then passed through to real cities like Venice and Rome. But it isn't like that at all.

It hurt me to discover it was a beautiful city, because I knew my journey couldn't end here. I had to get to Rome, at least. So Mario said. I had to restart my life, live somewhere, go to school, find work, meet people, make money, make friends, get an identity card, start fresh on the virgin shore after being tossed about on the crest of a wave and rescued by a man in a yellow Fiat. When I asked Mario that first morning in the car if he thought I could stay and settle in Trieste, in the first town where I'd felt freedom in the air, in my ears, he laughed and said, *Non è possibile,* shaking his head. It's hard for refugees in Italy, Luciana explained later. They're not welcome, understand? The government is tired of refugees. You must go to Rome, she tells me. You must ask for political asylum and then go to America.

I hadn't thought about going as far as America. All I wanted when I left my country was to escape the secret police and make sure I had at least two borders between me and all that madness so I wouldn't be run over accidentally on purpose in University Square. Italy was good enough for me. Before leaving Romania, for hours I studied a book about a boy growing up in a magical Italian place called San Michele. It was a tiny village with narrow, steep streets lined with beautiful white houses, and there was a villa on top of a mountain, with a balcony filled with white and pink climbing roses. There were misty blue hills in the background. Yes, Italy was good enough for me. I wasn't thinking that my wave was going to take me overseas. I hadn't known that refugees were like a plague that Europeans were trying to keep outside their borders.

Suddenly, I don't want to see any more of Trieste. What's the point, why get attached to another beautiful place when I've just torn myself away from my own country and family, from all of the places and people I've known? There is only so much tearing away I can manage.

But Letizia insists that I simply must see Trieste, even if briefly. Luciana agrees and adds that it will make them very sad if I don't want to take a tour of their beloved native city. I don't want to make my hosts sad so I tell them *Sure, I would love to see Trieste.* One bright morning with a sky so blue that it is violet in a way I have never seen sky in my life before, we set out to see the port, the churches, the Piazza dell'Unità d'Italia, the Castello di Miramare, and just to stroll on the quay along the Adriatic Sea. Piazza dell'Unità d'Italia is as majestic as its name: marble Baroque buildings, a group statue suggesting unity right in the centre, orangey and rose-coloured palaces. It all opens up towards the Adriatic. Only I don't want to see it. I don't care to feel any of this. I don't care to stroll along the walk that stretches out into the silver and mauve sea. But for a moment I imagine myself on the sea, gazing at the Piazza dell'Unità d'Italia from a moving ship, until the shore looks dreamy and hazy – a memory. I have a foreboding of sadness to come. Trieste could have been my final destination, not just a point of passage. I am in the heart of Trieste, and I can't feel it, I can't hear it: a heart pumping with a silent beat, for I am already far away on the sea. *E la nave va*, and the ship goes on. I am my own ship of estrangement and uprooting.

I tell Luciana, Letizia and Mario that I've changed my mind about Berlitz and James Joyce and that the next thing I wish to see is the railway station. Luciana shakes her dark curls and laughs at the idea, Letizia claps her hands in disbelief, but they all go along with my request, and we take a bus to the railway station. I want to see where I would have arrived, had I taken the train to Trieste. The real train to Trieste, coming from Belgrade, as Biljana had wanted me to do.

I am shot with a mixture of sadness and surprise when I see the elegant peach and white stone construction that looks almost like a castle. I could have descended here on this platform and walked into the shiny marble hallway. I could have glided under the Corinthian-looking columns and the rosy ceiling of this station, with my bag containing all my belongings, at dawn. I would have looked at the big clock on my left, and I would have noted it was already the next day, seven o'clock in the morning, starting everything all over in the free world. In Trieste. And what then? What would I have done then, where would I have gone then, not knowing one single soul in this border city that painfully surprises me with its melancholy beauty and languorous canals on the Adriatic? Maybe everything turned out as it should have.

There is a shabbily dressed older man with white hair leaning against one of the thick marble columns in the middle of the main hall of the station, holding a transistor radio. He reminds me of my father, only he is older and shabbier, maybe a poor person from Trieste. Suddenly a most heavenly music fills the station from his little radio: a soprano voice singing in Italian with such longing that my heart almost stops beating. A faint memory sneaks upon me. I remember one Sunday afternoon in the Atheneum where I used to go to classical music concerts with my high school, and a student of my mother's from the conservatory sang Susanna's aria in the garden from *Le Nozze di Figaro*. It is now only that it touches me, that I get it in its fully dishevelled beauty. Susanna is anxious and mad and longing for her Figaro. She wants to trick him. She is disguised as the Countess and pretends to be waiting and singing for the Count, but secretly she is calling out to Figaro. She talks about the pleasures of love in the fresh air. I stand transfixed in the middle of the station and cannot move. Everything that I have left behind and will never see or touch again glows painfully in my mind: the blood-red poppies and the orange marigolds in front of Aunt Nina's house, the pine and fir trees of the Carpathians and their endless blue chains, the green and violet waters of the Black Sea with its pearly shells. My mother with her delicate gestures always worried about something, my father's tall forehead and piercing blue eyes and his tender way of stroking my hair.

And in the centre of it all, Mihai is standing at our white rock. He is holding me on a cool summer night like the one Susanna is singing about. Our fiery embraces in meadows and on the side of streams at night amid the cricket song and the hypnotic flickering of the fireflies. Why did I have to tear myself from everything? It will never ever come back again. Susanna's voice curls and rises and falls in luscious trills as she waits for her Figaro, but for me it is all over. If only I had known what it would all mean the night when I eagerly got onto the train to Trieste. I am standing and staring at the old man with the transistor. Luciana and Letizia and Mario are surrounding me, gently trying to make me move.

My face is wet and I hear Luciana say *Poverina*, poor girl. Mario pats my back gently and says *Dai, dai*, come on, but Letizia takes me roughly by both shoulders, looks straight into my eyes, and says sternly: *Coraggio, ragazza, che è fatto, è fatto!* Be brave, girl, what's done is done! Then Luciana says she will make me minestrone when we get home, and minestrone takes care of all the heartaches in the world. I force myself to stop crying, and I try to think only of minestrone. I scrunch my eyes and promise myself I will never break down like this again, in the middle of a public place. What's done is done. I turn my head and look at the old man with the transistor: Susanna's aria is over and Figaro has come.

On the bus on the way back, Luciana points in the direction of the Castello di Miramare: *Guarda, guarda che bello.* Look how beautiful. I look at the majestic white castle rising in the distance above the Adriatic. I tell Luciana it is *molto bello*, in fact *bellissimo*, and patiently wait to pass by it, to pass by the canals and the churches and the narrow streets and get to Mario and Luciana's house. I refuse to leave the house for the rest of my stay in Trieste. Luciana keeps crossing herself and saying *Poverina* and *Madonna mia*, Letizia is proud of me because I am strong, and Mario tells them both *Lasciatela in pace per l'amor di Dio*, leave her alone for the love of God.

Luciana and Mario have friends in Rome who are going to help me. They'll take me to the authorities there and put me up in their house, in a suburb of Rome, until I get an answer. Things will turn out all right, *tutto sarà bene*, Luciana and Mario assure me. They send me on my way with a little bag of new clothes and some sandwiches of prosciutto and mozzarella. They wave at me from the train platform as the train pulls out. I stick my head out of the train window and wave at them until they look like three coloured specks in the twilight enveloping the Trieste railway station.

Roma, Amore Mio!

MARIO AND LUCIANA'S ROMAN FRIENDS are a handsome couple with a six-year-old daughter, Roxana, who has black hair and green eyes. She shows me her doll Ninetta and tells me that she is *cattiva*, a mean doll, and that she bites. I pretend Ninetta has bitten my finger and Roxana laughs, showing her new teeth. Then Roxana speaks a few very fast sentences that I don't understand, and I feel lost and embarrassed not to understand a six-year-old. Her mother, Marina, translates, telling me that Roxana wants me to help her give Ninetta a bath that evening and then put her to bed later.

I find out that I'm supposed to take care of Roxana while Marina and her husband, Vittorio, are at work. When school starts in a couple of weeks, it's my job to pick her up from school and look after her until her parents come home. It looks like I will be here in Rome for a while before I can move on. During the day, I am supposed to straighten out the house and sometimes shop for groceries.

I wonder what they'd planned to do about Roxana and their groceries before a refugee from Romania happened to appear. I don't ask; I haven't acquired enough Italian to formulate such a complicated question. I say *sì, sì* to almost everything and *grazie* before I eat their *spaghetti alle vongole.* I try very hard to swallow the spaghetti, feeling choked with loneliness and confusion every time I sit down to dinner with them in their little apartment in a building with huge balconies, in a suburb of Rome amid blue hills and pine trees.

My new hosts are both architects and leave for work very early every morning. Marina has a wardrobe for shoes alone, an entire wall of shoes of all shapes and colours. She says shoes are a woman's most important accessory, more important even than the clothes she wears, and she never wears the same pair of shoes two days in a row. I watch her with fascination as she tries on different pairs until she decides on one, and as Vittorio gets irritated and fidgets and pretends to leave without her. I think of my Bulgarian boots and my Hungarian loafers. I find it awkward that she has almost the same name as Mariana, the girl who died in a mountain accident before Mihai and I started our love story. I don't know whether it's a good or a bad omen, or whether I even believe in omens. But I cling to every coincidence and familiar detail.

The first day that I go out on their balcony is the first day I feel something resembling awe. The hills surrounding the town where Marina, Vittorio and Roxana live are blue like the hills I had seen in the book about San Michele. The dark, pointed and velvety green pines project themselves against the rosy sky of the morning, and the roofs are red and glistening in the sun. The buildings around us are of many pastel colours: oranges, mauves, yellows. I hear voices singing little operettas, but they're really just saying *Move your car out of the way. Signora Rinaldi has gone to Rome to buy the pasta for the day. School is starting soon.* I am enraptured by the sounds and the colours, and I try to understand and repeat in my mind every word I hear from people's balconies or from the street. I wave at the woman across the road hanging her laundry on her balcony. Everything is intensely colourful. It's like I lived in a black-and-white film before I came to Italy, with some bright spots of colour: the sparkling blue Black Sea, or the red raspberries, or the dark green fir trees in the Carpathians.

I tell myself I have to take it in my stride, take things as they come, that all is well. I am after all in Italy, practically in Rome. My adventure hasn't had a bad start at all, and I'm lucky to have found all these people ready to lodge me, feed me and help me out, as if I were the wandering princess from a story my mother once read to me. The princess would knock on some door, and the people would put her up and feed her and send her on her way again. She eventually gets to a magical kingdom where the prince of her dreams is waiting for her in a golden carriage surrounded by white doves. Only I've just left the love of my life, not knowing whether he's a prince or an ogre.

The days pass almost without notice as I take care of Roxana. She clings to me and constantly wants me to play with her dolls, wants me to draw, wants to comb my hair. Sometimes I just want to rest and think, or to take a stroll around the neighbourhood with Roxana, but her parents have told me I must never take her out by myself. They say I don't know the city, we might get lost, something might happen.

A month has already passed, and Rome is still summery in October. Vittorio tells me *Tomorrow we go to the Italian authorities.* He tells me first we must go to the police to declare my status, to declare I am not going back, and to assure them I am not planning on staying in Italy.

"They don't want any more immigrants in Italy," says Vittorio, "but they'll help you go to Australia or Canada or the United States."

The next morning, I ask him if we can please go to the Colosseum first, please, and then to the police and that other place with the political asylum. I want to see the Colosseum, which the Romans had built in their ferocious hunger for glory. The Romans who then invaded and colonized the Dacians, stole their words, and left them with only fourteen, and thus gave birth to my people! My tormented, violent, messed-up, poetic people, from whom I have run away for ever. I find it comforting that my origins are here, in this dizzying city. I am not so far away after all. Vittorio smiles his charming smile and tells me

Certainly. He seems more relaxed and talkative than usual, which makes me feel quite hopeful. I'm wearing a bright red dress that Luciana bought for me in Trieste, my first red dress ever, and a pair of shoes that Marina bought for me. She took me from one shop to another until she chose this particular pair – white with black linen bows on top. They are the most beautiful shoes I've ever owned, but they hurt my feet.

I stand in front of the Colosseum, feeling as if I could take off and glide and float above the city. I stare at the ancient walls curving around the gigantic piazza. The warm October breeze lifts my dress and caresses my hair.

Vittorio takes me to the most beautiful places in Rome. Piazzas where people raise their voices to argue and laugh over the splash of water spurting in powerful jets from jars held by satyrs and nymphs. Colourful tiny cars swirl in maddening circles around parks and piazzas, fountains and statues, and I'm spinning with them, around and around the city. The world is suddenly wide open to me, and I'm greedy to have it, all of it. I can do anything I set my mind to. I want to do everything. I am young and pretty in my flowing red dress, my white shoes with black bows.

Vittorio treats me to a delicious lunch of little round pastas filled with cheese and mushrooms, and then I order the biggest ice cream I have ever had, an ice cream of many colours like the houses you see from Marina and Vittorio's balcony: light green pistachio, mauve blueberry, pink raspberry. I am sinking in a river of coloured tastes and sights and sounds. I feel as light as spun sugar.

The Italian police smile at me all the time, especially when they find out I'm not asking for asylum in Italy. They serve me coffee and cookies and tell me I am *una bella ragazza.* Vittorio translates for me whenever my own Italian fails me. He points to the places where I must sign the forms, a stack of forms, and with each signature I feel Rome, beautiful, grandiose, dizzying Rome, slipping away from me. I picture myself finishing my studies at the Università degli Studi di Roma and becoming a journalist or an actress or both, but the pictures become blurry and dissolve. Why is everybody trying to send me so far away, as if the stories of secret police and food rations and dissident activities I tell them have put a curse on me? I overcome my sadness like the rambling princess in the story and move on to the next station of my journey: the organization that helps political refugees from Eastern Europe.

Everybody at this agency is serious and speaks in low tones. I hear English and French and Russian zigzag around the cluttered old office. Yet again there are forms to be filled out, explaining why I fled my country, what I did in Romania, how I got into Italy. Vittorio helps me write. I answer all the questions, trying not to linger too much in my mind on the faces and events behind each answer. *Just the minimum,* Vittorio says. *These people understand.*

I start sweating, and I feel terribly tired. It all seems endless, tedious and indefinite. There are so many things that start worrying me: how am I going to live in America where I don't know a soul, what am I going to do there, who is even going to give me a piece of bread over there, so far away, on a different continent?

Then a woman with glasses on a chain around her neck takes me into a small tidy room and interviews me. She says she's sorry she doesn't speak Romanian; their translator is out today. We try a couple of other languages and quickly settle on English. It occurs to me this is a test, and that I must prove I speak English before they'll agree to find me a home in America. She asks me about my father's time in prison and about my plans for the future. I try to be brief and clear, but she switches from one topic to another so abruptly I become confused. I haven't spoken this much English since my English literature classes at the university, and I wonder suddenly how much English my professor really knew and if I'm sounding like an ancient book. She asks me about the time the man pinned me in the doorway on the empty street at night and told me there are worse things than death, because it's mentioned on the form, the story I never even told my parents.

My English sputters out like a candle, and my lip begins to shake. She closes the folder on her lap and says, "That's all right. I think we have enough." She tells me that it works like this: They have to find a sponsor for me in America, because on the form that I have just filled out, of the three boxes, one with Australia, one with Canada, and one with the United States, I ticked the one for the United States. Every refugee has to have a sponsor, a person who will be responsible for her until the refugee can get started and take care of herself. It all seems very well organized, but somehow lonely and frightening. Who knows what sponsor person I am going to end up with, and in what city? She tells me it's best to name a specific city where I know someone or where people from my town have gone, so they can try to match me with a sponsor there. The whole process can take several months, so I must be patient. Then, when they find a sponsor and all the immigration papers are ready, this agency in Rome will pay for my plane ticket and *send you on your way*, the woman with glasses says.

"I want to go to Chicago," I say quickly, in one breath, as if afraid that someone will get ahead of me and take my place in an imaginary waiting line. It is the only American city I have a little bit of a connection with because of Ralph the librarian from the American embassy in Bucharest. I want to see the Chicago skyline and the Sears Tower.

The woman writes that down. She says she'll see what she can do.

"Chicago is a good town," she says.

I feel that this has been the longest day in my life. I am now a political refugee, on my way to America. This will be me for the rest of my life.

This is the day when people are going to start looking all over the gigantic United States to find the right person who will put me up and see that I have food and help me to get on my own two feet.

This is the day when I see the Colosseum and the Fontana di Trevi. When I eat ice cream like a rainbow, wearing my red dress and white shoes.

Vittorio is waiting outside the interview room. He looks tired, and I think he's been asleep. He asks me what I want to do for the rest of the afternoon. We can walk some more, or am I tired and want to go home? "Marina will be waiting for us with dinner," he says.

He's surprised when I say I want to go to a hairdresser and have my hair cut. He looks pained. "Why cut it?" he asks. I tell him I'm a new person now. I say that my long hair is useless and ridiculous, and I don't want it any more.

He watches with a look of pity and amusement as the waves of hair fall to the floor of the salon he found for me. I watch in the mirror as my hair disappears, the blond waves like those of my great-aunt Nadia who died of love with a faded postcard in her hand and her cat mewing on her shoulder, like those of Great-grandmother Paraschiva floating on the river Nistru in 1918. This is the hair in which Mihai buried his face so often during our moments of passion, and that he tucked behind my ear with a tender gesture. I watch with satisfaction as it falls on the shiny pink marble floor. When the hairdresser stops and holds up a mirror so I can see the back of my head, I tell him, *More.* I remember the dream I had of Mihai slowly slitting my throat and then my turning into a wild white mare. Better to have your hair cut than your throat cut.

I see my Romanian past in my mind, all its passions and fears, all the people and sounds and smells and tastes, being wrapped up in cellophane like a package for me to carry as I move on towards my future. I see my Romanian past as I saw Trieste that first morning, wavering upside down in the shimmering mirror of the canals.

As I wait for the refugee organization to find me a sponsor and to tell me when my immigration papers are ready, I become attached to my daily routine with Roxana, Vittorio and Marina, as if I were one of their family. I love waking up to the sight of pastel-coloured houses and blue mountains in the early light, drinking Marina's coffee, then watching her try on a dozen pairs of shoes and eventually choose one: the beige ones with a metal clasp, or the red pumps, or the grey soft ones. Once they leave I start straightening up the house, removing the coffee cups that Marina and Vittorio drank from, rearranging the shoes that Marina had tried on before deciding on one pair back in the rack, and then I have to take Roxana to school. I like to feel useful and busy while living among so many pastel colours.

At a dinner party Marina and Vittorio give at the apartment, I meet one of their clients, an Italian man whose wife had died the year before. He sits across from me, and I feel his insistent eyes on me. I look back at him across the table as he puts meat into his mouth. I look at him as he lifts his wineglass to his lips and swallows, as he bites into a piece of bread, as he spits an olive pit onto his fork. I focus on the grey hair at his temples, a spot of dried blood on his chin where he must have cut himself shaving.

He starts complimenting me about everything: the way I speak Italian, the colour of my hair and of my eyes, until Marina says to him, "Vincenzo, you beast! Stop pestering the girl. Can't you see you're making her uncomfortable?"

"She doesn't look uncomfortable to me," he says.

During dinner I have two glasses of Chianti, and my tongue gets loose. I speak in little rivulets of Italian words and am amazed at my own ability. I even make a joke, playing on two words that sound alike. I feel at home, as if I've lived in Italy for ever.

As the other guests are leaving, the Italian widower stops me in the hall and asks if he can take me out and show me Rome tomorrow. I tell him, *Sì, certo*. What else have I got to do but wait for someone among the millions of people in the city of Chicago to decide whether they're going to sponsor a refugee?

Over the next weeks, Vincenzo takes me everywhere. Sometimes he talks about his wife and about how much he loved her, but also how and with how many women he had cheated on her while she was alive. I begin to think he's a collector of women the way Marina collects shoes, all carefully lined up according to their colour, shape, and the occasions when they'll make him look his best. Marina and Vittorio tell me to be careful of Vincenzo. Roxana gets jealous when I go out in the evening instead of plaiting her hair or playing cards with her or playing with her mean doll, Ninetta. She tells me, "Vincenzo is a bad man. He killed his wife." Marina and Vittorio scold her for speaking like that and tell her to go to bed.

One night, Vincenzo asks me to marry him. He says I'll never want for anything, he'll treat me like a princess. We'll go on cruises, travel everywhere I want. We're at an outdoor restaurant on a hill overlooking the city. Italian music is drifting through the autumn air.

I feel a shiver of romance that doesn't feel like love, nostalgia for something, for someone. The image of Mihai and his green eyes shaded by dark eyelashes takes shape in my mind with more clarity than any time since we were last together, since the night we made love in the cave under our white rock. I stare at this man who has just proposed to me, whose face by now is so familiar that it doesn't make me shy. I tell him I don't want to be a princess. I want to be a journalist or an actress, or both. Can he arrange that for me? I say I'm going to America, to Chicago. I don't want a cruise around the world.

I tell him I already have a *fidanzato*, a great, great love living in Romania. We'll be together again someday, when I'm living in a high-rise in Chicago. We'll get married there, in the United States. I realize this is the first time I've ever had this thought.

Besides, I ask him, how many other women would he have once we've been married for a year, or maybe just a month?

He says that he would stop all that and be faithful to me and love me, only me. This strikes me as the biggest lie I've heard since the *Father of the Nation* told us we were living in a workers' paradise.

"Thank you, Vincenzo, for your proposal of marriage. And

how nice of you to offer to become faithful for me," I say in my most elegant Italian. "But I can't accept."

"You are quite a woman, Mona. You'll go far, I have no doubt of it. But maybe one day you'll remember me and regret your decision."

For a while, Vincenzo continues to take me out and buy me expensive meals, hoping he can change my mind. One day he buys me a red bag. I empty out my old bag on the restaurant table, everything that I carried in the yellow Fiat to Italy and held tight to my chest as the Italian border guard checked Mario's passport and thought I was his wife. I put it all back neatly into my new red bag. Afterwards I toss my old bag into a rubbish bin near the Piazza di Spagna. I find myself at the bottom of marble steps leading to the magnificent cathedral, surrounded by late-autumn flowers and little cafés where you drink espresso that jolts through your veins and eat multicoloured ice cream and little pizzas with anchovies.

Musicians with guitars and mandolins play old, heart-wrenching songs: a young man says he'll die ten times over for his brunette love with a red rose in her hair, but then he's angry and leaves her when she says she doesn't love him.

Very early one morning I call my parents from Marina's apartment. My mother answers and her voice strangles with emotion and tears. I realize I've just awakened her. A new grey day is starting in the little Bucharest apartment: the making of soy coffee, taking crowded buses to go to work, looking over your shoulder to see if someone is following you. She asks me timidly if I am fine. I tell her, *Yes, I am doing very well.* My father gets on the phone, and I'm relieved he isn't arrested or hiding somewhere. He is there next to my mother, who's probably wearing rollers in her hair. I can hear him smoking as we talk, with short furious puffs. We can't say much; we assume their phone is tapped. I can't give any names, any addresses. I just say, *It's getting cold up here.*

I tell them, *I miss you so much.* We hang up. I sit on the little chair next to the phone in Marina's apartment. I think of how much of me is gone for ever.

It's chilly, humid and rainy in Rome. I drink caffè latte or espresso every day in little bars and cafés to warm up. I stand one day in front of the Colosseum and stare at the noble, ancient curve of its stone walls. Vincenzo is next to me, shivering in his trench coat, hoping that maybe the cold and the rain will make me feel less confident about my future, that I'll change my mind about his proposal. The wind blows through me and through the white wool coat that Marina gave me, one of her old coats.

The next day I get the news that the agency has found me a sponsor in Chicago, *a nice older couple*, and I have a week until my flight. I cry when I leave delicate, porcelain-faced Marina with her many shoes, and dreamy, fidgety Vittorio, who had shown me the Colosseum for the first time and helped me become a political refugee and watched me have my hair cut off. I know I can never repay all these people from Trieste and from Rome who happened to cross my path like magical beings, and who have helped me and put me up and fed me for the simple pleasure of doing it. I know they don't expect me to repay them either, but that they are also sad I am leaving.

For our farewell dinner, Vincenzo takes me to a restaurant with musicians on Via Veneto. We dance to the music of Adriano Celentano. I feel particularly nostalgic when the song "Azzurro" is sung by the Italian singer trying to imitate Adriano Celentano. Vincenzo makes his proposal of marriage one more time, and again I refuse him as we swirl on the marble floor of the restaurant.

Roxana is crying at the airport and telling me she wants to come and visit me in Chicago. I hug Marina and Vittorio and hold Roxana in my arms one more time. *Tutto sarà bene.* In the distance, behind a group of American tourists, I see Vincenzo standing in his trench coat and smoking. He waves at me and sends kisses. I move on through the crowds to get to my airplane, my first airplane ever. A family with children passes in front of Marina, Vittorio and Roxana, and then I don't see them any more. I panic and I want to run after them, to hug them one more time, to beg them to help me settle in Rome, *Roma, amore mio.* To let me stay just one more season. But I am already in the line for the security check and a woman in uniform who looks like airport police pushes me ahead and barks at me to hurry up, *Dai, dai, presto.* I hold on tight to the red bag, and I move quickly.

PART TWO

In a Suburb of Chicago:
A Freedom Fighter

THE COUPLE WHO HAS SPONSORED ME to come to Chicago is a woman in her fifties named Gladys and a man also in his fifties named Ron. They are both silver haired. Gladys's face has a strained expression like she is sorry for something, and Ron's face is red and round. He works in an insurance company. She goes around in her car all day, not really working, not working for money, but meeting other women and doing volunteer work for the church, then preparing dinner for Ron. I discover they found out about me, and my need to be sponsored to come to America, through their church. This dumbfounds me. In the little Orthodox churches I used to venture into when I needed to calm my thoughts and get away from the images of the *Father of the Nation* and the three bearded *Marxist gods*, there were just old priests with long white beards and women dressed in black, kissing the icons and bowing to the altar. The saints on the frescoes and in the icons stared at you with puzzled, fixed eyes. I understand that I am a work of charity for Gladys and Ron. That's why they take me with them everywhere they go, to parties and dinners and to church, and present me as *the young lady from Romania.*

They live in a suburb of Chicago, not among high-rise buildings and roaring traffic as I had hoped, but in a little village near Chicago where there are enormous houses and empty streets. Every time I say I am going to go for a walk, Gladys and Ron look at each other amused. Nobody just strolls around out here. The pavements are narrow strips of paving at the very edge of the road. Sometimes I have to walk in the middle of the road, and people glare at me from their cars. Sometimes concerned drivers stop and ask me if I'm lost, if there's something they can do to help.

At their parties, everybody speaks about church things and then about pointless topics like the weather or the insurance business, about the dinner they are going to prepare for the special holiday called Thanksgiving, when everybody has to eat turkey and mashed potatoes, and then about the weather again.

They all ask me polite questions about my country and my parents. They ask me what language people speak in Romania, and whether there are McDonald's restaurants in my country. When I say there aren't any, they say they're sure Romania is a beautiful country, but they couldn't live there without McDonald's. Everybody laughs at the joke Ron makes about the lack of hamburgers in my country. I am not sure why this is funny, but in order to be polite I go along with the joke and say I can't believe I've actually survived all these years without eating a hamburger. Everybody laughs at my joke, too.

One day Ron takes me to the McDonald's near their house as if it were a great event. He gets me a Big Mac and hands it to me like a trophy. As I am eating the soggy bun and the dry patty of ground meat, which I eat with a fork and knife, not like a sandwich as Ron does, I am amazed. I tell Ron it's great, but I am actually thinking that it's funny how in America, everywhere you look, there are mountains of food that doesn't taste very good, but in my country we almost starved, yet when we did get to eat something, whether it was my mother's fried potatoes or a cucumber and tomato salad or a slice of bread with butter, it always tasted good. Or maybe it's just me sentimentalizing everything because I am so far away from my country, and the old Romanian proverb about the bread always being better in your own country, no matter how tough things may be, is acquiring its true meaning now. Mihai used to tell me this proverb sometimes when there was a discussion about people leaving the country. A quick memory crosses my mind like a flash: Mihai and I eating bread and tomatoes, him kissing me warmly, the feel of his hands on my back as I dance in his arms in my peach satiny dress at the New Year's Eve party when we started the new decade. I see his face smiling sadly and actually *not* saying the proverb or anything at all when the other guests told stories of escape. Then I am terrified that I will be overcome by memories and by missing everyone and everything as I was in the railway station in Trieste. I gulp down the hamburger furiously in a mad effort to close the door that has just dangerously opened in my mind. To keep away all memories for the time being. Ron takes my gesture as a sign that I really love the hamburger and offers to buy me another one.

"No, thank you," I say with a full mouth.

I'm possessed by evil impulses at Ron and Gladys's dinner parties and Sunday brunches. I say shocking things like *People are dying of starvation in the streets of Bucharest* and *They even kill each other for food.* I tell them I was a freedom fighter in an underground group. When they look amazed, I shrug and say I escaped from Romania wrapped up in a camouflage blanket in the back of a truck that was transporting beef to Turkey, because Romania is one of Europe's biggest exporters of beef. That's why the people are starving and killing for a little meat the size of those patties they serve at McDonald's. But our beef patties are tastier, I tell them, when we do manage to get our hands on one. Then I say that I used to work in the biggest theatre of Bucharest as an actress and that I studied politics and economics at the University of Bucharest. Everybody is puzzled by the fact that universities and theatres are still operating while people are hunting pigeons and cats in the streets of Bucharest for meat.

A heavy blanket of boredom spreads over me during these parties, and I feel unbearably sad. The worst are the Sunday mornings when everybody listens to a priest talk about not com-

mitting sins and about giving our lives and our souls to the Lord
Jesus Christ. When I was waiting in Italy for my sponsor to
materialize so I could go to Chicago, I had imagined a thousand
possibilities for my life. This wasn't one of them. I never pic-
tured myself being dragged to church and lectured to about
Jesus all the time and everybody being so polite that it made me
scared. They'd give me pamphlets with photographs of foetuses
mangled and covered in blood with big captions saying *Abortion
is murder.* I have no idea what abortion has to do with anything.
Why do people start talking about such a thing as abortion out
of the blue? Why, of all the possibilities in the world, did I have
to end up being housed and fed by people who keep using *Jesus
Christ* and *abortion* in the same sentence all the time?

I get really scared when Gladys and Ron ask me to convert to
their religion and accept Jesus Christ in my life, and when they
take me to their meetings in the church basement where they
talk about the evils of abortion and about how black people and
Jewish people are the Antichrist and are corrupting the country with drugs and abortion and homosexuality. They talk about
some Jewish conspiracy. They say the Communists will take over,
and the pornographers. They worship President Reagan. I don't
know anything about a Jewish conspiracy, but all this weird talk
in the basement surely seems like some kind of Jesus conspiracy
to me. On TV there is news about the bombing of an abortion
clinic by what the newscaster calls pro-life activists. *The explosion,*
says the heavily made-up newscaster with a smile, as if she were
announcing the building of a new school or the arrival of the
spring equinox, *resulted in the death of a doctor and serious injuries
of several nurses and personnel.* As we watch the news in the living
room Ron and Gladys look at each other with a strange look,
almost a smile. The expression *pro-life activists* in combination
with the news of blowing up a clinic, killing and injuring
people, leaves me dumbfounded. I wonder what the people who
are not *pro-life activists* get to do in America. I feel as terrified as
when the secret police had asked me to become an informer,
but it's even worse now because I'm supposed to be starting a

new life here, walking freely in the streets of Chicago, listening to jazz and studying to become a journalist. This is supposed to be my experience of freedom.

One day Gladys tells me to come with her to *spread the good news.* I wonder if someone in her family has just got married or had a baby or been given a job in the White House. I'm glad for the chance to go out for a walk, even if it's just around the little town with empty streets. Maybe if I'm lucky, I'll get to meet new people. But Gladys picks up her Holy Bible and a stack of her pamphlets. She starts knocking on people's doors to tell them about Jesus and accepting him in your heart and abortion is murder. People just close their doors in Gladys's face. Pretty soon she has a forlorn look like the whole world has turned against her. She walks down the road holding her Bible and pamphlets tight to her chest. For a brief moment I almost feel sorry for Gladys. I wonder what could have made her so misguided that she'd want to spend her life in this humiliation. But my pity for her disappears quickly when I think of my own embarrassment at being with her. I want to melt into the black asphalt of the streets just to be anywhere but here. I'd even rather be back in Bucharest with all the secret police.

At least there I felt some excitement hearing footsteps behind me and then a rush of victory when I reached the apartment, locked the door behind me, and sat down with my mother and father around our little table in the kitchen over some leek stew or boiled potatoes talking about metaphysical poetry. Everything here seems so dull and embarrassing. I experience a moment of hopelessness and think of Hamlet: *the whole world is a prison.* Chicago is even worse than Hamlet's Denmark, where at least there were murders, suicides, passions and dark, haunted castles. The America of this suburb seems submerged in a thick gooey substance with something poisonous mixed up in it, spreading like a pool. No grandeur, no beauty, no throbbing life.

I'm filled with hatred for Gladys. Why did she and Ron have to make me their charity case? I wonder if the organization in

Rome has any idea what kind of sponsors they're finding for people. I can't believe they do, remembering the woman with glasses on a chain around her neck, the sound of so many languages, and the colours of the weavings and artefacts from different countries on the walls. I want to write to them to watch out for the *nice couples,* to make sure refugees don't end up in scary religious groups instead of being properly sponsored, just being given a bowl of soup and a bed to sleep in.

Gladys furiously grabs my arm and starts back home, muttering about moral decay. I have to run away, I have to be free. I have to take the train to Chicago, which I haven't really seen yet. I have to find work, see the people walk in the streets, see the tall buildings, and cleanse myself of the sermons about blacks and Jews and abortions.

One night at the dinner table, I tell Gladys and Ron that I'm Jewish and that I've had sex with the black postman while they were out, and now I think I'm pregnant. I ask them where I can get an abortion. Just so they'll throw me out of their house with flowery wallpaper and baby-blue upholstery on the sofa. But they're nice and charitable. They believe what I said about being pregnant, and they tell me Jesus Christ will forgive me, that I should give up the baby for adoption. They say Jesus Christ will accept a Jew, too, if I repent.

I know I should feel at least some gratitude toward Gladys and Ron for having helped me come to Chicago, but I really can't bring myself to feel anything but nausea and boredom and fear, sensations I'd never experienced in this particular combination before.

One day when Gladys is out in her car doing her volunteer work, I leave the house and walk to the station where the Chicago train stops. I have a few dollars from the allowance Gladys gives me. I buy a round-trip ticket to Chicago good for one day.

The train leaves me somewhere that everybody calls the Loop, among gigantic buildings and a maze of overhead tracks. Everything whizzes by, roaring, hungry to get somewhere, climbing up towards the squares of grey November sky between the high-rise buildings. I've never seen people of so many different colours in one place, except for in a geography book in my school in Romania. It had a page with a big circle of people dancing around the globe, all dressed differently and with different skin colours, to show all the races living in harmony. I suppose it represented a Communist utopia where everyone lives together in harmony and peace under the red flag of the Communist Party. In Romania, the only people of a slightly different skin colour I saw were the gypsies who lived in camps in the country or in ugly buildings at the edge of the city. Everyone cursed them. Sometimes there were students from African countries, like my father's Senegalese student who exchanged Romanian money for the hundred-dollar bill I carried on the train to Trieste. Most people cursed the black students, too, because they were even darker than the gypsies.

A powerful feeling comes over me that this is the city in which I was meant to be born, that I am the victim of a cosmic mistake, not having grown up here amid all the roaring and colour. But then, on second thoughts, I think if I had lived here from the beginning I wouldn't be carrying stories of my relatives surviving bombs and eating roots and floating on rivers with mirrored music boxes. I wouldn't have known love in the Carpathians on carpets of wild berries or blue snow. In the whole messed-up, incomprehensible scheme of things, somehow this is just as it should be.

I feel a strange familiarity with Chicago, as if I've been here before, as if I'd seen these crowded streets lined with gigantic buildings that look like Cubist paintings somewhere in a dream, as if the swirl of people moving with focused steps and stubborn determination to make the most of this grey day had passed through my subconscious life sometime long ago. I roam the streets with a fierce curiosity and joy. I'm awed by Lake Michigan. I stare at the people I pass, trying to burn each face into my memory. This is a city fit for my hunger.

Buena Noche, Mi Amor!

A FTER MANY HOURS OF WALKING in Chicago, I enter a drugstore with a sign that says HELP WANTED. I assume it means they will pay for the help, but I'm not sure. If I'm going to run away from Gladys and Ron, the first thing I'll need is money. *See Manager Inside,* the sign says. I go inside and tell a woman putting bottles of shampoo on a shelf that I want to talk to the manager because I want to help. She's a black woman in a red sweater, and she says she is the manager. I ask her if they pay for the help.

"Honey, you'd better believe it," she says.

For the first time in the several weeks I've been in America, I laugh. The way the words just roll off her tongue is enchanting. She takes me into a back room and interviews me for about ten minutes. Her name is Rhonda. She's surprised when I tell her I've been in America for only a few weeks. She says my English is great, even though it's taking me a long time to fill out the form she's given me.

"Just bring it back tomorrow, honey, and we'll see what we can do for you," she tells me.

"Please, can you tell me now if I get the job? I can start right away. I want to work, because I need to get a place to live, and I need to start going to school. I am a political refugee, and I have permanent resident status, and all my documents are in order and, please, can I get the job? I would love to work in a drugstore."

It all pours out of me in one breath. She stares at me for a few moments with her arms crossed, and I can almost hear the thoughts rolling in her head. I think how I must look to her: a crazy woman from a strange country, wandering the streets of Chicago in some kind of desperation. She can't know the murky substance that I'm slowly drowning in. She opens her mouth in a big smile, a smile as wide and as white as that of my mother's friend Nora in the picture of her sitting in an orange tree somewhere in America, on the same continent where I'm standing at this very moment. She might as well be on the moon, because I have no address or phone number for Nora. I know I have to hang on to whoever shows me real kindness because I don't know anyone in this United States of America.

"Honey, you got it," she says in a special velvety way.

I'm so relieved, I become even bolder and ask her if she knows of a place where I can live, an apartment I could rent. She thinks about it, then takes me to the pharmacy counter and introduces me to Marta, who's from Mexico. Marta's round face reminds me of the beautiful woman I bought the bouquet of hyacinths from that cruel day in April. When Rhonda tells her I've just been hired and I'm looking for a place to live, Marta says, well, maybe she can help.

Marta speaks a different English from Rhonda. She rolls her *r*'s sweetly, just like we roll them in Romanian, and she turns *v*'s into *b*'s. Her speech has a playful twist, a delicate edge. I think of the swirl of a woman's skirt, of a nervous, graceful twist of one's hand in the air in a moment of excitement, like this moment right here for me in the Chicago dusk, amid so many coloured shapes in a drugstore where I've got my first job and maybe even a place to live on my own. I feel myself starting to push out shoots into this hard earth of Chicago, the first fragile, stringy roots.

The next day, while Gladys is out on her church work, I pack the few things I accumulated in Italy from the two families I lived with: the red flowing dress, the white shoes with black bows, two sweaters, and a blue skirt. I write a note for Gladys and Ron thanking them for their hospitality, telling them not to worry about me. I tell them I've found a job and an apartment in Chicago, so farewell. I linger for a moment to look at the living room with the baby-blue upholstery one more time. I expect to feel some kind of sadness or regret, but there's nothing. At the last minute before going out the door, I turn back and add to the note that I am grateful for what they have done for me, for sponsoring me to come to America. I plan to write to the refugee organization in Rome and tell them that I am making it all right and to warn them about my sponsors Ron and Gladys.

I move in with Marta and her six-year-old daughter, Daniela, until I can get into a studio apartment in her building at the end of the month when someone's moving out. Pungent, spicy smells of Mexican cooking rise from her kitchen and from other kitchens in the building. The hallways echo to the sound of people laughing and arguing in Spanish. Sometimes in the evening there is music somewhere in the building, music about love and death, *amor y muerte,* that makes me ache with nostalgia. It reminds me of the Italian musicians in piazzas singing about love and death in a different language.

I help Marta stir refried beans. I chop up tomatoes and onions to the sound of Mexican music. I make a green paste from the fruit avocado, dark green and shaped like an egg. I delight in the smell of Marta's kitchen and the taste of the green paste.

Sometimes Marta takes a few swigs of tequila right out of the bottle. I taste the liquor too, and it reminds me of the plum drink *țuică.* They both send an electric shock through your body like you've been struck by lightning. Sometimes Marta and I dance in the kitchen to the music of *amor y muerte,* and Daniela joins us, holding her mother's skirt. Marta picks her up and kisses her all over her face and dances with her, round and round, in the little kitchen smelling like onions and refried beans.

I sleep on the cot next to the bed where Marta and Daniela sleep together. At night, as I drift into the deepest sleep I've had since I was a child, after a day at the drugstore and after walking in the sharp Chicago wind and taking two trains, after cooking with Marta and drinking tequila and dancing, I hear the two of them speak softly to each other. Melodious chirping in the silence of the Chicago apartment, mysterious and comforting: *Buena noche, mi amor.* In the morning, Marta and I take the train to work together. Soon the Chicago winter starts.

Chicago Winter in Sepia

During my first winter in Chicago my feet get frostbite. I have a tooth abscess. My face swells and I look like a fish again. I writhe in pain for three days until the abscess bursts open and the pain goes away, then I have a dead tooth in my mouth. I'm still working at the drugstore as a cashier. I register for courses to complete my university degree, and I switch to the evening shift so I can attend classes all day. I take two trains and a bus to get to the university. There's graffiti on the trains that says things like *Life's a bitch and then you die.* The word *fuck* is written everywhere. You find out from the walls of these trains that *José is fucking Maria.* I am entertained every morning on the train as I try to picture these people who are having such an intense love life that they have to share it with the Chicago Transit Authority community. I earn money and learn the different stores on State Street and Michigan Avenue. I miss Italy. I miss the wide avenues of Rome, its special light, the pine trees, and the espresso coffee in narrow bars. I don't miss my country at all, only Italy. But it's not a painful kind of missing, it's substitute missing, because it's so much easier to miss Italy than my own country with everyone and everything in it that I love.

It's grey and cold in Chicago, so cold you think life will just stop and everybody in the street will simply freeze like mannequins for ever. The businesswoman in a black fur coat and sneakers will freeze as she searches in her bag for her car keys. The man playing a saxophone behind an empty hat will freeze just as he lifts his saxophone towards the dark Chicago sky. The homeless woman will freeze just as she is about to stick her hand into the trash can; the policeman guiding traffic with his hand raised will stay just like that. Everything – the taxis, the limos, the buses, the child running behind his mother who carries a grocery bag from Dominick's in each hand, will freeze just as he's about to catch up with her. This is how I see Chicago this cold winter: in black-and-white stills. I know there is something I should be feeling but am not. I don't let in any feelings that could distract me from making it through this winter.

I like my little furnished studio apartment. I visit Marta and Daniela often, when I feel lonely, when she feels lonely. I help Marta make guacamole, and we take turns swigging tequila from the bottle.

I study until late at night: English literature, religion, philosophy. Plato, Leibniz, the Bible, William Butler Yeats. I go to school very early in the morning so I can stay in the library and take out any book I want and watch students and teachers walk into the library. My teachers are amazed I've read all of Shakespeare and can recite passages by heart. I've even read *Tristram Shandy*. I am not certain they would understand that back home it was a matter of survival, reading until you became numb or euphoric. They don't know that people threw themselves from their apartment windows or hanged themselves in their living rooms when they couldn't pass the entrance exam for the university. Sometimes I have little private conversations with my teachers in class. I've never felt so important. My heart races just having a conversation about *Mrs Dalloway* with my professor while the other students watch us enviously.

I visit the financial aid office every day to fill out applications for scholarships, forms about my income and the income of my parents. I fill in many zeros, round fat zeros everywhere they ask about income and earnings and tax returns. I don't understand the concept of a tax return. I just tell the woman in the office that I'm a refugee and have no money – really, really no money – to pay for classes and that my parents are in Romania being persecuted. I even tell her about how I left Romania on the train to Trieste that wasn't truly the train to Trieste, and how I hitchhiked across the border into Italy with just my bag.

"No money," I tell her. "Just my bag and this book of my grades from the university and some pictures."

She stares at me for a moment. "You have a book of grades?" she says. "You mean a transcript? You took courses at a university in Romania?"

I know all the women in that office will talk about me when I leave.

A few days later, I get to speak to the dean of the university, who is all kindness and admiration. It feels like a dream, everybody taking me so seriously, being so kind. They've translated all the grades in my little book from tens and nines and one grade of six in Marxist economy. The dean gives me an official paper with many *A* letters and one *C* letter.

"It's very good," the dean tells me. "We're glad to have you."

I know my father won't believe me when I tell him about all of this. He'll be so proud that all my Romanian grades mean so much in America. He'll say, *Look how good Romanian education is! What a pity these bastards have fucked up our country like this.*

I don't like my job in the drugstore any more. I like being with Rhonda and Marta. I like making fun of the customers as we have lunch together in the little supply room in the back of the store. But I'm restless; I want to move on, to do something extraordinary like write a play that becomes famous, get my doctorate and become a professor. I want to be and do something that would make all my travails in America worthwhile, something that would fully justify my having torn myself from my own country and family. Sometimes, right before going to sleep at night, I think, What if I called Mihai right now, it's dawn in Romania. But what would I say, how could I explain everything, my leaving without saying a word to him? And what if he is cold and distant on the phone, that would be worse than not ever hearing his voice again. There is nothing we could tell each other over the void spreading across the Atlantic Ocean. I cut myself off from him the morning when I stood alone in his room staring at his bed and at the red slip spread on it and I made my final choice to climb back out the window and run to my train.

I don't like it when people ask me about my accent and ask where I'm from and how I got out of there. I don't understand why, when I say I'm from Romania, they always say, *Oooh! That's so interesting* or *Wow! That's great!* There's nothing intrinsically great about being from any particular country, I think. I never say it, though. Maybe when I'm forty, I'll just say, *What's so great about being from Romania or Albania or Patagonia, or anyplace? Where I'm from is none of your business!* Just to see how people react. But now I just smile and say thank you whenever someone tells me my accent is *so cute.* If I told them I'd been in the secret police in Romania, people would say, *Wow, that's great. I love your accent.*

Once in a while someone has heard of Nadia Comaneci or Dracula, or someone says they know another Romanian, and maybe I should meet him. I understand that my country is known for its gymnasts and vampires. I don't want to meet another Romanian. The few I've met just talk about making money and buying apartment buildings. They mix three words of Romanian with five words of English, pretending they've forgotten their native language. So far, I haven't met any of the sentimental exiles who weep in the middle of the street when they hear Romanian being spoken. Maybe I will someday, but I really don't care.

I like to wander in downtown Chicago and observe people and look at the store windows. Once in a while I go into a store and buy a really useless thing with the money I earn in the drugstore – a black patent leather belt or a little box with roses painted on it that opens when you push a button and inside is face powder on one side and a mirror on the other. Or I go into a restaurant and order myself a meal with a long name like *chicken cordon bleu* and eat it while I read a book. Every day is a thrill, even with the drugstore work and the cold wind, and the fear that I won't have enough money until my next pay cheque.

Sometimes there is sweet music in the street, flowing and undulating like a moan of love, like a tear falling on a lover's face. The man with a saxophone plays on State Street even when it's inhumanly cold, and his music is like the yearning and the sadness in that Romanian word *dor*. That's when it clicks for me, when I understand exactly what that untranslatable word means. It's what he's saying with his saxophone. I stand and listen to him after my classes, if I don't have to rush to work. One day I tell him he plays so beautifully he should play in a concert hall. He laughs so hard and says he won't never be playing in no fucking concert hall, he'll just be playing on fucking State Street. I say that's not so bad, because everybody can hear him there, and he says, *Yeaah!*

Slowly, in the Chicago cold, I learn how to live within freedom. I make a little place for myself within its wild vastness. And there is me, the little piece of me in the mosaic of America. Do you see me there? I'm the one with the maroon down coat from a secondhand store and grey boots that are too tight for my frostbitten feet. I'm right there, standing on State Street between the Russian woman selling apples and bananas and the Mexican man with the hot-dog stand. Do you see me now? I'm so excited I could just scream right here in the middle of State Street, so loud they can hear me all the way to Romania, to my aunt's kitchen where they're eating pickled tomatoes and wondering where that Mona could be right now.

All I need is to just make it through the winter. Some mornings, in the seconds between sleep and full consciousness, scrambled images of my past rush violently in my head: my parents whispering over a bowl of leek stew, Mihai in the rented room in Bucharest staring at me with tearful eyes, Cristina's dead body in the cemetery at the foot of the mountain. I have the distinct sensation both of being conscious and of dreaming.

In those eerie moments, an overpowering feeling of loss liquefies me. I still have another hour before I have to get up and start another Chicago day, so I will myself back to sleep. When the alarm clock rings its grating sound through my light morning sleep, I get up instantaneously and impose an unforgiving programme of forgetfulness upon my psyche. Just like a diet: no fried foods, no thinking of my parents, no sweets, no fantasizing about Mihai and what he might be doing at this very moment, no processed meats and no remembering the dream of only an hour earlier. I enjoy my morning hot shower, and I don't allow myself to think that my parents probably don't have any hot water, or that my mother would say not to leave the house with wet hair in the cold weather. I just tell myself I am lucky I can take a hot shower every day. I stuff all my schoolbooks in the worn-out backpack that Marta gave me and rush out of the building into the Chicago wind blasting in my face. I am making it through this winter. Yet somehow I am losing myself, too. The days when I'm not thinking of my past, I feel my heart is as frozen as my feet in the cheap boots I am wearing.

I have to think my way back; I have to hang on and try hard not to lose myself in the cold and in the Chicago crowds. I have to both hang on to something and survive.

I think of my birth. Summer in Bucharest, when the streets were filled with a scent of linden so heavy and so sweet that you'd want to be born again and again on a summer night filled with such smells. In the Chicago cold, I try to relive a moment that summer in Bucharest when I am inside my mother's womb, greedy for light, ready, frightened, eager for the world. I try to imagine my mother soaked in amniotic fluid, sitting quietly on the edge of the bed in her one and only black mourning dress that she wore to her mother's funeral a month before. Waiting for the morning. Waiting for my birth.

In order not to lose myself in this city of strangers, I carry a country inside my head. My parents' memories have become my own, as if I had lived their childhoods, their adolescences. I have collected the memories of my aunts and uncles, too, and my cousins, and the memories of characters in books I've read.

In the role of my father, I laugh at myself as I run to the nearest phone booth on a summer night in linden-filled Bucharest, pulling on my trousers and trying to light a cigarette at the same time. In the role of my mother, Dorina, I am puzzled at my own serenity as I sit on the edge of a bed waiting for the morning when my child will be born. I cry, not from the contractions of labour, but because my mother, Vera, has just died a month ago, and I didn't get to see her one last time. I am my grandmother, my mother, myself. We give birth to one another as we mourn for one another in the linden-scented night of old Bucharest.

America, America—
My Country of Refugees

B Y THE TIME SUMMER COMES, I'm no longer working in the
drugstore. I'm taking summer classes, and I get a job in
Uptown teaching English to refugees from Cambodia, Laos,
and Vietnam. They call me teacher and they bring me strings of
beads to wear around my neck and bowls of noodles and little
embroideries of red and blue people and birds in the mountains
that are embroidered by Hmong women from the mountains of
Laos. Although the designs are quite different, the bright reds
and blues remind me of the tablecloths and wall hangings sewn
by the peasant women in rural Romania. I place the Hmong
tapestries all around my bed so that they are the first thing I see
in the morning when I wake up: embroidered colourful people
and monkeys, exotic animals and birds among stylized mountains and trees.

The Chicago summer bursts in with its dizzying humid heat,
music pounding in the streets, car alarms, and white yachts
lined up along Lake Shore Drive. I work at night because all my
students work in factories all day. Some are eighteen; others are
fifty or sixty. Sometimes they come to class with their children.
Sometimes they fall asleep in class, and everybody laughs, pointing at the person whose head is dangling and whose mouth is
wide open. Past participles, *ring rang rung, sing sang sung*, posses-
sive pronominal adjectives, *this is my bag, that is your pencil.*

Words are soothing and funny in my mouth, and my students receive them like precious gifts, trusting my refugee English.

I drive a big brown Oldsmobile that I bought for eight hundred dollars out of my first pay cheque as a teacher. My American friends tell me I should be careful walking in that neighbourhood at night. I feel so high after each class that I'm never afraid to walk to my car. I feel like the queen of Uptown, sweaty from my four-hour class, with strings of cheap coloured beads dangling around my neck. Sometimes a few students walk with me to my car, and every word is a reason for laughter. We laugh in the Chicago night about our ugly old cars as police sirens slice through the thick summer air.

I had heard of Vietnam growing up, listening to the news, and hearing my parents and their friends talk about the Vietnam War. I knew of Cambodia as a place where people were much worse off than we were in Romania and where the famous French writer André Malraux did some kind of archaeological work and stole Khmer statues. I learned of Laos in my geography class – just another Asian country where people were also worse off than we were and about which my mother would say when I didn't want to finish off my portion of bean soup: "There are children starving in Laos and in Cambodia who would give anything to have this bowl of soup here." My father and all of his poet and artist friends always mourned the takeover by Communist regimes of these faraway countries and cheered America on to win the war in Vietnam.

I find out with great surprise from my graduate student friends that American soldiers performed what they all call atrocities in Vietnam, such as brutally killing innocent women and children and ravaging whole Vietnamese villages. Despite all of my knowledge of European literature, I feel so naïve and ignorant about so many other things, and I am almost embarrassed now to feel lucky that I have come to America, with its recent history of atrocities. I want to be able to juggle political concepts and jargon the way my friends do when they talk of the imperialist foreign politics of America. But it's ironic that they all warn me about the dangers of going at night into the Uptown neighbourhood where so many poor people and refugees live. If they feel so sympathetic to all the poor people and the refugees from all the countries, how come they are afraid to walk around there and why don't they also work in those neighbourhoods, I wonder.

I must have two of my wisdom teeth extracted on the same day, but I don't want to cancel my class. I never cancel classes. I am wearing a bright pink cotton dress, and my just-washed and blow-dried hair is sticking up in all directions like a cat in a cartoon that's got its tail stuck in an electric socket. I go into the classroom biting on bloody gauze. I try to teach my lesson: the conditional. *If I were rich, I would travel all over the world.*

"If I were rich, I would buy a new car and bring my mother from Cambodia to America."

As I taste the blood gushing out of the two holes inside my mouth, raw and sour, after I swallow the blood, I say, "To hell with the conditional. Why don't we just talk about you?" They laugh and say, "Aah! Teacher say *hell*!"

I find out from my students that Pol Pot's soldiers would cut out the hearts of people caught trying to escape through the jungle, actually rip the hearts of live people out of their chests, and that some of them have lost family members to that unspeakable lot. They are the lucky ones, they say. I don't know how to end this lesson that should have been about the conditional mood. I say, "I've never eaten a mango fruit." Several of them offer to bring me a mango the next day. "Mango very good fruit," they say. I know it makes them happy to give gifts.

Sometimes I want to steal everybody else's country and miss it. America is all about refugees, I realize. But I can't seem to be the proper Romanian refugee and miss anything about my own country. The conversations with my parents across the ocean are strained and interrupted by long pauses during which all I can think about is the expanse of ocean that separates us. The ocean that moves in its green immensity: the fierce sharks, the silvery dolphins, the algae, and myriad-coloured fish floating in rainbows. I am startled from my reverie when my mother asks something simple like "How do you like your classes?" There is a bulky lump of something stuck in my throat. It takes me a while to answer because I don't want to cry on the phone while I'm speaking with my mother who is probably also trying not to cry. The code question: *Did you get the red shoes?* which means *Were you able to do anything to obtain a passport to America?* receives the same whispered negative from my mother every single time.

Marta says: "Chica, you should find the Romanian church and meet your people. Talk your language, it would make you feel better, you know."

But I want to stay away from what she calls *my people,* somehow fearing that if I don't I'll be pulled back into the vortex of my nightmares and end up stuck on a dirty Bucharest pavement staring at tractors in a store window. I tell Marta *she* is my people, and we both laugh.

One day I go downtown before teaching to visit Marta and Rhonda in the drugstore. But I never make it to the Walgreens at the corner of Michigan and Chicago, because as I pass by the Marshall Field's store in the majestic marble Water Tower Place, I am suddenly drawn to the glitter of the cosmetics counters and decide to visit that section as if it were a museum. The glamorous women in the aisles trying to attract customers and sell their Clinique and Estée Lauder products look like mechanical dolls: they have perfect glossy pink cheeks, bright red lips, long black lashes that bat like confused butterflies, and hair that glistens. I feel strangely uplifted by this spectacle, as if I have suddenly entered a play, an American version of *The Master and Margarita,* and any minute, a gorgeous American Margarita is going to fly down in a flower basket from the golden sculpted ceiling, half naked, singing a throaty jazz song about American consumerism and her baby who don't love her no more. But instead, one of the doll women workers approaches me and asks me if I would like to have *a makeover.* I stand in the middle of the store and look at her puzzled because in all of the English and American plays and poems and novels I have read, I have never encountered the word *makeover* and I don't want to appear like the dumbfounded refugee that I really am.

So I say "Sure, thank you!" thinking that maybe a *makeover* means that they give you a bag with little envelopes filled with sample creams and perfumes for free, like I've seen other customers get. She takes me to the shiny counter studded with perfumes and with creams for every part of your face and with as many eye-shadow colours as there were ice-cream flavours in the *gelateria* in Rome where I ate my first Italian ice cream with Vittorio on the day I applied for political asylum.

She starts cleaning my face with cotton balls and different stinging lotions and then applies layer upon layer of creams and foundation and blush and eye shadow. I relax; the girl's slow movements on my face get me all stirred up like I haven't had the time or disposition to be in a long time. It strikes me that I haven't had sex with anyone in ages, I am not having sex with anyone, and it doesn't look like I will have sex with anyone anytime soon. I am alone in this cubist city and nobody loves me. Mihai's languorous face, the way he always looked at me after we made love, with strands of black hair falling over his forehead and the glitter of a smile in his eyes, appear to me from behind the watery surface beneath which I had pushed him long ago, on that afternoon in Rome when I had my hair cut by the Italian hairdresser.

An overpowering longing takes over me until I start shaking. The Clinique and Estée Lauder products sway in front of me, and I feel a pang of terror at the thought that this sophisticated makeover operation will cost me all the money I have in the bank till the end of the month. There are sudden and continuous streams of tears streaking down my thickly made-up cheeks, and the doll woman stares at me aghast because I have just destroyed her half hour of assiduous work on my face.

I manage to produce an almost inaudible whisper to ask: "How much?" The makeover specialist answers that it is free. I can't control the flood of tears damaging the makeover job on my face, yet I am ecstatic at the sound of the word *free*. I want to buy one product to show my appreciation for the kindness of this woman and of Marshall Field and Company. I can't decide on the product, my mind is painfully moving from one cosmetic product to the next, and I find it impossible to choose. Rivers of foundation and mountains of coloured eye shadow are dancing in my head until my eyes fall on a bottle of foot cream. It costs fifteen dollars, which is still more than I can afford, but in my happiness that I won't have to give my entire monthly salary for the makeover, the amount seems almost irrelevant.

I rush out of the Marshall Field's store holding my package like a trophy. My chest is heaving like a pump and strange wheezing sounds are coming out of my throat. Marta and Rhonda take turns holding me and making me drink little sips of ginger ale that I spit right out. I miss Marta and Rhonda, too, although they are right here next to me. I miss Mexico and Laos and Vietnam and all the Indo-Chinese mountains and jungles. I see Mexican minstrels with red scarves around their necks, playing languorous songs on their mandolins while the hearts of Cambodian children are hanging like peaches in the trees of the jungle.

I find myself in my apartment, burning with fever and coming in and out of something that feels like slumber. At some point there are tractors in my room staring at me with huge black, silent eyes. I am floating somewhere across the green ocean and am just about to drop inside its roaring waters and be eaten up by sharks. The remains of my body will be scattered into little pieces among multicoloured fish. Somebody is feeding me chicken soup. I think it must be Rhonda who keeps calling me honey. It's the only word I seem to understand. *Honey, honey, honey!* Everything has turned into sweet, creamy honey, and I am drowning in it.

Maybe I was never born in Romania, and I just imagined it so, after reading about Romanian culture in a book I had once bought at Barnes and Noble. Maybe I am actually Mexican from the sunny side of Mexico City, where the streets are lined with white stucco houses and cacti in bloom. Marta was my next-door neighbour, and we grew up playing hide-and-seek behind cacti and red bougainvillaea. Maybe I grew up in Nairobi amid millions of clashing noises and colours and women selling brightly painted baskets in the marketplace. I go into a dark tunnel filled with saxophone music, and then I come out of the tunnel and am floating on the river Nistru singing Beethoven's "Für Elise". I am sitting in the nook of a tree and watching the dirty waters of the river rush by me, counting the hours that I have left to live.

My mouth is parched, and I am drinking cold water from a porcelain cup. Slowly, the contours of my room start to take shape, and I remember that my name is Mona Maria Manoliu, that I was born in Bucharest on a summer day, and that this is my rented room in Chicago, which is now *my* home. I remember that I love Chicago. Marta and Daniela are sitting next to me on the bed. Rhonda is coming from the kitchen with a bowl of soup. I ask where is my foot cream, and Daniela hands it to me and says: "Here it is, Tía Mona."

"You were holding this for a long time, as if your life depended on it," adds Marta. Everybody in the room starts laughing, and I actually feel myself laughing, too.

Dancing with Tom

A FEW YEARS INTO MY AMERICAN LIFE, the dream I once had while watching *The Master and Margarita* in a Bucharest theatre starts to become reality as I pursue graduate studies in theatre at a sumptuous university by Lake Michigan. I learn about lighting systems and sound systems. I learn a whole new language for creating shimmering worlds on a stage, dialogue and movement, universes of feeling and gestures in violet and yellow hues. Fade in, fade out. The sound of storms, of dripping water, ringing telephones, a crying baby, a mewing cat. I can do anything. I can bring life to a dark, empty space, make the world, and then *poof!* Unmake and remake the world over and over again. With every new thing I learn, I am telling myself that it was all worth it; I am making it count.

I meet Tom McElroy at the library's circulation desk as he is borrowing Dostoyevsky's *The Brothers Karamazov*. He has a handsome profile, an aquiline nose, dark hair combed straight back, and a sexy moustache. He turns and looks at me as we wait for our books to be stamped. I notice the colour of his eyes: so blue, almost dark blue. There's a playful gleam in his eyes. I've never started a conversation with a stranger before, but this time I give in to my impulse.

"I love *The Brothers Karamazov*. It's one of my favourite books."

"And I love Western theatre," he says, glancing at the book I'm taking.

We talk for a while at the circulation desk, about Russian literature, heatedly, excited that we both know the same books. The woman at the reference desk is listening to our conversation. He says there's a party tonight for incoming and new students. I hadn't heard about it. I didn't know there were such parties. He asks, if I don't already have a date, would I want to . . . ?

"What's a date?" I ask.

"When you go out with someone you like for the first time," he says, smiling. "Or the second time, in fact."

I'm relieved he doesn't say anything about my accent or ask me where I'm from. I ask if he plans to ask for a second date. He starts laughing, and then I'm laughing because he's laughing. The woman behind the desk scowls.

At the new students' party, I dance with Tom for hours, like I haven't danced since Mihai and I danced on New Year's Day at Radu's house as the snow was falling relentlessly outside. My body is full, alive, and Tom's arms and chest are solid and comforting as he swings me to the different rhythms: rock and roll, salsa, reggae. This music beats through my body and makes me forget my worries. I realize I've been craving this for so long, to be held and swirled and held again, and Tom McElroy is just the man I need. He likes Russian literature, he hasn't mentioned anything about Dracula or Nadia Comaneci yet, he loves to dance, and he holds me as if he could hold me for ever. He is getting his PhD in psychology and works part-time as a high school counsellor as part of his training.

Within a month, I move into Tom's one-bedroom apartment in a redbrick building on the North Side of the city, on a quiet residential street lined with maple trees. Near our street there is a small green area that Tom calls a park, with large wooden structures for children to play and climb on. I like our Chicago street and our next-door neighbours, a Puerto Rican family with a five-year-old boy who always says *Hola señora* and then giggles.

By the end of the year, we've decided to get married in the spring. It's the mid-eighties, one more year and I can apply for my American citizenship. I feel comforted and content for the first time in a long while, maybe ever. I start wearing men's blazers and black tights, as if I've stopped caring about being feminine. I adopt the self-assurance and nonchalance of a man, an American man. I experiment with this new American me: boyish, shaggy haired, irreverent, and careless. I stuff Mihai's image deep down into the cellophane-wrapped keepsakes in my mind, where I cannot see his green eyes shaded by the longest eyelashes in the world. He is all squished up at the very bottom of the package where I keep my Romanian past.

We go to blues bars in hidden buildings on the South Side of Chicago, gritty and exploding with life and rhythm, and to rowdy Irish bars, because Tom is Irish and proud of his heritage. I prepare Romanian dishes for us, inventing as I go along, discovering almost with apprehension domestic pleasures I had never experienced before. In our chase for rationed flour and sugar, in the shadow dance with the secret police, domestic life in Romania was improvised and chaotic, swinging from the monotony of the same unsatisfying meal for the fifth time in a week to the intense joy of having found something new after queuing for two hours: two hundred grammes of cheese, a can of sardines, a kilo of peaches. Then there were the holidays, when the entire family mobilized to spend days in a tangle of queues winding through the city, just to accumulate enough ingredients for a Christmas dinner or a birthday party. Tom loves everything I make. He prepares dishes sometimes, *casseroles* from cookbooks and recipes his mother sends, or a special Irish bread named potato farl that is golden like the Romanian *mămăligă*. Between my theatre classes and teaching job, the inebriating rhythms of the blues and the modest excitement of chopping up green peppers and tomatoes side by side with Tom, I feel my little stringy roots spreading out, taking hold with a ragged determination like a stubborn plant sprouting through the Chicago pavement.

Tom and our graduate student friends teach me how to smoke marijuana and educate me about everything that is bad about America: the capitalist imperialism of great oil companies, hatred and inequalities based on race and gender. They tell me that freedom of the press is an illusion. Sure, you can swear at the president in a public square, but so what? You can't change anything, because the media is owned by the big corporations anyway. I discover the music of Bruce Springsteen and Sting.

One night at a party when I'm high on marijuana I do a headstand in the middle of a room full of people, my blue satin skirt billowing over my face. My gestures seem discontinuous, syncopated, like the movements of a marionette, like I'm seeing the seconds and the minutes unfold in separate streams, like the eight o'clock flower on my grandmother's grave blossoming with a *pop*. A vision of me as a child sitting with my mother on the Ferris wheel in the park with swans where we went the day the Russians invaded Prague passes in front of my eyes like a film clip. We keep going round and round on the Ferris wheel, which is moving faster and faster. Other such film clips pass by me, but the one I keep rewinding over and over again is one of Mihai driving a white car to meet me in Bucharest in front of the enormous white building called Casa Scînteii, the headquarters of the Romanian newspaper called *Scînteia*, the *Spark*, House of the Spark. This is the main Party newspaper that my father says is filled with lies, one bloody page after another. I am standing in front of the enormous white building wearing a yellow polka-dot dress that is too short and too tight, and Mihai keeps driving in circles by me without stopping, just waving a red scarf out of his car window. I hate the House of the Spark and I stand in the middle of the street, trying to make Mihai stop, but he is still driving in circles around me waving his red scarf, and then the film clip starts over in the room with people talking about President Reagan.

I love the song "Hungry Heart", singing it upside down as blood rushes to my head, because I have the hungriest heart you've ever seen, like Lady Lazarus in Sylvia Plath's poem – *I rise with my red hair / And I eat men like air.* I will eat all the flowers in the neighbourhood, like when I was seven and I vomited my lime-coloured bile, and I will eat the bad capitalists and the imperialists and the dishonest reporters, and I will vomit them all back out with my green bile, like the Big Bad Wolf in the story. Tom says we have to go home, that I'm not feeling well, but I say I'm feeling *just fine*, and can we hear that "Hungry Heart" song again?

Naturalization

IN THE SIXTH YEAR of my residence in the United States I
get to appear for my naturalization interview, in order to
become an American citizen. I am wearing my best dress, a red-
and-blue paisley silk dress that I bought at Carson Pirie Scott on
State Street before Tom and I went to a wedding party. I figure I
must look good and prosperous for my interview, to show that I
am worthy: a respectable permanent resident. Tom offers to
accompany me to the immigration office in Daley Center, but I
ask him to let me do this on my own.

As I am sitting before the immigration officer, suddenly my
aunt Ana Koltzunov comes to mind. The wild green Black Sea,
on that stormy summer afternoon when we got lost, bursts in
front of my eyes right here at the table where I'm being naturalized. The officer has just asked me something from the very end
of the questionnaire, about whether I would fight in a war
should the United States go to war.

The question takes me so much by surprise. I say, "On whose
side?"

The officer looks at me with mean eyes and wipes the sweat
off his flat, shiny face before he answers.

I correct myself and ask him, "What weapon?"

"Excuse me? Could you repeat that, please?"

"What weapon would I be using?" I ask. "I know how to shoot

a rifle. We shot a rifle every week in high school as part of our patriotic education, and I can do that. I can shoot a gun."

He isn't really following me. This is not the way naturalizing interviews are supposed to go.

"Does this mean yes? Is your answer to this question yes, that you would?"

To his utter horror I say, "Oh, I'm sorry! No, of course I wouldn't go to war. I wouldn't fight in a war, should America go to war."

My answer really baffles him. It irritates me how I had to pronounce the word *war* three times. I think of the two brothers across the bloody field lost and searching for each other as the sun shone aslant over the corpses. I think of Ivan taken as a prisoner of war and lost for twenty-five years. I think of my Bessarabian aunt who held me to her bosom in the rain, of her son Petea who made her so worried that she had forgotten the way home.

I tell the officer again, "No, no. I wouldn't fight in a war."

He asks whether I would help in any way, in case of a war, "such as care for the wounded. Be a nurse, for example."

When I answer yes to that part, he seems pleased that there's some common ground between us.

This scene stops making sense: the square, windowless room, the neon lights, the man with a flat, shiny face filling out a form and asking me questions about wars and the wounded. I think of the stories my father used to tell me about when he was a nurse's aide in the war, at fifteen. He saw the brains of soldiers with head wounds. He saw their brains pulsing through their crushed skulls.

I don't want to be naturalized any more. The word makes no sense to me anyway, as if I were unnatural. I want to get out of here. I think about telling him I have relatives who went to the USSR and engaged in forms of barter with the Russian population, and others who did time in the harshest of political prisons in Romania, and yet others who fell dead on the floor at the mere sight of the handwriting of a beloved person, and that a gypsy with raspberries was my relative, too – if I said all that, then he'd end the interview, they'd deport me, and I would never have to be naturalized again. What my fate might be if I were deported back to Romania is something so bleak and so frightful that the mere thought of it makes me tremble as I fidget in front of the naturalizing officer, feeling overdressed and ridiculous.

I think of the last time we saw Ana's son, Petea. It was many years ago, when he stopped by our house asking if we could put him up for the night. He looked haggard and haunted. The secret police were after him, but he couldn't tell us why and didn't want to get his mother in trouble. He told us not to tell Ana we saw him. Ana Koltzunov had tears in her eyes for the rest of her life. I think of Sergeant Dumitriu and of the shadows following me every night on my way back from school. I think of the scrawny man in the pastry shop, of the old man dripping brown soup into his beard, of my father's arrests. To where would I be deported? Where would they send me? *Mona Manoliu*, I say to myself, *it's better to be naturalized than to be deported back to that nightmare you left six years ago.*

The officer goes over to the next room and asks his colleague to join us. They whisper for a while in a corner of the office, and then they come over with strained smiles on their faces.

My officer says, "So, you're a conscientious objector. That's what you are."

He writes this down as the answer to the last question. I am finally naturalized as a *conscientious objector.* The long line of my relatives, with their stories of wars and floods, partings and reunions in train stations, look at me sternly, a row of stern faces, blue-eyed women and dark-haired men, neatly reflected in my great-grandmother's mirror.

Disintegration, Reintegration

A VOID SETTLES IN OUR MARRIAGE. Tom becomes more distant and irritable, as if now that we've been married for a couple of years, we can finally withdraw inside our own worlds and wait for old age like two strangers. I can't really point to the exact moment when Tom started treating me as a roommate instead of as his wife. Maybe it was the night when I went over to kiss him as he was reading Carl Jung's book on the collective subconscious and he pushed me away, saying he had a lot of work to do. His PhD orals were coming up, didn't I know that? Then it all escalated into a quarrel. I mentioned to him that, if anything, reading Jung and all that stuff about dreams and sexuality and the feminine and the masculine should make him want to kiss me more; then I blurted out that I had a great love in Romania, when I was young. He blurted back that I should just go back to that love in Romania. It was then that I felt the snap, a sudden rift. I was lonely, intolerably lonely, in our Chicago apartment. I wanted to pick up a suitcase and go. But I didn't really have anywhere or anyone to go to. So I didn't move from the armchair and thought, instead, to just give Tom some time; it will all get better.

Little quarrels that used to make us laugh and gave us an excuse to hold each other tight – *I'm sorry. No, it's my fault, forget it* – now stretch into hours, sometimes days, of debate and resentment, hostile glances, shouts and silences. Always silence. I feel that there is something I'm missing, as if I were doing something wrong all the time or as if something were always in its wrong place. Words get worn out, lose their meaning, and become empty sounds. *Light switch. Checking account. Toilet seat. That tone of voice. You clean up. No, you. Clean up, clean up, clean up, up, up.*

I think I've made a mistake. Nothing fits any more. Everything is a reason for a quarrel. When did this happen, how did it start? I'm all confused, because I don't see how I can get out of this. *This* is my marriage, and I wonder how I can survive for another forty years, fifty years . . . or just another year. Somehow *this* seems harder to escape than Romania or Gladys and Ron's house. Fate, some kind of cosmic randomness, dropped me into those situations. But *this* is what I have created and planned and promised myself with a clear mind and a pure heart.

I miss those first months with Tom, when we just laughed, listened to blues and squeaky Irish songs, chopped up vegetables, and talked about the glories of Russian literature and avant-garde theatre. I don't understand this new puzzle in my life or how to solve it. Sometimes I used to think that everything follows some kind of classic plan, that after overcoming many obstacles, the princess finally reaches her destination; there's a prince in a golden carriage surrounded by white doves who takes her to his calm, peaceful kingdom. A kingdom where she can rest after all her rambling and finish her theatre degree and delight in little domestic pleasures. I don't understand all this emptiness.

Mihai occasionally appears in my dreams, usually with his back towards me, sitting on the bench in front of my aunt's house or turned only halfway so I can see his profile as he is staring at something in the distance, on the other side of the street. Some mornings when I wake up not knowing where I am and I look at the back of the man sleeping next to me, I have the illusion, for maybe a fraction of a second just before coming to full consciousness, that it is Mihai's back moving slowly up and down in the rhythm of his breathing. We are finally together, it is not clear in what country and in what city, we are just suspended somewhere in the world, finally living our love freely, what I had once dreamed of.

When Tom rolls over and says *Good morning, honey,* I experience something like a sudden fall, a dull thump in my consciousness that brings with it a dull sadness, a dull sense of foreignness, everything dull, dull, dull, like a wedding without dancing.

It is around this time that my mother calls to tell me that the red shoes have arrived. My parents' immigration papers came through; they got their passports. They are arriving next month. It seems like my salvation. My parents will come and make it all better, solve all the problems in my marriage, and get Tom to straighten out.

I drive to the airport by myself. I don't want Tom to come with me. I want this reunion to take place just among the three of us, the way the disintegration of the family had taken place among just the three of us in the cruel April of hyacinths and daffodils in our Bucharest apartment when we decided I was going to try leaving that summer. It is May in Chicago, with warm gusts from Lake Michigan shaking the freshly exhibited yachts on Lake Shore Drive.

I'm sweating and having little earthquakes in my body, like the aftershocks that follow an enormous earthquake. *It's the earth settling,* people said after the '77 quake in Bucharest, whenever we felt more little shakes and were ready to rush down the stairs or jump out of the window.

I am standing in front of the large metal automatic gates at the international arrivals terminal, next to hundreds of other people who are waiting for relatives from all over the world and staring intently in the direction of the gates. Relatives from Poland and Senegal, from Vietnam and Burkina Faso, from Italy and Algeria, the whole world gathered at the gates for international arrivals. My head is buzzing from all the languages spoken around me, and I am counting in my head in Romanian, *unu, doi, trei, patru, cinci, şase,* counting seconds until I see my parents, not wanting to take my eyes off the gates, not even to blink, until my eyes are tearing from the effort of not blinking.

I see them before they recognize me. Then my father sees me, and his face beams. His hair is whiter, his figure more bent over. He's thin and old. My mother looks almost unchanged, though her round blue eyes shine bluer than ever. I let out a little scream, and my father starts to weep with jerking sobs.

The first thing my father says is "Our airplane almost crashed and fell into the ocean. I'll never take the airplane again, never again in my life."

"You're crazy. Don't listen to him, he's exaggerating," my mother tells me. "We just had a little turbulence."

"Turbulence?" says my father. "We were almost turned over and thrown into the ocean. That's all we needed, after all we've been through."

I laugh through my tears. It's like we've been separated for only a day, a long, long day during which I've moved about a dozen times, got married, finished one degree and started working on another, got a job and then another, and started having marital problems. And on that same long day, my parents had to apply to reunite the family according to the law for people who have first-degree blood relatives abroad. My father was dismissed from his job at the Ploieşti Institute, thrown out in a big humiliating scene in front of the whole university, and treated like a traitor to the country and the Party because he was leaving to reunite with his daughter in America. My parents had to survive without work until their emigration papers came through two years later. Aunt Nina, Uncle Ion, and Aunt Matilda helped them survive and get through the ordeal of waiting without jobs, without money. My father is dragging the enormous old leather suitcase that we always took with us to the seaside, and my mother is carrying a newer black suitcase that I don't know.

We talk nonstop on the way home in the car, our stories swirling together as we try to tell everything at once. "The secret police are meaner and stupider than ever. There's barely anything to eat. We practically starved for two years, survived on bread and potatoes, and even those were hard to find. Ceauşescu is building this monstrosity, the Palace of the People. Even the taps in it are golden and studded with diamonds. While the people are starving, can you imagine? He is in the last stages of his madness," my father says, squeezing shut his steel-blue eyes.

"The Securitate are swarming and squirming around like rats on a sinking ship," he goes on. Then he laughs and says as if he were telling the world's greatest joke: "They finally took their claws off me, the morons, once it was known I was emigrating, I was of no more interest to them. It's all over," he adds gloomily. "But something is going to happen soon," he says in his old prophetic way, "mark my words, something is in the air."

He asks what news of Romania we get here in America and is stunned to hear we don't hear much about Romania at all.

"Don't you listen to Radio Free Europe?" he asks.

"We don't get Radio Free Europe here," I say, almost embarrassed. "We get hundreds of stations and channels, though."

"What good are they if you can't get Radio Free Europe?" says my father, and I am glad to see that the humiliating years in Romania on the edge of starvation have not killed his spark, or his anger.

"Look, Mama! There's the Sears Tower, see? And look, Papa, there's the Chicago skyline, the Loop, see that?" I say proudly, as if the city belonged to me.

"Oh, so big, so modern," says my father. "Is that what all of Chicago is like?"

"Not all of it. It's a big, big city," I say. "You can find everything."

"Can I find work? Work in my field?" my father asks.

"We'll talk about that later, Miron, let the girl catch her breath," my mother says.

I am stunned by my father's question and by my own inability to give a reassuring or informed answer. What will my father do in Chicago at his age, with his background in Latin, Romanian linguistics and literature and with no knowledge of English whatsoever?

Tom is waiting for us at our window, waving from the first floor. I wave back at him, nudge my mother, who looks up through the car window, tries to smile and wave back. But my father is sitting in the front seat staring out of the windscreen without really seeing anything.

"We left everything just like that, a whole life . . . we just locked up and left with only a few things. The bastards must have already broken in, taken everything, and sealed off the apartment. To think of it, my mother's desk, all of my books . . . everything." His eyes are fierce with pain, anger, anxiety and every hard feeling on the face of the earth.

My mother tries to be light as she looks up at Tom, who is relentlessly moving his arms and smiling at the window. "Stop all this now," she says. "What's done is done, you wanted to leave more than anything else, remember?"

What's done is done, just like Letizia had said in the Trieste railway station, our fate sealed, our roots cut off, our past left behind. I lean over and embrace my father. He tells me not to cry, *We are all together now, what's there to cry for, it is just furniture after all.* Tom comes down to meet us and help us with the luggage.

But my parents' arrival does not perform the magic I am hoping for in my marriage. Now, with my parents living in our apartment and sleeping on the pullout sofa in the living room until they can get their own apartment, Tom and I are forced to argue in whispers, in the bedroom. Tom is exceedingly kind to my parents and does his best to help them with English, drive them around, and explain to them the news on TV.

Eventually my father gives in and starts classes at the same college where I've been teaching English as a second language. He takes the train every day to and from the college, holding the train pass my mother got him like a precious belonging in the front pocket of his blazer. He dresses up in his best suit every time he goes to his classes, as if he were teaching school himself. Sometimes we take the train together, but most often I go to work directly after my university courses. One day I run some errands after my performance theory class and end up at Howard Street station, where everybody transfers between Chicago and the suburbs. Close to the ticket area, I see a crowd and hear a lot of loud talking. I see my father standing in the middle of the crowd, with one of the train conductors taking him by his arm roughly and other people staring at him while he shouts in Romanian at the conductor to leave him alone and for everybody to go to hell. His face is red, his jaws are shaking in anger or as if he were about to cry. He has taken the train in the wrong direction to get to his English classes, has used up his ticket, and is trying to get through the turnstile in the wrong direction. He looks so desperate and diminished; his white hair is dishevelled, and sweat is pouring down his face on this sweltering Chicago September day.

I push all the people around him away, go straight to my father, whose eyes light up at the sight of me as if he'd seen his personal saviour. I tell the train conductor to leave my father the hell alone and learn to be more polite with people in the future, and I take my father by the arm towards the correct train track. He is shaking with anger and humiliation and tells me he does not want to die on American earth. As we get on the train and find an empty seat, he tells me he wants to be buried next to his people. He looks at me calmly and places his train pass neatly back in the front pocket of his navy-blue blazer.

My Lover Janusz from Belgrade

THERE'S A SUMMER WHEN my confusion strikes worse than ever. There are highways everywhere, and I'm riding on them, late at night, to my lover's house, in some distant part of Chicago. I still love my husband despite all the quarrels. I feel safe and secure next to him, but something isn't right.

I blame my estrangement on cultural differences. I blame it on my first love, who's not letting me love again the way I should. He blames it on his childhood and adolescence. We blame it on each other; we blame it on ourselves, on our parents, on and on. We struggle, we argue, we cry, we make up. I'm like Emma Bovary: *Oh my God, why have I got married?* But I'm not like Emma, really. I grew up in a Marxist country, after all. My biggest fantasy wasn't about falling in love; it was about killing our president. I think it's funny that even people who didn't grow up in a dictatorship still find ways to make each other miserable. I think it's funny that Tom is studying psychology and yet has so many problems of his own. Marta tells me it's classic, that many people who want to become therapists have plenty of problems, and that's why they choose that line of work: to get away from their own stuff. I tell Marta that makes sense, but I don't want to be the one dealing with Tom's problems; he can be his own therapist.

My husband is angry all the time for no clear reason. I get

angry because he gets angry. Then he says I get angry too easily. I tell him it's because I lived under a totalitarian regime and now I'm an exile. Why shouldn't I be messed up? I can't understand what he wants from me. He tells me we need to learn how to communicate better, and I have no idea what is wrong with my way of communicating, and I don't like talking about talking. Our arguments sound vacuous, and they remind me of the arguments of the people on *Dallas*, the one soap opera we used to get in Romania, between five and seven on Tuesdays. Although we used to watch the actors, their fabulous wardrobes and cars in fascination, we would always end up saying things like *These people have nothing interesting to argue about, they need a month of Romanian communism, then they'll have something to talk about.* And the following Tuesday, we would all sit in front of the TV again waiting for Pamela and Sue Ellen to roll their eyes and argue with JR and Bobby.

I start *seeing* someone else. I leave home on some pretence and drive the highway recklessly at night to *see* my lover. He is a Serbian man, a contractor I meet in the rain one evening. I'm walking in the rain past a historic building that's being renovated for condos, when I stumble over a bunch of bricks. I curse in Romanian, the worst Romanian obscenity I know. He helps me get up and tells me in Romanian *That's a pretty bad word.* Then he says: "You from Romania. I know a little Romanian. I am from Yugoslavia."

The word *Yugoslavia* gives me a little shock. I see Biljana and my two days in Belgrade, my hitchhiking escape that started at the train station. It all flashes through me as I stand in front of the Serbian man with a tanned, high-cheekboned face, a bit wrinkled and askew but somehow irresistible, and as I hear him tell me in a Serbian accent the few Romanian phrases he knows. He speaks English with an even thicker Serbian accent.

"I take you home. You all right? You hurt leg. Sorry! I work here, but workers not do good job and leave materials in street."

I tell him, "I'm OK. It's nothing. I have to go. Good night."

But he's worried and offers to take me home. I say, "Thank

you. I'm all right, OK? Please, my husband is waiting for me," and I run home.

Over the next few days, the image of the Serbian man keeps coming back to me. A yearning I'd forgotten has opened up in me, a weird and implausible longing for Belgrade. In the days to come, I keep passing by the building that is being renovated in the hope of meeting him. Which I do, several times. Many times. We have coffee he pours from his thermos, then one day coffee from a café. Then a snack, then one day lunch, then a glass of wine. I tell him my story. He is proud that his country had some role in my escape from Romania, and that I liked Belgrade, which I really never did. I just say that to be polite. Something in his manner makes me feel familiar and at ease. A current that passes between us when we sit in little cafés and laugh at memories of absurd events under Communist rule in our respective countries, and something in the way he flirts with me and kisses my hand over the cappuccino, makes me aware of what it is I am missing with Tom. We become lovers in his rented room at the other end of the city, past many highways and exits, on a little side street, and soon I become quite fond of Belgrade after all.

I live in a fun-house hall of mirrors. As I sit on the yellow-and-green sofa of our living room and watch Tom read his Russian and German literature and psychology books, multiple halls of mirrors reflect my many lives in a watery shimmer. There are always two images of Mihai. One has his face turned away, and I know it is the morose, unpredictable Mihai, the Mata Hari Mihai who betrays me by having shady dealings with the secret police and who denounces us and uses information about my father that he passes on to his superiors among the Securitate. He sleeps with Anca Serban and is probably responsible for the death of my childhood friend Cristina. The other Mihai looks straight at me, and his eyes are sparkling in the setting sun like emeralds. He smiles his most alluring smile, and he is a noble dissident working for an underground organization reckless in his acts of courage.

Janusz is walking towards me in this hall of mirrors and asks me to dance with him in a dimly lit Russian restaurant. We swirl among the tables in the fluid rhythms of a pop song about a lady in red, and his bony irregular face resembles that of a Hollywood actor. A Serbian Clint Eastwood. I let myself swirl on the little black and white squares of the dance floor. I get pleasantly dizzy and infatuated as my pink silk chiffon dress from a second-hand store on Halsted Street whirls in wide circles revealing my thighs. Afterwards we go to his rented room on the West Side of Chicago and make love until two in the morning. The highways are raw as I head back to my and Tom's apartment, the moon has a metallic glow, and the cars' headlights whizz by me like enormous fireflies. I am chipped like my great-grandmother's mirror, and my music box isn't playing "Für Elise" any longer.

Orange Moon over the Highway

THIS IS THE SUMMER WHEN my son Andrei is conceived. A merciless drought sets in across the American Midwest. The temperatures rise to one hundred and ten, and the sky is like white glue every day, with no forecast of rain. It's illegal to water your grass or wash your car, the radio says. Parks are as yellow as wheat as I speed by them on the highway to the house of Janusz, my Serbian lover, a refugee like me. It's comforting to love someone who isn't American, someone whose English is filled with awkward expressions that he translates directly from his own Slavic language. He says things like *I give you eat now food like in my country.*

The sweltering summer nights smell like scorched grass, overheated pavement, and petrol. The moon has an uncanny yellow tint to it as it hangs low and huge over the midwestern highway. My son is conceived in the worst drought of the century, when acres of parched cornfields, brown and brittle shoots, surround the city like a desert and nothing wants to grow. Except the round, pink nut in my uterus. A stubborn seed.

One evening I get into a huge argument with Tom, another psychological knot I can't untangle. It has something to do with the light not being turned off, which somehow triggers painful emotions from his childhood. I complain about always cleaning up, about the mess in the house.

"You goddamn husband you!"

English swear words still don't come to me easily, so I start breaking china. I compensate for my lack of English obscenities with the smashing of unwashed china from the sink. The dishes go flying all over the kitchen and one just barely misses Tom's head.

"Get the hell out of the house! Go get a lover or something!" yells Tom.

"I already have one – thank you for the suggestion – and am pregnant, too!" I yell.

The very second I pronounce the words, I know this is a big, big mistake. I instantly remember what Vincenzo, the Italian widower who wanted to marry me, always told me: *Remember this for ever, Mona: Even if your husband finds you naked and making love with another man, do not ever, but ever, ever admit it. Don't ever admit you've cheated on him. This is my advice to you for your future.*

He also told me, *Even if you don't want to marry me, I'll still watch out for you.* I thought it was funny at the time, as we listened to Italian minstrels play heart-wrenching love songs on their mandolins, but now Vincenzo's advice echoes in my head like the wisdom of Solomon, and my own spiteful slip echoes in its full, complete, unforgivable stupidity.

I'm a huge red lump of fury and surprise. Tom's mouth hangs open, and there's an endless, heavy silence. I wish there were some way I could take it all back, a convincing way to say *What did I just say? Forget it. I just said that to get back at you.* But my mouth stays shut, and I realize that since I really am pregnant, I can't take back that part. The suspicion is already there, the poison spilled out between us, over the mound of broken dishes at our feet. What's the point of saying anything any more?

I feel sorry for Tom as I watch him pacing around the room like a tiger in a cage. His face is red, and now he's yelling the angriest words he can think of. I am thinking maybe I should have just stayed in my stupid Communist country where I belonged. I never should have come into this man's life to mess it up.

He calls my parents, who have recently moved into their own apartment, and asks them to come over right away. He tells them on the phone that I'm a whore and he wants to divorce me. Before he finishes talking, I leave the house to clear my thoughts and try to decide what I am going to do. I find myself driving in the direction of Marta's apartment, near Ashland Avenue. Marta is reading with Daniela from a book of Mexican stories. As always, she is happy to see me and asks me if I want anything to eat. The smells of refried beans, guacamole, and fried tortillas welcome me and trigger memories of my first winter in Chicago. She makes me a margarita and heats up a burrito, and Daniela hugs me and tells me *You look sad, Tía Mona.* Marta listens to me tell her what happened: "*Chica,*" she says, "you've gotten yourself in some pickle. But a child is a child, if you want to have it, just be happy. It doesn't matter about the father. Things will sort themselves out. And Tom is not a bad man, you know. He will make a good father."

Marta's vague but positive advice helps me to calm down, and as I sit on the bed in her main room I suddenly feel a wave of something new, a different kind of joy and anticipation. As if that vague longing to have a child that I'd experienced on the train to Trieste as I was leaving my country and listening to the crying of the baby and watching her suckle at her mother's breast has suddenly awakened in full bloom. *A child is a child,* I repeat Marta's words in my mind, this is not a worse time than any other, my parents are here with me, and my marriage with Tom can still be salvaged. I am forging ahead in my studies and will soon have a teaching job. I am no longer the rambling, aimless thistle I had once thought I was. I rush back home feeling better and ready to tackle my problems with Tom and to plan for the new baby.

But when I get home, my parents and Tom are lined up on the sofa in the living room as if at a wake. My father's uncombed hair sticks up absurdly. I don't dare to break the heavy silence. I am staring at my swollen ankles. Then Tom starts calling me *whore, whore*.

My father asks, "What is *whore*?"

"Leave her alone," my mother snaps at him, then turns to Tom. "Calm down, we'll find a solution," she says, her voice low and conspiratorial.

"A solution?" yells Tom. "I don't want any solution with this whore!"

Then Tom starts crying. I bite my nails. Both of my parents light cigarettes. Tom is crying in big sobs and saying to me, "How could you? All the trust I had in you, all the love – it's all over now."

I start crying, too, and my mother tells me in Romanian that whatever happens, she'll help me raise the child. My father looks at me with deep sadness in his eyes, but in a flash so quick I almost miss it, he winks at me and smiles, as if to say *Don't worry, it's going to be all right, we'll stick by you no matter what.*

"Let's go to a marriage counsellor. I am so, so sorry I hurt you," I tell Tom.

I'm so proud of myself. I've learned all the important vocabulary for situations like this. I'm a real American.

He wipes his eyes and asks, "Why? Why did you do it? Aren't you happy with me?"

"Yes, I am happy. But . . . but I felt lonely, without love."

He cries some more and says maybe he deserved it.

"No, you didn't deserve it," I tell him. "I'm just confused. But I want to be with you."

"What about the baby?" he asks.

"We'll just have the child and raise it, that's all," I say, aiming to sound full of self-assurance.

My father goes over to Tom and slaps him jokingly on the back and says to him, "Whore." Then he laughs. Every time my father learns a new word, he has to repeat it several times. My mother tells him to stop saying stupid things, so my father asks her to tell him again what exactly *whore* means. My mother blushes and looks away, and then tells him the Romanian word for it.

My father lights up another cigarette, because he doesn't like anyone calling his daughter this. But he also understands Tom and is sorry for him, and that's why he chooses to smoke rather than to punch him, for example. We're all flushed. The Chicago heat is unbearable. This is the longest drought of the century. We're all trying to fan ourselves, and my body feels swollen with fluid.

Tom decides to stay. He says he'll try to forget what has happened. I know he'll never forget. But we go on with our daily routines as if everything were back to normal, whatever that line of normality might have meant so far. I am more and more drawn into the movements and rhythms of my own body. I take special pleasure in my new heaviness and in feeling my weighty steps on the ground, as if I can be sure no gust of wind or fate can push me away any longer.

As weeks go by I see that my father is not happy in America. The fact that I am not sure who the father of my first child is gnaws at my brain at night as I am trying to sleep. My father is not proud of me. He doesn't scold me. He stands by me because he would stand by me even if I had committed murder. But I can see he isn't proud as he'd been when I wrote beautiful compositions in school or when I passed my entrance exams at the university among the top ten. Of all the things he expected me to accomplish in America, having a child without knowing who the father is was not one of them.

My mother teaches all the languages she knows in part-time chunks at colleges and universities in the area: Italian, Russian and French. She is irritated with me for having made *such a mess* of everything. I tell her glibly that in America people make a mess of their lives and then they go to therapists. But she gets mad at my frivolous attitude and says this is no joking matter; this is another human life I'm bringing into the world.

My father tells her to shut up. He's sad all day long because he doesn't have the Communists to fight against, and because he doesn't have the music of his native language around him, and because he doesn't like the tomatoes in the supermarkets. They are tasteless, bad, bad tomatoes. I sometimes go shopping with my father in tiny grocery stores on Clark or on Devon, where women in brightly coloured saris and Russian men and women fill the streets in a constant flow. We buy a special kind of tomatoes called hydroponic that taste better and are juicier than the ones in regular stores like Dominick's. On those occasions, my father lightens up and asks me to buy him unusual things that he's never seen in his life, like hearts of palm and star fruit, or things that he has craved for years, like figs, dates, and Italian salami. He talks to me about their last years in Romania, how nightmarish everything was. "God knows what has become of all those people I used to work with, who knows," he says. "Maybe now they are preparing something really big. But I wouldn't know," he says, shaking his head. He felt he had to cut all relations with them before leaving, to not risk having his passport revoked. "Because all I wanted was to come and see you, my Mona," he says.

One day as we are buying tomatoes in a Greek grocery on Devon, my father looks at me and tells me I look so beautiful in my pregnant state, and then he adds out of nowhere: "That boy, that Mihai of yours, he was a good boy." I almost drop the double-headed weirdly shaped tomatoes that I am holding and the basket filled with jars of fish roe, dates and feta cheese. I stare at my father and ask him to explain himself, why is he saying this now, had he seen Mihai since I had left, does he know anything that I don't know? My father refuses to answer. He just repeats, *Mihai was a good boy, that's all,* and then he makes another unrelated comment: "I have one wish: I want to see my country one more time before I die."

The months go by. The rain comes, and the weather turns cold. I feel warm, pleasantly covered in fat. I dream of Eskimos cutting through the ice at the North Pole and eating the raw eyes of the seals they hunt, like I saw in a documentary on TV.

I've stopped seeing Janusz. I told him it was over. Sometimes he still calls, but I tell him to leave me alone. Tom says he has forgiven me, that it was his fault, too, no woman goes to find her happiness elsewhere if she is happy at home, he says. So he'll do his best to make me happy, he says, stroking my belly. Then he kisses me on the mouth, and I enjoy the feel of his lips on mine the way I used to in the first years of our marriage.

Execution on State Street

I NEED SOME LAST-MINUTE CHRISTMAS GIFTS so I go, as always, to State Street. It's early on Christmas Day, and I am desperately hoping I may find a store that is open, a little electronics boutique, for instance. I'm immensely pregnant, and I feel like a huge ball walking down the pavement, but it feels good to be out in the stinging air. I like to see the windows at Carson's and Marshall Field's decorated with mechanical animated scenes.

A group of children is playing African drums in the cold wind, *bud-um, bud-um, bum, bum.* It fills me with a feeling of warmth, familiarity and lightness. Why do African drums resonating on State Street on a cold winter morning make me feel so much at home? As if Romanian peasants carrying water from the well in the blue dusk are seamlessly connected to Africa, its heat and its unimaginable colours, carried halfway around the world by this group of children making music in the whipping wind.

As I walk a little farther down State Street, I stop and stand unmoved in front of Woolworth's. The president of Romania, Nicolae Ceauşescu, is on one of the TVs on display in the window. It must be afternoon on Christmas Day in Romania. Ceauşescu and his wife are sitting sideways at a desk in a dimly lit office, and they keep denying everything that the interrogating party is asking them. Ceauşescu bangs his fist on the table. Elena stares blankly in front of her. Then they are being dragged outside into what looks like a macabre yard and made to stand in front of a firing squad.

Those faces that looked down on us from every wall of every important building are now terrified and gaunt, begging for their lives. Some people – my countrymen – push them around, tie their hands. Nicolae and Elena, who watched us in our most intimate moments, whose secret police kept us terrorized and compliant, those two people who had us herded into squares and made us stand for hours in the sun, the rain, the snow, so they could listen to us cheering for them, are being dragged by angry Romanians out into what seems to be a wooded yard somewhere on the outskirts of Bucharest.

The children keep beating their drums, *bud-um, bud-um.* It's cold and windy on State Street. I remember my hallucination in Biljana's apartment, in my restless sleep that night in Belgrade, how all the people sitting and talking on my bed were saying that Ceauşescu's days were numbered. And now, Elena and Nicolae are hunched over against a wall, terrified, two ordinary people begging for their lives. A group of soldiers points guns at them; there's a bunch of shots following each other impatiently. Many silent shots, over and over again, as if the soldiers couldn't get enough of shooting the Ceauşescus. In the window of Woolworth's, the execution of the president of my country is replayed again and again. Now they are there on the ground, a small pile of twisted bodies and bloody clothes. There they are on CNN, lying in a pool of blood, their own blood at last.

How odd – instead of the bone-deep satisfaction, the limitless joy, I always thought I'd be feeling when this moment came, all I feel is pity and disgust. I hold on to my huge belly and feel the baby kick, a stubborn jolt of life.

Then I see images of tanks firing in the Palace Square in Bucharest and of people running in all directions. The CNN footage is edited so that one minute we see Ceauşescu's last speech in the big square interrupted by the roars of the people saying things like *Down with the tyrant,* the next we see huge crowds in the streets screaming against the Party and Ceauşescu and walking arm in arm in a huge compact and fiery mass. The next moment we see again people running for cover while others are shooting. And then again – the execution of Nicolae and Elena and their lifeless bodies lying on the ground of a courtyard. A full-fledged bloody revolution played and replayed on the television set in the Woolworth's window.

During the last couple of days, I have spent most of my time in my parents' apartment, and almost as soon as I would get home to Tom, I'd call for them to come over so we could watch the news together. "Now Romania is in the news all over the world," I'd tell my father proudly. But he didn't seem to hear anything that was being said to him and would keep saying how he wanted to be back in Romania, could my mother get him a ticket, right now. He was sure all of his old friends from the group he had joined for several years while we all lived in Romania prepared for what was happening.

After another replay of the execution, as I stand in front of the television set on State Street, I hear the almost inaudible voices of the commentators mention in passing the city of Braşov as one of the cities where people have been fighting in the street. An image of the city centre flashes by quickly, with people running alongside the walls of the buildings I know so well. My heart feels as if it's about to explode. I hold on to my pregnant belly, searching for balance. I can think only of Mihai. I imagine quick clips of him, as if in a slide show: Mihai in his room brooding and smoking Carpaţi cigarettes furiously. Mihai in the streets of Braşov, wearing his hiking boots, shooting at someone. Mihai in the streets of Braşov, again in his hiking boots, only he is the one being shot at. Mihai walking in the streets carelessly, recklessly, among bullets.

I walk farther down State Street, and stop in front of Marshall Field's. I stare at Santa's sleigh and the reindeer figurines moving in the store window. I'm wondering what's wrong with me, why can't I feel relief? All I feel is angry and exhausted. I stand motionless with my hand against the cold glass of the Marshall Field's window as Santa's elves and many reindeer rotate and turn towards a miniature golden sleigh, over and over again, and as drums are beating with a steady rhythm.

A New Destiny

I AM BACK IN BUCHAREST, lost in a district of factories on a grey November afternoon. There are no people in the streets. In my dream, I have the memory of America, of Chicago by the lake in the summer, and of my university classes, of me listening to the professor lecture about avant-garde theatre. I can see the lake through the window, and I'm feeling free and elated as a breeze passes through the classroom and touches my hair. But this is only a memory, and I know I will never be able to get out again. That's it, it's all over. They're going to get me now. I won't be able to leave again, not ever, ever again. Why, my God, did I ever come back? I don't even know why I'm back in Bucharest. Maybe to get my grade book from the university, or maybe to see Mihai. But Mihai doesn't exist any longer. He was crushed in the earthquake, under the building where they make cream puffs. I am sinking into a grey gelatin, and I scream so loud that I wake myself up. Tom is sitting up in bed. I am soaked in fluid.

My water has broken, and I realize I'm starting to give birth. But I feel so sleepy, so lazy. I don't feel like giving birth to anyone right now. Who can have a baby at one o'clock in the morning when they're waking up from a nightmare? I don't want to go to the hospital. I'll just go back to sleep. I'll feel better in the morning.

Tom is getting dressed already and telling me to get dressed. I tell him that I don't want to, I just want to sleep. But Tom insists. I curse at him. Then a sharp cramp cuts through my groin. I roll out of bed and get dressed.

When the contractions start in earnest, I'm out of breath. I fall asleep for ten seconds between the pains. There's nothing to say, nothing to think about or to want except for it to be over. Tom is holding my hand. The nurse asks me if I want a Popsicle, I tell her *Fuck the Popsicle!* My back, my groin, my belly are all erupting. I'm not screaming, just sighing, and I tell everybody to *fuck off.* Tom laughs.

The nurse says *Now you can push. Just one more half hour to go.* I feel my eyes bulging from the effort. Surely they're going to pop out. My eyes, my veins, my neck – everything is bursting open. Something is cutting me in half, and then that same something comes out, gliding. In less than a few seconds, all the pain stops. I have a boy. I have a plump, perfect boy, greedy for life and for my milk. A whole new destiny bursting into the world!

I am giddy and excited, grateful the pain is over. My parents come in trembling with emotion. My father, who was hoping for a girl, is surprised it's a boy. He thinks the baby is beautiful, like a bundle of light, and that he's never seen a baby like this. *And is he normal?* he asks. Tom is holding the baby.

We call him Andrei, because this name sounds nice in all the languages. After the worry of the last nine months, I am hoping so hard that Tom is the father. The baby's dark hair reassures me. But somehow it doesn't matter because I'm swelling up like a balloon in my contentment. I am fat and hard, and this is my baby boy, born in America on a spring day in the year 1990. A new decade, a new child. I hold Andrei all night long so that when he's hungry, he only has to open his mouth. The avid tug of his mouth on my nipple in the night fixates me in the fleshiest and sweetest corner of reality.

Pink Flamingos

WHEN MY COUSIN MIRUNA ARRIVES from Romania a few years after the Romanian Revolution of 1989, Tom, my parents, our little son Andrei, and I drive to meet her at O'Hare on a bright November morning. My parents lag behind as we walk the long concourses to the international terminal. Andrei is in the Terrible Twos, and keeping him under control becomes a battle while we wait for the plane that finally pulls up to the gate three hours late. I am startled to see Miruna coming out of the gate at a brisk pace and with a confused look after more years than I care to remember. She smiles her unique smile, her chicory eyes are watery, and she seems smaller than when I knew her.

As soon as we're in the car, Miruna squeezed between my parents, with Andrei in his car seat in the back while Tom drives, I propose we go to the zoo. For some reason even I don't understand, this is suddenly very important to me. We *must* go to the zoo. I want Miruna and Andrei to see polar bears, chimpanzees, flamingos. I have a million questions I'm dying to ask her. How was her first sexual experience? Who was he? Is she in love with anyone? What was the Revolution really like? Is it true people were just shooting wildly in the streets? Most important, I want to ask her if she's seen Mihai. But somehow I don't know how to begin after so many years. Besides, I'm so proud of my brown-haired, plump little son that I want to take Miruna somewhere that's more his world than ours, where he can show off and laugh and use his new words like *giraffe* and *pumpkin* and *snow*.

I can see from her look she doesn't understand my insistence on going to the zoo. Her eyes are covered with a film of weariness. She's exhausted from the long flight and bewildered by the blur of traffic on the expressway, but I see something else in her face: she's tired of everything. Gradually, after we get home, she starts talking. She tells me how for the last couple of years before the Revolution, when she was finishing her engineering degree in Bucharest, things had got so bad that people were just millimetres away from starvation. She managed to survive that period by eating pretzels and apples. There was almost nothing to eat, but she found a store in Bucharest – "You know, near where you guys used to live in your last apartment," she says – where they still made good pretzels like we would get in our childhood. And her father could still get apples from his family's orchards in northern Moldavia. She tells me about her first job as an engineer out in the country. She worked in a tiny unheated shack in the middle of a field so muddy that she had to wear rubber boots up to her knees just to get there every morning. I want her to tell me over and over again about the apples and the pretzels and the office in a sea of mud. She survived working in the bitter cold. She walked two miles of muddy country roads to get to an unheated office. She wore big rubber boots to get to her work. I am in awe of Miruna, remembering the little girl I used to play with, who has survived all this. My quarrels with Tom again seem so trivial.

I tell Miruna about how incredulous I had been on those December days about what was going on in Romania, and how our Revolution was the most violent in all of Eastern Europe, and how proud I was of my people. But then I add that I wasn't so proud of the way they had dealt with Ceauşescu. "Why did they have to kill them like that without a proper trial?" I ask.

"You know, Mona, while I was living in Bucharest," she says as I serve her some hot chocolate, remembering that it used to be her favourite drink in the world. Even in the summer on hot days, whenever we would go out into town with her sister, Riri, and her parents, and everybody got ice cream and cold sparkling water, she would always ask for hot chocolate. "Yes, while I was living in this apartment in the centre, next to the Military Circle, and I would sometimes stand on my little balcony and Ceauşescu would pass in the morning on his way to the National Assembly," she says, sipping her chocolate, her eyes closing from pleasure at the taste, "I would have this very clear image in my head of myself slowly pouring petrol on top of Ceauşescu's car and, immediately after that, throwing a burning torch over it and then watching his car explode and the two of them burn alive right under my balcony. And I would be the author of it," she concludes, looking very satisfied.

I stare at Miruna with my mouth wide open. This is a Miruna I had never known before, much different from the sweet and gentle little girl of my childhood.

"Can you keep me here for a while?" she asks. "I mean, I don't want to go back, I'd like to try to stay here, if you can help me. Things are moving very slowly back home. It's going to take time," she says. "And I don't have the patience any longer. I'm tired."

I am stunned but also ecstatic that Miruna has decided to stay with me in America; everything will be so much brighter and more cheerful with Miruna next to me.

"But how about Nina and Ion?" I ask. "Won't they be devastated if you stay?"

"Well, they'll get over it," she says, and again I am surprised by this new Miruna who is so cool and tough. "They have Riri, you know. She is stronger, she can take it, and she can wait until things get better. Besides, she doesn't want to leave anyway, she is happily married. Like you," she says and smiles. I smile back and do not say anything.

As I show Miruna the bedroom that she is going to share with Andrei, I can see how tired she is and that she doesn't want to go to the zoo; she just wants to be in bed. But the more I realize this, the more I make an issue of it, as if there's nothing in the world more important right now than going to the zoo. I can tell Tom is exasperated, but since the baby, he's been working hard to control his temper. Even my parents get into the argument, telling me I must be insane to want to drag poor Miruna to the zoo on such a cold day.

Miruna says nothing, but she looks more and more puzzled, trying to follow this argument in English and snatches of Romanian. She stares at me as if she's trying to decide what's wrong with me, if I've gone nuts or something from living in Chicago, but when my mother asks her what she wants to do, she's polite and says it doesn't matter, then meekly admits she'd prefer to stay at home. I tell her *no*, she can't. If she wants to live in America she's got to see what America is all about. So to the zoo we go, in our Mercury Marquis that Tom's parents gave us because *you have a family now*. Andrei is ecstatic and climbs into the backseat to play with Miruna's black hair. I point out the sights like a tour guide.

"See? This is Lake Shore Drive," I say excitedly. "Look at the high-rises. Aren't they beautiful? Down there is the college where I teach ESL. That's English as a second language.

"This is Lincoln Park," I tell her as we inch along behind taxis and buses, looking out at the leafless trees. "And here we are at the zoo!"

We put on our scarves and gloves and hats. We see the polar bears and the giraffes, so Andrei can say his new words over and over again, and the elephants and the penguins, whose walk Andrei imitates with amazing precision to the amusement of another family. We go to the flamingos last, as we always do. They're Andrei's favourite. The flamingos are in a huge glass cage in the winter, illuminated by yellow heat lamps, and their concentrated pink under the glass makes Miruna exclaim in wonder. She's never seen a real flamingo before.

We stare at the statuesque pink birds standing on one leg and twisting their long necks to look at us. Andrei is running around and around the glass cage, pointing at the flamingos, when I hear the woman nearby telling her daughter in Romanian *Uite mami ce frumoşi sunt* – Look, Mummy, how beautiful they are! It makes me want to laugh. Romanian parents sometimes use the diminutive for *mother* or *father* when they address their children. A Romanian family, apparently, is made up of a big mummy and a little mummy, a big daddy and a little daddy. I could never understand the logic of this when I was the little mummy, and it strikes me now as absurd and sweet at the same time. Then I realize that the woman has just spoken Romanian. I turn to look at her. She has a happy look on her face. I smile and ask her if she is Romanian, and then we ask each other what cities we're from. Amazingly, she's from Braşov, Miruna's town, Mihai's town. Miruna tells her she just arrived from Romania that morning, and the woman is impressed, her eyes wide and sparkling. She's been living in Chicago for five years. She is so happy that she's found another Romanian family in Chicago. I feel Miruna quivering with excitement next to me, as she starts talking heatedly with the woman, whose name is Lucia Vlad, about their beloved city, the streets they each lived on, the schools they each went to.

Meanwhile I notice that Andrei is getting more excited than usual and is screaming, "Mummy, mingo pumpkin!" He calls flamingos *mingos*, but I have no idea what he's trying to say. In the middle of the flock, two flamingos are copulating. Andrei keeps yelling louder and louder, "Mingo pumpkin! Mingo pumpkin!" Maybe he's trying to explain that the two flamingos glued to each other are round like a pumpkin.

There are pink feathers flying around, drifting in the cold breeze. Miruna says that the flamingos are like pink storks, and the Romanian woman agrees. They start talking about the villages around Braşov, how there are so many storks perched on roofs, the way they stand on one leg on the tile or the thatched roofs of old houses. The woman says maybe they're white flamingos. Miruna says she's flown halfway around the world to look at pink storks, and they both laugh.

The woman's little girl is also pointing at the two flamingos having sex. She jumps up and down. Andrei keeps saying, "Mingo pumpkin, mingo pumpkin!" over and over. Pink feathers are everywhere in the air, and we laugh so hard I have to crouch down so I don't pee in my pants. Miruna is laughing and crouching, too, and Tom is shaking with laughter as he chases after Andrei, trying to catch him. Andrei wants to go to the pumpkin flamingos to touch them, but Tom catches him and holds him up on his shoulder.

I look at my son. His chestnut hair is shining in the afternoon sun streaming through the glass. A pink feather is stuck in his hair, and his blue eyes are glittering with joy. The Romanian woman is holding her daughter's hand, laughing. After ten years, this has been my first contact with another Romanian exile. My cousin Miruna is right there next to me laughing about *pink storks*. I picture in my mind as clear as a photograph those white storks standing on one leg on the chimneys of peasant houses in a Romanian village as I'm looking and laughing at the pumpkin flamingos. I know Miruna is feeling joy and sadness together, just like me. She's thinking of how she left everyone and everything behind just yesterday. Maybe this is a good omen for the beginning of her journey as an exile, these funny, ethereal flamingos. Tears of laughter are streaming down her cheeks. I know they are also tears of sadness on her first afternoon in America.

But then, as we go to gather my parents from their park bench, Miruna holds my hand and looks at me guiltily, as if she's been hiding something from me. She whispers to me in a raspy voice, "You know, he died."

I don't get it. "Who?"

I almost don't pay attention to her because I am looking at Andrei running to his grandparents. Tom runs after him through patches of brittle leaves that cover the pavement.

"Miruna, who are you talking about?"

"Mihai died," she says in the same throaty whisper. "He died. He died in the Revolution."

Why does she have to say the word *died* three times? Somehow it still doesn't register with me. He died, he died, he died . . . three times, that verb in the past tense. What does it mean?

On the way to our apartment in the car, I look at the waves of Lake Michigan. I ask myself, *Why am I riding in a Mercury Marquis along a green lake with this man beside me, with my child, my parents, my cousin?* Then, suddenly, I get it. I will never be able to see Mihai again. Not ever again, as long as I live. I start sobbing in the car wanting him, aching for him. Why did everything have to be so twisted in my life, always a moment too late, a moment too soon? I sob in the car as we are rushing past the high-rise buildings on Lake Shore Drive. Tom looks at me as he drives. He has no idea what's going on. He probably thinks it's because of Miruna's visit, that my joy and relief at having her with me finally have tipped over into something else.

"It's over," I say aloud to myself through my cries. "It's finally over."

Andrei starts crying, too, because I am and because he doesn't know what's over. He thinks Miruna is leaving already, or that we'll never go back to the zoo again. He asks through his tears, "What, Mama?"

I don't know what to say to him. I hold his hand and tell him not to worry, it's nothing. I tell him we'll be home soon. Later, I put Andrei to bed, and I watch the early sunset out of his bedroom window, with Miruna standing next to me. I am thinking that in classic plays, like the *Iphigenia* that I saw in Bucharest when Mihai used to work at the tractor parts factory, everything happens during one full rotation of the sun, from sunrise to sunset: arrivals and departures, bloody sacrifices, murders, suicides and deaths, political upheavals, love. Everything during one full rotation of the sun.

My Own Little Wars

I t's dawn, winter grey dawn in Chicago, a month after Miruna's arrival and the news of Mihai's death. I slide in and out of sleep, restlessly rushing out of my usual nightmares and sliding back into more dreary fantasies. I find myself in the Piazza dell'Unità d'Italia in Trieste. It turns out everyone has been waiting for me, because when I appear in the piazza all the noise and the cheering stops, and the hundreds of people gathered there are staring at me.

Two men approach me and take me by each arm and make me walk towards the very centre of the piazza right in front of the big sumptuous palace. I find out that I am to be publicly beheaded. I am seized with terror and try to escape, but their hold on me is strong, and they force me to climb up the five steps that lead to the scaffold that is laid in gold and has red velvet on the square where they are supposed to perform the beheading. I am shaking and thinking of Andrei, who will have no mother, and what they will tell him about me when he wakes up and asks for me; how will they tell him that his mother ended up beheaded in a piazza in Trieste?

The executioner is standing with his back to me, wearing a classic executioner's hood, waiting for the moment. He turns slowly towards me and lifts up his hood, and I see it is Mihai, clean shaven and smiling. He stares at me both sweetly and frighteningly, the way he did in my dream in which he slit my throat. I know that I am being decapitated because I ruthlessly left my country and my love and my family and because I forgot about everyone, and that this is an act of vengeance. These are my people who are a vengeful and cruel people and who executed their president and his wife in an alley in Bucharest on Christmas Day. I ask Mihai if it was he who also killed Ceaușescu, and he nods with the same smile. *This is what we do with enemies of the country,* he says slowly, *all traitors and enemies, we kill them all, but we have prepared this special feast for you, because you are special, my love.*

Tom's arm is stretched across my chest, and he is snoring loudly. I try to breathe deeply and calm the rapid beating of my heart. I push Tom's arm away, and I rush into Andrei's room. He is sleeping on his back, with his mouth slightly open and an angelic smile on his face. I stare at him and try to shake myself from the frightening dream. I touch him gently to assure myself he is there, real and safe. As I go to the bathroom of our new two-bedroom apartment on Irving Park, I feel a wave of nausea rising up in my throat and a recognizable dizziness. Like when I was pregnant the first time. I throw up last evening's dinner and am crying at the same time because I hate vomiting and I didn't want to be pregnant again.

I remember my dream and find myself missing Mihai even in his executioner's cape and hood, his clean-shaven face beautifully framed by his black hair and his green eyes sparkling in the night as he looks at me next to the scaffold in Piazza dell'Unità d'Italia. *Mihai is dead, Mihai is dead,* I tell myself as I wash my face, as I have told myself every morning since Miruna gave me the news during our eventful visit to the zoo on the day of her arrival in America. I tell myself this sentence every day so that I can better get used to this news. A little bit more every day, but never fully, just like Zeno's paradox, never fully getting there.

I get dressed in a hurry and go to the Walgreens in the neighbourhood to get a pregnancy test. The Chicago winter air feels unusually stale and stuffy for this time of year. I come back into the apartment slowly, trying to be as quiet as possible and not wake Tom or Andrei. Despite myself I feel a strange sense of contentment when the test is positive. Maybe with this new child, who is definitely and unmistakably Tom's, our family will be strong and whole, a classic American family, our marriage will get better, Andrei will have a sister or a brother, and I will forget Mihai once and for all. He is dead, and I might as well get over the whole thing, live in the present, and be happy with Tom, Andrei, and our new baby.

But with each new month of my pregnancy I feel farther away from Tom. If only I could have seen Mihai one more time. Everything is so unfinished, and we never properly said goodbye. I drown myself in my work, trying hard to finish my doctoral thesis before the birth of the new baby, and I am focused like the other time on each new movement and the rising of fluids and the life inside my body. I go through the motions of our everyday life, which I pretend is a good and happy life and everything I had ever wished for. Miruna is now living with my parents; I even have extended Romanian family close by.

I defend my thesis on European avant-garde playwrights early in the new year, on a cold Chicago day, trying to control the heartburn mixed with nausea rising in my throat as the professors on my committee ask me complicated questions about performative choices.

Soon after I get my degree I manage to find a position in the theatre department of a small university in Indiana. *Crossroads of America* say the licence plates on Indiana cars. That's good enough for me. I am made for crossroads, always choosing this direction or that one, greedy and ambitious, always running up against new obstacles or creating my own. This flat land of crossroads is soothing to my heart. Indiana is a stone's throw away from Chicago, I console my family on a visit to campus. Andrei can see his grandparents every weekend. I have a teaching job, one chestnut-haired, blue-eyed boy, am expecting another child, and come autumn we will be renting a house on a residential street in a small college town in America.

And Mihai died in the Romanian Revolution, I suddenly think as we are driving back to Chicago. A random bullet hit him in the head during all the shooting on Christmas Day, Miruna said. A *hero*. But not quite a hero, since the bullet was random. Would he have had to be shot by a deliberate bullet to be a hero? It's not true that I've put him to rest in my mind, because I didn't see him dead, I've never seen his grave. I have never felt his absence in the city at the foot of the Carpathians.

Mihai and Mariana were both killed by head wounds, freak accidents, I think as we get out of the car in front of our apartment building on Irving Park. I'm almost jealous. It's as if the parallelism of their deaths makes their story compact and coherent, whereas my own story with Mihai hangs like a loose limb, across the years and oceans and foreign lands I've crossed. I touch my belly and stand in front of our car trying to be content. I kiss Tom and ask him what we should have for dinner and tell him I want my parents to eat with us tonight. Tom makes his broccoli-and-noodle casserole, and my mother prepares the Romanian meatballs that Andrei loves. I sit next to my father and tell him we should think of visiting our country soon, now that communism and Ceaușescu are dead. He agrees, but now only vaguely.

The summer when we are supposed to move to Indiana before I start teaching in the autumn, there are record floods in the Midwest. They will continue the next summer, too. Flood after flood, until the earth turns mushy and reddish, and crops and houses and vegetable gardens are floating everywhere. It seems I have brought with me the disasters my Romanian ancestors faced at the beginning of the century.

One evening when I feel so estranged from Tom that I might as well be living with one of the neighbours on Irving Park, I tell myself I have to absolutely free myself from this marriage or I will slowly suffocate and die. As I am reading a Brothers Grimm fairy tale with Andrei, Tom starts nagging me about a new credit card bill with purchases I made when shopping with my father on Devon. Andrei starts crying as he hears us fight again, and it is then that I tell Tom I want us to get a divorce, I want us to separate, there is no need for him to move with us to Indiana, I want to be free, free, free. I don't care about being pregnant with his child, I feel I have to do it now, not wait another moment, that if I wait until the baby comes, I might never have the courage to do it. It's now. I want my freedom now. Tom stares at me and says, both angry and resigned, "Fine, you'll have your freedom, if that's what you want."

Everything seems to be disintegrating, turning muddy and mushy. I have never achieved that clarity of thought I dreamed of on my train ride through the Carpathians so many years ago. Just more confusion. Giving birth, getting a divorce – they're all harsher when you're not on your native soil. You give birth and grieve and divorce, all in a foreign language.

I cry in big sobs when Tom finally leaves. We all have to leave our apartment before the end of the month, when I move to Indiana with Andrei. Tom has to stay in Chicago for another year to finish his graduate degree and his year as a counsellor at the high school. Then he might try to move closer to us and start a practice as a therapist, he says as he takes Andrei in his arms and kisses him on both cheeks. We both cry, despite all the fights and the recriminations through the years. I have a bad, sour taste in my mouth. He says he will come to Indiana to be at the birth, around the time when the baby is due. I realize this must be the single craziest moment in my whole entire life. *How many women actually start a divorce when they are pregnant with their husband's child*, I ask myself as I watch Tom ramble aimlessly around our apartment. And not a bad husband either, as Marta always said.

As we stand in the middle of the living room and Tom says good-bye to Andrei and I see our family break in the midst of packages and suitcases, I can't help questioning what my life is all about. I cry all night, feeling I've failed miserably. When you're a refugee and you fail, it's even worse. The whole point of becoming a refugee is to start afresh and succeed, to build a new life that's better than anything your ancestors imagined, better than anything you could achieve in your pathetic home-land burdened with communism and hunger and disasters. Your relatives in Romania have pictures of you at your gradua-tion and your wedding sitting on their mahogany cupboard. They think you're happy and your life is perfect, and you can't find a way to tell them the truth.

As Tom is loading the U-Haul, I realize that no one in my family, no one for a hundred years, has got a divorce. And here I am in the middle of the flat, muddy, flooded Midwest, alone with a small child in my arms, with no idea of what to do next.

I wonder what my grandmother would have said in such a sit-uation, the one who found her house ruined by the Russians, with big holes where the electric sockets had been and a couple of ripped-up dogs in the front room, the grandmother who scraped the ground for roots during the famine after the war to feed her children. She would have said, *Thank God we're alive.* That's what women in my family always said.

And I wonder what my maternal great-grandmother would have said, the one who saw her house torn apart by American bombs during the Second World War and dug through the rub-ble for her music-box mirror. She would have said, *Don't worry. We're safe. And look at this beautiful baby.*

My father regrets every day he wasn't there to work for the Romanian Revolution. He feels like a coward to have left every-thing for a country he doesn't even like. My mother suspects his dissident friends abandoned their secret activities more than a decade ago, after the execution of the generals who attempted a coup. They just faded away or were probably killed.

After dinner, whenever I visit my parents, my father goes back to the bedroom to write poems. He has an electric typewriter all to himself. He writes poems about an exile's suffering. He was happier when he typed manifestos on a forbidden typewriter. On Tuesdays and Thursdays he gives private lessons in Roma-nian to a woman named Molly who is preparing to go to Roma-nia; he doesn't know why. My father thinks she must work for the CIA, that she is secretly working to bring a new and better government to Romania. "Because this new government," he says, "is made up of just a bunch of recycled old Communists."

He talks about his childhood more than ever: the cherry and apple orchards, the war when he was a nurse's aide and he saw wounded soldiers' brains pulsing through their shattered skulls. Winters, sledding on the hills near his home. The time he jumped into a freezing lake to save a friend who'd fallen through the ice. Only his childhood stories seem to give him pleasure.

My father's stories also comfort me as I sink into the legal proceedings that eat up all my money and push me into depression. Listening to stories about the Second World War helps me feel less intimidated by greedy lawyers in Ralph Lauren suits. I figure if my family survived Hitler and Stalin, earthquakes, floods and famine, I can survive a few American lawyers. On a sad, hot and humid summer day in Chicago, I get into the U-Haul to move to our new house in Indiana. It is my father who gives me courage to go on and helps me make some sense this time: "Go, Mona. It's what you have worked for all these years, isn't it?" Then he quotes from a Romanian play: "*Zoe, Zoe, fii bărbată*, Zoe, Zoe, be a man!" I kiss him, put Andrei in his seat, and head towards Interstate 90.

Late in the summer, as we are settling in our rented house, the divorce and custody trials move to the Indiana courts. It all becomes senselessly fierce. The lawyers feed on our fears and vulnerabilities, Tom's and mine. Petitions and motions stuff our mailboxes. Just when Andrei is finally making full sentences in Romanian and English, I get a court motion made by Tom's lawyer that would take him from me and give custody to Tom. I read it standing in my kitchen as I'm about to prepare supper. Andrei is smearing tomato paste on his face and telling me about a boy named Steen who is mean and spits at everybody at nursery school. The motion says I don't care enough for my child because I take him to day care and use babysitters. I wonder how much lawyers and judges and the American government know about caring for a child at the same time you're working a full-time job. I don't see what's wrong with day care, where Andrei plays with other children and learns English, where he draws funny pictures of sharks and of himself in the garden with me, with a big yellow sun in the corner of the page and red tulips that are as big as the two of us.

Now more than ever, I want to eat up all the evil capitalists and lawyers I raged against that night when I was high on pot and did a headstand in my blue satin skirt. I have a she-wolf's hunger for blood, for lawyers' blood.

I am falling through a hole in the ice. Eskimos save me. They feed me raw seal eyes. I can't find Andrei anywhere. I go out of the igloo and in the distance I see Andrei in the blue down coat his grandmother gave him for Christmas. My steps are getting heavier and I am turning into a block of ice. I am freezing alive, yet I can feel everything and think clearly. I see the blue silhouette disappear in the distance with tiny, waddling steps.

I wake up screaming. Andrei is sleeping in the little bed in my room. I crawl in next to him and hold him against me. He wakes up and asks in Romanian, "*Ce mama?*" What, Mama?

"It's nothing, it's OK," I tell him. "Go to sleep, I love you."

He asks me if it's tomorrow yet. I say, "No, it's still today, but soon it will be tomorrow and we'll have to get up."

Midwestern Floods

THE SUMMER WHEN MY SON IONICA is born, it rains for an entire week in the midwestern town where I live and teach. An improbable omen, like something from a Latin American novel. Just like it did in 1918 in the Bessarabian town called the White Citadel. The rain taps day and night on the shingles until the roof gives in and starts to leak. We sit in the living room with a pail under the drip that comes from the middle of the ceiling, steadily, mercilessly.

For five days I sit in the living room nursing my new son Ionica and watching the drip, reading petitions and depositions and motions and court orders signed by esquires and honourable judges. Andrei tries to catch the drip on the tip of his tongue. It smells like wet plaster and rotting walls. The feeling of disaster lulls me into a state of indifference deeper than anything I've ever experienced before. Now that rain is coming into our house directly from the sky, my entire situation takes on a different light. Natural disasters along with the stack of petitions and court papers give me a strange sense of balance. I feel braver than ever, concentrated on the thought of pure survival.

Once a day I drive through town and watch, with a wicked sense of relief, the bulging rivers and the cornfields melting under brown water. Ionica's concentrated suckle at my breasts, the delicious pull of his mouth at my nipples day and night, gives me a hold on reality, a fixed point in space and in myself. Everything seems very clear: the drip from the ceiling, the regular suck at my breasts, Andrei's open mouth catching the drip, the words on the court papers and the signatures of lawyers and judges, the sound of the rain on the roof.

After a man with a long white beard who chews tobacco and calls me little lady comes to repair our roof, I sit with my two sons in the living room, happy that the roof is no longer leaking and that the sun is funny like an orange ball.

Soon after I start my new teaching job, Tom calls to tell me he is coming to Indiana to see Andrei and the new baby. I am anxious about the encounter and decide to scrub and clean the entire house, our rented house with a white wooden fence and an arborvitae in the front garden. I use up all the detergents I had brought from Chicago, and the recent smell of wet plaster from the floods and the leak in the roof is mixed with stinging Clorox and Windex smells and also with smells of baby puke and poop. I feel slightly queasy from the mixture of smells and the exertion.

Tom arrives in the evening and calls me from the local bed-and-breakfast to ask me if he can come over right now. He looks plumper than I remember him being, his hair is longer, and he is growing a beard. He walks into the living room confidently, pushing past the boxes with books and clothes and the new baby things, and Andrei jumps in his arms and screams, "Daddy, Daddy." He puts Andrei down and turns towards Ionica, who is sleeping in my arms with his head on my shoulder, and strokes his cheeks, saying he is a beautiful baby, so beautiful. Behind Tom comes a slightly older woman with red hair and very tight jeans, who walks into the house with the same self-assurance as Tom, goes past me, and heads straight to Andrei, trying to kiss him. Andrei turns his cheek away and puts both his hands on his face as if to protect himself. I stand in the middle of our new living room, among all our boxes and things, holding Ionica, and I say to the woman, "Excuse me, who are you?" Tom lets go of Andrei and informs me this is his friend Sandy, and can I please get Andrei's clothes and things ready for the road, since he plans to take him back to Chicago for a little while, Sandy can stay with him while he is at work in the morning. She doesn't have to work in the morning, and I do, and with whom will I leave the children when I am at work?

He elaborates and says he would actually like Andrei to live with him and Sandy in Chicago, and I can keep the baby. "It's a fair deal," he concludes. I am starting to sweat profusely, and I feel my milk let down furiously in my breasts. Yes, let's divide our children just like we did with the lamps, I think as I am trying to hold a steady point of balance in the middle of the room. You take the older child, and I take the little one. You take the green lamp from your mother, and I take the antique one with the iron stand. It seems to me rather improbable that I have actually married, lived for several years, and had two children with this man who is standing here in front of me saying such outlandish things. Sandy stares at me with an impertinent look, and I notice the thick black eyeliner around her eyes. She is attractive in what my mother would call a vulgar way. Feeling the tension in the room, Andrei comes to me and, clinging to my red knit skirt, says, "Mama, I want to go poopoo."

I take this as a good occasion to excuse myself and gain some time. I say with exceeding politeness, "Excuse me, please sit down, I will be right back." I push Andrei into the bathroom while still holding the baby. I sit on the edge of the tub while Andrei is sitting on the toilet, and I am thinking that maybe nothing that I ever did since that bloody train to Trieste was ever worth anything, that I would rather have had Mihai in my life even if he were to be secret police ten times over than find myself in this idiotic situation, this scene from a bad play: hiding in the bathroom with my two children while my husband, who has turned into someone unknown overnight, is laying siege over my life together with a red-haired woman who looks like a middle-aged hooker. But Mihai is dead, cold and hard as this marble here under my feet.

I stare at the bathroom window and at the black walnut tree

waving in the summer wind and fantasize about jumping out of the window with my two children and just starting to run across cornfields and wheat fields and among the majestic Indiana haystacks until I get tired and get to a different state – Kentucky, for example. Maybe in Kentucky, everything will get better for us. Ionica is shifting his position on my shoulder and is whimpering. I start nursing him to keep him from crying. I leave the bathroom to get the cordless phone in the hallway. I move stealthily like a thief in my own house, hoping Tom and Sandy will not hear or see me. They are sitting on the sofa in the front room, holding hands and staring out of the main window as if in a trance. Where did Tom find this woman, I think as I sneak back into the bathroom with the cordless in one hand and with Ionica nursing in my other arm, feeling like a circus acrobat. I call Marta. At first she says, "Ay, ay, the bastard, how could he do this to you?" But then in her typical practical and rational fashion, Marta tells me, "You know what they say, that possession is fifty per cent of the law. You have Andrei, *querida,* and the baby with you, just be firm and say he can't do anything without you first talking to your lawyer, just simply refuse to let Andrei go with him. Don't be intimidated, there is nothing he can do right now, there is no reason to take the child away from you, you're a good mother. Be tough, you can do it."

When I tell Marta about Sandy, she says, "At least he is not conventional, going after a younger woman, as other men would." I feel much stronger talking to Marta, who, before we hang up, says one last thing, "Mona, honey, he feels crazy right now, this is how men are, they go crazy when they see themselves suddenly without a wife, with no child, their family suddenly gone. Remember, as hard as it is, you have the kids around you, your life is fuller. But he is now alone in that apartment. Give him time, it will all get better, you'll see."

I come out of the bathroom with the children and tell Tom very politely that we need to talk to our lawyers first about visitation and that Andrei cannot go to Chicago with him right now. Andrei says he wants to stay with the baby and starts crying and pulling at Ionica's feet. Tom stares at me angrily, the way he did when he found out I had cheated on him, and says between his teeth: "You'll hear soon from my lawyer, Mona. Just you wait." I stare at him and Sandy and try not to say anything and not to be intimidated, as Marta has advised me. I just say, "Good-bye for now." Andrei, who is also sad that his father is leaving, goes after him and says, "Daddy, Daddy, when are you coming back to see us?" My heart is pounding as I pull Andrei and try to keep him inside the house. I feel spent from the effort and the tension, and as their car pulls away, I throw myself on the sofa in the living room, holding my children close to me and wondering what else the future has in store.

Dragons and the Social Worker

A SOCIAL WORKER COMES to have dinner with us to see how the children are getting along in my house, so he can testify in the divorce proceedings. The three of us are doing activities from a book. I go to the kitchen to prepare dinner. I just finished correcting one hundred and twenty-two exam papers the night before. Ionica woke me up three times in the night, one time to vomit the hot dog he had for dinner, another to drink some water, and then another to be changed because of his diarrhoea. I am tired to the point that the social worker, politely wiping his feet outside my front door, seems like an evil character from the Brothers Grimm stories I read to my children at night. Or maybe even the scaly dragon from the Romanian story my grandmother read to me, the story about magic golden apples. This dragon, who lives in a golden garden under the earth, abducts a beautiful princess. Eventually he gets chopped up into pieces by the youngest and smartest of the three sons of a king. The prince gets the magic golden apples in the end.

The social worker, with his neatly trimmed brown hair and a soft tweed jacket, with his nice-guy attitude as he tries to get the children to feel comfortable with him so they'll *open up*, seems like a cross between a cartoon character and a dragon. I am hoping my children don't bite each other's bellies or smear each other with snot or spit at each other the way they do when

I am too tired to pay attention to them. They get into fights about who took the string they found in the backyard or who's a butthead and who isn't. Ionica, who is now almost one and a half, has recently learned the word *butthead* in day care from a boy named Dante.

For dinner, I've made a Romanian cucumber salad and spaghetti with an Alfredo sauce I got premade in a pouch. The social worker likes the sauce so much he compliments me several times. When he asks me for the recipe, I tell him it's an old Romanian recipe that's too complicated to explain.

I ask Andrei if he remembers the tale about the salt in the food, a Romanian version of the King Lear story. The two oldest princesses tell the king they love him like honey and like sugar, but his youngest daughter tells him she loves him like salt. He gets so angry at her that he banishes her. She works for a year as a servant in a palace in one of the neighbouring kingdoms. The prince of this kingdom meets her, falls in love with her, and marries her. She invites her father to the wedding and prepares all his food herself – with no salt, just with honey and sugar. The king can't eat any of his food, and he gets angry. His daughter, the princess bride, stands up and tells everyone the story of how her father had chased her out of his palace because she had told him she loved him like the salt in food. Then the father realizes that salt is more important than just honey and sugar, and he feels ashamed. The king and his daughter reconcile, and everyone lives happily ever after.

Andrei tells the story to the social worker during dinner. It's his favourite story. Then Andrei tells the social worker one of the Greek myths he knows, the one about Hermes who stole Apollo's cows. This, too, is his favourite. The social worker is more and more impressed, and he comments on the cucumber salad and the Alfredo sauce again. He wants more spaghetti. He says I really have to give him the recipe.

All I can think about is the report he's going to give the court about *the mother's household*. Andrei starts mixing Greek myths and Grimm's fairy tales together until he's talking about sharks that eat people alive. Ionica starts screaming in his high chair because he thinks he's going to be eaten up by sharks, and I have to hold him and stand for the rest of the dinner to get him to stop crying.

I don't remember much of what happens after that. I remember the tiredness spreading all over me after the social worker has left and I look at the sink full of dirty dishes. Three of those dishes were the social worker's dishes. He is going to give recommendations to the court about Andrei's well-being and our living arrangements. The social worker's report, after one dinner with us, will determine whether I retain custody of my son. Exhaustion spreads through me like poison.

I want the blue snows of the Carpathian Mountains and their crystalline echoes. If only I could run away with my two children to the Carpathians and hide in some shepherd's house in a pasture where sheep graze. I stand in front of the kitchen sink clenching my teeth and staring at the dirty dishes. We would be living in the shepherd's cottage on top of the Carpathian Mountains where the air in the winter is so pure and so clear you can feel it with your fingertips. And we would eat goat's cheese that is smooth and white and salty-sweet. My two sons and I would sleep on a high straw bed, under a huge blanket called a *plapumă,* filled with goose down. I would feel them, peaceful and safe, breathing next to me on the straw bed, under the down *plapumă,* in the shepherd's cottage on top of a Carpathian mountain. Away from social workers and lawyers and judges and depositions and hearings and Alfredo sauce in plastic pouches. Under the stars of my own childhood, in the clear air ringing with cowbells and bleats of sheep and smelling of blue snow and dung and queen of the night. And I could speak the sweet, harsh sounds of my own language to my own children, without having to justify anything to a morose judge who mumbles his words into his beard.

The children start playing their cops-and-robbers game. I can't bring myself to wash the dishes. I join the game. Andrei and I are robbers, and Ionica is the policeman. I carry a sword and try to escape from the policeman chasing me. At some point, Ionica dashes out of the house and starts running down our street with his own golden sword in his hand, trying to catch other robbers who might have got loose in our neighbourhood. I run after him with my sword, calling to him hysterically in the cold November air. A neighbour looks out at us from her living room window. I'm in my slippers chasing after my toddler with a toy sword in my hand, shouting at the top of my lungs in a language that has never been heard before in this midwestern town of seventeen thousand people.

Tom's lawyer said in court that I habitually use obscenities to my children whenever I speak to them in Romanian and that is precisely why I use Romanian to speak to them in front of English-speaking people, so I can curse my children at will. Once, my *own* lawyer asked me if adultery is common in Romania. Is it a cultural thing, he wanted to know, and that's why I did it? But I have plenty of English swear words I learned riding the el my first winter in Chicago, and I tell him *Fuck you, mister, Romanians didn't invent adultery, you know.* At least my lawyer calls me by my family name, while Tom's lawyer just points at me in court and says *that woman.* I turn around during the hearings to see who is this *woman* he keeps pointing at.

The November air is fresh and chilly, and Ionica, with his plump little body and blond hair, running ahead of me on the crimson and orange carpet of leaves, is a beautiful apparition. It seems impossible to catch him. My steps are heavy, and he looks as if he might take off and soar into the chilly November evening with his golden toy sword held up to the sky, like the Romanian king Michael the Brave, holding his sword against the invading Turks, who must still be guarding the square where my parents lived the night I was born.

Then he stumbles and falls and begins to wail. Fear grips my heart, fear that neighbours are watching and will report this bizarre scene of *child abuse* to the police, fear that men in dark suits are going to walk into my house and take away Andrei and Ionica, fear that time is snatching minutes away from their childhood, rushing them away towards some unknown American future. I run to Ionica still holding my sword and carry him back into the house. He has somehow gone from crying to laughing in less than a second, and his face is red from the cold night air. He speaks to me in the language of Romanian shepherds, little sweet and harsh words, making the *r*'s into *l*'s, as all Romanian children do when they first start speaking. Romanian *r*'s are hard and round like cart wheels on cobblestones. It takes Romanian children a lot of hard work before they can pronounce their *r*'s, but once they do, they know the permanent delight of rolling the language over and over on their tongues, little rapid wheels, *rrrr*, hard and ticklish. Ionica can say only *l*, and he sucks his thumb all the time. He can run faster than either his brother or me.

Andrei helps me clean up and offers to wash the dishes. He uses too much soap, and the sink overflows with mountains of suds. He looks at me as if I'm going to scold him, but I just roll my eyes. A mountain of Palmolive suds is a more beautiful sight than the social worker's dirty dishes. Suds spill all over the kitchen floor. Ionica thinks they are marvellous. Andrei put suds on his cheeks to make a white beard, and his round blue eyes seem even bigger than usual. I wish again that we could all live in a shepherd's cottage in the peaks of the Carpathian Mountains. Instead, I tell them a bedtime story about shepherds living in little cottages on very high mountains, wearing huge coats made of sheepskin and carrying heavy sticks to protect themselves from hungry wolves and sheep robbers. Ionica asks me for a shepherd's stick to take to day care so he can fight with Dante, the boy who taught him *butthead*. We all sleep in one bed together tonight, with our gold and silver swords beside us for protection.

Indiana, Crossroads of America

I HAVE CHOSEN TO LIVE in the flattest, most boring landscape of the American Midwest, and I could call myself happy living in a university town where I teach drama and theatre. I love the flat, flat, wide, endless cornfields, where the sun rises and sets with a vengeance every day, having no mountains, no valleys, no undulating earth to hide behind. This space soothes my heart. I have the illusion, in its straight immensity, that my native land is just over the horizon. Just beyond that stretch of cornfield is the garden of my aunt and uncle's house in the Carpathians.

I bought my house on a whim, because it matched a white straw hat I was wearing one day when I was walking down that street and saw its FOR SALE sign. A delicate white house built at the turn of the century, it had round thin columns and a wide front porch. I imagined myself in it, in my white straw hat and in my pink linen dress, like an American midwestern woman in the 1920s, writing love letters on a rosewood escritoire. It made me want to have an American woman with an American past – a woman in a linen dress and straw hat sitting at a rosewood desk and daydreaming – as my great-grandmother. A woman who had been spared dictatorships, who never rode on cattle trains searching for refuge during the war or saw bloated bodies floating on a flooded river. I gave her a name: Jessie Gibbons.

She had bobbed thick black hair and dark brown eyes, and skin so soft and white you wanted to touch her face when you looked at her. The European wars were just a distant rumour to her. Her immediate concern was the ball at Ricky Danford's mansion on Sycamore Road. She wanted to wear the fuchsia satin low-cut dress, but her mother wouldn't hear of it.

I knocked on the door of the house and asked the plump, middle-aged woman who answered if I could look around. The high ceilings, the bay windows, the afternoon light flooding the rooms, the sculpted fireplaces, and the secret door in the kitchen that opened on to a secret patio with irrepressible ivy climbing everywhere – I immediately knew it. I had seen it somewhere in a dream. I often move around the house at night when Ionica and Andrei are asleep, each in his own room, and touch the banisters, the walls, the windowsills. I count all the things I've done that no one in my family had ever done, like working in the theatre, getting a divorce, smoking marijuana, hitchhiking in a yellow Fiat, owning a house with bay windows at the edge of a cornfield. I often imagine Jessie Gibbons getting ready to go to Ricky Danford's ball in her fuchsia dress and a long string of pearls, her dark eyes sparkling mischievously. She is fanning herself. It is hot and humid in the Indiana summer night, and it smells like honeysuckle everywhere.

In the silence, when my loneliness is sharper than ever, so many miles, so many worlds away from my birthplace, I feel my limbs stretch into strange shapes. They reach out past the walls of my house, past my street, past the welcome sign with its Elks and Rotarian logos announcing a population of seventeen thousand people, out into the world, across cornfields and the whitecaps of the Atlantic. But my arms, stretched thin as tendrils, crumble into dust just as I reach out to touch the lilac bush in front of our window or to pick a stem of the queen of the night. Just when I can almost touch the white rock on top of a mountain where the sun shining down on the clouds bathes Mona and Mihai in blue and pink light.

My arms become just arms, and I wrap them around my body.

I listen to the slow rhythm of my children breathing. I take turns lying next to each of them. I wrap my arms around their warm, sleeping bodies.

I wake up tired and grouchy from these nightly patrols. I drop spoons on the floor as I make breakfast and get the children ready for school and day care. As we sit around the kitchen table, I like to think we're a little nation of three people, a Romanian-speaking enclave in this little midwestern town; Ionica gets mad at me because I don't answer him when he asks for another bottle of juice. He calls me spider. It's the new swear word he uses when I don't pay attention to him. Ionica tells me I am "ten times spider, big black ten times spider".

I drag myself to the university to teach. Then it's time to rush from work and pick up the boys from school and day care. The judge has finally decided, after my psychological evaluation, to allow Andrei and Ionica to live with me and visit their father on weekends, holidays and for half the time in the summer. The court-appointed psychologist, a tired woman with lanky unwashed hair, showed me butterfly-shaped paint stains, and I had to tell her what they resembled, that is, the meaning of the splattered paint in the shape of butterflies and bats. I felt like I was back in first grade when we played with finger paints, squeezing colours from a tube and squishing them between folded paper. I invented beautiful gardens and meadows and seashells, and the psychologist took voluminous notes. Apparently, I was fit to raise my children after all. I wondered if there were any even marginally sane parents who said they saw mangled body parts of lawyers in black suits in those blotches of paint, after they'd paid twenty-five hundred dollars for the services of this depressed-looking woman. When the judge mumbled his decision, I felt sorry for all of us. I looked at Tom in his best suit and thought of my children sleeping next to me at night. Tom seemed sad as well and looked like the Tom I knew in our better days. He finally was accomplished and sure of himself, despite his melancholy air. He had shaved off his moustache and his face looked nobler than ever. I heard he had finished his PhD and opened his own family counselling practice in Chicago. For a quick second, I almost thought, Why didn't we try harder, why wasn't I more patient? Maybe everything would have worked out in the end, as Americans like to say. Everything except that I wasn't really in love with him. But I quickly shook myself from the thought, what's done is done, let's just get on with our lives.

Sometimes my limbs hurt as I lean over the kitchen sink and try to pull myself together to prepare another dinner containing all, or at least most, of the food groups written on the chart Andrei brought home from his health class: grains, meats, dairy, fruit and vegetables, no fats or processed sugars. Then I just make a big pot of *mămăligă*, the food of the Romanian peasants. Water, salt and golden yellow cornmeal. It has to be stirred a special way with a wooden spoon until your arm aches. People ate *mămăligă* five hundred years ago in my part of the world, just as I eat it now with my two sons in our kitchen on nights when I don't give a damn about the food groups they teach in school. We eat it with sour cream and butter, members of both the dairy group and the fat group, and my soul feels appeased, at least for the time of one dinner. A brief respite as the cornmeal fills me with its golden, heavy warmth. My children puff their cheeks at each other and grin.

Sometimes I'm angry that I do all of this alone. Where is that whole village raising your children when you need it? My body, collapsing on the bed, begs for sleep, and stretches out in its greed for sleep. Sometimes I feel like banging my head against every wall in the house.

Marta drives over from Chicago. She's now the head pharmacist at the drugstore where we worked together. She's moved into a bigger apartment. Daniela loves maths and drawing. She draws funny pictures of me and my two boys whenever we get together.

Marta takes over the kitchen and makes a dish of rice and vegetables. Daniela helps out with Ionica, who wants to kiss her all the time and wants her to draw a Tasmanian devil for him.

Ionica tells his brother that if he keeps tripping him the Tasmanian devil that Daniela drew will eat him up. I calm down a little. Tonight we are a big happy family speaking Romanian and Spanish and English. Marta and I drink a little tequila and laugh through dinner.

"You'll find someone who is worthy of you," Marta assures me, "you will marry again and be happy."

"I don't want to marry anyone," I tell Marta. "Not again . . . Maybe if you were a man I would have married you." We laugh and pass the bottle.

"You are strong. I don't know what will happen, but I know you'll make it. Don't worry," Marta says and hugs me.

I feel like Marta is my blood relative, one of the no-nonsense, feisty women in my family. If only she could stay with me, if she and Daniela could move in with us! But she has to get back to Chicago, to her work. I cry for hours after Marta and Daniela leave and I have to face tomorrow all alone again. Another week of gritting my teeth and hoping I don't drive off a bridge, hoping I don't drop dead in the middle of a lecture and have to lie there with my students staring down at me. The department chair would come into the classroom and stare at my dead body and say, *I knew I shouldn't have hired that crazy Romanian. I knew she would be trouble. Now what am I going to do with the body?*

Something goes wrong. The plot of my life has got too complicated; there's too much of everything. I have been too greedy, and now I am paying for it. I am tired and my brain is burning. A big hard knot sits in my throat all the time. I'm always scared of making some big mistake, of overlooking something disastrous. I dream, I have visions. I move in and out of sleep, and in the evening I let myself daydream for hours. But during the day I keep precisely to my schedule. Breakfast for the children, work, pick up the children, take them to piano lessons, soccer, birthday parties, cook dinner and get them to bed. Correct papers, balance the checking account.

I wake up feeling strange in my head, heavy and squeaky. I move in clouds of eccentric words and scarlet gestures that smell like the Romanian cornmeal mush, *mămăligă*, like the Black Sea the Roman poet Ovid described, like the Puerto Rican oregano I grow in my garden, like the French cancan, like scorched petunias on summer nights. Ideas have shapes and colours and bodies. Ideas dance on pointed shoes and make pirouettes in white and pink tutus. Ideas are blue and red and white and look like violet water lilies opening up through cracks in the smooth, cool surface of a pond.

Thank God I work in the theatre, where madness can be an asset. What would I do if I were an engineer or an accounts payable specialist? I move in and out of words with ease, in and out of languages: Romance languages, Germanic languages, Slavic languages. They slip off my tongue lightly and create iridescent and incandescent patterns like little fireworks. I let them float into the air in my classrooms towards wide-eyed students. I release them like balloons in conference rooms towards serious, bearded, grey-haired scholars who think I am *charming* but then never listen to what I say. I launch them on stages of school theatres towards weary audiences who yawn and nod asleep.

The Atlantic Ocean

M Y MOTHER LOOKS AT ME MISCHIEVOUSLY from a photograph my father took on the beach in Florida. They went to Florida in the summer a few years after their arrival in America, to visit an old colleague of my father's from the university who had also emigrated from Romania and had settled in Florida. It turns out that this friend, whom my father had thought was just another refugee, like himself, used to work abroad for the Romanian secret police. A year after my parents visited him, an assassin put a bullet in his head at the dinner table in front of his wife and children. It appears that the government actually sent some of their secret police abroad to follow people who were denouncing the abuses taking place in Romania. Two years after the 1989 Revolution, a Romanian university professor was shot dead in a lavatory at a Chicago university. My father said it was still the secret police in agony.

"He knew too much," my father says about his friend. "They had to get rid of him." My father is sorry for his friend's violent death, though he's shocked to discover his friend had been an informer all that time. He feels betrayed and sickened and sad to realize a friendship is gone in more ways than one.

My father is not well: his heart, his lungs, his kidneys, all of him is slowly melting, stopping. He looks haggard and has lapses of memory. Sometimes he is not sure whether he is in

Chicago or in Bucharest and asks my mother to go with him to the University Square, to his favourite tobacco store, where his friend Lucian with the amputated legs from a train accident is selling cigarettes and pipes. At other times he is fiercely lucid and talks sadly about how much he would have wanted to go back to his country to see what Romanians are doing with their freedom, to see his old friends. "My country, my country," he repeats. "You have to go for me, Mona. And for you," he keeps telling me. "You have to see and find out everything." He coughs very badly at night sometimes, and his face gets red.

One day when I am visiting Chicago in the summer with the children, he calls me into his room and starts to tell me something about a manuscript. "During those times, you know, I wrote something. You know, a sort of a book . . . I would like you to find out what happened to it." He stops there and starts coughing. When my mother comes in to give him his medication, he lights up another cigarette. My mother is furious and takes the pack away from him, crushing it in her hand. But then my father calls one of his Romanian friends he knows from the Romanian church and asks him to get him a new pack of Merits. He doesn't tell me more about this mysterious book, though I'm dying to find out more. But when I insist, my father coughs himself into a frenzy. I decide to let it go. Maybe he'll feel like talking about it later, another day, when he's coughing less. When he is suffering less. Eventually, one of his friends arrives and secretly gives him the pack of cigarettes and sits with him in his room, talking about how the Communists had destroyed the country and how all the Romanians over here in Chicago are worried about the Revolution not having changed things too much. "This new president, this Iliescu, he used to be Ceau-şescu's right hand," my father lectures in his room. "I bet the Securitate are now just like wolves in sheep's clothing, hiding and then appearing under a new face."

My father's friends, some of whom have actually gone back to Romania for short visits, tell him he is right, and that there are children sniffing glue in the streets of Bucharest now, and infla-

tion is so high that people who used to be professors and doctors and engineers are now barely surviving; some are even
becoming homeless. "Count your blessings that you are here,
Professor," his friends tell him.

One day, his friend Mitica says that there are people who are
saying it was better under Ceauşescu than it is now. "Maybe they
are right, Miron. At least then there was order," Mitica concludes. My father gets so mad at those words that he starts
shouting and coughing. He tells his friend to leave him alone
and go away, how could he be so idiotic to say or believe something like that, has he forgotten what Ceauşescu was like, has he
forgotten? "Order?" he yells hoarsely. "Order? Stalin brought
order, too, and also Hitler!" My father's friend leaves embarrassed, telling my mother that he'll come back to visit when
Miron feels better.

But the day I get back from Chicago, I am staring at this
Florida picture again, and there is my mother with her eyes as
blue as the ocean that stretches behind her, with her mysterious
sea smile. She gave me my wild love of the sea, the deep, irresistible love that draws sailors back for one more voyage. Calm
and restrained and proper as she always was, my mother became
reckless swimming in the sea. When I was little, she took me on
long swims so far out that the beach looked like a thin yellow
line. At all hours, when the sea was milky cool and violet at dusk,
smooth and sparkling in the morning, fidgety at midday, we
swam side by side beyond the lifeguards' whistles, the sounds of
the beach reaching us as a remote hum, the water sliding over
our bodies in smooth ripples. I see us together far away, gliding
away towards sunset on the sparkling green waters of the Black
Sea.

I pack our bags, one for me and one for Andrei and Ionica.
We go on our first holiday to the Atlantic Ocean, our first
American adventure together, to a place on the coast of North
Carolina whose name we all find hilarious: Nags Head. "Like a
place for witches," says Ionica. We take our breakfast on the bal-
cony, looking out at the ocean. We spend hours on the beach,

running, swimming, walking. Andrei runs after all the seagulls and imitates their cries, Ionica buries himself in sand. Let the waves roll.

We indulge in new little pleasures. We buy a Mexican tile with a sad guitarist painted on it. We eat Tex-Mex food in a special restaurant for the first time: tangy, spicy, delicious. Andrei tricks Ionica into eating brownies with Tabasco sauce, and to get back at his brother, Ionica puts a live hermit crab in Andrei's bed. There are shells and sand and live sea creatures in our hotel room. I laugh as I scold them and tell them to settle down.

I swim in the Atlantic Ocean and play in the waves with my energetic, shivering boys. At night we walk the boardwalk by the sea and pretend we live on one of the big, lighted cruise ships. We dream of going to Patagonia or Malta. I search deep for all the sources of strength and sanity inside myself as waves and foam and algae surround me and splash against my body.

We return to our midwestern town golden brown and smelling of salt water. I wink at my own face in the bedroom mirror. The day I start planting marigolds and petunias and parsley and tomatoes in the first garden I have ever owned, I daydream of coloured shoots. Stringy, snaky, coiling tendrils that grow out of my toes and fingers and weave a lacy canopy around me, the core that is me, a web of turquoise, fuchsia, yellow, scarlet, lime green. On the outside of this wildly coloured canopy grow plump tomatoes, round watermelons, leafy lettuce, fragrant basil. I am inside it all like a cocoon, warm and safe. As I walk down the streets of our town, people cheer me joyously and lawyers in black suits with squeaky voices drop dead at the sight of me like ugly flies.

I flush all the antidepressants down the toilet. I plant anything that strikes my fancy, without any particular plan: tomatoes and marigolds, watermelons and lettuce. I work without gardening gloves, getting the dirt under my fingernails and smearing it all over my hands. As my hands sink deep into the black earth, among so many roots, I miss my native earth and its special smells. I decide I have to go back to touch and smell and taste everything again, to assure myself it all actually happened, that I was in fact born and had grown up in a troubled country cuddled in the curl of the Carpathians and washed by the green waters of the Black Sea. At the hardware store, I buy seeds and fertilizer and that tool whose Romanian name is one of the fourteen Dacian words: *tîrnăcop,* hoe. My father's words about not being able to go back to his country before he dies keep ringing in my ears. The thought of Mihai having died fills me with sorrow as I stare at the dark earth with its coiling roots. Mihai must be buried in the cemetery at the foot of the mountain, where we buried Cristina. I must see Mihai's grave to fully understand his death, I think. I must see everything again, see and touch and smell everything. I want to go back.

Last Dance

M‍Y FATHER IS WEAKER, and his illnesses are getting worse by the day. He is sad and cannot remember recent things, though he remembers his youth and his childhood in great detail. The years of his exile in this foreign land have not brought him happiness or fulfilment. He never wanted to rid himself of the melodious words of his native language, and his freedom came too late for him. Chicago is harsh and cold this Christmas on the brink of the new millennium, just like my first winter when my feet were frostbitten.

He tells me I am the love of his life, my mother and me both. He is so weak, so small and frail. I hold him for a long time in my arms as he tells me he will die very soon. He says not to forget our country. "It's where you were born and grew up Daddy's girl. You go, Mona, go and see Matilda's grave, don't forget to see all the graves," he says. And then, a few days into this New Year, my father dies in his sleep, of heart failure, on a cold, windy Chicago morning.

It's a bad time, as bad as the year when I was eight or nine and everybody in my family seemed to be dying. But this is worse, because he is my father, and we're burying our dead in foreign earth, because I can't hide in my aunt's wardrobe and hug my bare knees for comfort. It's worse because my father died sad and confused.

We go back to Chicago for the funeral. Andrei and Ionica are puzzled by this death, the first they've experienced. They burst into tears at odd moments, and at others they laugh. They cling to me. They understand their grandfather died and won't be telling them funny stories any more, stories he made up for them at bedtime, stories about his childhood in the town in northern Moldavia. He won't be giving them more geography and history lessons about the countries of Europe, but really mostly about his own country, the crossroads of all the invasions and calamities in the world.

It's all raw and harsh and unforgiving. The Chicago cold, my father's stonelike, lifeless body in the coffin at the funeral home, in his best navy-blue suit. His room in the Chicago apartment, with all his possessions neatly arranged: the Pelikan fountain pen, the poems he wrote with it, the miniature English–Romanian dictionary, the books of Romanian poetry, the gold cigarette lighter. On the wall, the icon of the Virgin Mary that used to hang in his sister's Bucharest apartment, the one with the blood on her face from the Greek sailor who stuck his knife in it more than a hundred years ago.

There is no comforting my mother. She is dishevelled in her grief. Somebody calls from the hospital about *grief counselling*. It's the only thing she finds slightly funny. She doesn't even get it, it's so alien to her, these American words. My mother hangs up without a word.

We arrange for the funeral ceremony, pretending it's all correct and traditional, at the Romanian church in Chicago. There's nothing I can think to say to my mother to comfort her, except that it's a blessing he died in his sleep. People always want to die in their sleep.

We even have the special meal for the dead made of barley and powdered sugar. Miruna is with us, too, crying and holding my hand. She sits and reads with the children while my mother and I make some last arrangements for the funeral. We've never gathered this way in Chicago, family and friends, and now we're all sobbing. I am glad to have Miruna here like a sister, to not feel so alien and cut off. I tell her about the time when I was little and so many people in our family were dying, how she was a rosy plump baby eating the lipstick from her mother's bag and the lost kitten was mewing at the door. Her chicory-blue eyes give me courage.

Andrei and Ionica look sad and beautiful in their little men's suits. I feel proud of them as I see them through a blur of tears. They are alive and here next to me. They're shocked to see their grandfather's still body in the casket. Ionica hides behind me, and Andrei looks troubled. I tell them to say good-bye to their grandfather one last time. I embrace my father and don't want to let him go. For my children, I should be mature and grown up about this, but I'm not sure what that means. I hold on to him; my mother holds on to him. I want to crawl inside a wardrobe. Death is always ugly, but even uglier when you're so far from home.

I see my parents dancing at a New Year's Eve party with coloured streamers and confetti, one of the most beautiful couples in all of Bucharest, people used to say. I see them dancing at their twenty-fifth wedding anniversary, the year before I left. They are both radiant despite the shortages and the secret typewriter and my father's arrests. They are dancing in our little living room to music so luscious and old-fashioned that it gives the illusion of some luxurious, careless, happy time.

The coffin is being lowered into the ground. The January wind is blowing with a vengeance through our coats and into our faces covered with tears. My children are holding on to me and shivering. We throw the first handfuls of earth. We throw the last handfuls of earth as well. We are standing in the wind torn by our grief.

Both my father and Mihai are dead. The two men who most shaped my life. Now it is time to go back and deal with the ghosts.

Taking the Road Back Home

I RETURNED TO MY HOMELAND on the real train to Trieste, only in the opposite direction. I flew with my sons Andrei and Ionica to Italy, from where we followed the trajectory of my departure of twenty years ago, only backward. We strolled around the streets of Rome, and I showed them the Colosseum in front of which I had once stood in a red dress and white shoes with black bows feeling unattached and light like a red balloon. We ate colourful ice cream and *pizza margherita*, and I drank espresso while my boys drank blackberry Italian sodas in a café on a side street near the Fontana di Trevi.

Then we took the train for many hours during which Andrei and Ionica played cards and word games, tickled and spat at each other, while an older Italian woman stared at them sternly and while I greedily watched the landscapes rolling by, trying to recapture the feelings of twenty years ago. Trying to turn back time. When we arrived in the Trieste railway station I took my two sons by the hand and glided on the shiny marble floors of the elegant hall trying to relive the afternoon when I was in this same spot with Luciana, Letizia and Mario and melted with sadness at the sound of Susanna's aria from *Le Nozze di Figaro* that was playing on the transistor of an old man who reminded me of my father. Now there were several groups of Italian students listening to hip-hop and filling the resonant hallway with their loud, cheerful voices.

We strolled around the Piazza dell'Unità d'Italia, where Andrei and Ionica climbed on the group statue representing the unification of Italy. We ate green olives and scampi in the Café degli Specchi, Café of the Mirrors, and I couldn't help smiling at the irony: seeing myself reflected in the mirrors of a café in Trieste, twenty summers after my rushed and anxious passage through the city in the opposite direction. This time, I listened to the heart of Trieste, a steady and low-sounding beat, the regular steps of the poised Triestines and the nervous steps of new waves of refugees, from Albania, Turkey and Romania.

The morning our train crossed into Romania, dawn was sneaking through the humid pine forests of the Carpathians and jolted my body awake with a shock of recognition. Although there were no signs along the tracks, no announcements of stops with Romanian names, I knew I was on my native soil. I felt it in the way dawn filtered through the tall, symmetrical fir trees. In the way sunflowers swayed in the warm-cool summer air that caressed my face through the open window. I knew it from the smell of wet tree bark, pine resin, and the unique scent of the flower called queen of the night that opened up at dusk and filled the air with its dizzying fragrance until dawn all summer long. I knew it because all my limbs felt the right size, and because I could hear the echoes of my name, my laughter and moans stuck for ever in the valleys.

I came back avid for the smells and tastes of my childhood. Romanians had overthrown the Communist government and killed its leader. The customs officers were polite and didn't paw through our luggage. Bread and butter were available in the shops with no queuing, no ration coupons. *Mămăligă* was now served in restaurants where you could pay with a credit card and where people spoke on cellular phones about shady businesses. August 23 no longer meant anything to young people the age I'd been more than two decades earlier, when I fell in love with the boy whose girlfriend had died in a hiking accident, the boy with red fragrant lips, green eyes and black hair.

The files of the secret police were now being officially released and studied, and people were divided between those eager for revelations, vengeance and justice, and those fearful that the meticulous *work* they'd done during the Ceauşescu years – informing, threatening, intimidating, destroying *enemies of the people* – was going to be exposed, and they'd lose their positions in the new government.

More than the opening of secret-police files, more than the rocketing rate of inflation, Romanians were excited about their cell phones. So excited, in fact, that a family buried their dead father with a cell phone next to his head – just in case he wasn't completely dead and might want to call them. The cell phone started ringing in the night, in the grave. The ringing went on every night for a week, and the cemetery guard thought there were ghosts in the cemetery. He contacted the family. They had to unearth the tomb, open the coffin, and take out the cell phone. People who didn't know the old man had died were still calling his number. After the incident, a government statement reported on TV asked people to please refrain from burying cell phones with their loved ones. "Cell phones are for the living," concluded the newscaster.

I stopped in Braşov at my aunt's house directly from Italy, without bothering to go to Bucharest. With Aunt Matilda now dead, all of my parents' friends gone or disappeared, I had no one to see and was apprehensive to visit the city by myself.

After a few days in Braşov, which now looked to me even more beautiful and colourful than I had remembered it, I visited our white rock high above the city. The bells of the Black Church tolled as hauntingly as ever, and I saw us embracing in the purple twilight shrouding the red tile roofs of the city below us, as we had that August 23 so long ago. We had stayed here through the decades, enchanted, faithful. I called our names,

Mona, Mihai, across the wide valleys and forests. They burst out in all directions into wild echoes, as sharp as the rocks, spreading over the valley and town. This time I waited. I stood and waited for them to withdraw into the huge bell of silence enclosed by the mountains. So the sleep of infants will be peaceful, and lovers will no longer be cursed.

Watermelon After Twenty Years

I AM TWENTY YEARS OLDER, and as a French poet once said, "I have more memories than if I had lived a thousand years." I am climbing the stairs to Nina's apartment. My body is fuller from having carried my children, there is a powder of lines around the corners of my eyes, there is a fierce glitter in my look from my uprootings and the ambitions I've tried to fulfil; my limbs feel stronger and my muscles tighter, my hair is as unleashed as ever, only there are some fine strands of grey in it now. I hear Andrei and Ionica's voices as they play outside where I used to play and where I listened to Mihai strum his guitar on summer nights so fragrant you wanted to lie on the earth and scream with joy. I trip on a step of the grey-and-white marble stairs I've climbed so many times like this, hurried and breathless. *It's them, my own children,* I tell myself. Now I have a whole life in the American Midwest.

My children are playing outside with the children of those who were my playmates a few decades ago. Their screams in the summer afternoon resonate through the entire neighbourhood and through time. They blend with the smells of petunias and roasted peppers. A painful recognition flashes through me as I open the door. My uncle is just about to cut up a huge watermelon, the way he always used to when we were little.

"Take this piece here," he urges me, handing me a piece of

watermelon on his big kitchen knife. I eat the juicy watermelon with a piece of bread. The screams of my children and those of the neighbourhood children cross the afternoon. I see myself running like them, in the summer afternoon, swallowing the summer fragrances with an unquenchable thirst. Hide-and-seek – the thrill of holding your breath behind a door of the mean neighbour's cellar, smelling of cabbage. Rushing like a dart to the nearest tree to be the first, to win, to not be caught, twilight slowly falling and our mothers calling us to dinner.

My uncle asks me about my love life with a wicked smile. My aunt scolds him for being so nosy.

"What business is it of yours?" she says.

"I'm having a conversation with my niece here," he tells her, laughing.

I haven't told them that I actually divorced Tom; they still have my wedding picture on their mahogany cupboard in the living room. I just tell them that Tom still has work in Chicago and for the time being he is commuting to Indiana to see the children and that I go to Chicago during vacations. I keep things vague and switch to a different topic of conversation, like the downstairs neighbours. My aunt smiles and she stirs the cabbage soup that my children think is the best soup in the world.

We used to eat watermelon before dinner just as we're doing now. Meals have always been chaotic in my aunt's house. We start with dessert, then have soup, then a child comes in and wants to eat just bread and butter, then another comes in and wants fried potatoes, so my aunt starts peeling potatoes.

A neighbour comes to the door, and my uncle invites her in and asks if she wants a shot of *vişinata*, the sour cherry brandy only Romanians know how to make.

"It could wake up the dead," says my uncle. "But the dead are better dead," he adds. "Why would they want to come back to this, this . . . ?" My uncle Ion makes a wide sweep of his arm to indicate everything in the world.

The neighbour sits down, and my uncle pours some *vişinata*. Soon, my head is spinning. I count four different conversations going on at the same time: how it's better to just see your husband at the weekend, because then you don't argue about stupid stuff, how the prices of bread and petrol have gone up again, how my children are beautiful and speak Romanian so well, and how we should go to the cemetery to water the flowers on Vera's and Victor's and Paraschiva's tombs.

The neighbour leaves with a bowl of soup my aunt insists she take home for later. And then, my head spinning from the *vişinata*, I muster up the courage to ask what I have been dying to ask since I have arrived at the station. To ask about Mihai.

"Is it really true he died? How? What was he doing before he died?"

"Yes, it's true. What a senseless death," my uncle says.

Nobody knows any details. Nobody wants to talk about Mihai. It's as if he were a taboo subject. I hear my children scream and laugh outside in the garden, and for a second, giddy as I am from the sour cherry brandy, with the lacy curtains swelling in the afternoon breeze and everything almost unchanged in my aunt's kitchen, I have the illusion it has all been a dream and I just woke up from a nap. I will soon prepare my afternoon lies to be able to leave the house for a few hours to see Mihai, and I will say I am going to see Cristina downtown or that a group of kids in the neighbourhood is having a volleyball match at another kid's house. But the piercing sound of Ionica's voice from outside shakes me back.

I want to ask more. But my jaws are clenched, and the thought of my first love dying in the street hit by a random bullet from the wild shooting in the Revolution paralyses me. As I sit at my aunt's table, I remember my dream of the two moons. I have a sharp memory of Mariana. I see her toothless smile from my dream, though it was more than twenty years ago.

After we've eaten the watermelon, the French fries and the cabbage soup all in the wrong order, my uncle announces he has something to give me. He goes to the pantry where they keep the pickles, the sour cabbage, the preserves and the apples for winter. He comes back with a thick package of my letters and pictures that my mother had given him for safekeeping before they left for America. I take the package and hold it close to my heart, thanking him over and over and wiping tears from my eyes. I go into the bedroom and open it with trembling fingers.

The first letter is dated September 1979. Mihai is answering a letter of mine in which I must have confided to him that someone, a boy, was interested in me. He tells me not to be scared, that he trusts me, that no one can really understand what we want, the way we think and look at our future, that we have five more years to wait until I start and then finish my university studies, and he knows I'm young and I want to dance and go to parties, but what we have is so precious . . . Can I wait, will I be able to wait? Mihai asks in his letter. There is a drawing of me crying from the window of a train, big cartoon tears that fall on the platform. He is there, on the platform to catch them, they fall on his head like big balls, and there is a crack in his head. I laugh at the drawing.

I find a letter that has never been opened. It is yellow and has a few grease spots on the envelope. My name and address are written in small calligraphic letters. I open it curiously and start reading a strangely sappy love letter from a man who recounts all the things he would like to do with me and to me, and all the ways in which he loves my body and my face. The letter veers into the obscene. The ending promises a life of delights next to him in his native provincial town, with me as his wife and working as a schoolteacher. The signature on the back puzzles me: Stefan Dumitriu. My red carnation Securitate man! My shadow. He *was* in love with me, in his own sleazy way.

My children rush into the apartment, sweaty and red, asking for food, looking curiously at the package in my hand. They ask what I'm reading. *Old letters,* I tell them. *Old letters from old sweethearts,* Andrei says and laughs. My aunt asks them if they want cabbage soup and French fries and watermelon. They want everything.

Encounters Under a
Different Moon

I TRY TO FOLLOW TRACES OF MIHAI. Several of his friends had emigrated, but Radu, his closest friend, still lives in the same house. One fragrant, moonlit evening, I walk up the cobblestone street to his house – the house in whose walled-in garden we had danced and argued so many times. Time shrinks, and I become a seventeen-year-old girl. My hair is flying wildly in the summer night, my heart is pounding out of my chest, I'm running ahead of Mihai on the cobblestones, the sound of my sandals resounding like a little drum in the velvety air. I whistle a tune I make up, a love song, I tell him. I wait for him to get near, and then I run away up the street laughing. He can't catch me, but then he does and we stop and kiss in the middle of the street, just as Radu opens the door.

And now, I knock on the thick wooden door, and a heavy man with a red face and the grey stubble of a beard opens the door, an American cigarette in his hand. I'd forgotten my American past as I was rushing up the cobblestone street. But when I see the heavy man smoking, the reality of my American life pours through me. Husband, lovers, lawyers, highways under the moon, social workers, parched cornfields, flooded cornfields, tar and whisky on hot humid summer nights, raw freedom . . . the moon is the same, but the smells are different, and I am different and the same. But who in the world is this bearded man puffing his American cigarette?

"Is Radu home?" I ask.

"Radu!" he shouts behind him. "You have a visitor!" He kisses my hand, as many Romanian men still do, and tells me he is Dan, Radu's cousin. I smile and feel slightly more at ease.

It was in this yard that Mihai and I danced and argued about whether or not we would leave the country. It was in Radu's house that we danced all the dances in the world that crazy New Year's Day after which Mihai made love to me in the snow on the hill behind the house and after which Anca Serban scared me out of my wits by stopping me in the middle of the cold wintry night and telling me that Mihai was with the secret police.

"Who is it?" says a familiar voice, though it is rougher now. Radu appears from the darkness, also smoking an American cigarette. It seems that Romanians are now making up for all the years of cigarette shortages. He is holding a glass of what looks like whisky in one hand, and his other arm is around the waist of a woman in a black dress so tight and so low cut that I feel like tucking in her breasts so they won't pop out. I have seen women dressed like that everywhere on this trip. Freedom, it turns out, comes with popping breasts and glue sniffing and many, many American cigarettes.

Radu doesn't seem particularly surprised to see me.

"Do you remember me?" I ask.

"How could I not remember you?" he answers. "Mona Maria Manoliu. How lovely to see you again. Do you want something to drink?" he asks.

My need to talk about Mihai prevails over the unease I feel in the dark living room. I take a drink. Whisky, why not? Radu looks me up and down, and I remember how, two decades ago, he watched Mihai and me argue for a long time, smiling cunningly. We probably drank *ţuică* that night. The liquor spreads its warmth through my veins.

The night is sweet and fragrant. Music is playing in the garden, *Are you lonesome tonight?* We have moved into the garden from the dark living room, where it's cooler and we can see the stars. The woman with the tight dress stays inside.

Gradually, I ask Radu to tell me about Mihai. I want to know about the Mihai I never saw, Mihai when I wasn't with him. What did he do the other months of the year, when I was back in school in the capital? Who were his friends? And the rest: the years after my departure, the Revolution. How exactly did he die?

Radu's head snaps up. "Who told you Mihai is dead?" he asks.

"My cousin Miruna, when she came over to America soon after the Revolution. And my aunt and uncle, here, now, they both confirmed it. You mean you didn't know?"

Radu shakes his head and reaches for another cigarette. "He's not dead," he says. "He is very much alive. With a son, too."

A breeze passes by and cools my forehead. There are steps on the cobblestone outside the stone fence, in the street. The glass of whisky is shaking in my hand and the ice in it is jiggling. I am about to drop the glass. Radu leans over and places it on the little iron table between us. I stare at him in disbelief, look up at the orange, indifferent moon. Tears are flowing down my face. Radu leans over again and takes my hand. I try very hard to find my voice.

"Is this a joke?" I ask Radu. "This sounds like some bad American film where the hero is supposed to be dead and then he shows up with amnesia. If you're making this up, you're very cruel."

"Sometimes life has more clichés than the films," he tells me with a shrug. He puts out his cigarette in the copper ashtray.

"Why does everybody say he's dead?" I ask, irritated.

"Who's everybody? Your relatives, right? What do they know? They've always lived sort of isolated. It's true Mihai was wounded on Christmas Day, the day they shot the Ceauşescus. That much is true. He was shot in the leg. Ah, Mihai took to the streets on that day like a fiend.

"You know how gossip flies around here. There was such con-

fusion, such madness. There were so many false rumours during those days . . . We didn't know who was who and what was
what. We didn't even know who was shooting whom.

"Somebody must have seen him fall down and assumed he
was dead." A shadow of sadness and fatigue crosses Radu's face.
"I'm really sorry, Mona, but I haven't seen him in ages," he
concludes.

Radu lights up another cigarette, and his gesture reminds me
of Mihai and the way he always lit up a cigarette in our tense
moments or during a fight. I study his face closely in the moonlight. It took me about a decade to get used to the idea that
Mihai was dead, through the years of my marriage to Tom, having a second child, my legal battles, planting gardens, teaching,
directing plays. I was trying to understand the full enormity of
the fact that Mihai was dead and that any possibility I would ever
see or talk to him was nonexistent. What if Radu is playing with
me? What if it turns out he truly is dead, again?

"He has a son, you say? Is he married?" I ask.

"He's a widower. His wife died of cancer a few years ago. They
had moved farther north, in the Făgăraş area. Mihai was happy
to live at the foot of the mountain. They had a good marriage.
He was quite shaken by her death."

"Prove it!" I hear myself say to Radu, so loudly that I can
almost hear the echo of my voice in the little garden at the foot
of the mountains.

"Prove it? Prove what? Are you crazy? Who do you think I
am?" Radu answers, drinking up his whisky in an angry gulp
after which he slams the glass on the iron table.

"Yes, prove it, show me something to prove that he is indeed
alive," I insist and shove my whisky glass into his.

He laughs and gets up from his chair.

"You asked for it, Mona! Watch out, don't play with stuff like
that!"

He goes into the house and brings out his cell phone
together with a little notebook. He opens it and looks at it

briefly, then dials a number and hands me the phone, saying with a winner's smile:

"Here you are, you've got your proof, Mona!"

I don't know what to do with the phone, and as he places it in my hand I try to get rid of it as if it were burning. I hear the ring twice, three times, and then it stops. I hear a voice, a man's voice, saying: "Hello, who is it?" I drop the phone on the cobblestones of the garden, knock over the glass of whisky that spills all over my skirt. I lean over desperately trying to get to the phone and to hang up. The voice is still saying, "Hello, anybody there?" A faraway voice, deep, familiar, a little hoarse, a voice that I would recognize out of a million voices: its syncopated rhythm, elongated vowels, and then suddenly the rushed syllables at the end of the words, and that hoarse edge that used to drive me crazy with desire. I wait until he hangs up, and I hear the dial tone.

Radu comes over and holds me while I let myself cry for a good ten minutes, the way I have wanted to do for so long. I never had the time or the strength to let myself do it. I had always thought that if I did, I would never stop, and for the rest of my days I would do nothing else, instead of working, raising children, living. When Radu asks if I want to call again, I just shake my head that *No, I can't, not now.*

"All right. Let's start again. I believe you. You certainly produced your proof," I say, laughing. I want to know everything about Mihai, who he was during those years. The sound of his voice is still resonating inside me like a deep echo in a wide valley, *Hello, anybody there? . . .*

"What do you mean, who he was? It's taken you two decades to ask that?" Radu snaps, as if reading my thoughts. "Mihai was a good man. Something of a hero, you might say. But . . . you knew this, didn't you?" he adds, genuinely surprised. "You were the one in love with him. No?"

There is sorrow in Radu's voice. How could I not have felt it, sensed it, known it? Were my instincts so atrophied by fear and suspicion that I couldn't truly understand what Mihai was all about? But I saw him again, the black leather jacket, the green piercing eyes, and his rushed gestures. His sudden fits of anger when we talked politics.

I look Radu straight in the eyes. "I didn't have a clue of what was going on then; all I knew was that I loved him; that my father was doing all kinds of dangerous things, and . . . there was a night when a friend of Mihai's, Anca, told me he was secret police. She sounded so real, and so frightening."

Radu is staring at me with an ironic look, as if challenging me to convince him of something. The moon is now above our heads and it looks cold and unromantic. A different moon. I remember with a shudder the moment on the cold winter night when Anca scared me to death with her words.

"So you trusted some crazy woman in the street warning you about Mihai more than everything that you and Mihai lived together?" Radu says, crossing his arms.

"Go to hell, Radu, just go to fucking hell," I tell him. "Tell me the damn story, tell me what exactly happened then."

"All right, I'll tell you, although you are mean and you curse at me like a peasant," Radu says, laughing. "Mihai worked in the same group as your father did. I'm not quite sure whether they knew of each other before you two fell in love, or whether Mihai got in on it later. It doesn't matter. And yes, unlike you and your family and the Bucharest circles you moved in, Mihai was something of a Marxist, though I guess he questioned that often enough. He actually didn't think socialism was bad in itself. He just thought, well, that all the terror and censorship and secret police stuff were bad and that he had to do something about it. In that way he was sort of like the early Communists, who were the true believers. But he knew how you felt about all that, so he never dared to reveal to you that side of himself. That's why he could have given you the impression he was secretly working for the Party.

"They all wanted to protect you: your father, Mihai, even Cristina. And even Anca – in her roundabout way she inadvertently ended up protecting you."

"Why the hell did I need all of this protection?" I shout. "What was I, an eggshell or something?"

"You say that now," says Radu and he pours himself another drink. "But you seem to have forgotten how things were then. How we all felt under siege. That we had to be suspicious and hide things from each other all the time.

"It's true they wrote manifestos," Radu goes on. "They did try to send as much information and news about human rights violations to the people they knew at Radio Free Europe as they could. Once Mihai understood how the Party betrayed even the proletariat, the very class in whose name they were supposed to rule, he took on the dissident cause with a vengeance. Did you know about your father's manuscript? It was something like a report, a memoir of everything that he and others he knew had been going through. Like a testimonial. He wanted to be . . . well, sort of like the Solzhenitsyn of Romania. And Mihai tried to get that manuscript out into Germany through one of his German friends here in Braşov who had got a passport to reintegrate his family in Munich."

Radu seems genuinely saddened by the news of my father's death, though he had never met him in person.

"I have heard of him quite a bit from Mihai, I feel I almost know him," Radu says. I am moved that Mihai actually spoke about my father to his friends, as if he were a close relative.

"Yes, I heard my father once say something about a book, a memoir of sorts . . . very soon before he died," I say, remembering that moment in his room in Chicago when he was coughing and smoking himself to death. I ask Radu to please go on, tell me more, tell me everything he knows.

He is heated up by the story, and he seems to enjoy telling it. His face is flushed, his eyes are shiny, and his receding hairline gives him an almost patrician air.

I feel unusually calm as I am processing this. The dew starts setting in, and my arms feel moist.

"Well, you get the idea. The guy changed his mind at the last minute, and had to return this piece of writing to Mihai. The

Securitate knew there was a compromising book of some sort floating around but couldn't quite figure out what exactly it was. After Pacepa's defection they had all got somehow disoriented. And then at other times they would get violent and diabolic, to compensate for it. That's why they barged into your house that time and vandalized your apartment. We all heard about that night, Mona. But they were somehow without a clear direction." I am amazed that Radu knew so much about my life and our daily torments. Clearly, what I had thought my life to be then was a very different thing.

"Mihai left Bucharest because he wanted to protect you, not because he couldn't hack Bucharest. Well, it wasn't his favourite city in the world, it's true, and he did miss the mountains. But the real reason he left is because he wanted to distance himself from you and your father so you wouldn't be in any more danger than you already were. And for a while, around the time you left the country, he pretended to work for the Securitate, he would just meet up with some of them and tell them things they already knew, but with the air of it being something new. In any case, what mattered is that he tried to create the illusion they could count on him and this way sort of get them off his back. And yours. I believe he was in touch with Petrescu, your dad's former student, quite often. Mihai could be such a good actor sometimes."

"What happened to the manuscript?" I ask, stretching out my skirt to cover my legs, as I am getting chilly from the night air. I can't imagine it was anything that was going to produce a government coup. But I know it was important to my father; I am pretty sure it must have recorded the story of our sufferings during that time, the fear, the starvation, the cold in the winter, the overall despair. I know it from the wild look in my father's eyes that time when he mentioned it in between fits of coughing.

"Mihai kept it for a while. He took it back with him to Braşov after he left Bucharest. Then he gave it to Anca, who had promised him she was going to get it over the border into Yugoslavia. Anca was in contact with the woman who helped you escape – Bielna, Baljina, what was her name? I have no idea what happened with it from there. I should ask you, I guess, you were the one who met with this Serbian woman – did she ever tell you anything about it?"

"Biljana?" I say as my mouth drops open in shock. "What do you mean, Anca and Biljana? How did all of this happen, how were all these people in contact with each other? How was that possible?"

"Well, it was. We Romanians, we may be whores at times, but we aren't stupid. Romanians weren't nearly as organized as the Polish Solidarity with their Wałesa, for example, but there was some action going on. Some got caught, it's true, some disappeared or got killed, others got weak and informed on each other, but others didn't. The really smart and tough ones didn't, I guess. Mihai was one of them. He was lucky, too. Like in November 1987," Radu says with an almost dreamy smile.

"What in November 1987, what happened?" I ask.

I find out from Radu that in November 1987 the workers from the largest factories in Braşov were told they weren't going to get paid that month, so they started a mini-revolution of sorts. They took to the streets, barged into the city hall, broke the portraits of the leaders, threw chairs through the windows. And then the tanks came. Mihai was among the people inside the city hall, but he escaped from the overall chaos unharmed. Apparently in the late eighties, during the Gorbachev years, there were even Soviet delegations that would suddenly appear and stay in factories for periods of time, inciting the workers to revolt. Then they would disappear. The big Revolution was being slowly prepared from all sides, from the inside and the outside, it seems.

"The two had to coincide," says Radu, "the despair and the will of the people, the conglomeration of dissident movements and a certain revolutionary spirit, with the will of the bigger powers and the overall world climate. It all mattered, I think. Even your father's work, everything . . ."

"My father?" I ask.

"Yes, your father, of course. Although your father was something of a danger to himself sometimes, being so fiery and impulsive. On the other hand, that's what saved him, because they never fully took him seriously; they always thought he was just a loudmouthed literary poetic type who talked more than he acted. But he tried to do a lot, your father did. In the end, every little bit mattered."

I sit for a while staring at Radu, letting all the news work its way through my mind. He stares back, takes another sip from his whisky, and smiles at me. Mihai's voice with its hoarse edges is echoing in my head. If only I could turn it all back, relive everything but with the knowledge I have now. But what's done is done. Twenty years ago, in the Trieste train station, I heard Susanna was singing of the pleasures of love in the garden, when there was so much ahead of me, so much hope, and so much to live for. Susanna was with her Figaro just a few steps away, waiting to trick her only to reveal his love for her. It all ends happily for Susanna. But what am I supposed to do now?

What really happened to my father's writings, what happened with all of these people and this confused movement of dissent during the eighties, with all of its tentacles and meandering roads? Maybe Biljana still has the damned manuscript in her apartment in Belgrade, or maybe she did send it to Radio Free Europe and they didn't do anything with it. Maybe they did read parts of it, but it was all too late; the Revolution was already on its way.

Radu seems to be reading my thoughts and goes on. "Yes, it's possible that someone, maybe even Anca, met Biljana in the Belgrade train station and gave her the manuscript. By the way, Anca was madly in love with Mihai and would do anything for him. But mad as she seemed, she was a tough one. She was one of the few who actually played the double game for a while without getting caught. She had first infiltrated the Securitate and then gave the people in Mihai's group information about their intentions. The scare she gave you that night about Mihai was both a political move and one of love and jealousy. She wanted you to get away from him for personal reasons. But also everybody else, including Mihai himself, sort of tried to make you distance yourself from him – for safety reasons. It just about killed him, you know. Knowing that you suspected him. He just let that happen, I guess, and never tried to fully dispel your suspicions; he was doing the best he could. Your father's student, that Petrescu, he was his saving grace, you know. And yours, too. In all the madness you were sort of lucky. You had your lucky star, as they say," Radu says philosophically and laughs.

I remember Biljana's brown, elegant leather bag that she casually placed next to her and how she'd asked the conductor something at the last minute, something in Serbian, and how the Serbian words had seemed to me then so melodious in her mouth. I also remember being irritated by the fact she lingered, delayed the departure of the train by talking to the conductor. I remember the woman's scream with a sudden accuracy. That moment when I thought I was going to faint with fear, but then the scream came and the conductor let go of me and my coat. How I pulled down the window and saw the woman in the light summery dress running across the tracks. Could it all have been planned by these people who were somehow strangely connected to one another without my having the faintest idea about it: Mihai, Anca, Biljana, Petrescu, a mystery woman running across the tracks? Was Biljana's brown bag holding my father's manuscript right there in front of me? And why risk so much for something that was probably just an emotional report of our daily oppressions? But maybe Radu is right that it all mattered – it mattered that everything be known and recorded somewhere. All the years that my father was in Romania after my departure, he must have listened to his Radio Free Europe like a fiend, agonizing about his manuscript and hoping one night he would hear them read pages from it. No wonder the first thing he wanted when he got to America was to buy a short-wave radio.

"Do you get it now? Why Mihai was not there for you the morning you left?" Radu asks, like a detective reaching the end of an investigation.

I am back in Mihai's room that morning in late summer. His room is unusually tidy, his hiking breeches and boots are nowhere to be found, and my red slip is under the bed. Mihai knows I am planning to leave and has disappeared. He knows that if we see each other again this morning I might become weak and tell him everything; he might become weak and tell me everything. I might revoke all my plans and refuse to leave. The Securitate might get him because he is actually helping me leave the country, and they will realize that he is tricking them. Because he is aiding with the writing of some manuscript and is helping my father. A man from the village of Vulcan near Brașov has just been put in prison indefinitely for helping a relative leave the country. Mihai knows all too well about every possible danger. People are being arrested left and right. We might spoil everything at the last minute. Because if we see each other this morning, we will just make love the way we did our first morning several years before. We might just say to hell with everything; we'll both get ourselves caught right here in this bed, get caught and die together.

"It's almost two in the morning, you know," Radu says and offers me another drink. "I could pull out the sofa in the front room if you want to stay here," he offers kindly. I am more awake than I have been in a long time and beg Radu to tell me the rest: What is Mihai doing now, where is he, what happened to Anca, and why was Cristina killed?

"He loved this country so much, you know that," Radu says. "Though at times, when he needed to, he was better than anyone at pretending he didn't. Now he's helping sort out the truth from the lies in the secret files that are being opened," Radu informs me. "They are going after all the former

Securitate, have set up something called the National College for the Study of the Archives of the Secret Police."

Mihai goes for periods of time to Bucharest to study the files and to talk to the people from this "college", then goes back and hides in his "den", deep in the countryside. He has a bodyguard now. He travels under a false name, lives under another, Mihai Munteanu. Always these alliterations of the letter *m*, I think. Like my own name, Mona Maria Manoliu.

I find it funny that the organization is called a college. Maybe some people send their children there to study. Almost as funny as the family who buried their father with his cell phone next to his head.

"As for Anca . . . what more do you want to know? I didn't think you cared. You never tried, after you left Romania, to be in touch with us or with Mihai."

"I couldn't, Radu. I had to survive, you know. I had to put it all behind me, so I could move forward. It was the only way. But I've come back, haven't I? And of course I wanted to know, I never forgot anything." I don't tell him of my retroactive jealousy, or that I could sit here till dawn to talk about the past, about Mihai, about all of us the way we were twenty years ago.

"As I told you, Anca was something of an unusual bird. She had been caught having an abortion. You know how it worked: first they found you doing something illegal, then they offered to let you go if you'd squeal on somebody else. But she outsmarted them for a while. It wasn't the same for poor Cristina, though. She was cornered from all sides because of her relations with that Tunisian guy, because she was trying to leave the country, and because she had also tried to do some work for Mihai's group. She was a friend of this young doctor from Vulcan who was resisting the internment of prisoners of conscience as mental patients. She was planning to marry the Tunisian student and leave. But she was too . . . too fragile to handle it all; there were too many things going on at the same time. She broke down. There was nothing Mihai could do to help her in the end. She had got herself too entangled. She either was pushed to the brink until she killed herself or they actually did it and staged it as a suicide. I tend to believe it was suicide. Ah, there were so many then – it happened more than you could have possibly imagined.

"It was all a mess. Nobody knew what was what," says Radu. "But one thing is sure," he continues. "Mihai never sold out. And he was smart through and through. And," he adds, lighting another cigarette, "he was faithful to you, although Anca was always after him, as were other women! Anca ended up badly," Radu continues. "She married someone in the group who turned out to be an undercover secret police. He beat and mistreated her. I have no idea what's become of her."

So I had been somewhat right in my delirious fantasies the summer when I had the hair-pulling fight with Anca in the middle of the street. Radu didn't mention one other possibility, that of people becoming political in order to get closer to someone they loved. Love and politics always get mixed up with each other. And then love is usually the loser. My dear Cristina was the loser and the victim.

I think of the sugary letter from Dumitriu that I have recently discovered among old letters. Thank God love didn't win there. Maybe Dumitriu helped me, too, by being too much in love to act and denounce me in my attempt to escape. Maybe all he wanted was sex and marriage in a little Romanian village. It seems too easy, though. These were men who beat you senseless over a suspicion of a manifesto or ran you over in the street without a moment's hesitation, without even slowing down the car.

My fate depended on so little, a thin thread. An American bomb falling a few inches to the left. A yellow postcard with a few rushed words written in prison. A stone kicked out of its niche and rolling on a hill. A student studying Symbolist poetry. A woman's scream on a train platform. The train slowly moving on. While I felt so adventurous and courageous that night, a whole network of forces that could have destroyed my life for ever was in place.

Radu tells me that Mihai always kept a photograph of me laughing on a mountaintop. It drove his wife crazy, until one day when she ripped it up. Radu says Mihai was furious; he loved that picture. But he can't blame the wife either.

I know exactly the photograph Radu is talking about. Once, Mihai brought along his parents' camera, an old Leica with a huge lens, when we hiked to our mountain. He took dozens of shots of me lying on a bed of wildflowers, hiding behind a tree, leaning against our white rock, climbing atop our rock. Mihai had loaded the film wrong, and all the shots were exposed onto the same frame – all except the final shot of me climbing atop our rock and laughing. I am laughing because I could barely keep my balance, and I thought I was going to fall crashing down through the treetops all the way to the foot of the mountain.

Radu is still talking, saying how soon after he got married, Mihai started reading all the literature and philosophy he could get his hands on.

"It was like he was trying to reach you," says Radu, "to understand you.

"And as for those Communist bastards, he beat them at their own game," concludes Radu proudly.

I wish I had known that side of Mihai. Why couldn't the two of us have done dissident work together? We would have been two revolutionary lovers. We could have typed revolutionary manifestos together that said: *Romanians wake up, Romanians the day of freedom is near, down with the tyrant!* We could have walked into the People's Palace with the old Romanian flag, me and Mihai at the front of a large group of angry revolutionaries, followed by riotous crowds yelling *Down with the tyrant, freedom, freedom, no more Securitate!* We would have been carried on the arms of the people, and then I could have stood right in front of the *Father of the Nation* in a purple shiny silk dress, wearing a pair of dark sunglasses, and I would have pointed a gun from among the guns that our dissident organization has been collecting, right at the dark heart of this illiterate Nicolae Ceaușescu, Comrade, Son and Father of the People. Mihai and I would have lived in history as the saviours of the people.

I stare blankly at Radu as I am having my revolutionary fantasy. As if he once again guesses the gist of my thoughts, he says, "No, Mona, he did well. He was right to not involve you. Don't you realize how worried he was for your life? You were a pretty clear target. You could have been killed . . . just like that," Radu says and snaps his fingers.

The music keeps playing, and I taste my own tears. I am soaked in tears, sweat, bad whisky, and the dew that's settling on the grass. On this August night, so fragrant, so confusing, my love turned out to be real after all.

I embrace Radu and thank him for everything. I feel warmth and gratitude towards Mihai's old friend who has helped me get the last pieces of my story together. Before leaving, I decide to ask one last question.

"By the way, whatever happened on that hiking trip, the year of the earthquake, when Mariana died? You were with them, weren't you?"

"By the way of what?" asks Radu, and his face suddenly changes from the relaxed, ironic expression he's had all night to a look of intense pain. "How is this connected to anything, Mona? You're driving me crazy," he adds with a bitter smile.

His change makes me even more curious. There seems to be a bottomless bag of secrets for me to open up tonight.

Radu sips slowly from his drink. "I loved Mariana, you know. She was my great love, and Mihai found out on that trip, he overheard me telling her about my feelings and got really angry." Radu's eyes are shining in the night, and his face is crossed by grief.

"You know how he could get mad, don't you," Radu goes on hesitantly. "We got into a fistfight on the slope. Mariana was running ahead of us and wanted to get away from both of us, she said we were crazy and was crying and going down the slope. We fell down as we were fighting . . . one of us must have kicked the damn rock that went down and hit her. I thought Mihai was going to either kill himself or kill me that day."

"And . . ." I start.

"That's all, Mona," says Radu. "There is nothing left, nothing more. Let's get together again if you are still in town. But it's enough for tonight, please."

I pull back, realizing I've gone too far with all my questioning. Discovering Radu's hidden love story was the last thing in the world I had expected before I came over. I had always thought him to be a cynic and a womanizer, but that was the cover he had used all along to hide his secret about Mariana. Mihai's brooding moments whenever he remembered Mariana, particularly at the beginning of our love that summer, appear now in a new light as well. He *did* feel guilty and angry at himself for the fight on the mountain and probably could never forgive himself for it. Maybe it's also what pushed him into all the reckless acts that came afterwards. I embrace Radu one last time and rush into the silent, deserted street.

I am running on the cobblestone road going down the hill from Radu's house. The new moon is setting, and my hair is flying wildly. I am seventeen and I am forty, both. My heart is pounding, my face is wet, and I'm not sure if they're tears of sadness, fury, or happiness. It's all of that. My love was not a hero, but he wasn't a villain either. He had been a Marxist in a Marxist society gone bad, but more honourable than the corporate capitalists of the capitalist society I'm living in now. He had been indifferent to my intellectual passions, but then he set out to read all the literature in the world when it was too late for me to care. He taught me how to dance. He taught me the secrets of the Carpathians and of my own body. He always carried the picture of me laughing on a mountaintop. I carried the picture of us morose on the November day in Bucharest, in my bag when I crossed the border on the train to Trieste.

There were serious reasons to love him. I hadn't just been *in love with love* as so many people had told me. I had loved Mihai Simionu, from the town with the Black Church in the Carpathians, an engineer who played the guitar and wore black leather jackets like the secret police. Or like a daredevil biker. We had both been truthful to ourselves and to what we had wanted to be; we had both deserved that moment of complete beauty above the city, coming out of the stormy afternoon changed, with rain on our faces.

As I am running on the cobblestone street, a sentence that Radu uttered earlier keeps rolling in my head: *For a while, around the time you left the country, he pretended to work for the Securitate.* I keep repeating it over and over again and the possibility that Mihai knew I was going to leave only now appears to me in its full magnitude. Something like an illumination comes over me. Mihai felt somehow that I was planning to leave. He was more sensitive to my hidden turmoil than I had given him credit for. I rewind everything back again to the night before my departure from Braşov, two days before I took the train from Bucharest.

I am falling through a deep tunnel like Alice in Wonderland, everything passing by me in reverse order. Images of myself and of the people in my life moving backward flash at me from all directions, in the deep tunnel where I am sliding in a breathless free fall. It all moves faster and faster and I know that soon I will hit the ground with a thick thump and millions of pieces of myself will be scattered to the stars.

Perhaps Mihai left the apartment that morning because he wanted to make it easier for me. Or he left the apartment because he didn't want *them* to see we were still together. Did he want to create the illusion of a breakup, so that they trusted him more? Had he taken it upon himself to follow me, and let them believe *he* would stop me at the border, or that he would send someone to stop me? Perhaps he misled them all along, letting them believe he was getting information from me and telling them what they already knew about my father. He found out from them that I had asked for a passport and that they were planning to stop me. Or maybe my own father had told him and they were both doing their damnedest to create as many distractions as possible, so I could cross the border unharmed. That's why Mihai had smiled sadly when I told him I had to go back to the capital to start the onion- and potato-picking work earlier. He knew I couldn't live in confusion and fear any longer. Most important, he had feared for my life, and after Cristina's death he wanted me away from all danger. Even if it meant parting with me for ever. He had read my mind before I had even articulated it to myself during that New Year's Eve party when he said, *You'll leave me one day, won't you?* He was both reckless and meticulously careful. My Mata Hari lover had played it all up. He had tricked everyone without getting caught. If only he had given me a clue about it as well.

Now that at least some of the fog surrounding Mihai has dissipated, my heart can rest from all the tumult of the last twenty years. Perhaps my own country will become the country I had once missed so deeply in the composition I had written more than thirty years ago. And maybe I will get used to having two countries, to having no country, to being my own country, and stretching across the Atlantic Ocean, one foot in the Indiana cornfields, the other in a berry-filled meadow in the Carpathians, like a huge baobab tree.

The Encounter

THE NEXT DAY I CALL RADU AGAIN, and I ask him what I had so much wanted to ask the very minute I found out Mihai was alive: if he can arrange for me to meet with him.

"A meeting between you and Mihai?" he asks, surprised. "What for?"

"Don't ask, just do it, please. If you can. It's important. I have to."

I hear him sigh. "OK. But you know it's not easy to get to his house in the boonies. You'll have to put aside a whole day."

"As long as it takes," I tell him.

"I'll try. But you owe me big time!"

"I know. I'll have to invite you to America and buy you all the whisky in the world."

"That will do. Wait for my phone call. What a pain in the ass you are, Mona!"

Radu calls me three days later. My plans are to go back to America in another three days. But when he calls and says Mihai is waiting for us, I can think only of the next few hours.

I change my clothes six times before I decide what to wear. If I wear pink it's too cheerful and girly; if I wear red it's too femme fatale; if I wear trousers, he won't notice my ankles; if I wear something too elegant he might think I am flaunting my wardrobe; if I wear something too old and nondescript he will think I'm doing badly in America. I wear a white linen dress. Little blue earrings and a pearl necklace. A little makeup, but not too much. Fuchsia lipstick. Red sandals that don't match my lipstick. A dab of French perfume.

Andrei and Ionica are worried that I am leaving them for two days. They beg to come with me. I say we'll do something grand together when I get back, like go to the big mountaintop they can see from the town. Ionica says he wants to climb on foot all the way to the peak of the highest mountain to see black goats. My aunt and uncle wave to me from the balcony and tell me not to worry as I get into Radu's car, a battered dark blue Dacia, the classic Romanian car.

We drive on winding, rutted roads through little villages with stone houses and thick stone fences. The Carpathians, overlapping one another, wait patiently ahead of us in a pale blue haze. Radu plays the car radio, Romanian music, until it fades into static.

The music and the landscape wash over me in waves. The deep green countryside, the dirt roads, the women with babushkas standing in front of their gates watching the cars go by. Red and yellow flowers in the window boxes. Red tile roofs, white storks perched on the chimneys. I smooth out my white dress. I stare out of the window. I look at myself in my pocket mirror and adjust my lipstick. I look at my watch and count the hours.

Radu looks over at me. "It's a long way," he says. "Are you hungry? Do you want to stop?" I shake my head. He drives steadily, squinting a little.

The blue mountains never seem to get closer. We pass endless wheat fields rippling in the wind. The sun feels warm and soothing in my lap. The fields are full of people wearing brightly coloured clothes. I move among them as they welcome me with gifts: earrings, necklaces, scarves, apples and pretzels.

"We'll get there in half an hour," Radu announces. "You've slept quite a long time."

I wipe the sweat off my forehead, the lipstick off my mouth, drink an entire bottle of water, and sit quietly for the rest of the ride, with my hands in my lap.

The landscape has become wilder, more primitive, as if we're in some mythic time in the midst of rocky, uninhabited mountains. I think of the Smoky Mountains. I think of my white house in the midst of cornfields. I want to have an American and a Romanian house.

I stare at my red sandals and at my painted toenails. Mihai used to like the shape of my toes and sometimes kissed them one by one. But then they were never painted with bright red polish.

Radu takes out a slip of paper from his breast pocket and looks at some scribbled directions. He enters a little village of old stone houses with water wells in their front yards. He drives through it and turns onto another dirt road. At the end of the road, at the foot of a magnificent peak, is a pale green stone house with a wooden porch and a garden with climbing red clematis and grapevines all around. Mihai is sitting on a chair on the front porch, looking out into the woods and smoking. I get out of the car. I walk slowly towards the house. There is a waterfall on the side of the mountain that swallows up all sounds, including my own steps on the gravel.

Every quiet step seems like a huge leap over time and large spaces. I am walking on the thin gravel path leading to the house, and the contours of the man sitting on the porch appear clearer with every step. I have always laughed at movie scenes in which important encounters are filmed in slow motion. Now I feel like someone inside such a scene. Only this is not a scene. This is me, Mona, walking towards Mihai, who is sitting on the porch of a green house at the foot of a snowcapped peak deep in the Carpathians. His dream came true. He always spoke about living in a place like this.

There are wild red and blue flowers on the side of the gravel path. Mihai is wearing a blue shirt and green trousers. I have never seen him wear two bright colours at once. His hair is cropped tidily, and he has the beginning of a beard. There are grey patches in his short hair. The waterfall is getting louder, and Mihai hasn't seen us yet. As I look at him with all the attention I am capable of mustering, I also see myself as if in a mirror: the lines around my eyes, my hair flying in all directions, my eyes in which Mihai used to see little stars at once a bit paler and yet more fierce than they used to be. I stumble over a pebble and I notice a slight, almost imperceptible shift in the position of his shoulders. I know that Mihai is finally aware of my presence, but he is taking his time.

A thought crosses my mind as I am getting close to the house and as I start going up the wooden steps. I should buy a house like this one with clematis and grapevines all around it and a wooden porch, here in the middle of the Romanian nowhere. For me and my children when we come back next summer. Mihai lets out a swirl of blue smoke and looks up. He looks at me.

✗

ACKNOWLEDGEMENTS

In completion of my novel, three amazing women played the role of fairy godmother: first is my agent, Jodie Rhodes, who discovered me, stood by me, and whose extraordinary passion for her writers, her insights and integrity, should be a model to all those who practise her profession. Without her unrelenting belief in my ability as a writer and her irrepressible energy, my novel might never have seen the light.

The extraordinary writer Sandra Cisneros has touched my destiny in a magical way with her inspiring and brilliant mentoring, pushing me to transcend my own limits. She is the fairy godmother who guided me toward narrative complexity.

My brilliant editor, Robin Desser, is the fairy godmother who taught me to stay in the castle of storytelling clarity and not be chased out by redundancy and excess. With immense patience, devotion and intelligence, she has guided me toward making this book the best that it can be.

Dennis Mathis also deserves profuse thanks for his valuable insights, suggestions and editorial guidance. Our many conversations are remembered fondly.

I am also grateful to Ellen Mayock for her staunch professional support.

I owe many thanks to my dear friend Paul Friedrich for his sustained moral support and to my beloved mother, Stella Vinitchi Radulescu, for her precious advice and belief in my work.